THE BITTEREST WINE

THE BITTEREST WINE

A novel about a French family's conflicting roles during the German Occupation of Provence and famous writers and poets who inspired resistance.

LIZ KONOLD

ISBN: 1517688167
ISBN 13: 9781517688165

Dedicated to Jim, Asa, Ryan and Lucas,
Julie, Allisen, Harley and Natalie
who exemplify family in all its diversity and joy.

"Our bitterest wine is always drained from crushed ideals."

ARTHUR STRINGER, 1874-1950
AMERICAN POET

"Do not suppose that this is the end. This is
only the beginning of the reckoning.
This is only the first sip, the first foretaste, of a bitter cup..."

SIR WINSTON CHURCHILL
OCTOBER 5, 1938
~ FROM HIS SPEECH TO PARLIAMENT
REGARDING THE MUNICH AGREEMENT

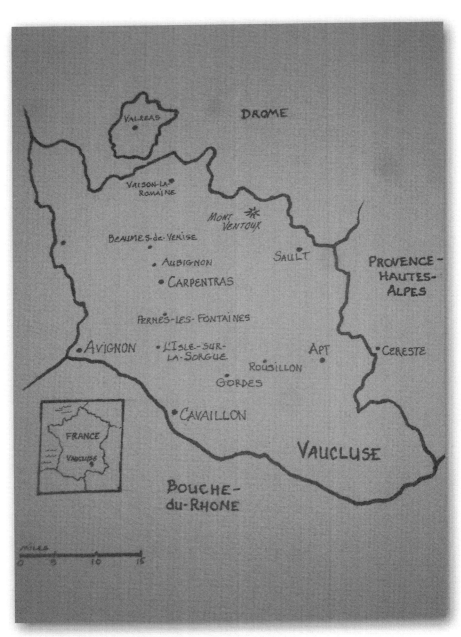

VAUCLUSE DEPARTMENT, PROVENCE

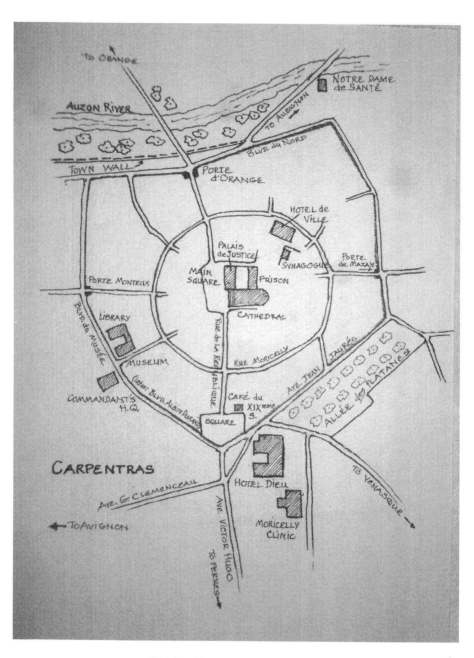

CARPENTRAS – CENTRE VILLE

PORTE D'ORANGE, 14TH CENTURY   CARPENTRAS, FRANCE

PREFACE

This book is the result of my finding a small monument under an olive tree next to a parking lot in the town of Carpentras, France. It states:

*'On this site stood the Café of the 19th Century,
rallying point and one of the major sites of the
Resistance in the Vaucluse from 1940 to the
Liberation (August 25, 1944).
The owners were René Dulfour and Marcel Alibert.'*

This led to information about Maxime Fischer who fled from Paris to Carpentras in 1940 and co-organized a local resistance group called the *Maquis Ventoux*. I learned that René Char, a renowned Surrealist poet, joined the local Resistance and was in charge of parachute drops on the south side of Mont Ventoux. I found other writers and poets involved in keeping the idea of eventual liberty alive.

As I spent time in Carpentras, the capital of the Vaucluse and my summer home, I heard more stories of what it was like living during World War II. From research as well as personal interviews, I learned of diverse points of view, various methods of coping, unrelenting hardships and horrifying events that shaped people's lives. Gradually the idea of this novel took form.

'The Bitterest Wine' is about choices people made during a chaotic period, combined with the poetry and prose of famous writers whose passion to fight against oppression inspired others. Fictional characters intertwine with real people (listed in the appendix) and actual events as liberation nears. I want to emphasize to readers that I have tried to be as accurate as possible; however, in many cases my imagination made up for lack of specific information. Since wine is such a major part of the Vaucluse, this is a thread running throughout the book. Even during the Occupation vintners worked to systematize and improve the quality of what they produced.

I hope that these stories convey the complexity of life in wartime and the importance of 'avant garde' thought and poetry that kept alive the prospect of *egalité, fraternité et liberté* during a very bleak time.

The author

RESISTANCE IN THE VAUCLUSE

Twenty-eight-year-old attorney Maxime Fischer knew enough to get away and stay away from German-controlled Paris in June 1940. As an anti-fascist Jew with crippled arms from a bout of polio, he was far from the Aryan ideal. He headed for the Vaucluse in the southern 'free zone,' a department of Provence also known as the *Comtat Venaissin* during five hundred years of Vatican ownership. The *Comtat* was known for centuries as a sanctuary for Jews fleeing persecution.

Instead of returning as most Parisians did, Fischer stayed in Carpentras. In early 1942 he began organizing a Resistance network with his new partner, Lieutenant Colonel Philippe Beyne.

Fischer went looking for Beyne a day after Pearl Harbor and the Americans entering the war. Their encounter at the Hotel du Louvre in Sault did not start auspiciously. The Lieutenant Colonel, portly, in his mid-forties, wore a dog-eared army jacket with a faded Legion of Honor rosette. He slouched against the bar, leaning on his elbows as he slurped wine. The hero of the famous 'Red Devils Regiment' of World War I had a two-day growth of beard and mumbled his words as he and the bartender talked. He'd lost his position as the town's tax collector for his anti-fascist beliefs and this apparently had taken its toll.

At first Fischer was unsure if this man was the right one, no matter how highly regarded he might be. Still he sidled up to the legionnaire, ordered a glass of wine and casually spoke with him, occasionally to the rumbling of Beyne's stomach. Fischer outlined his idea of recruiting men to fight against the Nazis. Beyne nodded his head, listening, not responding.

Finally Fischer bluntly asked, "Are you willing to help me?"

Colonel Beyne thought for a minute then agreed.

It is hard to imagine less likely characters putting together one of the major resistance groups in France than these two men.

They named their group the *Maquis Ventoux*. Code names were selected to protect identities. Fischer chose '*Anatole*' in reference to the writer Anatole France. Beyne selected '*d'Artagnan*' in fondness for one of the three Musketeers.

At about the same time, an engineer trained in explosives, Jean Garcin, was organizing the *Group Franc* network south of Mont Ventoux. He chose the code name *Commander Bayard* after a magic horse in French legends that could change its size to fit the number of riders. On the north side of the mountain, the *Maquis Vasio* began to form around Vaison-la-Romaine. Men joined for a variety of reasons: being Jewish, communist, anarchist, Socialist, Freemason, Spanish Republican or for French honor. Some were minor criminals evading the law.

At first there wasn't much to do and few enlistees, then during the winter of 1942-43 a flood of refugees arrived in Provence seeking places to hide or a way out of the country. The *Maquis* found them shelter, made false identifications cards, provided maps and contacts.

In January 1943 a man code-named *Max* parachuted into Provence with instructions from General de Gaulle to unify the motley collection of partisans. A former municipal politician from the Midi-Pyrenées, Jean Moulin established MUR, the *Movement Unis de la Resistance,* from Marseille to Lyon. The disparate Maquis groups became coordinated networks, with commanders and divided responsibilities.

It was thanks to drafting Frenchmen into forced labor by the Germans, in February 1943, that ranks began to swell. Dozens of young men in the region flocked into the mountain to contact Resistance groups. In late spring 1943, Beyne supervised about six hundred recruits—by August 1944 it would be close to two thousand. The networks trained in guerrilla warfare: striking, harassing and disappearing.

Camps were established in remote ravines and forested hillsides. Maquisards robbed German convoys of armaments, food and clothes. Farmers and shepherds siphoned off some of what they produced to help supply, feed and care for the men. On Mont Ventoux, a man with an ambulatory cinema going from village to village picked up foodstuffs stashed in an electric transformer and delivered them to hidden sites for retrieval.

The *Maquis* expected that one day that they would be called upon to help the Allies liberate France and they planned to be ready. They sabotaged and faded away, the 'shadow army' that became a serious threat to the Third Reich during the last year of the German Occupation in Southern France.

Maxime Fischer and Colonel Philippe Beyne

PART ONE

SEEKING ESCAPE - 1978

As the train clacked toward the south of France, I watched a youthful looking face shimmer and undulate in the window, superimposed over a blur of fields and vineyards. Blonde-streaked brown hair rippled around smooth cheekbones. The suggestion of a smile waffled above a firm neck.

Minutes later in the train's restroom mirror the same face stared back at me, with drab bangs sliding over one eyebrow and pale lips tightly pressed together. There were tiny furrows between the eyebrows and more than a few gray hairs among blond-streaked brown. Reading glasses bobbed on a neck chain as I washed my hands. With a wry grimace I admitted that, regardless of the flickering image, this trip would not recapture my youth.

This self-chosen exile was penance for having believed my life was almost perfect and to heal a heart that was stomped thin. I'd jumped at a semester's sabbatical to avoid a new, ambitious department chair at the private college where I'd worked for fifteen years. My topic was 'French Surrealist writers of the Resistance' during World War II.

The smell of dust and mildew from the Sorbonne's library archives and the Museum of the Resistance lingered in the scarf around my neck, remnants of the days spent flipping through decades-old papers and books. As I focused on my research, nose-to-microfiche, summery Paris had sizzled beyond the iron grills. Now I was heading toward Provence. Clouds, puffy white against a blue sky, soared above rippling fields of wheat that melded into neatly trellised vineyards. The occasional field of *tournesols* with wide yellow petals and brown faces followed the sun like satellites on green stems.

My seatmate, an elderly lady who napped with her mouth open, had left at Lyon. The place remained empty perhaps because the vacationing French were already ensconced in holiday rentals along the coast. Across the aisle a man in his mid-thirties had been glancing over with a smile and raised eyebrow. To avoid his gaze I reached for a book in my bulging canvas bag. Pulling out *The Magnetic Fields*, the first Surrealist publication, I opened it and kept my head down as I reviewed how it all started.

The authors, André Breton and Philippe Soupault, had been twenty-two and twenty-three years old, angry, disillusioned and recovering from the horrors of World War I. In rebellion against established literary guidelines, they locked themselves in an apartment for eight days and wrote whatever popped into their heads. They tapped into abstract images, remnants of dreams, passing thoughts, bits of overheard conversations, psychic sensations, anti-rational thought. I re-read a snippet at the top of a page:

> "...*The bells, or perhaps it was the trees, struck the hour.*
> *He thought he heard the voices of his friends speaking:*
> *"The office of lazy trips is to the right," they called to him,*
> *"and on Saturday the painter will write to you....Everybody*
> *loves a fire; when the color of the sky changes it's somebody dying."*

The department chair was eagerly fluffing up the feathers of our flock of professors, exhorting us to complete terminal degrees and publish, publish, publish. My article on André Breton escaping arrest was in the process of being printed in a lesser-known literary review. Had Breton and his family been on a train similar to the one in which I traveled when he fled to Marseille? I could relate to his sense of unease at being forced to leave the familiar.

Some writers had died during the war; others shortly after. In 1960, Albert Camus had been killed in an automobile accident; however, René Char, who had organized parachute drops around Mont Ventoux, was still alive although in ill health. He lived near Carpentras and I hoped to meet him.

A conductor in a dark blue uniform walked through the second-class car announcing the next stop. I smoothed my blue seersucker skirt and gathered up my purse and book bag. Tugging on the typewriter case above the seat, I managed to get it to the shelf's edge. The man across the aisle stepped over, lifted it and followed me to the vestibule, looking pleased. As I fumbled for my suitcase in the luggage area by the exit he grabbed the handle. My new acquaintance carried them to the open door, stepped out and thumped both on the ground with a jaunty '*voila, Madame!*'

Was he about to follow me? I stiffened, hoping my grateful '*merci, merci,*' was not encouraging him. Then he stepped onto the train with a wave, saying that it was his pleasure to help a lovely lady.

"Ah, yes! I'm in France..." I reminded myself.

The heat, sparkle and flash of August in Provence blurred the shapes weaving along the platform of the faded depot. Hearing my name, I shaded my eyes with my hand and saw a woman frantically waving a wide-brimmed straw hat, shouting, "Claire Somerset! *Chérie*, I'm here!"

Abandoning the baggage on the platform, I strode toward Sophie as she ran along the train. We had been best friends for thirty years.

"*Alors*, I am so happy to see you! It has been too long." Sophie plopped her hat on her head.

"It's so wonderful to be with you again, sister-of-my-heart!" My childhood friend and I touched cheeks once more.

"The car is in front of the station—I'll take your cases." She grabbed the book bag and typewriter whose weight made her arms look inches longer. Her tanned legs in high-heeled sandals swished a flowery flared skirt as she briskly led the way to a dark blue Renault-Cinq.

After stowing the baggage in the trunk, Sophie concentrated on threading the car through Orange's central streets. The magnificent Roman amphitheater, its wall towering over the main road, attracted thousands of visitors every summer. In the late afternoon, cars filled up every street leading to arteries out of town. Traffic was tangled. The useless bleating of horns from confused tourists and frustrated locals surrounded us. Under her breath Sophie muttered epithets, 'merde' prominent among them.

At a roundabout the Renault emerged and sped east, windows down, a warm wind tossing our hair. I felt jet-propelled from Paris's busy intensity to Provence's somnolent beauty and soaked in views of tidy villages with wrought iron belfries on stone steeples, irregular patches of black-green woods, fields of rolled hay and sun-splashed tile-roofed houses. In the distance the granite top of Mont Ventoux, muted by a halo of hot air, looked snow capped.

Sophie turned slightly, "Frankly, Claire, you look like you need a vacation. But no wonder. I was so shocked and sorry to hear of your divorce. When you and Ted visited us four years ago I never guessed that there was anything wrong."

"Neither did I. It is such an ancient story but one you never expect to happen. The typical tale of the middle-aged male falling for a younger woman and, as Ted put it, feeling like a new man."

"Hmmmphh." Sophie snorted. "In France, we adapt to situations like that. A man would never desert his family here."

"That's because you're Catholic. Your religion and culture hold families together. We've gotten into a very 'me-centered' nation. My husband changed a lot after he went through a self-help course called *est*."

"Est? I've never heard of it," Sophie questioned. "You wrote that Ted went to a psychology workshop. I thought that it was part of his job."

"Almost everyone in the San Francisco Bay area is into humanistic, change-your-life programs. A number of our friends had gone to 'est,' Erhard Seminars Training. They thought it was wonderful and they gained all sorts of insights. Ted tried it and his insight was that he needed to start life over with another woman."

I looked to my right, wishing away the lump in my throat.

"The surprise was that she was one of his former students with whom he'd had an affair several years ago. Ted and I try not to be acrimonious for

JT's sake." I sighed, "There are times when I think murder would have been simpler."

Sophie glanced over, her eyebrows raised, "Ah, don't worry. You will feel differently after a few weeks here in the Vaucluse."

"Mmmm, maybe." The thought of returning was already depressing.

"What about John-Theodore? Did he manage all the changes without being too upset?

"Yes. JT was focused on getting into college so the divorce was more of a nuisance. You know that he's at Yale University on the east coast? I went with him to freshman orientation before I flew to Paris. We talked yesterday and he seems happy, likes his roommates."

"*Merveilleuse!* So you now have time for yourself. I hope that we will have many chances to reminisce about our good times growing up together!"

"Dear Sophie, I often think of our crazy days in Paris."

She laughed. "When we tried our first cigarettes and nearly vomited our lunch? And those darling boys who seemed so well behaved but kept reaching for our breasts? We did have fun!"

It was September 1946 and I was barely thirteen. Dad's civil engineering firm had assigned him to work on reconstruction of bridges and transportation systems around Paris. My two younger brothers and I arrived in a damaged country, feeling lost, isolated and faced with an incomprehensible language. Our mother, having minored in French, worked with refugees as a volunteer and ignored her three at home.

Sophie was the only girl in my class at the *college* brave enough to try and talk with me. She later said that she was intrigued by an *Américaine* who spoke English and had access to chewing gum. That we were two girls surrounded by brothers, Sophie had four, was an immediate reason for commiseration.

We made an odd pair: I was tall, lanky, fair-haired, shy; Sophie was dark, petite, animated, given to dramatic flights of fancy. She became my self-appointed French tutor. Soon we were inseparable, giggling over boys, sharing secrets, completing each other's homework. Our friendship over the years had never wavered.

Barreling along, the gears of the Renault complained as it passed farm machinery and slow cars. As we drove into Loriol-du-Comtat, Sophie turned down a road toward the Dupré's farmhouse. Beyond a row of poplars I saw familiar faded blue shutters closed against the heat. Higgledy-piggledy rock and stucco buildings meandered on either side. Tree branches flopped over the roof. Dust-laden lavender plants, faded geraniums and spidery white flowers on long stems surrounded a patch of sunburnt lawn. Spindly Oleander bushes, *lauriérs rosés,* were splayed against a rock wall.

We carried my baggage over the stone path and into a cool salon. An iron chandelier above a round table lit up the comfortably messy room. A worn tweed couch and a smattering of chairs faced a low table in front of a carved stone fireplace. The place looked just as it was four years before.

Sophie headed for a circular stone staircase. "I've fixed up Suzette's old room on the first floor for you."

I hefted my belongings and followed her. Although the rooms upstairs were shuttered from the sun, they were significantly warmer than those below. My eyes adjusted to the dimness and hints of the surroundings became sharper.

Hand-hewn beams striped the ceiling. Tiles in designs of green, yellow and dark orange paved the floor. On the bed a white linen sheet embroidered with a design and the initials of Sophie's grandmother lay tucked over a Provençal quilt, a *boutie.* Mosquito netting attached to a tin crown lay behind the ornate headboard. A rush-seated chair stood by an armoire with a mirrored center door.

I breathed in the perfume of old stone, furniture polish and a scent of lavender. As I plopped my typewriter on a table I realized how much I had missed Provence. It was a different country not only in the sense of place. This time it was a chance to avoid my former reality, perhaps create a new one, although I wasn't sure how.

THE EXILE
ANDRÉ BRETON

By the summer of 1940 the port city of Marseille teemed with frantic people: the wealthy expecting special treatment, the corrupt hoping to skim from the unsuspecting, the poor begging for relief, sailors and prostitutes living for the day. Fishermen and merchants raised prices due to demand as refugees from every class and country in Europe arrived, increasing from 650,000 people to over one million in a matter of months.

André Breton, his wife Jacqueline and their four-year-old daughter Aube had fled Occupied Brittany for the south-eastern 'free zone' in August, as soon as he was decommissioned as a first lieutenant medical officer in the former French Army. At age forty-four, his wavy hair was turning gray and his distinguished features showed the effects of anxiety and stress. Clutching two suitcases, he looked toward the family at his side.

Jacqueline, a respected artist, ever composed and coping, held the hand of their four-year-old child and a third suitcase as they stood at the bottom of a staircase leading to a magnificent villa overlooking the Mediterranean sea. Above the gate was inscribed *Villa Air-Bel*. To the right of the gate was a hand painted sign saying *Chateau Espére-Visa* ('Hoping-for-a-Visa Castle').

Varian Fry, an American journalist who specialized in analysis of political situations in Europe, had arrived in Marseille with a list of two hundred notable Europeans that his organization, the Emergency Rescue Committee, was to help escape from the Nazis. The Bretons were among these lucky few. Breton knew that this was due to his contacts in New York with whom he worked on Surrealist art and poetry shows in prior decades. Because of his outspoken anti-Fascism and as co-founder of the Surrealist poetry movement of the 1920's, André would likely be arrested if he stayed in France.

Between serving in World War I and the 1939 attempt to stop the German invasion, Breton had seen enough carnage and destruction. He was not looking to become a hero in middle age. Yet he was adamant that the artist, the writer, was obliged to expose the under-belly of society's worst ills. He loved his country and was torn apart by this latest conflict, remembering the horrors that he saw when he first served as a young doctor in a neuropsychiatric hospital during the First World War.

He wrote to a friend: '*America has become necessary ...only in the most negative sense. I don't like exile and I have my doubts about exile.*'

Hiram Bingham, the sole US State Department officer cooperating with the ERC in direct opposition to the American Consulate's official stance of 'non-interference,' worked tirelessly along with Fry. When legitimate passports were unavailable the two men turned to forgers and the black market. They steadily increased the number of desperate immigrants piling onto ships and boats exiting *Vieux Port* toward Gibraltar, unloading a number in North Africa. Others were helped across the Pyrenees to Lisbon where the Unitarian Service Committee arranged for passage abroad. Originally asked to assist two hundred escape, these two men would eventually help over two thousand successfully flee France.

Fry, thirty-three years old, had arranged for the use of an eighteen-room mansion for himself, his staff and specific guests. The Bretons had rooms on the same floor as Victor Serge, a Belgian-Russian journalist and novelist, his mistress Laurette and his petulant teen-age son, Vlady. Other inhabitants were Fry's French assistant, two American women involved with the ERC, a cook, a nursery maid from Spain and a housekeeper with a drinking problem.

Those fleeing persecution came and went: poets such as Tristan Tzara, René Char, Benjamin Peret with his Spanish/Mexican artist wife Remedios Varos; artists such as André Masson, Victor Brauner from Romania, Oscar Dominguez from Spain, Yves Tanguy and his American wife--a haughty artist named Kay Sage. Many were desperate to get out of France before being ensnared and unable to leave.

The Bretons filled out immigration forms. The American heiress Peggy Guggenheim paid for the family's expensive *Nansen* passports issued specifically for refugees. André, Jacqueline and Fry discussed various ways of getting out of the country. They did all that they could to arrange passage, yet months went by and they still languished in Marseille.

André's creative spark caused the house to hum with activities that helped ward off the misery of waiting. He read classics out loud or challenged residents to games such as 'Murder,' 'Truth and Consequences,' or 'Exquisite Corpse.' The latter name came from a line in a game invented by the Surrealists: '*The exquisite corpse will drink the young wine.*' Each player would write a line of a poem, fold the paper and hand it to the next person. After the players were done, the poem could be added to and changed.

In the winter, strong winds and freezing temperatures buffeted the villa. Still the situation there was far preferable to the squalid conditions in the *Panier* area west of the *Vieux Port*, crammed with people desperately seeking a way out of France while hiding from the police and the Gestapo. Many of those fleeing were victims of the anti-Semitism rampant in France as well as in Germany. Most were considered 'dangerous anarchists' by the Nazi controlled Vichy government.

Victor Serge wrote in his journal: '*Here is a beggar's alley gathering the remnants of revolutions, democracies and crushed intellects... In our ranks are enough doctors, psychologists, engineers, educationalists, poets, painters, writers, musicians, economists and public men to vitalize a whole great nation.*'

On December 3, five months after the Bretons settled into the residence, gendarmes arrived and ransacked the Villa looking for anti-fascist propaganda and illegal refugees. André unfortunately had left a drawing, a doodle, lying near a poem on which he was working. The statement 'this terrible idiot Petain' was written below a stick figure and a rooster, France's symbol. Breton assured the police that he had written *'putain,'* the French word for whore. He insisted that the sentence did not refer to the 84-year-old hero from World War I who had been appointed president by the Nazis.

The police closed the Villa and carted André and Victor to a cargo ship requisitioned to hold an overflow of prisoners. After sleeping on a bug-infested straw mattress for four nights, the men were surprised to be released as soon as Maréchal Petain returned to Vichy after his visit.

By spring, Yves Tanguy and his wife Kay, Salvadore Dali and his wife Gala, and the American photographer Man Ray had already arrived in New York. Max Ernst, a German-Jewish artist, had escaped from a prison near Aix-en-Provence and was avoiding arrest by moving from place to place while waiting for a passport. Marc Chagall, his wife Bella and daughter Ida were hiding in Gordes until they could leave safely.

As time went on, Breton started writing a lengthy prose poem titled *Fata Morgana*, illustrated by Wilfred Lam, a Cuban artist who also was waiting for a visa. To escape the household clamber the poet worked in the greenhouse next door, at the home of the elderly landlord Dr. Thurmin. Only five 'proof' copies were printed.

In one Breton wrote *'to my friend of deepest reflection, to René Char, to the just and divine.'* One of the original Surrealist writers, Char dropped in now and then to work on anti-fascist articles with Breton as well as to criticize two colleagues with whom they no longer interacted, the communists Louis Aragon and Paul Eluard. A tall, self-assured, athletic man eleven years Breton's junior, René Char also was evading arrest. André and he often discussed the options of going or staying.

"I'm leaving so many of my colleagues behind! Do you think less of me for fleeing?" Breton anxiously inquired.

Char shook his head, "André, you have a family, a child. How could you risk their lives at a time like this? The rest of us will carry on our resistance to fascism as best we can. You, Philippe and Paul will forever be the inspiration to see beyond 'what is' to 'what might be.' I treasure this latest work of yours. A thousand thanks!"

Breton made a fist. "When in New York I'll do whatever I can to convince the Americans that they must help stop Hitler's rampage."

In mid-spring 1941, Varian Fry pulled André and Jacqueline into the library. From his briefcase he pulled out three passports and tickets for passage on the *"Capitaine Paul Lemerle,"* a beat-up old junker scheduled to leave March 25.

"It's the best that I could do, André," Fry removed his glasses, his usually neat suit wrinkled, his bowtie slightly awry. "At least it will get you out of France and a very dangerous situation."

Jacqueline grasped Varian's hand in both of hers, "We cannot express how deeply grateful we are to you and Mr. Bingham for all that you have done."

André seized the American's shoulders and kissed him. He looked at the tickets and exclaimed, "Ah, we are definitely going to Martinique, *ma chérie*. No need for all these sweaters and coats, at least."

Fry handed over a sheaf of papers. "Here is what you will need to pass through customs in Marseille. In Fort-de-France you will have to go through another process of applying for asylum in the USA. The Serges, Monsieur Lam and the eminent anthropologist Claude Levi-Strauss and his wife will be on board with you. They have received their documents and, if I'm not mistaken, are busy packing for the trip."

Jacqueline added, "That is exactly what we need to do."

The family passed through Customs without a problem although their documents were reviewed thoroughly. Officials pawed through suitcases and wooden boxes of artifacts André had collected from travels in Mexico with Frida Kahlo and Diego Rivera.

The ship was stacked with containers, satchels, suitcases, and rows of refugees in varieties of dress. Annoyed deckhands prepared for departure, coping with overcrowded decks amid the wheezing of the rusty bucket of a vessel. Victor Serge, in his inimitable fashion, described the boat as *'a can of sardines with a cigarette butt stuck on it.'*

Passengers cheered as the ship heaved from the dock and chugged its smoky way toward Oran, Algeria to unload the first of the travelers. The Bretons, with their daughter Aube held up between them, waved back at their friends, knowing that they might never meet again.

Fata Morgana *(an excerpt) (2)*

Tell me
How to prevent oneself while traveling from having
  in the back of one's mind the pernicious thought
That one is not going where one would like to
The little square fleeing surrounded by trees
  imperceptibly different from all the others
Exists for us to cross it at such and such an angle in real life
The stream in this very curve as in no other of all
  the streams
Is the master of a secret it cannot make ours in a rush
Behind the window this one faintly luminous among many
  others more or less luminous
What *is happening*
Is of prime importance for us perhaps we should go back
Pluck up our courage and ring
Who is to say we wouldn't be welcomed with open arms
But nothing is verified everyone is afraid we ourselves
Are almost as afraid
And yet I am sure that deep in the wood under lock and key
  turning at this moment against the glass pane
There opens the single clearing....

A 'Fata Morgana' is an unusual and complex form of a mirage that is seen in a narrow band right above the horizon.

André Breton   1896 – 1966

THE VAUCLUSE - 1943

APRIL:

The morning held an April chill that would give way to a pleasant afternoon. Vendors and buyers at Friday's market were dressed in well-worn jackets and coats, hand-knit scarves and assorted warm hats. The rubbing of hands and stomping of wooden-soled shoes and sabots accompanied the hubbub of conversations that became muted when German sentries or the police meandered by. Chickens and ducks squawking in their cages, and horses neighing by their wagons added to the cacophony. Barnyard smells mingled with dried lavender and honey.

It seemed that most of Carpentras' fourteen thousand residents plus those from neighboring towns had descended *en masse*. A constant bobbing of heads as cheeks swiped in greetings gave a rhythmic, dance quality to the milling throng.

François Laurent arrived with his mother and younger brother Maurice in the family's farm wagon, their only transportation since their 1934 model truck had been confiscated the year before. Old Clotilde, the one horse left for their use, was staked to graze on a grassy patch by the Auzon River below the town's north wall. Walking up a hill, the trio crossed a trench that now surrounded the city and went through the *Porte d'Orange*, the last remnant of its once numerous 14th century towers and turrets. Crowds orbited in front of tables with meager piles of produce, eggs, cheeses, jams. Each of the Laurents carried a sack of food for relatives and friends.

"Francois, give my greetings to Amélie." Juliette Laurent smiled at her oldest son. "Maurice, Uncle Xavier will be at the café near his apartment. We'll meet you at noon at the Café of the 19th Century."

She kissed her sons and walked down the main street to meet Florence Gilles-Martin. Their grandmothers had been sisters and, as second cousins, they had remained close over the years even though Juliette was eight years older. The Laurents' farm supplied the Gilles-Martins with extra produce, olive oil and wine beyond what ration books allowed.

Francois Laurent wandered among the throng, stopping now and then to shake a hand, kiss a cheek. When he came to the large square in front of the city hall hung with satiny black and red Nazi flags, he saw a constant stream of men in their early twenties strolling by a notice, mumbling to each other.

Francois joined the crowd, jostled for position and frowned at the sharp words on a notice stating that all able-bodied French men between the ages of sixteen and sixty must now work in German factories or farms. A previous effort to recruit three 'volunteers' in exchange for releasing one 'prisoner of war' had failed miserably. The newest edict was called the *Service de Travaille Obligatoire,* the STO. Posters were distributed throughout France with phrases such as 'papa is working in Germany to earn money for us' over cartoons of a smiling mother and child.

Starting on March 27, men born in 1920, 1921 and 1922 were to be drafted first. Police would show up at a young man's home or work, give him half an hour to gather a change of clothes, a spoon and a fork and then say 'goodbye.' Immediately he would be taken to Avignon. After a medical examination he would be sent to Germany. Families of those who avoided the STO were subject to fines, confiscation of ration books and arrest.

Francois ambled toward a fountain where two of his friends stood. Compared with Michel Perrin, who was tall, slim, with straight brown hair,

Francois resembled an athlete: muscular, sure-footed, dark unruly curls and a dimple inherited from his mother's side of the family.

"Well, I guess that we were born at the wrong time!" Michel griped. He stamped out a cigarette with a well-worn boot as he brushed hair back from his forehead.

"Benedict used a hammer to smash his knees so that he'll have an excuse to get out of it." Francois added, "I'm not willing to go that far."

Gaspar, short and slightly rotund, smiled grimly, "I've decided to see if I can be exempt by working in one of our coal mines or in the forest cutting trees."

Francois and Michel looked at each other--they weren't going to work for Nazis in either France or Germany. The law was new enough that officials still had to research and organize the lists of eligible recruits. By the time gendarmes arrived at their homes, the two of them would be gone.

Francois whispered to Michel with a wink that he was taking some things to the *Boulangerie Bertolini*.

His buddy nudged his ribs, "To see Amélie! You lucky guy."

On a side street, Maurice Laurent sat with his great uncle at a café table in a sunny corner. Xavier Chevalier's wife, Adèle Laurent, had died in childbirth two years before he had joined up to fight in the Great War. He looked far older than his fifty-eight years--his hair turning silver, his face lined--as much from a wound and damaged lungs as from age.

"*Mon cher petit*, are you and the family managing to stay safe at the *Domaine?* Things seem to be getting worse for us here in town."

"Yes, Uncle Xavier."

Maurice knew to not divulge the Laurents' wartime activities. His great uncle was a pacifist, which he mentioned often, and had many friends who were staunch Petainists supporting the old Marechal. They rationalized that 'peace at any price' was better than war. Chevalier wrote for the local paper and often his lyrical poems, glorifying nature and the rural life, were pub-lished in it.

"I brought you something to read," Uncle Xavier rummaged in the pocket of his jacket and pulled out a beige book with a red title. "It's by Jean Giono, my favorite writer. I hope that you'll enjoy it."

Maurice took it, knowing that Giono, too, was a pacifist, thought to be cooperating with the Germans.

"Thank you. I'll return it when I'm done." Maurice pocketed the book without looking at it. "*Maman* asked if there was anything special that you wanted, the next time that we come to town."

"Ah, your always thoughtful mother. How nice. Well, let's see, I suppose that if you have an extra bottle of your muscat wine, but I don't want to be a burden."

Maurice stood, "You're family, Uncle Xavier. You'll never be a burden." He leaned over and kissed the man's cheek as he struggled to stand. "We'll bring you some more food in a couple of weeks, and the wine. *Au revoir.*"

The young man scampered down the street, in a hurry to find his friend Josian Rousseau whose family had a radio hidden in the attic of their four-story, narrow townhouse. The Rousseaus, and the Napiers who farmed near the *Domaine de Lauritaine* with their illegal radio, passed on news from Radio London. General de Gaulle constantly kept alive the hope of liberation as he broadcast news of the Allies progress in North Africa. Few of the French Military Police (the *Milice*) or the Germans would have suspected twelve to fourteen-year-old boys of being conduits of subversive information as they rode around on their bicycles or played sports.

That evening Francois Laurent and his schoolmate Michel sat behind the small-paned windows of the *Grand Café du 19ème Siècle*, sipping at their wine and waiting anxiously for a contact in the *Maquis.*

Their contact, Roland Najarian, was a member of the *Parti communiste français*, PCF. Being in the PCF had been illegal in France for several years and he was subject to immediate deportation to Germany or worse. As soon as the Nazis occupied the 'free zone' in November 1942, he joined the Resistance. The gaunt young man sauntered into the café, removed his beret and greeted the owner's daughter, Madame Alibert, at the zinc-covered bar of carved walnut. While chatting, he looked at reflections in the mirror and confirmed the two *refractaires* that he was to interview. He signaled to her father, René Dalfour, for a glass of wine. An ever vigilante Roland then walked over and sat with Francois and Michel.

Francois was surprised. "Hey, Roland! It's good to see you."

"So, guys, what's going on?" Roland asked.

The two young men looked at each other. Michel took the lead, "Ummm, Francois and me, we don't want to leave for Germany. We're here to talk to someone about staying in France."

"It turns out that I'm the one."

Roland looked up as a glass was placed on the table.

"*Bonjour, mon ami*," Monsieur Dalfour said.

"René, good to see the café is open. We had very a dry August."

Roland referred to the café being closed for a month after Dalfour illegally joined others in a rousing rendition of the *'Marseillaise'* on Bastille Day, at the town's World War I monument.

"You and everyone else, although I took the family on a vacation for the first time in years," Dalfour lowered his voice. "I have a note for you."

Roland nodded and turned back to Francois and Michel, whom he knew from having played Rugby on opposing teams.

"We could use both of you, but you've got to realize how difficult and dangerous it is. This past winter we had to eat whatever we could catch, including snakes. We nearly froze, lived in abandoned buildings and remote farms, melted snow to drink and bathe. We've lost guys because of traitors and not being cautious. This isn't a game."

Francois whispered, "If we stay, we'll be sent to Germany and I'm not about to help the *Bosch*. We want to fight these bastards, especially since the Allies are winning in North Africa and they're on their way to free us."

Michel looked concerned, "How does this work? What will we do?"

"Because so many are joining us, we've built new camps in the forests. You'll be in a group of ten to fifteen men under a commander. We're confiscating clothing and food from the Germans so that we won't go through another rough winter."

Roland hesitated then continued quietly, "You'll be taught how to sabotage, to move around without being obvious. You'll get fake names and identification cards. We have a couple of people avoiding the STO by working as gendarmes who tip us off when they hear of a raid. Even so, it's no guarantee that someone won't turn you in."

He looked around, "Right now there are three main groups in the Vaucluse. One is the Maquis Ventoux, directed by *Anatole* and *d'Artagnan* from Sault. You may know *Anatole* who lived here, an attorney named Maxime Fischer."

"I met him," Michel said. "He was one of our neighbors."

Roland nodded. "Another unit is the *Groupes-Francs* headed by a *Commandant Bayard* whose family have paper mills in Fontaine-de-Vaucluse. Then there's *Groupe Kléber*, with a woman as their leader. She and her network help stay in touch with the families. The *Maquis Vasio*, up around Vaison-la-romaine, control the northern part of the mountain."

He sipped his wine and scrutinized the young men. "You'll need to come up with a phony name to protect your real identity. I'm *Petrarch*." He looked over his shoulder, "And Monsieur Dalfour is *Maxmillian*."

Francois spoke quietly, "So now what do we do, *Petrarch?*"

"What about your family?" Roland looked at Francois. "Aren't you needed for food production?"

Francois nodded his head 'no.' "Maurice is almost fourteen and he's able to help. Besides, some farmers have had their only son picked up. I'm on the list."

Michel grunted, "My dad works on the trains that carry foodstuffs and armaments between Marseille and Avignon. He's seen the cattle cars filled with people being sent to the German camps. There's no way he would let me go."

"All right. I can vouch for you." Roland leaned forward. "The day after tomorrow, at ten o'clock at night, there will be a truck on a side street across from the Jewish cemetery. If you plan to join us, be there. Bring warm clothes and blankets."

Michel retorted, "I'm ready. Here's to kicking the Germans out." He sheepishly looked around the café.

Francois mumbled, "The Nazis and their henchmen are paranoid about losing, and they're reacting more viciously than ever."

"You're right, Francois. And, don't forget, our own countrymen are helping them. The *Milice* will turn in anyone that they think looks suspicious. You've heard about the anonymous letters of denunciation. All it takes is one person being careless and doing something as simple as cooking extra food or buying a different sized shirt. They could be shot on the spot." Roland spoke bitterly.

René Dalfour appeared at the table.

"My young friend, I see that you are the one stuck with the bill tonight." He put a small plate with a folded paper next to Roland's hand. "Apparently it is your turn."

The other two were amused and thanked Dalfour for being so observant. The café owner leaned over. "You need to leave."

Roland put the bill on the table's edge when he opened it. He pulled out a folded piece of paper about one inch in diameter and tucked it inside his pocket as he took out money. Turning he mumbled, "We should all leave. I'll go upstairs while you go out the front."

Roland walked to the bar and paid the bill. Francois saw two gendarmes lean toward each other at a corner table. As Michel and he started toward the door, one of the police got up and headed in the same direction. A stony-faced man in a beret watched Roland walk upstairs.

Roland read the note by match light in the dark upstairs hall. A *pianiste*, a radioman, had received a message that a shipment of munitions was being routed by rail from Orange to Jonquieres. Roland memorized the message, touched a match to the paper then rubbed the ashes into the floor with his shoe.

The partisan pulled his cap over his eyebrows. Walking into a back room, he exited at a window above a narrow ladder attached to the wall that led to an adjoining roof. From there he scaled down a thick water pipe. Once in the dark street he headed up a lane, wending his way to an old water reservoir on the east side where he'd parked his motorcycle.

MAY:

The clanging echo of St.-Siffrein's bells announced lunchtime to the residents of Carpentras. Weaving into the final peals was the beat of boots as German soldiers thumped along the stone lane toward the boulevard surrounding the once fortified town center.

Florence Gilles-Martin pulled back lace curtains at a window overlooking the street. Sunlight filtered through the filigree, a brief moment of beauty in the dullness of the day. After seven months of Nazis occupying Southern France, residents were in a near schizophrenic state attempting to create a sense of normalcy, beset with food shortages, underlying fears, a deep sense of helplessness. She waited until her husband and daughter entered the street then let the curtains fall.

Florence placed food on the table as Henri and Gigi came in the apartment door and hung up hats, coats, placed books and bags, chattering amiably. She greeted her daughter with a kiss, caressed her hair and smiled at her treasured child. She and Henri spoke pleasantly as they pulled out chairs and sat at the dining table. They bowed heads and made the sign of a cross while Henri said his usual mealtime homily.

The Gilles-Martin family was luckier than most, as their cousins lived on a farm and provided additional foods. Also Henri, an amateur violinist, had joined the *Kommandantur*'s chamber orchestra after the Germans arrived in town. Occasionally leftovers from a party were doled out to the musicians; sometimes extra ration cards were provided. Today's meal was a duck breast in a wine sauce. A portion that normally might serve one had been sliced so that the family could enjoy the impression of a gourmet dinner. Florence gave Gigi an extra slice and she took one less.

Henri uncorked a bottle. "We're low on wine, Florence. Would you ask Juliette Laurent for some the next time that you see her? I'm sure that they have a plenty even though they try to hide it from the authorities."

"Of course, dear," Florence responded. "Juliette said that she would also have some eggs for us this Friday. And a bottle of olive oil."

"We can't survive on their olives and oils, can we?" Henri shrugged. "Still there are definite advantages to having farmers in the family, even if their politics are questionable. We need to remember Marshal Petain's admonishment that we must pull together during these difficult times."

Gigi's father took a bite of the meat and smiled at his daughter, "We can certainly tell that your mother did not cook this duck."

The ensuing silence did not register with Henri as he dug into the boiled Jerusalem artichokes that formerly fed farm animals but now replaced potatoes. "Florence, surely there is something you could do to this….slop, to make it more palatable."

"Yes, Henri," was Florence's meek reply.

The family did its best to enjoy their main meal of the day. They asked their daughter about her school, discussed the weather, the rationing of meat, bread, cheese, wine. Florence recited ingredients for a soup that would be their supper. Henri periodically interjected reasons why it was important to support such frugality.

Dessert was a cheese course of *chevre* spread on thinly sliced bread, drizzled with honey that Cousin Juliette had brought. Their 'coffee,' ground from such substitutes as barley, roasted tomato seeds or roasted carrots, was served in fine china cups in an attempt to keep hardships temporarily at bay.

At the end of the meal Florence removed the dishes and washed them at the metal sink in the tiny kitchen. She was a petite woman with a penchant to look down or to the side when responding to others. Her dark brown hair was rolled at the neck in a style of the times and held back from her forehead by hairclips. Her eyes, when she looked up, were large, a golden-brown, with a tendency to blink.

Henri sat in his chair by a front window, his round glasses sliding down his nose as he read *Le Ventoux*, the town's Vichy-approved paper. Occasionally he brushed at a thin, neatly trimmed mustache above pursed lips. Gigi was in her room, finishing homework for her class at the *college*, which she attended with others aged eleven to fourteen years.

After doing the dishes, Florence sat in a chair opposite her husband. She picked up a basket of yarn, pulled out needles and worked at adding length to the sleeves of Gigi's sweater from yarn unraveled from one of her old ones. Her actions needed to be as normal as possible so that Henri would not be suspicious. She waited, on edge, for him to leave for his German class at the high school.

She felt her usual vague irritation that most of the room's furnishings were from Henri's family home in Metz: a heavily carved sideboard with a hunting scene, a chunky-legged dining table, chairs with solid backs and brown tapestry seats. On pea-green papered walls were prints of paintings by Jean-Francois Millet and members of the Barbizon School. Behind her husband's chair was an ornate Chinese-style stand with a copy of Michaelangelo's *David* in white marble, Henri's favorite *objet d'art* that he'd purchased in Italy.

Florence had never liked what they had inherited. Before the war she occasionally splurged on magazines with photographs of modern designs including the décor of Jules Leleu. He used curved and inlaid wood and had created the interiors of famous ocean liners such as the *SS Ile de France*. The use of tubular steel by leCorbusier seemed clean, simple. Danish modern furniture had started making its appearance a few years before the war. The one item in her home that she treasured was her deceased mother's well-worn kitchen worktable.

Henri checked his watch, rose and walked to the hat rack by the door. He was developing a slight paunch, even with the rationing, and his light brown hair was combed back close to his head. He shrugged on a brown jacket with meticulous care, brushing a bit of lint off a sleeve.

"I shall be back for supper around eight. The chamber concert group is practicing tonight, remember?" He spoke with his back facing his wife as he put on his fedora, picked up his violin case and opened the door. "And please, dear God, don't serve any more Jerusalem artichokes. I'll pass gas for two days!"

The door gave a crisp but quiet slam.

Florence had thought that marrying someone with Henri's intellect and education offered a chance at a better life. She was flattered that he was interested. It soon was clear that he wanted her to be nothing other than a housewife, an indentured servant who would take care of him and his widowed mother. Lately his angry outbursts were more frequent. She thought that some of this could be his concern over what might happen if the Allies invaded France.

Florence listened to Henri's footsteps descend the stairs. She put down the yarn and needles and reached for a book hidden at the bottom of her knitting basket. She was almost finished with Baudelaire's *Les Fleurs du Mal*, and checked some penciled notes in the margin. Florence stuffed the book inside her handbag, put on a straw hat with a red ribbon and faded flower then called out to Gigi.

"Darling, it's time to go. The bells are ringing."

Gigi dumped books into her bag. She was glad when her father left as the atmosphere between her parents was tense. They never argued anymore although she remembered, as a young child, hearing her mother dissolve into sobs when her father got angry. She thought that some of the unhappiness and tension was because of the scarcity of food and clothes, or the possibility of an invasion.

The young girl walked to the mirror and straightened the collar of her white blouse. She turned to the side and puffed out her chest to make her breasts appear larger, then sighed and slumped. It was a losing battle. Her straight dark hair was still in braids, tied with pieces of crocheted yarn. Her father wouldn't let her cut and curl her hair like Simone, a girl that the boys liked. She put her uniform jacket on, shrugged a book bag over her shoulders and joined her mother.

Florence noticed her sad expression. "Would you like to cycle out to the Laurent's place this weekend? Cousin Juliette always needs help gardening. Perhaps she'll want to do some canning."

Gigi shrugged but smiled slightly. "Will Maurice be there?"

Her mother nodded, "I'm sure that he will be around, helping his father. How nice it is that you have a cousin close to your own age." Florence mentally winced, as she felt guilty that she had not produced a sibling for her child.

The two walked together until Gigi turned off to her *college* and Florence turned toward the *rue des Halles* and its various shops. Gigi supposed that her mother was going to stand in line to buy food, join a group of volunteers at the *Hotel Dieu* to roll bandages or meet friends at a café for a drink. Florence instead headed toward the library on the west side of the heart-shaped *centre ville*.

She walked into the courtyard and up familiar steps to the hushed room. Taking a seat at a far table, she pulled out her book. Several people wandered among the shelves, looked at books and eventually went to the desk where Madame Poitier stamped the due date. During these troubled times the library was a haven for many who had not used it before. The librarian kept her sanctuary just that and was known for being as neutral as one could be.

Previously, Florence came to the library about once a month to read parts of a novel. She never took one home as Henri might think that she had too much time on her hands. In early March as she picked up a slim volume by Voltaire, the janitor stepped from the door to the off-limits section of the rare book collection. He paused then whispered to her that it was one of his favorites.

Florence was startled that a janitor was conversant with Voltaire then realized, in wartime, many people did different jobs. She dipped her head and said that she didn't understand much of it. He looked surprised, then Antoine Dupont introduced himself and offered to explain it to her, if she would like. He was finished for the day and they could sit in the courtyard and discuss it. Their meetings began that effortlessly.

Sometimes they sat in a small room that doubled as a storage closet and a place to heat water for *ersatz* coffee or tea. In good weather they sat on a stone bench outside, hidden by overgrown bushes. On occasion, when the curator was gone, they would sit in his office. Dupont remarked on her insatiable curiosity and wondered why she had not gone further in school. 'Poverty' was her answer.

This day her mentor arrived with a box of repaired books. He greeted Madame Poitier then nodded to Florence as he headed for the 'staff only' area. She meandered to shelves that partially hid the entrance, looked at several items until no one was watching then opened the door.

Antoine and she greeted each other with perfunctory two-cheek kisses. Florence sometimes wondered if Antoine had Irish ancestry. His wavy hair had a reddish tinge and his eyes were somewhere between sea-blue and alpine gray. His nose was typically Gallic, slightly curved, and his lower lip was plumper than the upper, his chin slightly pointed. She liked standing beside him, feeling taller herself, as he was at least three inches shorter than her husband.

For Florence it was the first such intellectual friendship of her life and she treasured the kind man's tutelage. Both were reserved and shared little of their private lives. Antoine knew that her husband taught German at the *lycée* and played in the chamber orchestra. She knew that his wife had died from pneumonia in 1940. After the Nazis occupied the 'free zone' the previous November, he had moved to Carpentras for this job.

Florence sat down on a folding chair and brought out Baudelaire's poems, turning to one that puzzled her. As they discussed its meaning, the dynamics of the phrases and the descriptive words, Florence felt transported to a different place for a wonderful moment in time. There was no war. There was no sad marriage. There was this new world opening up to her.

She tentatively stated, "Most of the poems in *Fleurs du Mal,* 'Evil Flowers,' seem to display anger and frustration."

Antoine explained, "His father was much older than his mother and died when Baudelaire was young. Apparently the poet never got over his mother's marrying again. As he grew older he grew bitter, ran up huge debts and had many affairs. He became addicted to laudanum and opium and drank to excess. To sum it up—he was not a happy man."

"I guess not!" Florence laughed quietly.

"This particular book of poems got him into a lot of trouble," Antoine seemed amused. "They don't seem so outrageous today but he was sued because some were considered decadent and morally impure."

"Yes, I can see that. However, I liked one called 'The Enemy.' It is about how rapidly one's life speeds along. Perhaps it also is describing his sadness at a wasted life?"

Turning to a page, Florence pointed to the poem:

And who knows if the new flowers of which I dream
Will find in this soil washed from a seashore

The mystic food that will create their vigor?
Oh torment! Oh torment! Time eats life,
And the obscure enemy that erodes our heart
Grows and fortifies itself by the blood that we lose. (3)

Antoine looked pleased, "I think that your interpretations are good. You are becoming more analytical, more able to read between the lines. Doesn't it also make you think of today, the uncertainty, waiting for an unknown ending?

Florence nodded rapidly, "Yes, right now time is eating our lives. We live in a limbo, surviving on hope."

After a half an hour of discussion, she closed the book and Antoine clasped his hands. "I think that it is time that we turned to some of what Beaudelaire termed 'the modernists.' I brought you one of my books by André Breton and Pierre Soupault. These poets used a technique called 'automatic writing' in this experimental work that they called *The Magnetic Fields.*"

Florence pulled her pencil from her purse and wrote a few words in a school composition book as Antoine stood to heat water for their drinks.

"Surrealism and Dadaism had a huge impact in the 1920's. You've seen Surrealist paintings by Salvadore Dali and Juan Miro?"

Florence nodded, remembering pictures in the magazines.

"Like the artists, these poets broke traditional rules about writing rhyming verse with clear and understandable meanings." Antoine smiled at her. "This will be a major leap for you, jumping into this verbal quagmire! I'll be interested to see how you interpret these modern poems."

"A quagmire? I do know that a lot of art and literature after the Great War was considered shocking. But somehow I don't think that I'll be shocked, considering the past few years. The picture that you showed me of Picasso's 'Guernica' and the story behind it made me weep. We hear of similar massacres in our own land."

Antoine handed her a cup and Florence stirred in a sugar cube, aware that this must have been a 'black market' purchase. He sat down and leaned toward her, his elbows on his knees, the cup and saucer held up between them.

"You mentioned that your husband has become close to the German officers in Carpentras." Antoine looked serious.

There was a long pause as their eyes met. For one instant Florence felt a twinge of defensiveness.

"Yes, he speaks German fluently and enjoys using it."

"I hope that I'm not misinterpreting this, but I sense from our conversations that you are not especially supportive of Germany ruling our country. Do you discuss political views with Henri?"

Florence let out a sarcastic laugh. "I'm not supposed to have any political views as far as Henri is concerned. No, we never discuss this. And you are right. Henri is supportive of Germany ruling Europe. He likes the discipline and order, enjoys Goethe's poetry and Wagner's music."

"And you?" Antoine looked directly into her eyes.

"I am French to the core," she stated firmly. "My family history goes back centuries here in the Vaucluse. One of my ancestors fought for the Pope in the battle against the Counts of Toulouse that made this land Vatican territory in the 13th century. Henri's family is originally from Alsace-Lorraine. Since it has gone back and forth between France and Germany, he is more used to that culture than I am."

"I feel that you are trustworthy, Florence. You are a good person. Because of your husband's views I'm sure that you would not be suspected of being anti-German." He paused. "If possible, I need for you to do something for me."

Florence felt her cheeks tingle then responded, "Of course. I'll be happy to do it if I can."

"The only thing, it could be dangerous." Antoine's hands trembled slightly. "You have a daughter you must think about and you must say 'no' if you have any doubts at all."

Florence blinked then said, "What is it?"

"First, you must promise that you will not tell anyone what I tell you. Especially you must not tell your husband."

She leaned forward, puzzled. "So what is it that you want me to do?"

"You may have guessed that I haven't always worked as a janitor. I am a librarian specializing in ancient texts and rare books."

Florence looked wide-eyed.

"Because of my interest and expertise I also became an expert on printing. I was fascinated by the inks, the techniques, the different kinds of papers. Our paper mills, such as the Garcin's in Fontaine-de-Vaucluse, produce beautiful examples." Antoine continued quietly, "Once Germany invaded and refugees poured into Provence, I became a counterfeiter. I made fake identification cards and documents for people fleeing the country. Now I work for a Resistance group based here, doing the same."

There was no conversation for almost a minute as the two sipped their tepid drinks, then she whispered, "I see."

He put down his cup and leaned back. "I think that I am under suspicion and am being followed. I need someone that I can trust to act as a courier, someone who is not obviously known to be close to me."

"What do you mean by 'courier?' What would I have to do?" Florence's cup rattled as she placed it on the saucer.

JUNE:

Gabrielle Laurent sat sipping an odd tasting *ersatz* coffee while reading part of a local paper that someone had left on the café table in the town of Cavaillon. The dailies were now smaller in size and she irritably thought irritably that it seemed like everything was shrinking, from the papers to the people. Her own clothes hung inches too wide on her body.

She cast a desultory glance at an article about one of the terrorists who had been arrested in Lyon, a Jean Moulin. She yawned and turned to a page with a series of recipes on different ways to cook rutabagas, something she'd never eaten until the past two years. Having grown up in the middle of vineyards and olive groves, her family raised their vegetables in their large *potager* that never had been planted with what was considered animal fodder. It was at times like this, sitting alone with too much time to think, that she missed her parents, her younger brothers Francois and Maurice, the gentleness of growing up on the family farm, the *Domaine de Lauritaine*.

A shadow loomed over her paper and she looked up at a well-dressed, middle-aged man carrying a briefcase.

"Madamoiselle, please, I would like to speak with you."

Gabrielle shrugged and gestured to the chair opposite her, her lips in a tight grimace. She was used to strange men watching her hungrily, rude whistles and crude approaches. Normally she would ignore them or brush them off but, with the Gestapo openly occupying the Hotel Splendid down the street, it was wise to not offend anyone. Denunciations to the Nazis could be based on any imagined slight.

"I believe that you are working at the law offices of Boyer and Lavalle as their secretary?"

She nodded. It had been the offices of 'Boyer, Lavalle and Bloch' until Monsieur Bloch and his family left the area for who knew where. His partners had removed the brass plate on the ornate front door and replaced it with a painted sign. Gabrielle had helped box up letterhead and envelopes with the former title, for storage in the cellar.

The man reached into his pocket and pulled out a card. "I work at the City Hall, and we need a new receptionist and typist. The pay will be an increase for you. I hope that you'll consider the job."

She took the card, looked at the name then glanced up.

"I have already spoken with Monsieur Boyer and he is ready to accept your resignation. As you know, their business has decreased. He stated that his wife would be able to replace you."

"It sounds like I have no choice, do I?" Gabrielle bit at her lip to keep from saying anything more.

The man ordered a coffee and then proceeded to outline to the stunning auburn-haired young woman opposite him the precise duties of her new job. It's no wonder the deputy mayor had recommended her, after meeting her at the law office. And, on top of that, she actually was a terrific typist. She would provide the right tone for the Vichy Administration of Cavaillon as they worked with the German officers charged with finding and getting rid of terrorists.

JUNE:

Anthony Eden, British Foreign Secretary, chided General Charles de Gaulle in a light tone that 'he had caused England more difficulties than all their other allies combined.'

Since arriving in London in 1940 this little-known soldier, designated a general three weeks before he departed France, had been broadcasting to the French on the BBC. Branded a traitor and condemned to death *in absentia* by the Vichy administration, his incitements to the French to resist, to not believe German propaganda, were obviously of significant influence. Many had responded to his call.

The British had grudgingly acknowledged him as the leader of 'Free France' and growing numbers of French citizens now supported his own sense of destiny. The biggest 'thorn in his side' was the opposition to his leadership by the Americans: to be exact, their president Franklin D. Roosevelt who was trying everything within his power to sideline the unconventional Frenchman. Few of those living under the German Occupation had any inkling of this drama unfolding during the planning for an Allied invasion.

Roosevelt and de Gaulle, with Prime Minister Winston Churchill an uneasy middleman, continually clashed over who would be in the final position of power in France: the American military under General Dwight D. Eisenhower or this obstinate Frenchman. The Allies, Roosevelt primarily, preferred General Henri Honoré Giraud, a much more cooperative man, to lead French troops assisting the Allies. De Gaulle wouldn't budge.

On May 30, 1943 de Gaulle arrived in Algiers and was greeted by thousands of enthusiastic followers. He had come to meet with a committee of French military and diplomats to iron out a possible 'shared' position with Giraud. By June 3 the group had formed a new 'French Committee of National Liberation' (FCNL) and, according to Prime Minister Winston Churchill who observed and reported, it looked like the 'bride and bridegroom' were heading toward détente if not domestic bliss.

By June 10 it was clear that a divorce was on the horizon. De Gaulle resigned and then Giraud threatened to resign. Chaos reigned. Churchill attempted to mollify an incensed Roosevelt and downplay reports in the papers of de Gaulle's increasing support from the French. Communiqués and political behind-the-scenes manipulations continued on all sides for days, with little result.

By the end of the month, the cool head of General Dwight D. Eisenhower prevailed and de Gaulle was named head of the FCNL and half of the military in North Africa. Giraud was to lead the other half.

Roosevelt then invited General Giraud to the United States, presenting him to the American public as the next leader of France.

SWIMMING IN WORDS - 1978

The Saturday after arriving, I spent the day at the Duprés' home. After lunch Sophie and I walked down to their pool built of rough cement and hand-dug in a field along the Auzon River. Multiple sensations caressed me as I slid over the side: a cool minty shroud of water, coarse cement grating my feet, hot air on my face. After several laps I swam to the edge and climbed out. A breeze wafted across nearby fields so that the heat felt good as I lay on my towel.

Sophie slid into a corner of the pool and sighed. She leaned back, elbows resting on the *terre cuite* tiles. Her lithe, bronzed body belied the fact she was the mother of four. Short dark hair, reminiscent of Leslie Caron's, surrounded an oval face bare of make-up, her only adornment a tiny cross on a chain.

"Dear Claire," she pouted, "I wish that you'd picked the apartment in Loriol instead of the one in Carpentras. Our village is so close."

"Living in town means that I can use the buses and won't need a car." I rose up on an elbow. "Thank you for checking out those other apartments and for contacting Madame Charpentier."

The town had been a market crossroads during Roman times. At the inner core it was a medieval city, reigned over and expanded by the French Popes in the 1300's. When an earthquake in 1738 caused extensive damage, successful industrialists rebuilt their homes in grand style using fortunes from tanneries, quarries, textile and grain and paper mills. Old houses were razed and elegant townhouse mansions, *hotels particuliers,* were constructed fifty years prior to the French Revolution. After the Revolution, most of the wall-encircled town's eleven convents were destroyed, converted to apartments or replaced by even more mansions. Someone said that eighty of these grand homes were in *centre ville* alone.

Madame Charpentier's *hotel particulier* was divided into three apartments, one on each floor. Her nephew and his wife had gone to Paris for a temporary job and they were glad to have some income for the two months that I needed their place. It retained bits of elegant 18th century ambiance, although contemporary thin walls and doors cheapened the interior.

"How do you like the place?" Sophie asked.

"It's very romantic and historic appearing. But the kitchen is plain old fashioned," I teased my friend. "The stove burners and the oven's pilot light have to be lit with matches. Hot water comes from a tank above the sink. The tiny *frigo* has a freezer that might hold a carton of ice cream. I certainly can't cook for a crowd!"

"*Non, non!* Anyway, you know that the French rarely entertain in their own apartments unless with very close friends. That's why we have so many good restaurants."

"Dear Sophie, I'm kidding. I'll do very little cooking."

She toyed with a corner of her towel. "Georges and I are planning a dinner next weekend so that you can meet some of our friends. The weather will be perfect for an evening supper."

I knew Sophie well enough to suspect an ulterior motive and looked at her quizzically. She ignored me, rolled onto her stomach and rummaged around in a colorful straw bag. After withdrawing a packet of cigarettes and a lighter, she looked over with big grin.

"I think that it's time for our second favorite sin."

This tradition grew from our pact to quit smoking in our late twenties. This single fall-from-grace celebrated being together again. We inhaled deeply as the flame caught each tip and, in unison, said "aahhhh."

Sophie propped herself on her elbows and narrowed her eyes. "So, have you met any interesting men since the divorce? You've never mentioned anyone special."

I breathed out a waft of white. "No, there's no one special. In fact, no one at all."

"You haven't dated anyone at all?" She looked surprised.

"Of course! At first I needed reassurance that I was still…attractive, I guess. However I have not met any men that interest me. Most are divorced and usually I can see why." I counted on my fingers, "There was an alcoholic, charming but unreliable. There were a couple of men who liked chalking up conquests. I dated a psychiatrist who, I realized by the third date, was certifiably crazy. One fellow was chained to his work; it was all he could talk about. Most needed to spend time with children and it seemed that we all were occupied with our own lives. I'm waiting for a classically-educated millionaire!"

Sophie and I laughed although mine was more of a snort.

"Were any good at sex?"

"I only slept with a couple and haven't been involved for six months." I looked at her over my sunglasses, "One of my friends complained that the men she's dated either have a brain the size of a pea or a cock the size of a crayon. I'll take her word for that."

"Ooo la la," She winked and sat up.

"I'm not ready for anything serious, Sophie. I have this project and then I need to settle into the condo. I'm looking forward to the next couple of months with time to relax and refocus. The last thing I need is a man to complicate my life."

I took a puff and exhaled a handful of cares.

———

After supper, Georges, Sophie and I sat under a *tonnelle* of wisteria in their courtyard. Streaks of red and gold filled the darkening sky, a breeze drifted in from the faraway Rhone River. Their mixed Spaniel-Shepherd, 'Chance,' lay panting at our feet.

Georges looked at me through tortoise-shell frames below his receding hairline and I could sense his kind demeanor, as a well-respected pharmacist in Carpentras. "So, Claire, I hear that you had a good time in Paris doing research."

"Yes, if you call doing research 'a good time.' I spent hours in the Sorbonne library and at a museum out in the 19th arrondissement. The best part was meeting Samuel Beckett who sometimes greets the public at his hotel in Montparnasse. A professor with whom I was working introduced us."

"Beckett? Who wrote *Waiting for Godot?*"

"The very same! He continued to live in France after the war and writes everything in French. He's about seventy years old and a charmer. His Irish brogue made him appear almost elfin."

"I didn't know that he was in the Resistance," Sophie stated.

"He is reluctant to talk about what he did. However, my professor friend told me that he narrowly escaped being captured. Most of those in his group in Paris were tortured and killed."

"Did you get much information about other writers in the Resistance?" Georges questioned.

"Quite a bit. The majority, actually all of them, were hot heads and radicals after World War I. Most became communists and a few remained so even after learning of Stalin's atrocities. As you know, they were close friends of famous artists who illustrated their books--Braque, Picasso, Matisse and so on." I paused. "They were so young yet they've had an immense impact on modern writers and artists. Ezra Pound, Ernest Hemingway and F. Scott Fitzgerald were influenced by their ideas and came to Paris to be part of their world."

Georges frowned, "But during the Second World War these men weren't young firebrands anymore."

"No, most were in their forties, successful, married, some with children. They fought for an ideal even though it could have cost them their lives. Their language changed and became more patriotic, more approachable, more lyrical." I toyed with my wine glass. "Poetry and politics have often been combined to publicly state disagreement in an abstract way so that the artistic

camouflages direct condemnation. Some poems sounded like they were written in code."

"Surrealist poems can be quite strange," mused Sophie,

"The prose was like random thoughts and ambiguity personified. It took
work to try and figure out what they meant. I've memorized one of Paul
Eluard's, a co-founder of Surrealism:"

After years of wisdom
During which the world was transparent as a needle
Was it cooing about something else?
After having vied with returned favors squandered treasure
More than a red lip with a red tip
And more than a white leg with a white foot
Where then do we think we are?   (4)

"That's impressive, Claire!" Georges tipped his glass.

Sophie blew a kiss. "*Chapeau!* Hats off to you! What does it mean?"

"Like abstract art and atonal music, such images are open to personal interpretation. I think this one meant that, after a peaceful, cooperative period,
people became self-centered and focused on competition, then were shocked
when life changed for the worst."

Georges interjected, "Or one can read a poem rapidly and accept the
initial image and reaction, simply to enjoy the rhythm, cadence. Perhaps we
French are more used to accepting experimental expression as it is deep in
our culture."

"True! Teaching my students has made me realize how un-poetic
Americans are. France was the center of education, culture and creativity at a
time when the United States was busy with expansion and building up indus-
tries. What culture we did have came primarily from Europe."

I held up my glass so that Georges could refill it. "The popularity of poetry here is significantly greater. It is a common method of communication
whether between individuals or public entities. While we were expected to
memorize poems as students here in France, I find it rare in America."

Not to be outdone, Georges grinned, sat back in his seat, looked off into the landscape, and launched into a singsong baritone:

"In the winter, we shall travel in a little pink railway carriage with blue cushions. We shall be comfortable. A nest of mad kisses lies in wait in each soft corner. You will close your eyes, so as not to see through the glass the evening shadows making faces, those snarling monsters, a mass of black devils and black wolves.

Then you'll feel your cheek scratched...a little kiss, like a crazy spider, will run around your neck...And you'll say to me: 'Find it!' bending your head--and we'll take a long time to search for that creature-that travels a lot..." (5)

Georges touched Sophie's neck with his finger and traced a half circle under her ear. She gazed at her husband's impish face and grabbed his hand.

"My dear romantic Georges! That was the first poem you recited to me and then you proceeded to use it to your advantage."

Their eyes crinkled, their lips touched.

"See! That's what I mean," I pointed with my glass. "I cannot imagine an American man going to that much trouble. He'd probably memorize something like...baseball team scores. And here, your husband quotes... Rimbaud?"

George replied, "Yes. I did all sorts of crazy things to impress the love of my life." He paused, "I think that I still do."

"And don't stop, my darling," Sophie kissed him again. "Claire, tell us what you plan to do with the research."

I thought a moment, tapping a finger on the table. "Vietnam, your French Indochina, is our most recent military foray. It will be a long time before our nation recovers from this first televised war. It greeted us in our living rooms every night, immediate and graphic even though at a great distance. But the German occupation of France was more than nightly news on a TV screen. It was everyday life."

I turned to Georges, "I'm thinking of including André Malraux even though he was in Indochina when Surrealism started. He's now known more as a politician than as a writer. Did you know that he toured the United States in 1937, trying to raise money for the Spanish Republicans fighting against Franco?"

"No, I didn't. Although there has been some controversy about his past, Malraux was one of the heroes of the Resistance. I'm sure that you know he was wounded and captured, and his brother died in Dachau."

Sophie added, "Of course, you know that he loaned the 'Mona Lisa' to President Kennedy after his visit in the early sixties."

"Jacqueline Kennedy was responsible for arranging it, I believe. She and Malraux would probably have hit it off."

"But he wasn't technically a Surrealist, was he?"

"No. About the same time that the Dada and Surrealist movements were in full sway, he was in jail in Southeast Asia." I chuckled. "He was caught trying to abscond with temple reliefs to make money! But this, too, might make him relevant since he was in France-occupied *Indochine* and wrote novels about his experiences."

"I read his *La Condition Humane* at University," Georges added. "It painted a grim picture of France's mistreatment of the people in Vietnam and Cambodia."

"I'm impressed that so many of these writers and poets spoke out against the repression and horrors of war. Some died in prison, others took up arms. They were warriors and I think that our kids today can relate to this. Kids? Some of my students are returning Vietnam Vets."

"Here you still see men without limbs, women wearing black, families without grandfathers. Many have vivid memories of what was experienced. Yet talking about what happened is difficult. We French were involved in a civil war within a world war. I think that it takes a long time after such an experience to restore the soul of a country," mused Georges.

"When Sophie and I were students in Paris it seemed like everyone was in a hurry to get past the deprivation. There was a rush to restore buildings and bridges and move on."

"It took longer here in Provence," Georges reminisced. "Because our region is agricultural, improving infrastructure, electrical power and better transportation between villages came more slowly. Add in remnants of old grudges and conflicts from the war, progress was often blocked."

Sophie patted my hand, "Georges, Claire needs to take a break from the stress that she's faced. Let's not dwell on the past."

"You are right! I'm going to relax and spend time with some favorite friends." Our three glasses clinked together. "I have an appointment to talk with a friend of René Char, who may be able to set up an interview with him. Char even received a commendation from General Eisenhower for coordinating parachute drops of supplies around Mont Ventoux."

Georges looked over at me. "Ah yes! Char is quite a presence. He apparently still has a number of liaisons."

"Meaning?" I asked.

"Even though he's over eighty it hasn't slowed him down when it comes to attracting women. He's a superlative example for us French!"

Sophie playfully swatted his arm. "In your dreams, *mon cher!*"

I asked Sophie, "Is it my imagination or are a lot of old houses and farms being modernized since I was last here?"

Sophie grimaced. "Yes. We know a family from Brussels that is renovating a *hotel particulier* in the center of our village. Foreigners buying and fixing up houses in Provence are causing prices to increase."

"Last year, in an attempt to protect our region from outsiders and the building madness that wrecked the Cote d'Azur, the communes in the Vaucluse and Alpes-de-Hautes-Provence established a huge preserve, the 'Regional Park of the Luberon.' Now no buildings or vacation homes can be built there," George looked pleased.

Sophie added, "But some of the changes are helping our economy and forcing us to modernize. Did you know that a nuclear power plant is being built north of Orange?"

"Good heavens," I exclaimed. "That really will change things. I also noticed some of the main roads are being widened."

"There are plans to construct an express train from Paris to Marseille that will go two hundred miles per hour. *Incroyable!*" Georges shook his head.

Sophie tapped my hand. "I mentioned that we have invited friends over for dinner on Saturday. After you get settled, you can help me shop at Friday's weekly market."

"Ah, yes, new roads but no supermarkets."

"Not yet. We like to know our butcher and baker, where we are sure of getting the freshest items and can order what we need. There's a fishmonger in the rue des Halles and my favorite patisserie is on the *rue de l'Évéché*. I plan to serve *pintade*, guinea fowl. You can help me cook!"

I raised my glass in agreement.

"Georges, didn't you tell me that the weekly market has been continuous since the 12th century?"

Georges nodded as he patted Chance.

I turned to Sophie, "I didn't bring any dressy clothes. I usually wear jeans, shorts and t-shirts and only brought one skirt."

"*N'anquiete-pas*—don't worry, it will be casual. After the market we'll have lunch and wait until the dress shops open!"

"You have just touched on my darling wife's favorite past time, shopping for clothes," Georges laughed as he kissed Sophie's hand.

THE VAUCLUSE - 1943

JUNE:

It had been almost two months since Francois Laurent had joined the Resistance. He vividly remembered his family's farewell, the anxiety, the fear. His father had repaired his boots and oiled the old revolver that had been hidden in the *cave* when the gendarmes took their rifles.

"Do what you must to defeat the *Bosch* but keep your head down. Don't take any crazy chances," his father had warned.

Maurice, an inch taller than his mother, his face lengthening from a child's oval to a young man's chin, had slapped his hand on the kitchen table. "I wish that I could go with you, Francois. You know that I'm a good shot!"

Their father had spoken sharply, "I can't manage the groves and vineyard without you, Maurice! Even if most of the oil and wine goes to the Germans, the family needs the rest."

His mother had reached around his shoulders, holding him close, softly saying, "*Mon cher infant*, I will pray for you every day."

His parents kissed him goodbye. Then Maurice embraced him, thumping him on the back. Francois had strapped on the backpack and picked up a suitcase, promising to send letters through the *Group Franc Kleber*. He then stepped out into the night, walking toward a path in the *garrigue*.

Michel and he met Jacques and two others by the Jewish cemetery, as told. They were blindfolded, put on the back of a farm truck and covered with blankets. In some remote ravine they had bedded down in an empty farmhouse. There they were interrogated, had photos taken and picked a code name.

A terse man in an old Citroen coupe drove them up the mountain. He had swung around curve upon curve without headlights, on a route with no visible signposts. If a spy attempted to infiltrate and report on locations he would have had little luck. At the 'red barn' the recruits were questioned further, told more about life in the Resistance and given their false identity cards before being moved to a training camp.

Roland Najarian looked up from his lunch in the latest campsite to see Francois Laurent and Michel Perrin with Jacques, talking, gesturing. He continued slurping the stew in his metal dish. Laurent pulled a tin pan from the strap on his suitcase and walked to the fireplace. He waited politely for a spoonful of stew to be plopped into the plate, picked up a chunk of dark bread then looked around the room.

Roland motioned with a shrug of his shoulder to the other side of the narrow wood bench as he slid over. "So you managed to get here to 'camp deluxe!' What am I supposed to call you two?"

"Michel is *Baptiste,*" Francois brightened, "I'm *Androcles.*"

"Ready to tame a lion?" Roland chuckled softly. "How did training go at *des Ecoles?*"

"Good thing that I'm a farm-boy and am used to hauling and hunting, *Petrarch.* It wasn't so bad for me but I felt sorry for guys straight from school or office jobs. They were sore and bruised from the hand-to-hand combat and weren't used to firing guns. But we're now ready to do some damage."

"You may be disappointed," Roland's smile creased his cheek. "You'll be doing a lot more gathering than hunting. We're busy collecting food for the winter. You know Gaston Cat in Carpentras who owns the trucking company?"

"I've seen his vans before."

"He's 'collaborating' with the Germans, transporting stuff for them so he gets more gas, but he's also one of us. The nice stew and bread that you're eating? That's thanks to him and a few other men who stole almost four tons of food from a German storage depot between Carpentras and Pernes-les-Fontaines last month."

"That's fantastic! Rationing is severe. People are only allowed three liters of wine per month, a tiny chunk of cheese, almost no meat. I read in *Combat* that the Parisians are starving." Francois frowned. "Yet the German Army pretty much gets all it wants!"

"The Allies are parachuting in stuff like tobacco and chocolate. Not often, but enough to make us want to win sooner than later."

"Yeah, at the training camp we learned how to light and extinguish fires for the drop zones. We practiced how to disappear after collecting what was dropped. Or if we were being chased." Francois rummaged in the back pocket of his pants. "Here's my ID card. I'm…uh…Didier Martin, nineteen years old, and a woodcutter."

"You'd better know that by heart," Roland cautioned. "Not all the Germans and Milice are as stupid as they look. Get your suitcase and knapsack and I'll show you where you're supposed to bed down. Tomorrow you will get your first assignment from our section chief, *Centurion*. How are you at digging latrines?"

Roland laughed and slapped Francois on his back, amused by the new recruit's look of disgust. A booklet dropped from Roland's pocket. He reached down and picked it up.

Francois queried, "So, what are you reading?"

Roland held it up, "Ah, nothing much. Some poetry by a fellow Armenian, Missak Manouchian, who lives in Paris."

"Really?" Francois was surprised. "I didn't know that there were any Armenian poets. Is he one of the Surrealists, the modern writers?"

"No. He didn't arrive in France until fifteen years ago after Breton and the Surrealists had pretty much disbanded." Roland paused, "He's a Communist. So am I."

Francois was intrigued. "I know there are a lot of you guys in the Resistance. I hear that members of the *PCF* will be shipped to Germany if they get caught."

"My brother's in prison north of Paris for moving a *Roneograph*, a mimeograph machine, and having purple ink on his hands. My dad was arrested, tortured and died from his injuries so I had to go into hiding. Hey, it's been worth all the rough spots to be able to harass the Nazis. A couple of nights ago another guy and I poured wet sand into a staff car gas tank when the guard went to take a piss. Hope the motor is ruined for good!"

Francois gestured toward the book that Roland was holding. "What kind of stuff does he write? Anything about war?'

"A lot of it, and some about the Armenian genocide, about living as an immigrant. It's in Armenian." Roland tucked the book back in his shirt pocket, "Are you finished eating? I can show you where you'll sleep."

Antoine Dupont peeked in at his daughter Sylvie as she helped Madame Poitier with the dishes then tiptoed to the front room. He pulled back the blackout curtain a fraction and peered out. The apartment was located at an 'L' where the street made a sudden turn so it was easy to see any activity or an unfamiliar person lurking in a doorway. All seemed normal and quiet.

Dupont walked downstairs into a dim ground floor, using his flashlight. He turned into a hall toward a back terrace then reversed to a thick wood door leading to the cellar. The top cellar with vaulted ceilings had been built in the 18th century when many houses in town were re-constructed after the earthquake of 1738. An original, lower cellar had been dug in the late 14th century when the Avignon Popes left their imprint on Carpentras, including its fortified walls.

The first cellar was actively used. There was a ringer washing machine, a stone sink, a pile of suitcases, a large trunk, boxes of Madame's personal items and books, a stack of wood, two chairs with unraveled seats, narrow shelves holding jars of preserves and bottles of wine. On the far wall, a tall cabinet was fitted into a space between two stone half-pillars. It held books covered in newspaper, rusted tools, dusty baskets with unwanted locks, keys, wire, junk.

Antoine's use of the second cellar came about accidentally. He had planned to use the attic for his counterfeiting equipment until he brought the empty suitcases downstairs. Exploring the basement with a flashlight, he noticed the faintest curve of what looked like a keystone between the pillars at the top of the cabinet. He discovered old-fashioned iron wheels behind each corner of the cabinet's baseboard. Pulling on the case, he found a low archway leading to narrow stone steps that circled down and off to the side to an unused *cave*, probably intended for making wine in its day. He cleaned and oiled the wheels and now the cabinet rolled easily.

Antoine had pushed a new electrical wire attached to the main fuse box into seams between the stones, covered it with plaster, run it behind the cabinet to bolts screwed into the staircase's rock wall. It looped to a light in the center of the dirt-floored room. He'd brought in a damaged library table that was tucked in a corner. A small bookcase held a variety of metal and wood boxes next to a deep stone cistern, dark brown and cobwebbed inside.

Now Dupont gently pulled the cabinet out, slid into the narrow opening then walked bent over, down the steps. His contact in the Resistance had sent him a simple order: a matter of filling in new names on identification cards, gluing on photos, forging signatures that had been gathered and stored on cards in a box. The work would be completed in less than an hour.

After the Germans occupied northern France in 1940, thousands of refugees roamed Provence. Some hoped to 'hide in plain sight' with false papers. Others searched for a way to leave France and paid dearly for passports, visas, and *cartes d'identités*.

At first Antoine did favors for a few people that he knew well. He doctored a passport for a young friend who planned to cross the Pyrenees into Portugal and escape from there. Then someone who knew the friend asked for help. When the United States' evacuation of famous writers, artists and scientists expanded to include many more desperate people, Antoine worked feverishly on fake documents, for which a few recipients had paid him handsomely. Although he never was in direct contact with the man called Varian

Fry of the Emergency Rescue Committee in Marseille, Dupont suspected that some of his documents helped Fry's ERC clients.

Antoine amassed official stamps, bribing, paying and stealing to get what he needed. He bought solvent on the 'black market' to erase old names and insignia on used passports and cards. Friends helped by giving him documents that could be reproduced. When boxes full of blank identity cards were unloaded at Avignon's *Hotel de Ville*, one 'accidentally' fell out and found its way to Dupont. He found that he enjoyed perfecting what he considered his art.

However, by mid-1942 Antoine began to fear for his life in Avignon. He contacted a colleague, the curator and director of the d'Inguimbertine Library in Carpentras, who arranged for him to work as a janitor under an assumed name. He had earlier helped the director, his son and the Rabbi when they moved the Torahs and historic items, such as the antique chandeliers, from the Synagogue to the library's basement, where they were hidden among other artifacts.

Within days of meeting Madame Poitier at the library, the Duponts were invited to move in with her instead of living in a hotel. She could use the rent and felt safer with a man in her home. Antoine felt protective of the kind woman and worried that his clandestine work might put her in jeopardy. Florence Gilles-Martin also concerned him. He was taking a huge risk asking her help yet he needed someone unlikely to be suspected of aiding enemies of the Nazis. He would not expect her to do anything risky. Acting as a courier to a few trusted contacts and funneling documents was all that he would ask.

He enjoyed Florence's enthusiasm as they discussed poetry. That she liked the Surrealists surprised him. He expected that someone so traditional, so 'housewifey,' would have preferred readily understood, rhyming prose.

As he guided the bookcase back into place and used a tiny broom of twigs to brush the sandy floor, he thought of a poem by Philippe Soupault. A founder of Surrealism, he had become a well-known Parisian journalist who had moved to Tunisia where he ran a French radio station. Antoine rummaged in a box of his favorite books. He pulled out a volume of Soupault's and flipped through pages to find a poem that vaguely reminded him of the work that he and others in the Resistance were doing:

> *Tomorrow is Sunday*
> *One has to learn to smile even when times are grey*
> *Why cry today when the sun is shining.*
> *Tomorrow we gather with friends*
> *With frogs and birds, mushrooms and snails,*
> *Do not forget the insects, the flies, the ladybugs,*
> *And every noontime I will await the rainbow*
> *Violet, indigo, blue, green, yellow, orange, red,*
> *And we will play hopscotch.   (7)*

JULY:

Ordinarily *boulangers* were required to make brioches and baguettes according to traditional recipes handed down from generation to generation. With the shortages, new styles of bread were based on whatever grains were available. The Bertolini Bakery was an exception. Carpentras' German commandant had selected it as his supplier so the bakery received additional white flour and the finest milled grains. Their customers also benefitted from this alliance, as uncomfortable as it was.

Amélie Bertolini stood next to her father, handing out half loaves. Madame Bertolini collected the money and ration coupons at the brass cash register that, amazingly, had not been confiscated for German armaments. The huge bronze statue of Bishop d'Inguimbert that once stood in front of the town's hospital was not so fortunate. It had been pulled down and shipped to a foundry in Lyon.

Anne-Marie moved to her husband, "Can you two manage while I do some shopping?"

"Of course, *ma chérie*. Amélie can handle the money." Émile paused for an instant. "If you want, take time for a coffee."

Anne-Marie picked up string shopping bags and her purse, stopping to take a remnant of a light brown croissant, and left by the front door. She walked past tables and stalls toward the *allée des platanes*, heading to the produce area.

Within half an hour she was done, the bags weighed down with vegetables and some late-season peaches. Anne-Marie turned back toward the *Grand Café du 19ᵉᵐᵉ Siècle* where contented shoppers sat, pleased at having struck a good bargain or found a needed item. She chose a table in a corner and ordered syrup-flavored mineral water.

When the Germans invaded northern France in 1940, they arranged with Mussolini and his army to oversee the southern or free zone. Although the Italians stationed in the Vaucluse were fascist troops, they had much in common with local families of the same heritage. They shared a language and a culture. Anne-Marie couldn't remember any problems other than their tendency to flirt openly and party loudly. But things changed dramatically when German soldiers had replaced them the previous fall.

She would never forget the wide, frightened eyes of the little girl from Belgium who looked up toward the window where she stood watching. SS soldiers had forced the Jewish child and her father into the back of a truck, battered suitcases thrown in after. The neighbors who had sheltered them stood on the sidewalk, the wife in tears. Her husband restrained her as two soldiers with guns drawn stood on either side. When Anne-Marie backed up behind the curtain, tears rolled down her cheeks, she was aware of faint sobs, her mind numb with self-blame.

Émile tried to reassure her that it could have been any number of people or circumstances that led to their arrest, as the Vichy government tried to fulfill their quotas. There were collaborators in town more than willing to ingratiate themselves with the Germans. Someone angry with the neighbors over some petty incident could have denounced them anonymously. He pointed out that her friend Florence's husband was likely one of these.

Anne-Marie knew that many local Jewish families were being hidden in town and throughout the countryside. Even the dreaded Pierre Laval, head of the Vichy government under Marachel Petain, seemed reluctant to turn over French Jews as, according to the French Constitution, their citizenship trumped their religion. In addition, sheltering the 'Pope's Jews' had remained a deeply ingrained tradition in the Vaucluse since the fourteenth century. The oldest Synagogue in France was in Carpentras, although it now was vacant and, from the outside, looked like any other residential building.

Yet this haggard looking man, a refugee with his six-year-old daughter, had been hunted down, captured, arrested. Anne-Marie reviewed conversations with Henri Gilles-Martin that could have caused him to be suspicious. She remembered stopping once in mid-sentence and changing her phrasing, so swiftly she thought, that he could have mistaken her pause as nervousness.

Then there were the interrogations by Gunther Schmit, who used their son's internment in a prisoner of war camp as leverage. Had an inadvertent slip-of-the-tongue been enough to result in the destruction of four people's lives?

"Anne-Marie, didn't you hear me? You look like you were in a trance. Are you all right?" Florence Gilles-Martin sat down and signaled for a coffee. "I hope that you haven't heard bad news."

"Oh, Florence, I'm sorry. No, we haven't heard anything for over a month. Even Schmit won't tell us if Étienne is all right." She gazed at the soulful eyes of her friend who constantly deferred to her husband, a demanding and stiff soul.

"Perhaps you and Émile can come by for a dessert? It would be so nice to spend time with you." Florence's smile seemed surprisingly relaxed.

"Ahhh, yes, that might be possible. I will talk with Émile."

How many more excuses could the Bertolinis give to avoid being around Henri, whose political diatribes grew more inflammatory every time they met? Anne-Marie patted her friend's hand as she got up to leave. "Let me know when you would like us to come."

Florence watched Anne-Marie walk away then looked around. Antoine had told her that she should sit at this particular table, at this particular time, and wait for someone in the network to contact her. As she sipped a coffee, she observed the passing crowd.

On market day, there was a going-to-church-on-Easter mood, a social atmosphere. Worried faces, glum and uneasy looks were replaced by smiles and the constant bobbing of heads, the congeniality of exchanging news, the warmth of laughter singing across a square. This was the way life ought to be, Florence thought, not with rigid gray-green automatons looking suspiciously at everyone. Some of these recruits looked weary at their posts. Do they, she wondered, think of home when doing their duty for the Fuhrer? Do they think of their mothers and sisters when they watch a crowd such as the one that wandered among the vendors' stalls? Are their hearts so hardened that they look upon us as inanimate objects to be controlled?

Poems were becoming her companion and solace. Florence reached into the slit in the lining of the straw basket and pulled out a book. Antoine was right about Surrealist poetry being difficult to understand, but she was growing to appreciate their writings. Louis Aragon's poems, ostensibly love poems for his wife Else, were thinly veiled critiques of the German Occupation. Florence had found the book the day before in a dusty box at the back of a second-hand shop. She bought it with some food money allotted by Henri. He would be furious if he knew, particularly since Aragon was not only a 'modernist' but also a communist.

She opened the book to a page marked with a slip of paper, to a poem called 'Else at the Mirror.'

Combing her golden hair I thought I saw her
With patient hands quenching an incendiary
It was in the very middle of our tragedy
   And during a long day seated at her mirror
   Combing her golden hair it seemed to me
   It was in the very middle of our tragedy
   Playing an air on her harp without a tremor
   During all that long day seated at her mirror
It was in the very middle of our tragedy
As the week's heart is set on a Thursday
And during a long day seated before memory
She saw them dying far off in her mirror. (8)

Florence sighed contentedly and began to re-read the poem, savoring the sounds. The subliminal message was one of comfort as well as indictment, patience tinged with resentment. The interweaving of words and thoughts were becoming more understandable. That Antoine was confident that she was not only clever but also capable of handling tasks for the Resistance amazed Florence. He had approved of her code name *Ariadne*, the goddess of mazes and labyrinths. He said that it suited her.

Sensing someone next to her, she looked up at a sweet-faced nun, no older than twenty-three or four, her winkle crisply white against a faded black robe. The novitiate held her hands together and bowed slightly.

"*Bonjour Madame*, may I have a moment of your time?"

Slipping the book into the basket, Florence motioned for the young woman to sit. She stared, thinking that there was something very familiar about her. "Yes, of course. What perfect weather we are having, aren't we, Sister?"

The nun smiled broadly and leaned closer to the table. "You don't recognize me, do you?"

Florence sat back with a puzzled look. "Madeleine? But...but...I didn't know! When did you take your orders?"

Madeleine shook her head, "I'm no longer 'Madeleine,' I am *Sister Monique*. However, my orders are not Vatican approved. You might say that they have been superseded by those from London."

Florence frowned then her eyes grew round. "Oh!"

"We understand that you are helping with transfers and deliveries, *Ariadne*." Sister Monique put her hands on the table and bent her head, almost as if she was ready to recite the Rosary that she held over a black book. "I want you to give this prayer book to our friend, *L'Imprimeur.*"

Florence looked down as Sister Monique opened the top pages, revealing a hollowed out center with photographs inside. "Of course, Sister. I will be happy to share such....spiritual thoughts." As she reached for it, Sister Monique placed her hand over Florence's.

"Let us bend our heads in prayer and I will give your further instructions.

THUNDERBOLT - 1978

As Georges and Sophie's guests arrived I removed my apron, smoothed my new yellow linen sundress and entered the living room. Georges introduced me as 'their friend from California, Professor Claire Somerset.' I met the Merciers, another pharmacist and his wife who lived in the village. Then Ambrose Grimaud, an attorney-*notaire*, and his wife Simone appeared with a bouquet of flowers. Last to arrive was a farmer named Maurice Laurent, with a bottle of wine from his vineyard.

He had a handsome, weathered face with dark gray curly hair. While shaking his hand I felt a mild shock, a tingle, run up my arm. He looked at me in surprise, holding my hand a second or two longer than necessary. His eyes opened slightly then he smiled shyly and tipped his head as he, too, said '*enchanté.*'

I returned a polite "It's a pleasure."

Relieving Sophie of the flowers, I headed to the kitchen and put them in a vase. My light-headed, heart thumping reaction to Monsieur Laurent was a surprise. After filling the vase I carried it outside to the table.

Sophie's entertaining was quintessential Provençal. Hand-painted dishes and three wine glasses were ranged at each seat. Good silverware, passed down from her grandmother, added a touch of gleaming elegance with forks turned to show ornate backs. Initialed linen napkins were folded in squares on each plate.

As we wandered into the courtyard Georges handed out flutes of champagne. Sophie and Monsieur Grimaud debated qualities of city council candidates while the Merciers and I listened. I tried not to glance toward Maurice Laurent as he and Madame Grimaud discussed the current heat wave.

When Sophie announced 'à table,' Georges guided me to a seat to his right. I watched Maurice help Jeannette Mercier with her chair then sit next to Sophie. His broad shoulders and tanned, muscular arms under the rolled-up sleeves of his white shirt showed clearly that he was used to working outdoors.

Linen napkins swished from the table to laps. Georges passed a bottle of *viognier/bourboulenc* blend as Sophie brought out the first course. Talk centered on wine and the coming *vendange,* the grape harvest. There was concern about the heat. We turned to Maurice Laurent as he stated that the muscat grapes would be ready to pick within a month. Several offered to help amid light-hearted jesting about the effort required for a few bottles of wine. He quipped about the difficulty of getting cheap labor and then having to feed the workers.

Conversation evolved from politicians to the economy, the real estate market to summer trips, intermittently returning to a discussion of food and wine. Ambrose Grimaud asked me about my visit and I explained that this was my sixth trip to Provence. I was finishing research on writers involved in the Resistance. I mentioned my appointment to talk with Claude Lapeyre, a friend of René Char's.

Jeannette Mercier spoke, "I'd heard that they were good friends."

"Yes, evidently Professor Lapeyre and Char walk together several times a week. He's a great fan of Char's poetry."

"Hmmmm, " she responded noncommittally. "I never could quite see the appeal. A lot of it seems rather vague."

Her husband leaned toward her, "My dear, he was one of the Surrealists and they're supposed to be vague. Isn't that the point, Claire?"

"They do leave a lot up to the reader's imagination. However, I'm interested in how their writing evolved as they got older, as they became members of the resistance movement."

"We are rather proud, actually, of our *Capitaine Alexandre*." Ambrose Grimaud wiped his mouth with a corner of his napkin. "I know men who worked with him up on the mountain. He was a wily fellow, keeping two steps ahead of the Germans. I also believe that he was nominated for the Nobel Prize in literature."

"Yes, during the early 1960's, but others received the award."

After a couple of 'humphs,' talk veered off to vacations taken earlier in the month. Soon Sophie brought out the platter of guinea fowl with mushrooms--*pintade aux cepes;* thin beans--*haricots verts;* a casserole of potatoes with *chevre* cheese and *crème fraiche.*

A little after ten o'clock Sophie presented a peach tart from the patisserie. Afterwards came espresso. Georges then poured the Laurent's *Beaumes-de-Venise Muscat.* He whispered in my ear that this wine had received its AOC designation during the war. I nodded as if I understood.

Conversation, light and filled with laughter, continued until after midnight when the guests departed amid required kisses. I breathed in a musky perfume as Maurice leaned over and brushed my cheek. His parting words were *à bientot,* equal to 'until later.' I could only nod my head as I gazed into brown marbles.

As Sophie, George and I carted trays of plates and dishes, glasses and utensils into the house, Sophie mentioned that they had met the Laurents years before at a wine festival in Beaumes-de-Venise. Maurice had lost his sweet wife the year before.

Georges said, "His brother was in the Resistance and worked with René Char part of the time. Francois still limps from his wound. However, many of the former *Maquis* won't talk about what they experienced."

"It's understandable that many people prefer not to remember," Sophie added. "The atrocities committed were horrifying. Part of the road encircling Carpentras is named for a farmer in nearby Sarrian, *boulevard Albin Durand.* French military police used Durand's mechanical saw to cut off his limbs because he was suspected of sheltering members of the Resistance. A local doctor participated, giving him shots to keep him conscious. It's a gruesome story. Yet, even under such ghastly torture, this man never betrayed a soul."

I know that I looked shocked.

"Retaliations by the Resistance weren't much better—there was inhumanity on both sides," Georges grimaced.

Sophie snapped, "But nothing the Resistance did was remotely close to what the *Boche* did!"

"Claire, much of this controversial history was not exactly swept under the rug but not openly discussed either." George shrugged, "You can see why De Gaulle wanted to focus on rebuilding France's pride.

As I dipped a wine glass under the hot water, I pondered what I was uncovering, delving into wartime stories. Some were heroic and inspiring, others were disturbing and appalling. Just as the French had dealt with dramatic changes, over the past decade the American women's movement had shaken up established values and roles for women. I was beginning to re-examine my own view of what I wanted from life.

I felt caught between my Republican-upbringing and messages from Bella Abzug, Gloria Steinem, Germaine Greer, and Betty Freiden. I had subscribed to *Ms. Magazine* and found the contents constantly challenged my previous beliefs as wife, mother and second-tier professor. With J.T. in college, I could pursue a Ph.D. and teach at a larger university. My darling father suggested, much to my surprise, that I move to San Francisco, buy a Kinko's copy shop and go into business. Or, I occasionally daydreamed, I could chuck it all and work in one of the new Napa Valley wineries.

THE VAUCLUSE – 1940-41

THE ESCAPE ARTIST:

When René Char returned to L'Isles-sur-la-Sorgues from his short service in an artillery company during the 'phony war' of 1939-1940, he knew the commissioner of police in Avignon had him under surveillance. In addition to concern that he was a communist, he was suspected of publishing and distributing pro-de Gaulle pamphlets. In late December, ignoring the pleas of Char's friends and his record of exemplary military service in two wars, the police chief got a warrant. The family house was searched from top to bottom.

On his way out, one of the policemen whispered, "You must leave right away. We plan to arrest you tomorrow."

Georgette Goldstein Char was as likely to be arrested as her husband, since a statute published that October legalized rounding up Jews. Their other great concern was Albert, René's older brother, who was a supporter of Marechal Petain. René pulled his wife aside.

"*Chérie,* I'll bring the suitcases to our room. We have to go, now."

René was used to looking for quick exits. As a child he had often snuck out of his family's bourgeois home, *Les Nevons,* in order to escape the blows and insults of Albert. He would scamper through L'Isle-sur-la-Sorgue to the simple house of a kindly, white-bearded man who regaled him with stories about rural Provence while he cleaned a pistol or rifle. René listened to other old men entertain each other with far-fetched tales of younger days roaming the *garrigue*.

As he got older René ducked out of *Les Nevons*, his backpack filled with rations, to spend days walking in the country. He met hermits and gypsies, fishermen and farmers, men who spoke Provençal, as had his father. He admired these men who knew the constellations and recited old poems, who helped him see horizons beyond the parochial values of his home. His other refuge was at the *Hotel Palerne,* the neighboring home of the Roze sisters: Louise, his godmother, and Adele. A library brimming with books and two tolerant spinsters provided a haven from the rigidity of his family's way of life.

Now once again he was looking for an exit.

Knowing what was likely to happen, in early 1941 Char began to create places where he could hide. He rented an apartment in Aix-en-Provence where his mistress Greta lived with her son Christophe Tzara, then rented two others, in Gordes and a smaller village near Gordes.

Char chose the hamlet of Cereste as his base because he knew the town from the time when he and Georgette had stayed there during a severe illness in 1936. Barely past the border of the Vaucluse, in the Alpes-de-Hautes Provence Department, it was remote and rustic. The residents of the hamlet were taciturn and proudly self-sufficient.

Once established, he became a good friend of the Pons family who lived almost across the street. Their home backed up to one owned by a member of his resistance group, *le reseau Action.* There was the Taupin's place where he and Georgette had lived before. His home and headquarters were across from a granary that was surrounded by convoluted passages. Other safe places to hide were at the Roux family's house, at the local grocery store or in the rented room of Irenée Pons, a mechanic who became his driver.

The house in Cereste was simple. It had one large room downstairs with a fireplace and a stone sink. Up narrow stairs were two bedrooms and a bathroom with a tub. Surrounded by crisp, country air redolent of the wild herbs of the hills, encircled by birdsong and tranquility, René was energized. He adapted well to country life with no running water, an outhouse and a fireplace for heating and cooking.

Georgette was aware of René's various romantic liaisons and had accepted that her brilliant and charming husband would not be faithful. She knew of his affair with Greta Knutson Tzara from when they had vacationed on the coast years before. She knew that Greta was in Aix-en-Provence and that René visited her now and then. Within months of arriving in Cereste, she became suspicious that he was involved with someone in the village. By summer 1941 the tension between them reached a breaking point.

"Look, *ma chérie,* you need to go to Paris and convince your mother to change from Goldstein to our name due to the anti-Semitism. Also you may be safer there than if you stayed here with me. You know that I must be on guard and move around."

It was not a gentle parting although her husband was right. If the Gestapo stepped up their pursuit of the *Maquisards,* she would not only be in danger but could be a liability. The capital certainly had more appeal than living like a peasant in this isolated spot. Georgette packed her bags, grabbed her fur coat and took the bus to Avignon. By the time the train reached Paris, she had accepted that their marriage was over.

René began contacting men and women in the area who believed as he did, that France must find a way to exit from the forced occupation of Nazi troops. Fascism grated upon people who had embraced democratic ideals for one hundred and fifty years.

Char kept a journal and corresponded with friends but resolved that his prose would never be published as long as Germany occupied France. He continued to put thoughts on paper with the expectation that, when France was liberated, writers would once again have freedom of expression.

René Char, center rear, with members of his 'reseau' at a parachute drop zone.

<u>Refusal Song - Beginning of the Partisan</u>

"*The poet has returned for a long span of years into the naught of the father. Do not call him, all you who love him. If it seems to you that the swallow's wing has no longer a mirror on the earth, forget that happiness. He who worked suffering into bread is not visible in his glowing lethargy. Ah! May beauty and truth ensure your numerous presence at the salvos of liberation!* (9)

THE VAUCLUSE - 1943

JULY:

Roland was right. *Maquisards* spent a lot of their time on daily tasks. Somebody had to fix and cook the food, clean up around campsites, cover the latrines with lime or dirt, run errands, deliver messages. Standing sentry duty was a relief, as Francois felt like he was at least in a position to prevent an attack. Betrayal was a constant worry.

In June word came from Lyon that *Max*, the man sent by de Gaulle to coordinate the resistance groups, had been captured by the Gestapo and was in Montluc Prison in Lyon. The SS officer in charge was an especially sadistic torturer. Once Klaus Barbie finished with Jean Moulin, he would be dead. Others in his group were also imprisoned. There was concern that information about section chiefs and camp locations had been compromised.

In early July *Colonel Bayard*, head of the *Group franc du Vaucluse*, obtained a false ID card stating that he was a member of the Lyon police department. He went to the prison and confirmed the arrests, deportations and deaths of those captured. As far as he could tell, not one of the brutalized men had confessed. Moulin died on the train to Germany from injuries suffered under intense torture.

Roland told Francois that Montluc was where his brother had been sentenced to death.

"Is your brother...ummm...all right?"

"I don't know, we haven't heard anything for months." Roland looked down at his hands. "He was rounded up with my dad in 1941. After our father died from being beaten, we were sure that Anton would be shot. However, because he was the eldest and now responsible for our family, he was kept in prison. Then I went underground because of being a communists."

Francois sat down next to Roland. "Why are you a communist?"

Roland sighed, "It's kind of a long story. In 1915 my father, an uncle and an aunt barely escaped the Armenian massacres in Turkey. Their parents paid to have them smuggled to Italy, where they took a train to Marseille. My grandfather and his two brothers died in a labor camp and my grandmother, her sister and two of their cousins died on a death march into the Syrian Desert."

"I'd heard about the massacre but you're the first Armenian I've talked to about it. So what happened to them?"

"My papa, my Uncle Serge and Aunt Adelaida walked one hundred miles north from Marseille to Chateauneuf-de-Gadagne where a colony of Armenians live. My father changed his name from Jahan to 'Jean' and got a job in a paper factory. The family already spoke French." Roland looked pensive. "He said that their life in France was very different from the academic life that he knew growing up. Working conditions were harsh, with unfair laws. They joined the Communist Party to advocate for a five-day, forty-hour work week, two weeks of vacation and decent wages."

Francois nodded, "My family owns land where we farm, make wine and olive oil. It's hard work but at least we control our own lives."

"After the Russian Revolution a lot of people were attracted to Lenin and Marx. Many intellectuals and artists of the time joined the PCF. Like Manouchian, the poet I've been reading."

Francois fiddled with a twig. "I don't understand, though, why you'd stay a communist when it became so dangerous."

"It felt more like a game of 'hide and seek,' nothing that dangerous at first. We used pots of leftover paint or tar to write slogans on walls. We distributed illegal copies of *L'Humanité*. Then a guy our age was arrested and beaten to death in Lyon. Innocent townspeople were shot in place of 'terrorists,' as the Germans called us. Our family had already almost been exterminated so Dad and Uncle Serge told us to stop what we were doing. Then Anton was arrested because he helped a friend move that *Roneo*."

"Yeah, I remember when this really turned bad and the Germans reacted with unbelievable cruelty. So why didn't you change parties, maybe become a socialist?"

"We felt that it was our duty, I guess. We believed in a 'passionate and generous working class' that was supposed to uphold liberty and independence. It took a while for the rest of the country to realize that what we'd said about fascism was right."

"And boy, were you guys spot-on! How long do you think it will be, before the Germans are forced out?"

"I think it will be a year or so. We should place bets on it."

"And who would we trust to hold our money? For a year?" Francois slapped Roland's shoulder. "Besides, as a communist wouldn't you want it divided up evenly between everyone?"

"Very funny, Francois. No, we'd have to give it to the Central Committee and we'd never see a *centime*. It would be used to print posters." The two boys giggled.

Centurion walked up to the men. "Having a good time, guys?"

"Just kidding around. Do you need us to dig a latrine or something?"

"Actually, we've got a more interesting assignment. Four British aviators bailed from their bomber and were rescued, south of Avignon. They were picked up and driven to Carpentras by Gaston Cat. We are to get them to safe houses up on Mont Vonteux. Come over to the shack. We've got planning to do."

Centurion spread a map of the Vaucluse on the rough pine table and pointed with a stick. "The pilots ejected from their plane after it was hit by anti-aircraft fire. They landed in a field here, not far from Saint-Remy-de-Provence. Farmers hid them until Gaston picked them up in his delivery truck. A doctor has performed surgery on one, in the kitchen of the house where he's staying in Carpentras. So we have to deal with one wounded man."

Centurion explained that the pilots would be delivered to Bedoin the next day in Gaston's van. From there the aviators would be taken inland, then picked up and flown to North Africa to rejoin their outfits. Roland and Francois were given detailed instructions.

Early on Bedoin's market day, four Maquisards traveled to the town along different routes. Centurion and Baptiste rode with a sheepherder taking lambs to the market. Androcles and Petrarch rode double on a beat-up but functional motorcycle. The pilots arrived before dawn in Gaston's van. They had false identities from *L'Imprimeur* and new clothes: baggy pants with suspenders, berets and caps. Two wore the wooden peasant shoes called *sabots*. Their recent hosts had taught them more French, augmenting what they had learned at flight school. The injured man grew a light beard that was sprinkled with limestone dust so his use of a cane would not seem odd. He was taken to a house where he'd stay to recover before being passed on to a guide. *Petrarch* met his pilot at a café on a side street, buddies sharing a glass of wine at a back table although neither could understand the other. They left by a back door, hopped on the motorcycle and headed for Malaucene, halfway up Mont Ventoux.

Francois Laurent was waiting at a vineyard a couple of kilometers north of Bedoin. When Gaston stopped to relieve himself, two aviators crept up the trellised rows to meet the man they called *Androcles*. Francois couldn't understand the flyers' conversations. They seemed confused by the map that he used. There was a lot of gesturing, a lot of *merci* and *oui* from the Englishmen. They clearly understood whenever Francois said 'danger, or 'let's go' or 'stop.' One wore British-made boots. Francois thought that this was because he was tall and his feet were big. If they did run into the Vichy police or Germans, those boots would be enough to have all of them shot on the spot.

At first both men acted tense, jumping at any noise. The further they walked into secluded parts of the mountain, the more they relaxed. They followed a steep path into bushes and trees of a narrow canyon. At dusk the group arrived at road above a remote safe house, a former stable with a hole in its roof gaping like an evil eye, the rock walls of a the corral tumbled in disarray. As much as the change of pace was welcomed, it was with relief that *Androcles* watched the pilots clamber down the path toward the ruin. There a sheepherder would take over and lead them south.

Under a half-moon, Francois walked back to his own camp, an easy two-hour trek. He arrived to a welcome reception and claps on the back. Roland wanted to know if he'd met someone pretty along the way. A couple of the other guys continued the ribbing, releasing tension after a harrowing day.

The next morning Centurion had news.

"The Englishmen safely arrived at their first stops and will be moved around until they can be picked up in a *Lizzie* and flown to Algeria." He paused. "However, the Gestapo are on their trail and a couple of guys in Carpentras have been arrested, our friend Gaston Cat among them. We are relocating our camp early in the morning so pack your things. Sentry duty is to be doubled tonight."

AUGUST:

The blistering heat of summer cascaded across the Rhone Valley without a sign of either wind or rain. Groves of olive trees, genetically programmed over centuries of Mediterranean seasons, weathered this in their persevering way.

In a large grove directly in front of him, Jean-Pierre Laurent saw green fruit turning a purplish-brown under the protection of silver green leaves that augured well for a harvest in November. Olives were their most important crop, upon which the families in the region relied.

A dozen or so apricot trees, on a narrow piece of terraced land along the gravel road leading to the *Domaine de Lauritaine* buildings, had been harvested in June. Sunbaked leaves hung like bits of tobacco, on trees with twisted old bodies, waiting to drop at the first autumn chill.

The grapes were Jean-Pierre's concern now. He turned northwest and stood with his hands on his hips, a cigarette dangling from his mouth, his face shaded by a stained cap as he surveyed four precious acres of muscat vines, along the border of the commune of Baumes-de-Venise. For the past decade he had been part of a group of vintners in that region, north of Carpentras, striving to get their *Muscat de Frontignan* varietal wine designated as a *cru*, the top category, under an *appellation de controlée (AOC)*. The final application and selected bottles from each participating vineyard had been submitted the previous year to Baron Leroy de Boiseaumarie, founder in 1935 of the institute that awarded the AOC designations. Documents and cases of Muscat had been sent to the committee overseeing the requirements just weeks before the Germans swarmed into Provence. Since then, the Baron and the committee had ceased making decisions.

In order to improve reputations and have prestigious names, wine regions throughout France were regulating their production. Several AOC 'crus' had been granted in the Cotes-du-Rhone between 1936 and 1940. A 'cru' designation allowed the use of the town's name on the label. Winegrowers from Tavel only produced rosés. Chateauneuf-du-Pape vintners could choose among eight different red grapes and five different whites for their blends.

At *Domaine de Lauritaine* extra barrels of the Muscat were in the farmhouse's hidden cellar, unavailable to Nazi officers who assumed their *droit de seigneur* in confiscating whatever pleased them. And this perfected dessert wine pleased them greatly.

Jean-Pierre called to his teenaged son who had been his shadow since infancy. Maurice alternately stared into space or was in the way when his father had some project going. He had hands too large for his skinny arms, feet that caused him to trip, a nearly constant dimple in one cheek. As he walked over to a vine, Jean-Pierre motioned for Maurice then squatted down and picked up a handful of soil and rocks. It was so hot that he quickly sifted it through his fingers. Lifting green leaves with crisped edges, he reached for a bunch of yellow grapes clustered together as if safety was in their crowded numbers. He plucked several and bit into them.

"Voila, Maurice. Taste these! There is no need to check the sugar content. Can you tell that they are almost ready to pick?"

The boy did as he was told, gazing thoughtfully into the distance as he sought to remember the texture, taste and essence of the fruit.

Later in the week, Jean-Pierre and a dozen others involved in promoting this grape would meet with Louis Castaud of *Domaine de Bernardin*. Castaud, the leader of those championing the Baumes-de-Venise Muscat as a *cru*, might know if there was action toward the AOC designation. Those in this pioneering group would share opinions on the likely date of harvest and ways of avoiding the full allotment demanded by the Germans.

After the devastating Phylloxera epidemic of the late nineteenth century, thanks to the introduction of native California rootstock and the process of grafting, France was again leading the world in the creation of fine wines. Jean-Pierre remembered his father and grandfather discussing grafting techniques with Messieurs Paul and Émile Fenouil at their seed store and nursery, located on a flat terraced spot between the city of Carpentras' high retaining wall and the Auzon River. Many times they had driven a wagon in to pick up cartons of rootstock and cuttings, and get advice.

The father and son lumbered up steps toward an upper terrace of Grenache vines, planted by Jean-Pierre's grandfather. Removing his cap, Jean-Pierre wiped his forehead and face with a grimy handkerchief. Replacing his hat, he bent to survey velvety purple clumps that were beginning to wrinkle. He tasted a couple, spitting out the seeds.

"What do you think of these, my son?"

Maurice mouthed a few of the grapes, biting, chewing.

"We might harvest these earlier than usual." He sounded tentative.

Jean-Pierre nodded, "Good. We probably will have to move up the *vendange* a week or so."

Blended with syrah grapes, these vines would provide the table wine, a palatable *vin ordinaire*. An extra barrel would be siphoned off for the family from what the Germans allowed, to be kept in their hidden cellar.

Maurice turned and plodded down another row of vines, heading north, periodically looking under a leaf and trying another grape. Jean-Pierre watched him for a few minutes, musing that his second son had been born with earth under his fingernails, unlike his older brother.

In the pasture to the southwest Clotilde huddled under a tree, her neck dangling limply. Only an occasional twitch or swish of a tail made the mare seem alive. Juliette Laurent, wearing a broad-brimmed straw hat, was in the kitchen garden plucking beans from trellises, dropping them by handfuls into a basket in her other hand.

"Juliette!" Jean-Pierre called as he walked past the *noria*, a hydraulic pump that brought water up from the creek. He noted that if rain didn't arrive soon, he would need to turn on the pump and irrigate the vegetables. Juliette Laurent smiled at her stocky, tanned husband, waving her hand.

"*Ca va?*" she called out.

Her dark hair was in a bun, with tendrils dampened by sweat edging her attractive, unlined face. A beige garden smock covered a faded sundress. Her wooden sabots were dusted by red-brown earth.

"I guess so," Jean-Pierre commented as he came up to her and nuzzled her neck with his mustache. "The muscat should be ready in a month but I think we'll also have to pick the other grapes in six weeks. I hope that this heat wave breaks soon."

"Look over to the *Dentelles-de-Montmirail*," Juliette pointed. "I think the tops of the trees are starting to move at the edge of the mountain. Maybe a mistral is on its way."

Jean-Pierre shaded his eyes and squinted to the northwest.

"Maybe," he commented laconically. "We can hope that it brings a shower with it. Is this what we're having for supper?"

He pointed at the basket, filled with beans, a few carrots, some radishes, a turnip.

"I'll make a *salade composée* and an *omelette*. It's too hot to cook much else." She looked at him and bit her lip. "Still no word from Francois?"

"No, chérie, nothing. But that is good news, you know. He's probably safe at the resistance camp, wherever that might be."

Tears suddenly filled her eyes. "And Gabrielle, too? No word from her in over three weeks. I am so concerned about her being in Cavaillon, with so many Gestapo there."

Her husband frowned, "Juliette, what do you expect me to do? I can't rush down and drag her home. Gabrielle is an adult and she should be able to use good sense! Besides she's not especially political. We have enough to worry about here at the Domaine."

Juliette touched his arm, "You are right, but we all have to be so careful. Speaking of that, Florence sent a note asking if she and Gigi could come out on Saturday and help me with the canning. As usual, I think that they want more fresh vegetables and wine."

Juliette saw her husband's expression turn sour.

"I know, darling, I know, but Henri is not coming. He has his usual rehearsal or meeting to attend. They can't possibly suspect that Francois has joined the Maquis. We'll talk about news that he's sent from Germany to keep up the pretense. If needed, we can show them the fake document."

John-Pierre rubbed the side of his face in weariness.

"*Mon dieu!* A son fighting in the *Maquis*, your cousin married to a collaborator, your uncle a pacifist, your parents hiding out who-knows-where, our daughter working in a town where the Gestapo is based. We've hidden fugitives in our cellar. All we are missing is a communist in the family!"

"We haven't hidden anyone for over six months," Juliette looked sideways. "*Anatole* probably has either found easier places or the numbers have diminished."

Jean-Pierre sighed. "I need for Maurice to start repairing and stacking the harvest baskets and oiling the tools. It will give him something to do besides brood about not being old enough to be in the Resistance."

"I've also asked him to ride to Monsieur Napier's with eggs to exchange for honey, for the jam. He can find out the latest news from them about de Gaulle and the Allies. And there's always weeding to do in the kitchen garden."

"When he comes back, tell him to meet me in the barn."

Her husband pulled out another cigarette from the pack in his pocket, frowning at the odd herby odor of those he had learned to concoct. Juliette watched him for a few minutes, adding Jean-Pierre's impatience and barely controlled outbursts to her list of worries. The Allies had just invaded Sicily and were establishing control of the Mediterranean. She was torn between hope and fear as she and her family waited for liberation. The upheaval would be worth the risk, yet the anticipation was like pressure in a champagne bottle waiting for the *bouton* to be loosened.

SEPTEMBER:

Xavier Chevalier sat at a table for two at the edge of the café's terrace, his head tipped up toward the sun, his eyes closed. The heat of mid-August had faded and a rainstorm two days before had allowed the softness of autumn to emerge. The elderly man basked in gentle warmth and gentle thoughts.

On the table next to an empty wine glass lay a book by Jean Giono. It was a novel that Xavier had read years before. With paper being rationed fewer books were being printed, and Monsieur Chevalier enjoyed re-reading his favorites. Giono's descriptions of the rural landscapes were sensual and tactile. Xavier could descend into the lushness of a time and place he wanted to remember as real. Stories like this one and memories of the Provence of his childhood made the Occupation endurable.

The book was *Jean le Bleu*, published in 1926 and based on Giono's childhood in Manosque, a town on the south side of Mont Ventoux. In the story, Jean's mother was a laundress, his father a shoemaker. He becomes an adolescent shepherd who reads the *Iliad*. Before the war, in 1939, Marcel Pagnol had made a film based on *Jean le Bleu* called 'The Baker's Daughter,' starring the comedian Fernandel. Xavier remembered it as a delightful escape from the tension of the times. He agreed fully with Giono's view of the world:

> *"From the time we began to build houses and cities,*
> *since we invented the wheel, we have not advanced*
> *one step toward happiness. We have always been*
> *in halves. As long as we invent and progress in*
> *mechanical things and not in love, we shall*
> *not achieve happiness."* (10)

The sound of a chair scraping startled Xavier and he turned to see Henri Gilles-Martin smiling down at him, a glass in his hand.

"Monsieur Chevalier, may I join you?"

Xavier bobbed his head and gestured, "I'm happy to have company. And how are you, on this lovely autumn day?"

Henri looked around, paused then smiled quizzically. "Yes, it is a nice day. Sometimes we forget to stop and enjoy the moment."

Xavier did not say anything although he certainly agreed.

Henri continued, "Well, things seem to be settling down now that vacations are over and school has started. I'm glad to see that the Milice are in evidence, keeping things in order. It's important that people be protected from the terrorists, you know."

Xavier nodded in agreement as he signaled to the waiter to bring him another glass. "Ah, yes. The constant feeling of being in danger is not pleasant. I greatly miss the days when we could walk wherever we wanted, at any time we wished. Those days of plenty, when we profited from the bounty of this beautiful land."

Gilles-Martin looked at Xavier with a squint, not sure what to make of the remark, then spoke sharply. "If everyone joined in supporting Marechal Petain's goals for returning France to traditional values, emphasizing our heritage and family unity, then we would be able to walk about freely. Our problem is communists and foreigners who do not respect our laws."

Chevalier bent his head, humming to himself. Henri leaned back, "Are you all right, Xavier?"

"I, ummm, I don't like to talk about war and our daily problems." He grabbed for a glass on a startled waiter's tray. "Merci, monsieur."

"Well, of course, I know that you believe in 'pacifism.' However, there are times when one must confront evil and stand up for what one knows is right."

"Certainly, certainly." Chevalier answered in between a sip. "Now that the students are back, you must be quite busy."

"Oh yes. I find it reassuring that our young people today are being given more guidance. Once the Vichy government was organized, we reinstated a course in religion and there is much more emphasis on physical activity. I'm sure that you have seen the *Chantiers de la jeunesse,* the youth workers, exercising and practicing parade skills in their uniforms down in the *allée des platanes.* Also I am pleased at the progress of the students learning to speak German." Henri let out a satisfied sigh.

"Yes, ummm, the students. I like young people." Xavier picked up his book as he set the empty wine glass on the table. "I'll see you at orchestra rehearsal, Henri. Do give my warmest regards to your lovely wife and daughter. I see them when Juliette is in town, from time to time."

It was Henri's turn to murmur 'hmmm' as he watched his wife's relative hobble off toward what he imagined was a dingy apartment where he probably played his clarinet and read books. Although Florence addressed him as 'Uncle Xavier," he was really some distant cousin by marriage. The whole family was strange, Henri mused, a burden that he'd had to endure since he had married dull little Florence.

A TABLE FOR TWO - 1978

Carpentras attracted few tourists. Perched on a high ridge, the old *centre ville* did not have major historic buildings for guidebooks to feature. With a population of twenty-some thousand, residents primarily worked in family businesses or agriculture, in an area nicknamed 'the garden of France.' It was a quiet place to live.

Feeling like a spellbound tourist I exulted in walking through the streets. My fingers traced hand-hewn stones, trying to picture the people who built the walls, those who carved the designs in stone or wood, who forged the iron of balconies and gates. The cobalt sky in the narrow lanes hovered like a wide silk ribbon. Where others might see decay and obsolescence, I saw layers of history that gave me perspective, a sense of the brevity and preciousness of life.

Taking a break from sorting through notes, writing, and eating sandwiches at the kitchen table, I wandered into a bistro mid-week after the Dupré's dinner party. A slate board propped on an easel at the entrance listed the *menu du jour.* The proprietor walked toward me, a white napkin tucked over his black pants. I saw him glance over my shoulder to see if I had a companion.

"I'm alone," I mumbled and was guided to a table by a fountain tinged by green moss under a vine-covered arbor. A young *serveuse* brought a smaller version of the slate board and asked if I wanted an *a la carte* menu. Declining, I selected three items, a glass of rosé and a carafe of water.

A number of tables were already occupied. At one, a large man had tucked a blue and white checked napkin under his double chin, in addition to the restaurant's napkin over a rotund stomach. He was telling a story to his friend across the table, a dark-haired fellow with a brushy mustache, a Gallic nose and receding chin. A slim wife with short henna-colored hair and round spectacles sat quietly across from another woman, with a chignon and hoop earrings. Their husbands carried on a subdued but spirited conversation, consuming their food with gusto, periodically clinking glasses in agreement. This camaraderie lightened my heart, made me smile.

Then I saw Maurice Laurent seated across the terrace. He stood, shaking hands and talking with two people. The owner brought a bottle of wine cradled in his hands and the foursome seemed to be discussing it. After the couple moved on, Maurice sat down as the man uncorked the bottle and poured a glass. He took a sip and they continued talking.

Replacing my glasses, I reached in my purse for a composition book full of notes. Holding it in front of my face, I read a poem of Louis Aragon's, unsure how to react, wishing that I'd washed my hair that morning.

> *"I'll reinvent for you my rose as many roses*
> *As there are diamonds in the waters of the seas*
> *As there are past centuries adrift in the dust of the*
> *earth's atmosphere*
> *As there are dreams in just one childish head*
> *As there can be reflections in one tear."*

I peeked at Maurice. He was looking toward me with a puzzled expression. Lowering the book, I hesitantly acknowledged him with a nod. He nodded back. I looked at my notes, uncertain. When I glanced up again, Maurice was walking to my table.

"Bonjour, Madame. I hope that I am not intruding if I say 'hello' and that it was nice meeting you at the Dupré's."

"*Non, non,* not at all." I closed the notebook and slipped it into my purse. "How nice to see you again. I am surprised that you're in town, as you must be getting ready for the harvest."

"I needed to talk with one of our vendors. Besides one needs to take time to enjoy a bit of life." He smiled charmingly, "I hesitate to ask and please feel free to not accept, but may I join you?"

I felt my face flush and instinctively pulled at a strand of hair as I stuttered, "Certainly."

As he sat down, Maurice signaled the waiter and asked that two glasses and his bottle be brought to the table.

"We just opened our 1976 red. Would you like to try it?"

Maurice filled my glass. Clinking rims, we both said '*santé.*'

"Do you know why we touch our glasses when we drink wine?" Maurice asked. I shook my head.

"Many centuries ago in Europe, if one dined with powerful people who had something to gain by one's demise, there was a certain amount of risk. Poison could be slipped into the wine glass of a disliked guest. Thus it became a custom to pour a bit of wine from one glass to another so that one knew the wine was safe to drink. It meant that you were among friends."

Maurice held up his glass.

"That's a great story," I exclaimed.

"I don't know if it is true or not, but I do like the thought."

"Here's to being among friends," I tipped my glass.

"Yes, I hope that this will become true with us."

Maurice's candor surprised me. This was not typical of the usually reserved and well-mannered Frenchman. However, conversation was easy. Maurice helped when I searched for a word in French. I enjoyed hearing about his work as a farmer and a winemaker. He talked about the *Domaine de Lauritaine*, the changes he was making to improve their red wines as part of an *Appellation d'Origine Controlée* or AOC.

"I don't know what is meant by AOC."

"Ah, well, France is known for its rules and bureaucracies. In the middle of the nineteenth century, the wine industry established a system in the Bordeaux and Burgundy regions that controlled the kinds of grapes and the percent of each grape allowed. When someone talks about, for example, a Medoc wine from the Bordeaux region, we understand that it is primarily made from cabernet sauvignon grapes. If it is a St. Emilion, it is primarily merlot. Today only three other grapes are allowed in Bordeaux wines: cabernet franc, petit verdot and malbec."

Maurice held up his glass.

"If it is a Northern Cotes-du-Rhone red wine, syrah is the primary grape with grenache noir blended in. In the southern region, where my vineyards are, we use the reverse: grenache noir with with syrah in a smaller amount. There are also other red grapes that can be used: mourvedre, cinsault, carignan, muscardin and cunoise. Our Domaine's label is under the AOC Côtes-du-Ventoux."

He turned the bottle's label toward me.

"That sounds really complicated! The USA uses a much simpler method. For years beverage companies have produced what we call 'bulk' wine, labeled either 'red' or 'white!' However, a number of wineries are focusing on producing a single variety such as cabernet sauvignon or syrah."

"You seem to know a bit about wine," Maurice queried.

"I live not far from Napa Valley. Have you heard of it?"

Maurice thought a moment. "No, I don't think so."

"Ah," I said. "There have been wineries in that valley for over one hundred years. Some famous brands are Inglenook, Christian Brothers and Charles Krug.

Maurice wrinkled his forehead. "No, I don't know them. We don't drink California wines in France. At least I've never had any. We have enough of our own," he laughed.

"So I suppose that you've never heard of the 'Paris Tasting' two years ago?"

Maurice looked puzzled.

"In 1976 several new Napa Valley winemakers entered a contest in Paris comparing American and French wines. In the United States this 'Paris Tasting' was big news because the wine that the judges picked as best was a California Chardonnay."

Maurice looked amazed. "*Non!* That's not possible. In comparison to our wines? Who judged it, country café waiters?"

I reacted sharply, "The article I read said that they were top wine critics, sommeliers and *restaurateurs* picked by the wine shop owner who organized the tasting."

The silence between us seemed heavy until Maurice shrugged and leaned forward in his chair. "Well, they didn't taste our wines. What do Paris wine shop owners know, after all? They are focused on Bordeaux's big reds and Burgundy's two grapes. They should have included a Cotes-du-Rhone blend such as a *Chateauneuf-du-Pape.*"

"I'm sorry to say that I don't know much about the wines of this area. You are right. American wineries seem to be focused on Bordeaux varietals or Chardonnay and Pinot Noir."

"*Tant pis!*" Maurice exclaimed. "Too bad! Now I know that you must come visit my place to taste a few really good blends. You seem to have liked the one today."

I was amazed to see that the bottle on the table was empty. Without noticing I continued to sip whenever Maurice refilled my glass. Glancing at my watch, I saw that two hours had slipped by without my realizing it.

"It went perfectly with the duck leg and its cherry sauce."

"If you are available next Saturday afternoon I could give you a tour of *Domaine de Lauritaine* before the picking begins."

After a second's hesitation I agreed. Maurice and I discussed the details of when and how, then noticed that the owner was stowing the slate menu board behind the bar, the server was clearing all the empty tables. Only two others were still occupied. Clearly, lunch was over.

THE MAN OF MANY NAMES
LOUIS ARAGON

L ouis never really had his own name. His given name, it turned out, was one that his biological father chose—after a town that he visited in Spain. A former ambassador to Madrid, a senator, married and head of another family, the man went out of his way to ensure that his bastard son was never publicly acknowledged. His foster mother and sister told him that he was an orphan that they had adopted. As he was leaving to fight in the First World War his 'sister' informed him that she was really his mother and his father was a famous politician.

While trying to elude the Nazis, Louis Aragon assumed a variety of names. Using a new identity every few months or so seemed perfectly logical, in the scheme of things. The current one by which he was known in the remote mountain village of Saint-Donat was Lucien-Louis Andrieux. He enjoyed the fact that for the first time in his life he was using his father's real surname. The old man, long ago deceased, would not have been happy.

Known as the 'poet of the Resistance,' he published under names such as 'Francois-the-furious' and 'Jacques Destaing.' He and his wife Else changed locations, names, identities and even appearances every few months. In 1942, in

Lyon, they were known as Monsieur and Madame Castex or the Maysargues. This 'new' Monsieur Andrieux and his wife, now called Elisabeth, had escaped from Lyon for Saint-Donat in July 1943.

During World War I, Aragon worked as a medic in the *Val-de-Grace* hospital. Young men were carted in on stretchers with missing limbs, gaping wounds, burnt faces and lungs, unconscious or screaming. He felt helpless in the face of such incurable injuries. In 1919 he met André Breton, another young doctor, in a bookstore in Paris and they talked for hours. They had similar tastes in literature and the arts, and were stunned by the war casualties that they encountered in the hospital.

After the Armistice each was honored with medals and lofty sentiments. They contacted each other and established a scholarly review called simply '*Literature.*' Surrounded by other writers and artists, the pool in which they swam was full of nutrients that stimulated creativity, generated the desire to change the world, and opened their minds to unlimited possibilities. He, Breton and Philippe Soupault churned out their heartaches and disillusionment through subconscious thoughts, automatic writing and other experimental methods. They welcomed Tristan Tzara, founder of the Dadaist movement in Zurich, when he stepped off the train in Paris. Although they had parted ways over political--and literary--differences long before the Germans invaded in 1939, Louis Aragon thought of these colleagues with fondness tinged with remorse.

As a young soldier he was ordered to fire upon striking miners who refused to work in tunnels under proven dangerous conditions. Louis refused. His sympathies were with the workers. Aragon had abandoned belief in God soon after his first communion and, in his teens, became an admirer of Marx and Lenin. By 1927 he was a member of the French Communist Party (PFC). Currently he was an editor of their newspaper *L'Humanité* as well as a member of their resistance group, the *National Front.*

Louis met the Russian beauty Else Triolet at a Montparnasse café in 1929, shortly after his translation of Lewis Carroll's '*The Hunting of the Snark*' was published. Due to Else's contacts, Louis was warmly received at the Association of Revolutionary Writers and Artists' conference in Moscow.

They wed just before he was mobilized in 1939. Since then his gracious and loyal wife, an established author in her own right, had provided the steadfastness that he needed.

Aragon's aristocratic looks belied his intensity and courage. While serving as an army medic during the 1939 'phony war,' he led thirty soldiers in a daring escape from German forces. After France was defeated, he was awarded the *Croix de Guerre* and a medal for acts of bravery. Immediately after, he and Else headed for Nice where they hoped to be safe. There he wrote the prologue to a book of paintings by his friend, Henri Matisse.

In mid-1941 Louis and Else illegally crossed from the 'free' to the 'occupied' zone to attend a writers' conference in Paris and were arrested. Although eventually released, they came close to deportation. This grim experience made them more committed anti-fascists and more cautious.

Getting published during the German Occupation was difficult. Everything was subject to censorship. As well, lead for typesetting and paper was scarce. Many big houses such as Gallimard in Paris reprinted books by approved writers and occasionally featured new ones provided the subject was non-political. However, small and more mobile underground companies could print what they wished, in limited and covertly distributed editions.

One such publisher lived a double life, editing poetry and articles for the Nazi-controlled Vichy government at the same time that he printed anthologies of anti-fascist prose. Pierre Segher, energetic, intelligent and innocuous appearing, had published his first review in the 'free zone' of Provence as a demobilized soldier in 1939. He called it *Poetes Casques*, 'for poets of the resistance, open to all voices.' Louis Aragon was one of his first subscribers, submitting a poem called 'The Separated Lovers.' Segher then established his shop *Les Editions du Tour*, in Villeneuve-lès-Avignon across the Rhone River from Avignon.

The Aragons met Pierre and Anne Segher in 1941 and they ended up staying in the Segher's 14th century tower apartment, once part of a wealthy Cardinal's villa. Pierre told them of his youth in nearby Carpentras, his introduction to great literature, his haunting of the town's d'Inguimbert Library. He and Anne had met there as students. At the age of sixteen, because he had to earn a living, he became a salesman of hotel and restaurant furnishings in Avignon.

In 1942 Segher printed Aragon's famous anti-fascist prose, 'The Eyes of Else.' In May 1944 one of the young publisher's books titled 'Poets of Today,' dedicated to Paul Eluard, was distributed. The second edition was dedicated to Louis Aragon and a young member of the Maquis who hid the Seghers when the Gestapo were on their trail in July 1944.

In September 1943 Louis Aragon had another collection of poetry publshed, this time by Eluard's *The French Library*. The best part—it was printed from type that was stolen from a shop owned by Pierre Laval, the detested Nazi collaborator in the Vichy Government. Laval had made his fortune as a publisher in Clermont-Ferrand. Two members of the Resistance got into his print shop, packed up boxes of lead letters and carried them on a train down to Eluard's shop in Saint Flour. The next day, two couriers left carrying suitcases bulging with thousands of copies for distribution throughout France.

This day in the spring of 1944, Louis looked out from his latest quarters toward mountains covered with snow. The scattered gray roofs were no longer capped with white although it would be a month before a true spring arrived in this valley, 3500 feet above-sea-level. His third novel, *Aurelian*, was finished and he was ready to start on the fourth, which he planned to call *Les Communistes*. His hero in *Aurelian* was a young man deeply affected by both world wars and involved in a tragic love affair. Loosely autobiographical, he knew that it would not be published until after the war ended, but he also knew that could be very soon.

Louis turned toward the door as he heard footsteps. Else's beautiful, calm face peeked in. "*Mon cher*, lunch is ready."

Louis walked over and kissed her. "As always, darling, you call and I will do your bidding."

She laughed and kissed him back. "Then do come on."

They walked down to the kitchen where a table was set for two. The warmth from the stove was a welcome change from the chill of the upstairs. Louis removed his coat and hung it on a hook. Else had concocted soup from scraps of the week's meat and bits of vegetables, served with oddly speckled bread and a slice of cheese.

At a knock at their front door, the couple looked at each other and did not move. The knocking continued and they recognized the voice of their neighbor, Monsieur Alphonse. "Are you there?" Pause. "Are you there?"

Louis let the gray-mustached man in with a whoosh of frigid air. He bolted the door as Alphonse stomped his feet and slapped his gloved hands. "*Zut alors*, it is cold enough to crack a rock!"

Else stood and shook his hand. "Monsieur, would you like a bowl of soup with Lucien and me?"

The wizened face looked concerned for a moment, "I am sorry to bother you! I didn't even think…." His voice trailed off as he became aware of the aroma engulfing the kitchen.

Else sensed his eagerness under a vain attempt to be polite. "Sit down, dear friend, I will get you a bowl."

Alphonse did not hesitate and tucked a napkin under his chin. Else winked at her husband, both of them fairly sure that their neighbor had just finished a meal at home.

"So, Monsieur Alphonse, I presume that you have news," Louis leaned forward in his chair.

An avowed socialist, Didier Alphonse spent most of his days at the town's hotel with his cronies, veterans from World War I. The Aragons/Andrieux often learned of events from him before the news hit the paper, from who was newly engaged to who was recently arrested.

"Ah, oui, I have good news! I found out that an Englishman parachuted in to Mont Mouchet to help get ready for a deluge of arms. The liberation has to be coming!"

"That is good news, Monsieur," Louis smiled at Else. "This will certainly help the Maquis, so long as they stay out of reach of the Nazis. It also seems that collaborators are as frightened as the Nazi officers are aggressive. That makes for a dangerous blend."

Alphonse mopped at his mouth. "But, Monsieur and Madame Andrieux, writers of novels, that is not a dangerous career I would think."

"*Non, non*," Louis said quickly. "Still, one should be cautious."

His guest looked serious. "Did you know that I was interrogated in December right after that group of *Maquis* was killed? The *Milice* thought that I might have known one of the boys. I only knew that his family sold cheeses at the market. Still it was not a pleasant experience having a wild-eyed former street sweeper scream at me, spitting his garlic breath in my face. I have to keep a low profile, you know."

Louis did not dare look at Else for fear of smiling, as he was sure that they both were trying to imagine Monsieur Alphonse keeping a low profile, anywhere. His reputation as a teller of tall tales and speaking his mind was hardly subtle.

As Louis sat there, enjoying the anecdotes of their guest, he felt almost relaxed. He and Else just might make it; they had been incredibly lucky so far. Their fellow poet and friend René Tavernier in Lyon, who covertly published Aragon's anonymous poems in his various revues, had once again offered to let them stay at his home. Else was already packing in anticipation of another flight.

I Salute You My France *(excerpt)*

I salute you my France where winds become calm
My France of forever, that geography
Opens like a palm branch to the sea breezes
So that the bird from afar comes trustingly
I salute you my France where the wandering bird
From Lille to Roncevaux de Brest to the Mont-Cenis
For the first time was made aware
Of what it cost to abandon her nest.
Country alike for the dove and the eagle
Where songs and courage share equal space
I salute you my France where wheat and rye
Thrive under the sun of diversity. (11)

Louis Aragon (1897 – 1982) with Else Triolet
and Pierre Segher at Villeneuve-les-Avignon in 1941.

THE VAUCLUSE - 1943

SEPTEMBER:

Florence seemed more robust and animated as they worked together. Antoine didn't mention this but did compliment her on a nice-looking new outfit. She confessed that the skirt was made from a pair of Henri's pants with worn-out cuffs. She didn't tell him that Henri had not noticed.

As they sat and talked in the closet space, Antoine scratched his chest. "I'm getting hot."

He pulled off his suspenders, removed his shirt then pulled up an undershirt. Bandages swathed around his chest were held together by safety pins. He unfastened them as he turned and unwound the gauze. Florence helped by rolling it. Against his back was a thick envelope. Florence held it as the last of the fabric fell away, and looked at Antoine expectantly.

"Well, I guess that you know what this means?"

"My next assignment!" she stated.

"Another clandestine and dangerous assignment."

At the look on Florence's face, Antoine reassured her, "*Non, non,* this delivery should be easy. Were you told when and where to take these?"

"Yes, I spoke with Sis…another courier."

"Good. My contact obviously likes the job that you're doing. You've managed discretely considering your husband's position."

They sat and talked about was involved. Florence, distracted by the light brown hair on his chest, looked up and focused on his face. Her partner stopped and, mid-sentence, put on his shirts and pulled up the suspenders.

"How did you like André Breton's 'Manifestoes of Surrealism? Did it help you understand Surrealist poetry better?"

Florence looked pensive. "I haven't read much about Freud, but Breton must have been influenced by him. Dreams and psychiatry evidently influenced his writing."

"His experience as a medic in a psychiatric hospital during World War I may also have contributed to this."

May I read a quote that I liked?"

She opened a book with slips of paper sticking out. "He says *'I have always been amazed at the way an ordinary observer lends so much more credence and attaches so much more importance to waking events than to those occurring in dreams. Man... is above all the plaything of his memory.'* " And here's another," she continued without stopping: " *'The mind of the dreaming man is fully satisfied with whatever happens to it. The agonizing question of possibility does not arise.'*

She looked at Antoine, puzzled. "Do you believe that dreams are equal to reality?"

Antoine did not answer immediately then said, "The mind is very powerful. Whether one has dreams, uses imagination or distorts a rational view, in many ways it all melds together to make a person who they are and what they believe."

"Ah, and Breton mentions that. My favorite part, so far, is this." Florence read softly: " *'Man proposes and disposes. He and he alone can determine whether he is completely master of himself, that is, whether he maintains the body of his desires, daily more formidable, in a state of anarchy.'*"

"Why do you like it?"

"I had never really thought about this before." Her voice was a whisper. "The ability to change, to change things."

Antoine tried lightening the mood. "That's what reading and education do to a person! The next thing I know, you'll be writing poetry."

Florence closed the book without answering. Antoine looked at his watch and announced that he had to leave. He had been assigned extra work at the museum. She put the documents in the hidden compartment of her shopping bag and gathered up her things. They kissed cheeks and he watched as she opened the door a crack, waited for a minute and then waved slightly before sliding into the main reading room.

Antoine's assignment was to clean the museum across the courtyard three days earlier than usual. The *Kommandantur* had requisitioned it for a private party with three of his top aides and some women from one of the brothels on *rue du Refuge*. Beds were to be installed in partially concealed areas among the art works. After an unsettling few weeks, the officers intended to spend an evening of debauchery away from prying or insubordinate eyes. The *Kommandantur* wanted one evening of light-hearted fun before enduring what he anticipated would be more months of problems.

Conflicting information from Berlin and Paris, not to mention Marseille, about diverting the two best divisions to the west coast was causing confusion. Older veterans, some barely recovered from wounds, and difficult troops conscripted from Eastern countries challenged his officers' ability to keep up morale and discipline. Damage by terrorist groups required continual repair of telephone lines and railroad tracks. Parachutes were reported around Mont Ventoux although nothing had been found by his patrols. Forays into villages with threats of destruction were not effective in ferreting out troublemakers. The German commander was frustrated and wanted to relax, if only for an evening.

When Antoine entered the Museum's foyer, he found a grim-faced secretary and two volunteers packing the remaining *objets d'art* that had not already been hidden from avaricious hands.

"*C'est la guerre,*" he thought as he headed to the sink in the basement.

SEPTEMBER:

Étienne Bertolini crawled to a corner of the dark cell. His second attempt at escape had been thwarted and the beating had left him with a broken index finger, a gash on his forehead, bruises down his back and along his left thigh. He felt blood ooze from his mouth and reached up to touch it.

With relief he realized that it was due to a missing tooth and not from an internal injury.

He pushed up against the cold wall, trying to focus on his surroundings. Beams from the camp's searchlights flickered through a high window. Across from him were two mounds under ragged blankets.

Étienne breathed deeply to check that no ribs were broken. He was sure that, after being given meager rations, he would be put back in his work detail. Laborers were needed to harvest the potatoes and turnips in fields surrounding the camp and a village nearby. Although prisoners of war were not supposed to work, by international law, as the Nazis drafted their own men into the armed services they were replaced with POW's and conscripts shipped in from France.

Étienne did not know how much weight he had lost over the past three and a half years but his once muscular body had wasted to almost skeletal dimensions. His previously wavy brown hair was shaved within one-quarter inch of his scalp. His even features, aristocratic nose, wide-set brown eyes and easy smile were reduced to a stretched-skin version of what had been a good-looking young man.

He wrapped a thin, smelly blanket around his body as best he could, trying not to touch the throbbing finger. He had learned in this hellhole that pain, a great deal of pain all at once, had a way of becoming a remote irritation. Sensors shut down and passing out was a relief. The young man leaned back and soon dozed fitfully.

A creaking door and the thud of boots woke him. Pale sunlight streamed in the narrow window. Étienne heard guttural words, unintelligible at first, then phrases indicating that bowls of maggot-infested gruel would be shoved under a groove in the iron-covered wood doors. He recognized the voice of Sigmund, a vicious thug with a stout body, a twisted mouth on a pugilistic face. He thought that the other guard might be Herman, who was tall and fair-haired, blue-eyed, mildly retarded and willing to do what Sigmund dictated. They had enjoyed beating Étienne although the commandant made it clear that he was to be left in good enough shape to work.

Sigmund's brutish face appeared behind an opening as he slid back the metal cover and barked, "*Achtung*. Up, stand at attention."

Crawling on all fours, Étienne pushed himself upright. He saw one blanketed form emerge, grope the wall and stand up. There was no motion from the other blanket.

Sigmund barked again, "You! Stand up or you'll get another beating."

There was no response.

"Look under the blanket. Is he alive?" Sigmund was gruff.

Gerard, a railroad worker from Lille, had been captured after his train of armaments was sabotaged. He shuffled to the inert shape and pulled the blanket back from the battered face of a man with gray-flecked brown hair. He felt the man's neck and shook his head.

"*Mort*," he said.

Sigmund grunted, stated that he'd be back and slammed the peephole shut. Étienne turned to Gerard, whom he knew drove tractors. "Are you all right?"

The other man nodded.

"Why are you in here?"

Gerard's head drooped. "Stealing bread. Carlos was sick and missed his share. I tried to take it to him but we got caught."

Étienne sat up as they heard boots pound their way back into the jail. The door opened and four guards entered. Sigmund and Herman stood with Lugers in hand as their colleagues rolled Carlos onto a stretcher, placing the dirty cloth over his face. They lifted the carrier and marched out of the cell. Sigmund slammed the door and locked it.

The noise of inmates gathering in units on the parade ground could be heard. The murmur of French, Spanish and Polish voices merged with shrill German commands and sounds of motors as drivers hauled away work crews. Étienne had learned German at the *Lycée* and was nearly fluent. Few in camp knew how much he understood. The sudden bang of a door and the grind of the lock shocked him into awareness. Next to Herman stood Klaus, one of the guards at his bunkhouse.

Klaus muttered, "You nuisance! Why did you cause trouble again? You are on barracks cleanup today and I'm short handed."

Étienne forced himself to stand and totter toward the door. He looked at Gerard who stared, expressionless. He looked at Klaus, nodding toward the other man. The guard barely moved his head in a 'no.' Klaus grasped Étienne's elbow roughly then let it become a support. They walked into bright sunlight with Herman following. The two crossed the packed dirt between the jail and the barrack. Étienne felt his limbs loosening as Klaus pulled him along.

Under his breath the guard spat out, "What a stupid, stupid thing to do! You are damned lucky to be alive. If I had been on duty the night that you pulled this stunt I would have been transferred. That *kapo* Sebastian was whipped and Oskar has been sent to the front. You idiot!"

Étienne whispered out a 'sorry' between clenched teeth.

When they climbed the wood steps into Barrack 13-C, Klaus helped Étienne sit on wood slats of the first bunk. He scooped water from a bucket, handing it to the prisoner.

After consuming a second ladle, Étienne closed his eyes for a moment then spoke, "*Dankeschön.*"

"Yah, Yah," the gray-haired, wrinkled, sad-faced man said in an exasperated tone. "*Dummkopf.*"

Klaus had been in the camp as long as Étienne had lived there. He was stern and followed the rules, yet he was not one of the sadists who gravitated to this kind of work. He confided to Étienne that he had been a prisoner of war in Great Britain for almost two years, during the Great War. Although there were hardships he was treated decently.

A cautious friendship sprang up between them. Quiet conversations were snatched at intervals. Over time the two discussed literature, music, their families. Klaus's daughter had died in the 1918 flu epidemic and a son had been killed on the Russian Front. His remaining son had lost half a leg when his Panzer Mark IV tank caught fire in the Libyan Desert. He was home, moody and depressed, adjusting to an awkward prosthesis.

Étienne told him of paternal great-grandparents who came from Italy, of sheepherder ancestors, of a grandmother who married into the Bertolini 'baking' family. His mouth watered when he described his parent's bakery and choked up when he showed a snapshot of his sister Amélie. Klaus looked at the photo for many minutes and declared that she reminded him of his daughter. Étienne's other photo was of his sweetheart Laurianne, who mailed him hand knit scarves and sweaters and sometimes tucked in a poem from one of the underground papers. When he learned that guards confiscated the food she sent, he told her to not send any more.

As the war stretched for over almost four years, Klaus's certainty in Hitler's ability to rule Europe began to waver. He had quietly mentioned his weariness at the fighting, the damage and the fear. Etienne had simply listened.

As Klaus handed Étienne a broom he spoke like a stern father. "You must not try this again, promise me!"

"I'm not sure how much longer I can hold up. I don't know...," Étienne bowed his head.

"You must. The war will finish sometime, maybe sooner than we thought." He softened his voice. "The Americans have invaded Italy. Our troops on the Russian Front are not doing well. I think maybe there will be a truce and you can go home. You need to be patient. Don't push your luck."

Klaus frowned and shook his finger. The young prisoner sighed, his shoulders slumped but he nodded his head up and down and began to sweep the soiled hay into a pile.

SEPTEMBER:

As usual on Friday, the *allée des platanes* and the major squares of Carpentras teemed with vendors ready to haggle. Buyers lined up, measuring out coupons from ration books, sorting their francs and centimes. Once described as a 'shower of noises, full of peasants and poultry,' Friday's market was now like 'game day' in the Vaucluse. A certain amount of side business would be conducted as long as it was done discretely.

Florence Gilles-Martin sat under a *platane* tree by the 19th Century Café, waiting for Anne-Marie Bertolini and Juliette Laurent. Although the air on this fall morning was cool, her underarms and palms felt sweaty. She breathed deeply to calm her nerves, trying not to glance at the new, generously sized straw bag at her feet. In its fake bottom were identity cards and documents from *L'Imprimeur*. On top of these she had placed a red scarf and her purse.

Most of the transfers had gone without incident, but *Ariadne* suspected that she had been followed to one rendezvous point. Henri, happily, neither seemed aware of her trips to the library nor curious about what she did with her time as long as the apartment stayed clean, his shirts pressed and meals were served promptly.

Juliette waved as she came around the corner from the rue de la Republic carrying two tattered cloth bags, obviously weighed down with bottles. Plunking down opposite Florence, she apologized for being late. Uncle Xavier had been chatty when she delivered his usual oil and wine. Maurice was taking a bottle of olive oil to Josian Rousseau's family, an excuse to spend time with his friend and get the latest news.

"*N'inquiete pas*, Anne-Marie isn't here either. Let's go ahead and order something."

Just then Anne-Marie rushed up, still wearing an apron.

"Sorry, we received a special order from the *Kommandantur* and Émile is in a dither about getting enough flour and butter. Fortunately it is not a large event and Amélie wasn't asked to work." She frowned, "Is everything all right, Florence? You look pale."

"I'm fine. You are the one I worry about." Florence raised her eyebrows, looking questioningly across the table as her friend looked away.

"*Non*, still no news from Étienne. Perhaps the *Croix Rouge* has not been able to get mail from their POW camp due to train delays."

Florence said softly, "I can only imagine how worried you are, as Juliette is with Francois working in a German factory. I would be out-of-my-mind if my son were in a place so far away."

"Well, we try not to attract notice so we don't ask many questions. Here you are, as I promised." Juliette reached for her bag and pulled out two bottles of wine.

A stocky man wearing a beret, farmers' dungarees and leather boots with wood strips as soles, sat inside the café by a small-paned window directly behind the women. He held a newspaper in front of his face with his good right hand, his withered left arm dangling at his side. He identified the courier *Ariadne* by the hat that she wore, yellow straw with a red flower. After finishing their coffees, the three kissed cheeks and left in different directions. *Anatole* folded the paper as best he could and put it on the table. He grabbed his shopping bag that held some turnips, rutabagas and a few eggs. Lacy green carrot tops cascaded over the basket's edge. A list, identity cards and instructions for *L'Imprimeur* were under the false bottom. He nodded to René Dulfour behind the bar as he sauntered outside.

Walking a good distance behind Florence, he watched the red flower bob among taller patrons. He passed her as she talked with a woman at a vendor's table. He wandered through the stalls to a dairyman's truck with the cheeses displayed on the back end. They exchanged coupons, money and a few words. *Anatole* observed Florence walk by with her basket, now also showing a splay of carrot tops, as she headed toward the mushroom vendor's stall. She had tossed a red scarf around her neck. He took his time, pausing to speak to a couple selling crocheted dishcloths and homemade jams.

Several people were in line for the mushrooms, which were almost depleted. Florence was third and glanced around at the crowd, although Anatole didn't think it was unusual for someone waiting for service. He constantly checked for the *Milice*, himself.

Noticing *Anatole*, the courier placed her straw bag on the ground to the right of her leg. A woman behind her with a cranky three-year-old walked around to the other side, shushing her child, oblivious to the fact that she was usurping Florence's turn. Maxime Fischer took advantage of the distraction and placed his bag next to Florence's. The similarity of the two was no coincidence.

After Florence purchased the limit allowed, she leaned over and picked up the basket that her contact had put down. She put the newspaper-wrapped mushrooms inside, hooked the bag in the crook of her arm and turned to leave. She barely glanced at *Anatole* although her forehead was puckered, her cheeks pale, her mouth pinched.

Anatole placed his purchase in the much heavier basket and made his way out of the crowd. He headed toward a mud splatted *gazogene* car that used wood charcoal for fuel, its thin tires needing repair. The driver had contacted a young woman in the *Kleber network* whose duty was bringing news to families of men wounded or killed. At least this time, mused Anatole, there was only a boy with a broken leg. He plopped into the passenger seat, nodding to *Ignace*. Within minutes the car began its journey toward Sault.

Maxime Fischer's rare appearance in Carpentras or, for that matter, any of the towns down on the plain, had been uneventful. As the Resistance numbers swelled it was critical to know what was going on. He had been given a message from London for *Capitaine Alexandre*, in charge of drop zones on the southern side of Mont Ventoux; another for *Colonel Bayard*, in charge of sabotage south of Apt. He'd tried to find out about Gaston Cat who was still under arrest, without much success. He'd replenished his medical supplies from one of the doctors in town. He'd successfully retrieved documents from the new courier who seemed unlikely to attract attention.

Lighting cigarettes that had arrived in a drop earlier that week, *Anatole* and *Ignace* drove in companionable silence. *Anatole* blew smoke into the air and watched as it clouded the beauty of the surrounding countryside. The Allies would be arriving in less than a year. Where or when he had no clue, but he and *d'Artagnan* would have their troops ready and waiting.

As Florence turned from a narrow lane into the square near her house, she was surprised to be confronted by three soldiers searching grocery bags. A half dozen irritated shoppers stood with terse expressions as their purchases were probed, before they were allowed to leave. Florence waited her turn as a bead of sweat trickled down her spine.

IT GOES WITH THE TERROIR - 1978

In the late afternoon on Saturday, Maurice waved as he stood at the side of a run-down car, a pale green, well-used *deux chevaux*. I walked to where he'd parked in the *allée des platanes*, again aware of an odd tingling sensation as we kissed cheeks. His scent, whatever it was, was appealing. His profile reminded me of a Roman statue, the curls, the slightly curved nose, well defined lips.

We headed down the hill by the Porte d'Orange toward fields of fruit trees and grapevines. Along the way I got a lesson in viticulture. Maurice explained again that only a few areas scattered around the slopes of Mont Ventoux were awarded *Appellation d'Origine Contrôlée* status as a *cru*, the highest rank in the Cotes-du-Rhone. Wines designated as *cru* used the name of their town on the label, such as Tavel, Gigondas and Chateauneuf-du-Pape, the oldest and best known. The next level was 'Cotes-du-Rhone Villages AOC' with the name of the town such as 'Sablet.' The least prestigious wines were labeled just 'Cotes-du-Rhone Villages' and 'Cotes-du-Rhone.'

"Our family's red and rosé wines are under the 'AOC Cotes-du-Ventoux,' which was granted in 1973."

I asked, "What does that mean, exactly?"

"Cotes-du-Ventoux is a region of fifty-one communes or parishes with over one hundred thirty different producers. Because we are on the slopes of Mont Ventoux, the 'giant of Provence,' our *terroir* has microclimates and soils from ancient seabeds that influence our blends. I'll explain more as we taste the wines."

We drove through the center of the village of then turned toward Mont Ventoux. Maurice explained that a deep frost in 1956 had wiped out the olive orchards throughout most of the Vaucluse. Instead of producing olive oil, they became vintners. After pulling out dead and deformed trees, he and his father had planted more vines to add to what they already had. Their vineyard was in the 'Malaucene basin,' an area that was more protected from the Mistral winds than those further south, toward the Durance River.

"My father passed away a year after we got the AOC. But he lived to see our vineyards granted two prestigious *appellations d'origine contrôlée*. We are very proud of our *cru,* the *Beaumes-de-Venise Muscat* that you tasted at the Duprés. But our AOC Cotes-du-Ventoux red wine is also making gaining a reputation. Regulations call for at least half the *mélange* to be grenache grapes and no more than thirty percent syrah."

He and his son, Julien, were experimenting with adding a combination of mourvedre and cinsault to get the perfect blend. The grapes were grown as organically as possible, using natural fertilizers, no pesticides, allowing the *terroir* to be in control. Maurice was obviously proud of his family's generational involvement in agriculture and good reputation. He was passing on the same values to Julien, who had just finished a degree in chemistry, and Joseph, studying biology at Montpellier University. His daughter, Marie-Laure, was at a music conservatory in Paris.

"Julien will inherit the Domaine and has decided to emphasize the scientific side. He spent a year working at a top Chateauneuf-du-Papes *vignoble*. He and his new bride, Martine, live in Jonquières,"

Maurice looked over at me and I had trouble focusing on his words instead of those limpid brown eyes.

"I tried to talk them into living here at the farm but Martine teaches at an a primary school in Orange. Julien works with me and is very good at figuring out the chemistry. He's gradually learning about vine and crop management."

"There's a lot to the business of agriculture."

"It is more complicated than many people think." He pointed to his right. "There's our farm, the house is right behind those trees."

We drove between stone pillars with a wrought iron arch that spelled out the name *Domaine de Lauritaine*. Both young and twisted, thick-trunked olive trees were on either side of a sloping gravel driveway. On the left was an orchard of apricot trees, devoid of fruit. To the right was a neatly terraced vineyard, heavy with dark purple grapes.

"*Lauritaine?* What does that mean?"

Maurice chuckled, "A distant ancestor combined his name, Laurent, with that of his wife's name, Barbitaine, when they built the house in 1742."

"Your family his lived here since then? That's amazing."

"Yes, considering the Revolution and various upheavals, the wars, we have been lucky. My older brother was supposed to inherit the place but he didn't want to farm and became an accountant instead. Family members share in the profits or buy each other out so the old place has been in our hands for over two centuries. I'm the seventh generation to live here."

The house with dusty, uneven apricot-colored tiles, a facade with faded blue shutters, was an emblematic Provençal calendar scene. Oddly shaped, added-on structures were stacked in different levels on either side, fitted into and following the terrain. A crusty farming implement, a tiller, sat in a bed of wildflowers in front of a jagged, low stone wall. On the left side, an arch in a crumbling rock wall led to a patio. This was dotted with large glazed pots that held gray-green lavender plants or heat-scorched geraniums.

Maurice parked the car by an open barn filled with farm equipment, to the left of the house. A dog of undistinguished lineage, resembling a Beagle and a Russell Terrier cross, rose from the shade of a tree and gave a deep-throated bark. He sidled up to Maurice as he opened my door.

"This is our dog, Simon," Maurice knelt and let his pet lick his cheek, lovingly patting the dog's back. "He's been with us since the children were teenagers. Now he's my companion, two old bachelors managing on our own."

Maurice stood and gestured toward the arch that jutted from the side of the house. "This was the entrance to an original building, probably from the 1500's, as is the terrace floor of quite worn stones. Be careful as you walk. It was already in ruins when the farmhouse was constructed. Would you like a glass of water before I show you around?"

"Something cold would be good."

We walked through the arch to a rustic table under an enormous *platane* tree, with a trunk almost the width of a California redwood. It leaned inwards, shading almost a third of the terrace. I sat in an iron chair in need of sanding and paint and waited while Maurice went into the house. I removed my straw hat and smoothed wind-blown hair with my fingers. Fanning myself with the hat, I reveled in what I loved about Provence: the timelessness of ancient stone, the careless beauty of nature casually and bountifully displayed.

The Laurent's house had a dilapidated elegance to it: chipped stucco with rocks showing through, a broken patio chair leaning against a wall, rusty garden tools dropped, unclaimed, a withered rose bush climbing above a window. I thought of the contrast between the neatly manicured lawns and trimmed hedges of suburban California houses and the random disarray of rural France. Through my muddly thoughts, Aragon's wartime poem wandered....

Oh month of flowering, month of transformations
May that is without cloud and knife-sharp June
I will never forget the lilacs and the roses
Nor those that, in Spring, keep their shapes... (12)

Maurice arrived with a white tablecloth over his arm and a tray on which he'd placed a pitcher and two juice glasses, two wine glasses and a bottle opener, along with half of a baguette. We arranged the items; he poured some water then raised his glass in a salute and we drank thirstily.

He pointed to the vineyard terraces that stretched down to the narrow road and explained, "This is the syrah vineyard. Our olive grove was there before the frost. As you can see, those vines are not ancient ones. Behind the barn are the grenache vines that my grandfather planted, about one hundred years ago. Let's start where we press the grapes and store the wine."

We walked back through the arch and to the left of the equipment garage, past an entrance to a low building with steps leading down to it. A tile-roofed barn with a sliding wooden door stood separately. Pushing the door aside, Maurice helped me step into a dim room filled with wooden tanks and barrels. The perfume of fermented grapes, the heady smell of wine, was powerful.

Maurice clicked a switch and overhead lights went on. He pointed to two large stainless tanks and remarked that these were for the syrah and grenache; the smaller tanks were for the muscat, the cinsault and mourvedre. Oak barrels with notations on them were stacked along each side. The floor was cement except for a wooden platform where a long table sat against one wall, dotted with various beakers, bottles and testing equipment. Notebooks lay about, a clipboard hung from a nail.

At the end of the building was another sliding door. Shoving this aside, Maurice continued his narrative, pointing out the de-stemmer and crusher on a cement pad next to an upper road. Behind the road stretched a vineyard on a slight hill. We walked around the side of the wine barn and he pointed to our right.

"That creek borders the muscat vines on the other side which are considered part of the Beaumes-de-Venise commune."

We meandered across the road and through vines into the first row of apricot trees neatly spaced in the reddish soil that flowed down to the road leading to Beaumes-de-Venise.

"Come. Let's select some bottles from the cellar."

He took my elbow and we walked back to the balustrade leading down rocky steps. Beyond was a low arch, the entrance to a narrow stone building. Flicking on a light, Maurice and I walked past some dusty barrels on the left. In the back corner, behind a protruding wall, was a curving stone staircase that led down to a door from centuries before.

"Be careful, Claire," he cautioned. "Part of this cellar was built at the time of the first house. The steps are worn and slippery in places."

He reached for my hand and helped me down. Taking a large iron key from a hook in the wall, Maurice turned it in an ancient lock and bolt system then raised an iron bar and pushed. With a creak the door swung wide and the scent of wine poured out. He flicked another switch that lit up fluorescent bulbs on the ceiling. Maurice reached for a flashlight on a shelf to his right.

Come on," he motioned as I stepped into a long vaulted cellar.

Diamond-shaped wood shelves ranged along both sides of rough-hewn rock walls, full of horizontally placed bottles. Boxes marked with the Domaine's logo were stacked in the middle of the floor. Immediately to my left was a deep stone vat with a dark brown interior. At the end of the cellar was another door, narrow and more modern. Maurice walked to the left, pointing his flashlight at various labels. He pulled out a bottle.

"This would be a good one to taste. It's a new blend, two years old and ready to drink. Ah, and here's a rosé." Walking to the opposite side, he flashed the light on dusty bottles with faded, yellowing tags. "These are older vintages--some from the 1960's. I think that this 1966 has held up well."

He handed me a bottle.

"And back here," he moved to the shelves at the far end, "are the muscats that we've reserved from the 1940's. We also have a couple of cases of Chateauneuf-du-Pape and a great red from 'Seguret,' recently given an AOC 'Cotes-du-Rhone Villages' designation "

He rummaged down the shelves, checking labels.

"Is there more wine in that room?" I asked, pointing to the modern metal door.

Maurice walked over and opened it. He hit a switch and a light in the middle of a beamed ceiling lit up what looked like an extension of the first cave. Maurice moved inside and I joined him.

"My wife kept her jams and preserves there. For the most part though, we use it for storage."

The room had the same rock walls darkened by mold and dust. Directly in front of me were stone treads that curved up inside a supporting tower. There were two wide shelves at the far end and one looked like it had a mattress on it. Dust frosted barrels lined the left wall. Narrow shelves to the right of the staircase contained a smattering of jars, old appliances, kitchen junk, rejects that appeared no longer useful. In a corner, a stone sink with a brass spigot jutted from the wall.

I turned to Maurice with a puzzled look. Maurice noticed and grimaced slightly.

"This is where the original cellar connected to the main house. I'll explain later why we divided it into two rooms during the Occupation. In the meantime, let's try out these wines."

The lusty *cigales* concert kept pace as the summer sun eased west. Maurice and I sat under the tree, tasting from each bottle. We swirled, inhaled, sipped. Much of the wine was spit on the terrace's grass edged stones but, I will admit, a good amount was swigged. Baguette pieces lay scattered on the tablecloth.

We discussed aromas: berry, earthy, stone fruit, a touch of smoke, leather, tobacco, dirt? What food would be enhanced by each?

"Your new blend would be perfect with a Compté cheese."

Maurice said it was perfect with anything!

In between discussing the wines, our talk was interspersed with bits of information about children, marriages, a death and a divorce. I leaned back in the chair. "Maurice, I think that your wines are delicious! And the rosé--I never tasted one with such depth."

"*Merci*," he said seriously, as he waved his arm toward the vineyard below the house. "We may have one of the best vintages this fall in several years. The summer was cooler than usual. And this nice heat at the end will bring our sugars up just enough without making the wine too overpowering."

"When did you get the AOC *cru* designation for the Muscat?"

"It was actually granted in 1943 but we did not find out until after the war, in 1945. My father was one of those working with a fellow winemaker, Louis Castaud of the *Domaine des Bernardins*, in promoting the muscat. Gradually, though, others in the region realized the importance of improving the quality and gaining recognition. *Papa* also was concerned with preserving the land, not using pesticides, being sustainable, *biologique*."

"Ah, *bio*, organic. That is planning for the future."

He leaned forward on both forearms and looked at me, saying, "So, are you staying here in the Vaucluse for long?"

I glanced away. "I'll be here until the middle of October. I'm spending a semester doing research in order to make modern poetry more interesting to the students that I teach at Sir Francis Drake College, a small private school in my hometown."

"You said something at the Dupré's about writers who joined the Resistance."

"Yes, a number of the Surrealists became involved, as did other modern writers. They already were expressing the dichotomy and senselessness of the post World War I era and segued from this to anti-fascist themes. They worked with artists such as Picasso, Matisse, Duchamps, and musicians such as Eric Satie." My voice trailed off, "I sound like I'm giving a lecture."

I twirled my glass, wondering if Maurice particularly cared.

"It's interesting how times of crisis cause some people to re-evaluate their views, others to become more determined to preserve the old ways of doing things. But what do you expect to find here in Provence?"

"I hope to talk with the poet Réne Char. In a couple of days I will meet with a good friend of his to learn about his early years."

"My brother Francois' crew worked on parachute drops that Char organized."

I leaned forward, "I would love a chance to talk with him!"

"I can ask Francois if he'll do that, although he rarely talks about what he did."

"When I was in Paris I had a chance to meet the Irish playwright Beckett who won the Nobel Prize for literature in 1969. After barely escaping from the Gestapo in Paris, he lived in Roussillon. Toward the end of the war he again worked in the Resistance, although he is reluctant to make much of his life as a *Maquisard*. I find these writers' experiences intriguing."

I felt a bit awkward, again twisting my glass.

"I'm glad that you find French men intriguing." Maurice's smile was mischievous. "Sometimes we seem very steadfast, *de pied ferme*."

"In English we call that being a 'stick in the mud.' And, no, I don't find most French like that, at all."

Maurice put down his glass and began to cork the bottles. "Would you like to see the *mas* from inside? Remember, I told you there was a story to go with the second cellar."

THE VAUCLUSE - 1943

DROP ZONES:

In September 1943 Camille Rayon, known as *Archiduc* in the *Armée Secrete (AS)*, returned to Southern France from de Gaulle's London headquarters. He was to establish landing sites for containers that would be dropped throughout Provence in preparation for the Allied invasion. The man he selected to organize the *Basse-Alpes* area was the six-foot-four-inch, thirty-seven year old poet René Char who was living in a remote hamlet on the mountain.

René was blunt. "If you want me to manage this area of Mont Ventoux, you must understand that I expect to have a large margin of independence. I'm not an easy person."

Rayon understood. "René, I have confidence in you."

The Valensole plateau on the mountain's southern edge, fifteen hundred feet above sea level, resembled a high, flat Kansas plain that tapered up against the Alps of eastern Provence. Wind swept the plumes of grain below a lavender blue sky that melted into dark gray jagged peaks. Remnants of once abundant almond orchards were tucked around the edges of the plateau like bits of lace.

In November a group of men stood at the side of a field prickly with wheat stubble. They wore a variety of farm hats, common work boots and sabots.

A couple leaned on scythes, one held a long-handled ax. The man in charge, now known as *Captain Alexandre*, stood several yards into the field, arguing with the owner. The problem was an enormous wide-branched walnut tree, smack in the middle. Both men gestured with their hands, pointing and interrupting each other.

"There is no way that I will permit that tree to be cut down! Look at it. It is magnificent. It has stood for over a century. *Non! Non!* Never!" The farmer folded his arms in determination.

"Monsieur, " the *Captain* spoke softly, "I know that you want to help France regain her freedom. In the next few months, the Allies will be parachuting in arms, ammunition, food, radio operators. We have to support them when they arrive. The planes will fly in low and may need to land in an emergency."

The farmer folded his arms, his expression dark.

Captain Alexandre swept his arm in a grand gesture, "Look at this level, hidden field. It is a perfect landing site except for the tree. Imagine a plane full of Frenchmen returning to defend their home, a load of munitions that can be distributed throughout the Vaucluse. The pilot knows that they have been hit by anti-aircraft and he sees this perfect place to land. Only when he does, the plane slams into that tree and everyone, everything inside, goes up in flames."

Char stopped to light a cigarette, letting the silence expand. "Do you want to be responsible for that loss?"

The farmer mused on his run-ins with the Germans, the confiscation of his farm animals, the worry over his nephews in the STO. He sighed, shook his head.

"This horrible war! All the losses that we have suffered and even more to come." He lowered his head, his shoulders slumped. "All right, cut it down."

As the farmer walked away, Char turned toward the men at the edge of the field. He raised his palm and nodded his head. He had won this particular battle but did not feel any pleasure in destroying a living thing of such beauty and age.

Archiduc admired his friend, as did the young *Maquisards* who worked with him. He was known for his strategic planning skills, his tireless energy, his compassion and congeniality. He touched the poet's shoulder. "Good job, René. We can bring our team back tomorrow morning to remove the tree. What shall we call this landing site? We've already got 'tourist,' 'vineyard,' 'spitfire.' 'the long field.'

The poet looked to the sky. "I'll think of one after we're finished."

The next day a crew of men with double-handled saws, pick axes, crowbars and shovels arrived in vehicles from bicycles to a butcher's van. Tree branches were attacked first and cut into useable firewood. Workers carried and stacked logs in the van and a truck. Soon two-handled saws were needed for the big center branches. Cutting through the immense trunk took until past noontime. Bit by bit the elegance of the ancient tree was reduced to a tall stump.

After a lunch break, as the men lounged on the edge of the pasture smoking and relaxing, René explored the base and looked for the main root. He found and isolated a thick piece that wound at least thirty feet further. Probing with a shovel, he began to excavate the root. Then he hit something that sounded metallic. Brushing aside dirt he saw what looked like rusted iron. Motioning the crew over, Char pointed out his discovery. At first they thought it was a piece of old machinery. As they dug further, a human bone was found then another and another under bits and pieces of metal. They realized that they had unearthed the remains and armor of a soldier, perhaps from a century or more in the past.

A piece of a walnut shell was found in what appeared to be the pocket of a leather vest at the top of the man's femur. René liked the coincidence and tried to convince the men that this was precisely where the tree had sprouted.

Archiduc later asked, "Do you have an idea for a name yet, René?"

The poet thought for a moment.

"*L'abatteur.*" He grimaced as he looked back where the magnificent specimen had stood.

"Ah, yes," Camille Rayon nodded. "One who slaughters or cuts things up."

Within weeks, reliable British Lancasters, nicknamed *Lizzies*, began dropping canisters and men. René Char wrote in his journal:

> *"The airplane descends. Invisible pilots heave off the ballast of their nocturnal garden then press a brief light under the armpit of the apparatus to signal that it is done. Only the gathering up of the scattered treasure is left. The same for the poet... (13)*

OCTOBER:

Looking at herself in the full-length mirror on the armoire's door, the young woman turned and peered over her shoulder to make sure that the seams in her silk stockings were straight. She bent down and adjusted one behind her left knee then made a pirouette and smiled broadly.

Gabrielle Laurent was reluctant to wear the expensive hosiery to work, as much due to snide comments as the concern that she might snag the precious hosiery. However, she was sure that Colonel Von Hellmann would pass by her desk at the *Hotel de Ville* that morning to talk with Monsieur Fournier, deputy mayor of Cavaillon. The handsome, blond, blue-eyed officer had always been extremely courteous to her, a lowly receptionist-secretary in the entry. Over the previous few months he had taken time to talk with her in his excellent if accented French before he went upstairs.

Because he was one of the dreaded Germans occupying her country, Gabrielle was prepared to detest the man. Instead, from the day that he walked through the door to introduce himself to the Mayor, she thought that he was one of the handsomest men that she'd ever seen. He was tall, with polished manners, a charming smile, probably in his mid-forties. He did not appear threatening, even in his crisp label-ridden, silver encrusted uniform.

Oberst Dieterich Von Hellmann was in the habit of bringing a little gift every couple of weeks to Gabrielle as well as to the Deputy Mayor's private secretary. Sometimes he brought a tiny bottle of perfume from a house in Paris, a silk flower for one's hair or hat, most often a box of chocolates or other candies. Last week he arrived with a flat package for Gabrielle that he slid under a file on her desk while he waited to be summoned. Inside were the stockings.

Gabrielle leaned close to the mirror to ensure that her lipstick was on straight and none was on her teeth. She stepped back and looked at herself with satisfaction. Girls like her grow up accustomed to people smiling at them, bashful boys flirting with them, hearing the elderly compliment parents on their child's good looks. As well, they saw their reflections in comparison to other girls, realizing that their even features, well-spaced eyes, plump lips, coloring, were those that defined beauty. Her naturally wavy, auburn hair, green eyes and perfect skin were due to nothing other than pure luck, a genetic godsend. Yet, as with many an attractive young women, she tended to think that it was her entitlement to have such attributes.

She wore a form-fitting green sweater and a pencil-slim dark brown skirt. Four-year-old brown leather pumps with three-inch heels were polished to a high shine. She had on pearl and gold earrings that her *mémé* and *papi* gave her when she completed secretarial school in Avignon. She was sure that she appeared much older, more mature, than her twenty-four, well almost twenty-four years. Picking up her handbag and swinging the suit jacket over her shoulders, Gabrielle walked confidently downstairs and toward the city hall.

When Colonel Von Hellman arrived Gabrielle was sitting with her ankles crossed to the side so the stockings were visible. She made sure that she appeared busy and kept typing away, unconcerned about mistakes. She would correct them later. She waited until the carriage of the typewriter clanged back to the start of the page before looking up and greeting the German with a wide-eyed blink and a soft "bonjour, monsieur l'Oberst."

Von Hellman chuckled and lowered himself to the chair beside her desk. "Bonjour, Mademoiselle Laurent. I believe that I am a bit early for my appointment with *monsieur le deputé*. I hope that I am not disturbing you if I wait here for a few minutes." He leaned close to her face, looking directly at her with pale blue eyes fringed with dark blond lashes.

Gabrielle felt an overpowering urge to lean forward and kiss lips that appeared defined and sensitive. Instead she responded by leaning fractionally closer. "It would be my pleasure. Shall I notify Madame Moreau that you are here?"

The German paused and smiled, "Perhaps not yet. I would like to talk with you for a minute."

Gabrielle did not move and stared back, smiling.

"I think that, considering all the difficulties of the times, you might not have much of a social life let alone decent meals. Would you be my guest for dinner next Thursday evening?"

Gabrielle had trouble breathing and gasped, torn between her attraction to this man and her fear of what he represented. He was one of 'those' who harassed her family, who had drafted her and her brother to work for them. But he was right that there was not much social life. The boys her age were gone, either conscripted by the Germans or hiding in the hills. It would be one dinner at a very nice restaurant, and she would certainly enjoy that. Besides, she rationalized, in her position it was safer to be neutral. This would simply be an extension of her work, being pleasant to someone important to the town administrators.

"How very thoughtful of you, Colonel Von Hellman." She paused, tipped her head to the side, "That would be nice."

"If you give me your address I will call for you at eight in the evening, Mademoiselle. In the meantime here's a little something that you might enjoy."

He reached into his briefcase and brought out a beautifully wrapped package that he placed on her lap under the desk. He leaned over and whispered in Gabrielle's ear, "I will wait impatiently for Thursday to come."

Moving back, his voice changed. "Now I do need to handle an important matter. Perhaps you will be so kind as to alert Madame Moreau that I am here."

Gabrielle was suddenly all business as she dialed the extension. Von Hellman stood, placed his insignia-covered hat on his head, tipping it to her as he strolled toward the stairs. Gabrielle noticed one of the security guards staring at her. When his lascivious grin commenced, she abruptly looked down and started typing. She knew that she might as well throw this letter away and start over as there were so many mistakes in it.

OCTOBER:

Before dawn in St. Lambert's forest, south of the Nesque River gorges, a group of three Maquis squatted on logs and rocks. They were eating a breakfast of dark bread, persimmons they'd filched from the edge of a farm and ersatz coffee brewed over a tiny fire. Two other men stood as sentries on rocks nearby, using binoculars to scan the terrain.

Francois took a moment to savor the beauty of a forest in early fall, the odor of crushed leaves, the warm breeze, the squealing cry of a bird as it flew down into a ravine after a prey. It seemed like he had been in the Maquis far longer than six months. Francois liked this group of guys, especially his new friend Roland from whom he was learning about poetry, and he loved living on the mountain.

Most of their days were spent doing routine work. They cut wood and occasionally hunted game or tracked down an errant goat. Gathering chestnuts and wild mushrooms was an autumn pastime. They checked out oak trees hoping that a winter truffle would be found. Sometimes a batch of eggs would be scrambled up for dinner with thin slices of this 'black gold.' Then there were the foodstuffs stolen from the Germans in Carpentras. The Vichy governments' concept of "starving out the Resistance" did not seem to be working.

Word had arrived that a convoy of clothes, destined for the *chantiers de la jeunesse,* was on its way to Gordes. The Vichy-directed program was intended to teach young workers military skills, develop them physically and inculcate them with the Nazi doctrine. Their wool capes, shirts, pants, heavy boots, socks, and berets would provide the Maquisards with not only warmth but also matching outfits.

Colonel Bayard and his *Groupe Franc* needed additional support to waylay three trucks. He contacted d'Artagnan, who asked Centurion's cell to help. This would be the first major mission since the aviators' arrival in August.

Most of the time, Francois and the others cut phone lines and worked as sentries on roads near parachute drops. They helped hide and distribute weapons sent by the Allies. Occasionally one of them delivered a message to a Resistance member in a nearby town.

Centurion's men finished their meal, picked up their rifles and marched a further six miles on winding trails. They reached a farm road heading toward the town of Gordes, a town plastered at a forty-five degree angle on a steep escarpment of the northern Luberon Mountains. There they met the *Group Franc* cell that would take charge of the trucks. They broke into teams of two and confirmed plans to meet at the ambush spot.

The *Maquisards* took positions behind trees, rocks and walls and waited until the trucks chugged up the steep hill. From a remnant of a ruined house, *Androcles* and *Petrarch* shot into the air above the cab of the second truck as others attacked front and rear. The object was to capture the goods, not kill the drivers. Six men were rounded up, their hands in the air, their guns on the ground. *Group Franc* members jumped into the trucks, turned around and headed down the mountain for the safety of the Chateau Javon near Sault. There the clothes would be handed out to those who stopped to 'give their regards' to the owner.

Francois helped blindfold and tie the hands of six prisoners then marched them into the *garrigue* to the west. After heading toward the stone huts called *bories* they went north and crossed back over the main road into *le foret de Mars*. The captives were to be led in circles to a spot where it would be safe to release them. As they meandered it became apparent that no one among the captives was a fervent fascist. They were men caught in the vortex swirling around France, anxious to survive, to care for their families, reluctant to talk about themselves or politics. One of them periodically cried, tears dampening his blindfold.

A former quarry worker with an injured hand, sturdy, tanned, in his early twenties, was the only one who willingly spat out his dislike of the Germans. Shortly after noon, the man asked to talk with Centurion about staying with the *Maquis*. Led away from the group, he was interrogated by Centurion and Petrarch. When he returned, his hands were untied, his blindfold removed.

He sat at a distance from the five other prisoners, blinking, looking around, a slaphappy grin on his face, motioning with his crippled hand a 'hello.' Later in the day, *Centurion* and *Baptiste* returned to camp with their newest recruit to report on the mission's success.

Francois and Roland found the work of guarding the captured men boring yet tense. Sporadically they touched the end of their revolvers to a neck as a reminder to behave. A boy known as *Mardi* was their lookout, staying at a distance, using binoculars to check for danger. When he whistled a particular birdcall, Francois moved his two prisoners off to one area and made them lie down. Roland led the remaining three to an opposite location. In the early evening they found a half cave, hollowed out from the limestone side of a cliff, camouflaged by a scraggly chestnut tree and accessed by a narrow trail. Apples and water were portioned out as the group waited for dark.

Roland pulled out his heavily thumbed book of poems and sat reading, biting into an apple.

Francois whispered, "What's so interesting in this book?"

Roland stopped chewing, "Sometimes Manouchian gives me a new perspective on the problems that we face; sometimes I just enjoy his way with words. I can translate one for you."

Francois murmured, 'sure,' and leaned back against the rock. The five blindfolded prisoners lolled close by, seemingly used to the routine of moving, stopping, moving, stopping, and resting when they could.

Roland flipped a few pages and paused, reaching for the right words in French, and spoke softly. "*Bien*, here's one. When others asked him why he does what he does, why he fights for people who seem to have no rights and little hope, he says in part:"

> *I intermingle them thus to my own personal suffering,*
> *Preparing for the poisons of hate a pungent serum —this other blood*
> *that flows through all the vessels of my flesh, from my soul.*
> *This elixir, would it seem strange to you?*

It makes me less conscious of the tiger, when teeth and clenched fists,
all kinds of violence, occur as I walk through the streets of a metropolis. (14)

"Do you get it?" Roland bent over to look at Francois's face.

He whispered back, "Sure, yeah, really I do. I mean, he's trying to fight against a brutal enemy but without hatred. I think that he hopes that things will change. Right?"

Roland didn't answer immediately then said, "Umm-hmm. Like us, right now. We are trying to do something about getting rid of tyrants. In the long run, we hope that we all will be able to live in peace."

A prisoner to Roland's right leaned over, listening. He shook his head slightly in agreement. Time passed, Roland reading, Francois and the prisoners dozing, *Mardi* at his post next to the tree. At dusk, the five men were escorted toward Roussillon. Guided down a narrow path to a dirt road, they were ordered to sit with blindfolds on for fifteen minutes or they would be shot.

Immediately the three Maquisards ran up the dirt road and branched off onto a trail leading into the shelter of their mountain. They made their way back to camp, having accomplished their goal. When winter came, the clothes could mean the difference between staying and fighting or giving up and going home.

A TASTE MUCH SWEETER - 1978

After we finished tasting the Domaine's wines, I helped gather up the glasses and followed Maurice past the double French door into a wide tiled hallway. On the right, a comfortable sitting room with a pair of rumpled leather couches, piled with an assortment of pillows, slouched in front of a stone fireplace. A chair covered in faded tapestry sat by the window, a plush-seated armchair next to it. It hadn't been modernized to any degree, content with shabby gentility.

Through double doors on the left was a dining room. Rush-seated country chairs surrounded a rectangular slab of dark walnut in front of marble fireplace. A pen and what looked like an accounting book were beside a stack of mail at the end of the table. At the far end was a buffet with a rack of hand-painted *faience* dinner plates.

Maurice walked on through a doorway at the end of the hall that led to the kitchen. After we put the bottles and glassware on a counter, he walked over to a door. He motioned me to come closer and opened it.

"What does this look like to you?" he asked.

The floor inside of antique cement tiles in a typical Provençal pattern matched the kitchen's, with cabinets starting about three feet above it. A vacuum cleaner, a mop and bucket, a couple of brooms and, in the back, battered-looking suitcases and a box of wine took up the space.

"A utility closet, I guess."

"This is actually the entrance to the *cave* down below."

Maurice began to remove the cleaning utensils, suitcases and box, putting them to the side. He jiggled up a tile on the edge then reached for a metal ring sunk into the wood underneath. With a strong yank, the floor started rising up as a pulley contraption behind a back wall creaked and a trap door became evident. Directly below were the triangular curved steps above the pressed dirt floor that I had noticed from the main *cave*.

"What is so mysterious about this? I see that it is convenient to be able to get to the wines and store things without having to go through the old cellar. Isn't this typical of most farm houses?"

Maurice lowered the trap door, pushed the tile back in place, and began to place the contents inside.

"Originally the cellar was one large room with steps going directly down from this door. During the war my father and a couple of friends in Beaume-de-Venise needed a place to store casks of wines that were being used to obtain AOC labels." Maurice continued as he replaced the items he'd removed, "*Papa*, my brother and I built the rock wall separating this part of the *cave*. We used dirt and coal dust on the rocks to match them to the originals. *Papa* built the trapdoor and put cabinets up above to make it look like a closet."

He went to the sink to fill a teakettle. "Tea or coffee?"

I chose coffee then waited for him to continue.

"During the Occupation, we hid people down below even though living conditions were pretty miserable. Once I stayed there, as did Francois and his wife, Amélie." Maurice bit at his lip. "My father was arrested because we were suspected of harboring fugitives. We lived in fear, much of the time."

Touched by Maurice's obvious discomfort, I placed my hand on his arm, "It must have been awful. I'm so sorry."

He put one hand over mine as he placed the coffee pot on the counter. When he leaned toward me, I did not back away. I closed my eyes when he moved his hand to my cheek. Maurice's kiss melted my body and I felt that tingling sensation. As our tongues probed, we gripped each other. Kissing spread to ears, eyelids, my neck. I ran my fingers through his curls.

He chuckled as he hugged me tightly and began stroking my breasts through the cotton blouse. I moved closer and swung my hips back and forth against the protrusion in his jeans. There was a half moment of reflection as I thought that this was so unlike me. Was it the wine?

Maurice's hands undid my blouse buttons and reached under my bra. I pulled on his belt and buckle, managing to unlatch them and unzip the front of his pants. Maurice let out a groan as his stiff velvety skin filled my hand. He stopped, looked at me then grabbed my arm. Holding up his pants with the other hand, he pulled me through the doorway and up the stairs leading to the bedrooms above, both of us laughing like giddy adolescents.

I awoke in a strange room and for a fleeting second thought that I must be dreaming. Sunlight filtered through a gauzy curtain across a patterned tile floor that I didn't recognize. The walls were light gray-green and I gazed at an armoire with one door open showing a line of shirts or blouses. None of them were mine. Then I moved fractionally and felt the warmth of a back pressed against my own. Ah, yes.

Maurice turned toward me, murmuring, "You're awake?"

I nodded and snuggled into his enclosing arms, breathing a contented sigh. He kissed and licked the side of my neck. I wiggled my hips.

"Ready for more?" he whispered.

I chuckled as I turned toward him, "Don't you think that three times in one night is enough?"

"Evidently not!"

He seemed as surprised as I was, as he pulled me close. We dissolved into a much slower and less zealous rhythm that definitely lacked the passion of our previous lovemaking.

Satiated, we lay in each other's arms, my thoughts weaving between light-headed dreaminess and the idea that a shower would feel really good. Maurice tipped his head above mine and looked toward a table by the bed.

"I need to take you home. The family will be arriving in an hour."

My eyes widened. "The family?"

"Every Sunday we gather here for lunch. I would love for them to meet you but perhaps this might not be the best time."

I stared at him for a moment then burst out laughing. "I'm awfully glad that you told me now and not an hour later!"

I tossed back the sheet and sat up, looking around the room that had been dimly lit, in shadows, or plain dark during the night. My clothes lay haphazardly on a chair and Maurice's pants were on the floor nearby.

Antique dressers, a wingback in a Provençal print, a table with a lamp, were ranged around the walls. There were four doors and I had no clue as to which one led to a bath or shower. Maurice smiled at me and reached for my hand, pulling me toward his side of the bed.

"Follow me."

I clambered across the bedclothes and we went into a sunny bathroom with an old-fashioned claw-footed tub and a modern corner shower. Within twenty minutes we soaped and rinsed each other, washed our hair, dried off and dressed. Maurice led me back down the stairs and offered to make coffee. I looked at my watch.

"Do we have time?"

Maurice grinned, shook his head a bit, "Not really. Unless you would like to meet my mother today."

Maurice drove up into town and parked, illegally I was sure, since the *allée de platanes* was occupied by the second-hand and antiques market on Sundays. I pulled my hat down low as I got ready to leave the car. We hadn't talked much and kissed lightly before Maurice turned away after walking me to the door.

I leaned against the heavy oak entrance for a moment. Feeling limp and skeleton-less, as I started upstairs I muttered, 'Vive la France!

THE EDITOR
ALBERT CAMUS

In October 1943, Paris was bathed in the glow of a perfect autumn. Ochre-brown leaves of chestnut and plane trees blanketed parks and lined streets. Fall odors pervaded each avenue: crushed leaves, fermenting apples and pears, smoke from roasting chestnuts. The Eiffel Tower looked as elegant as ever silhouetted against a crisp sky. The silvery Seine was lively, reflecting back an azure dome.

A cough still lingered and periodically Albert slowed his pace or sat down, using a handkerchief to stifle ragged puffs of breath. Although he had been discharged a full year before from the hotel-sanitarium north of Lyon, he knew that it could still be months before he would breathe normally. He knew that he looked even thinner than other emaciated Parisians.

In 1942 the tuberculosis that had dogged him as a teenager returned and doctors in Algeria sent Albert Camus to recuperate on a high plateau in France, the *Viverais*, known for its 'good air.' It was the home of summer *pensions*, pious Protestants and reticent peasants. While recovering, the young writer learned that Jewish children were being smuggled in and hidden in boarding schools, orphanages and remote farms. He became involved with neighbors who believed in non-violence, as did Camus, and worked tirelessly helping children escape deportation.

The longer the war continued, the more it confirmed to Camus the bizarre juxtaposition between man searching for meaning in life in an indifferent world, a universe over which he had no control. He had concluded that one could commit suicide, could exist on faith or could embrace the absurdity and live fully.

This day he walked past barges tied up along the Seine and sat on a bench near the Pont d'Alexandre, a gray fedora shading his face. He removed the coat that his friend Michel Gallimard had given him and luxuriated in a moment of tranquility. His job as a manuscript reader at the Gallimard Publishing Company provided enough, along with royalties from earlier publications, to live comfortably in a hotel in the seventh arrondissement. He missed his wife Francine who was back in Algeria, yet found great pleasure in being around so many creative thinkers.

Albert's love of words had been a huge surprise to his partially deaf, illiterate, widowed mother and his illiterate and domineering grandmother. Hard working domestic servants, they never understood his strange stories, his flirtations with communism and anarchism, his free spirit, his desire to write. Albert excelled in school and, in spite of a bout of tuberculosis, completed the equivalent of a master's degree at the University of Algiers.

Friends had brought his writing to the attention of André Malraux, whose works were published at Gallimard. Even with the shortage of paper in wartime, Malraux' influence had helped Camus get his novel *The Stranger* and his essay, *The Myth of Sisyphus*, published the year before.

Albert's friendship with Jean Paul Sartre, the existentialist philosopher and writer, was especially close. They had similar views about the absurdity of life, the difficulty of making sense out of chaos intermixed with control. He had directed Sartre's play 'No Exit' until Sartre could hire professional actors and a well-known director. They enjoyed each other's company and the odd pair, one tall and nice looking, the other short, fat, with broadly spaced eyes, would regale each other with stories about escapades, women, and philosophies. At least three times Jean-Paul had told Albert his ever-changing story of getting out of a POW camp with forged documents that claimed he had a disability.

Often after work, Sartre writing prolifically at a sidewalk café table and Camus editing and revising manuscripts in his office, they would meet at Brasserie Lipp or Café de Flore. Simone Beauvoir might join them although she and Albert were occasionally adversarial, as if each was competing for Jean-Paul's attention. When the couple got into sexually tinged confrontations, Albert would look away or leave.

Today Albert waited for a woman who worked on the underground paper *Combat*, of which he was editor. She knew him as *Albert Mathé*; he knew her as *Auger*. *Combat*, a pro-de Gaulle and pro-social democracy journal, now distributed 250,000 copies each month throughout France. The Communist paper *L'Humanité* often had articles deriding the politics of *Combat*. This competition for the 'hearts and minds' of the populace was symbolic of the final race to see who would govern the country after the war was over.

However, Albert enjoyed reading Louis Aragon's articles and poems in *L'Humanité*. He'd met the Aragons in Lyon when he was working with their mutual friend René Tavernier and other Resistance writers on the National Writers' Committee. He had debated with the Aragons their respective views on politics, poetry and writing. Else, almost twenty years older than Albert, had been flirtatious to the point that Louis raised his eyebrows more than once. Later Albert received a note from Else stating, *I have the impression of having made a declaration of love to which you have not responded. I love you like a brother.*

The young man was greatly relieved.

Inspired by discussions among these writers, Camus wrote and published the first of four anonymous 'letters to a German friend.' In these essays, he combined existentialist philosophy with entreaties, rationales, that France would never be conquered by power and threats.

Letter to a German Friend (#1, July 1943, excerpt)
"I belong to a nation which for the past four years has begun to relive the course of her entire history and which is calmly and surely preparing out of the ruins to make another history and to take her chance in a game where she holds no trumps. This country is worthy of the difficult and demanding love which is mine. And I believe she is decidedly worth fighting for since she is worthy of a

higher love. And I say that your nation, on the other hand, has received from its sons only the love it deserved, which was blind. A nation is not justified by such love. That will be your undoing.

And you, who were already conquered in your greatest victories, what will you be in the approaching defeat? (15)

He watched as Auger sauntered along the quai from the west, thinly elegant in a gray suit, her hair coifed in the style of the times. As he stood up, she greeted Albert Mathé with perfunctory kisses. She sat down and spread out on the bench, on a piece of paper, grapes and four steaming chestnuts. From her large purse she withdrew a half bottle of wine and two water glasses. She handed the bottle and a *tire bouchon* to her companion and asked if he would open it.

Auger, the executive secretary in charge of *Combat's* publications, had arranged for a safe location in which to produce the newspaper. Her parents' former maid was a concierge at an apartment complex in the eighth arrondissement, not far from the Gare St. Lazare railroad depot. Behind her office was a large room where the staff could type, edit and compile the weekly in safety. Couriers would then take copies to a dozen or more shops scattered around France for printing and distribution.

They commented on the weather and reported on states of health as they casually checked out people in the vicinity. Then they launched into the reason for the meeting.

Jacqueline reached into her purse and carefully pulled out a packet of cigarettes and an envelope, sliding them over to Camus. The pack was open, with several cigarettes inside. Camus brightened and took one out, lit it with matches from his shirt pocket then placed the cigarettes and matches into the pocket. He allowed himself a long, satisfying pull and slowly let the smoke emerge from his nostrils, avoiding the voice in his head telling him not to smoke.

"The microdot is on the 'i' of the brand's label." She added, "The envelope has more information that we want published in the next issue. Some are reports of resistance successes in Provence and retaliations by the Germans.

There's one about a massacre in Provence. I don't envy you having to edit that, Monsieur Mathé."

"It might be easier for you to bring articles to my office for me to review. As you may have guessed, my real name is not Mathé. It's Albert Camus. I work at Gallimard on rue Sebastien-Bottin. Since it's a publishing company, it might look less obvious when you drop off things. There I use the name Albert Bauchard."

"Camus? The author of *L'Etranger*? Oh my goodness! I loved your book. Are you writing anything new?" The woman looked in awe at the thirty-year-old man with his furrowed brow and drawn cheeks.

"It's hard to fit in my own projects between proof reading at Gallimard and editing *Combat*, but I've started a novel called 'The Plague.' "

"A fitting name, considering 'the brown plague' under which we currently live," she commented sarcastically. "I look forward to reading it in what we can hope will be better times. By the way my real name is Jacqueline Bernard, although it's always best to refer to me as *Auger*. We are delighted to have you in charge of the journal, Monsieur Camus."

Camus laughed, "It's still 'Albert.' Also, please don't say anything to the other staff, as I want to continue to be known by Mathé. By the way, I think that I've convinced a couple of my friends to help us—Jean-Paul and Simone. They have interesting perspectives."

"You'll be the one to decide if what they write is appropriate."

Jacqueline suddenly stood up and leaned over to peck Albert's cheek. "I should leave you as I see that there's a group of what may be Gestapo heading this way. See you soon."

She turned and walked briskly toward nearby steps. Camus watched her shapely legs, lined with brown pencil in imitation of silk stocking seams, as she climbed toward the busy street above. He continued to sit on the bench, finishing the cigarette as his right knee began to shake, waiting to see where the Germans were heading. He was relieved to see them stop at a barge and confront the captain. Within minutes the skipper was roughly removed from his boat and pushed between uniformed agents toward stairs at the other end of the quai.

The journalist stood, put on his coat and walked west, fingering the pack in his pocket, anticipating a full night ahead as he reviewed and edited the information and articles that the envelope contained. Pulling his hat down, he climbed the stairs, stopping now and then to cough, a handkerchief making it hard to identify his face.

⸻⟨∞⟩⸻

Camus continued leading his double life, finishing up his book and writing a play called 'The Misunderstanding.' Maria Casares, the beautiful daughter of a former prime minister of Spain, was a featured actress. She and Albert rapidly became lovers as well as co-conspirators in the Resistance. Although members of the Resistance were caught, arrested, tortured and killed on a daily basis in Paris, the playwright/editor and actress moved about freely and publicly—to a point.

In late March 1944, a significant number in the *Combat* network were arrested. However, the group was rapidly rebuilt and Camus' team continued to publish the paper. Their young printer, who also set up the distribution system of *Combat*, was arrested three times. The first two, he was released or escaped. The last time, in June, he was wounded and committed suicide rather than undergo another bout of torture. Jacqueline Bernard, *Auger*, was also arrested in June and sent to the Ravensbruck concentration camp.

Fearing that her address book could be decoded, Albert Camus went underground along with Pierre and Michel Gallimard. They bicycled to a rustic house owned by another Gallimard editor fifty-some miles from Paris. There was no June 1944 issue of *Combat*.

In August, as the Allied armies and LeClerc's Free French Division arrived at the outskirts of Paris, Camus and his friends returned to the city. De Gaulle's provisional government (GPRF) announced that, as soon as the Germans left France, over fifty daily collaborationist papers would cease publishing; only papers of the Resistance would be allowed. Albert met his staff at the former *Paris Zeiting* building. Camping out in their new upstairs offices, they followed the American and French armies advance, as they put together the first issue of a free press.

The new motto was 'A Single Leader: De Gaulle; A Single Fight: Our Liberty.' Camus and his writers emphasized that the country needed to look beyond liberation and start thinking about what sort of country they wanted to rise from the ashes of humiliation and sacrifice. His theme included fairness, justice and rebuilding the honor of their beloved country. The first issue came out on August 21st, a single page with pictures of Paris scenes and the announcement that it would be a 'daily' newspaper.

His editorial, signed with an 'x,' stated that 'Freedom has to be earned and has to be won. ... The liberation of Paris is but one step in the liberation of France.... The combat continues.'

In the meantime, barricades and battles filled the streets of the City of Light. Students manufactured Molotov cocktails in university laboratories and tossed them into the tanks and trucks of German soldiers. Weapons taken from dead Nazis armed more citizens. Snipers stood on rooftops and shot from behind the barriers.

Then *Combat's* fifth issue, August 25, had a headline stating 'AFTER FOUR YEARS OF HOPE AND STRUGGLE FRENCH TROOPS ENTER INTO THE LIBERATED CAPITAL.' In his editorial, Camus wrote: 'Those who never lost hope for themselves or their country are finding their reward tonight.'

⸺⸺

Letter to a German Friend *(July 1944, excerpt)*

Now the moment of your defeat is approaching. I am writing you from a city known throughout the world which is now preparing against you a celebration of freedom. Our city knows that this is not easy and it will have to live through even darker a night than one that began, four years ago, with your coming. I am writing

you from a city deprived of everything, devoid of light
and devoid of heat, starved, and still not crushed.
Soon something you can't even imagine will enflame
the city. You are the man of injustice, and there is nothing
in the world that my heart loathes as much. But now I
know the reasons for what was merely a passion. I am
fighting you because your logic was as criminal as your heart. ...
This is why my condemnation of you will be sweeping;
you are already dead as far as I'm concerned....., I can tell
you that at the very moment when we are going to destroy
you without pity, we still feel no hatred for you. .... We cannot
guarantee that we shall not be afraid; we shall simply try to be
reasonable. ... and we want to destroy you in your power
without mutilating your soul. Even now I expect nothing
from heaven. But we shall at least helped save man from the
solitude to which you wanted to relegate him. Because you
scorned such faith in mankind, you are the men who, by the
thousands, are going to die solitary.
And now I can say farewell to you.   (16)

Albert Camus   1913–1960

THE VAUCLUSE – 1943

OCTOBER:

As soon as work was over on Thursday evening, Gabrielle rushed home and grabbed her robe and towel. In the bathroom down the hall, she put money in the meter to heat a few inches of water. She lathered herself with a scrap of lavender-scented soap hoarded for special occasions. After pinning up some curls, she went through dresses that she brought from home, those that she considered suitable for a working girl, and picked one in dark maroon wool. It was long-sleeved, form-fitting, with a matching fabric belt and wide brass buckle. She opted for her pearl and gold earrings.

The exquisite Hermes scarf that the Colonel had placed in her lap lay on her bed in its tissue-paper lined box. A card had accompanied the scarf with, to her surprise, a poem copied in perfect black script. She picked up the card and read it again, seeing a different side to this enigmatic officer. Gabrielle was not quite sure what to make of what he'd written, yet was rather touched:

> *April*
> *Eyes tell, tell me, what you tell me,*
> *Telling something all too sweet,*
> *Making music out of beauty,*
> *With a question hidden deep.*

Still I think I know your meaning,
There behind your pupils' brightness,
Love, truth are your heart's lightness,
That, instead of its own gleaming,
Would so truly like to greet,
In a world of dullness, blindness,
One true look of human kindness,
Where two kindred spirits meet.
    And since I'm lost, in what entrances,
    Studying those mysteries,
    Eyes, may you be drawn to see,
    The intention in my glances!
              Goethe (17)

Tossing the card onto her dresser she picked up the scarf. Gabrielle fondled its quality, its luxurious softness, then wrapped it around her neck and tried a couple of ways of wearing it. She opted for rolling it and tying it like a necklace with the ends hanging in back. The muted colors of brown, deep red, gold and green complemented her dress and her hair. Brown heels were all that she owned, although she would have preferred black ones to go with the wool coat that had belonged to her mother. As she stood before the mirror to check her hem and hosiery, she hoped that she looked good enough to be on the arm of an important older man.

Von Hellman was prompt and businesslike as she greeted him at the front door. This evening he wore formal black slacks with his uniform instead of his usual jackboots below breeches. Taking Gabrielle's elbow he guided her to the car's back seat; a young chauffer sat in front. She made sure that her silk-stockinged, well-shaped legs lingered before drawing them inside the car. She noticed the Colonel glancing down.

Conversation was casual, references to her work, the cool weather after the latest mistral, a compliment on how nice she looked. At the restaurant the chauffer opened their doors, the Colonel's first and then Gabrielle's. Inside, a trio played Strauss waltzes, candles gleamed, crystal chandeliers sparkled and the painted paneling was of a distant era. Waiters in white shirts and black bowties slithered between linen-covered tables set with an array of glasses and silverware.

The maître-de greeted Von Hellman by name, clicking his heels, bowing obsequiously, and showed the couple to a corner table by a window. Gabrielle was aware of glances as they passed, a blur of men in gray uniforms and dark suits, women with fancy hats or jewels in their hair. Some of the men nodded at her escort who tipped his head in return.

The maître-de helped Gabrielle remove her coat, took it to a hat rack then returned with two leather-covered menus. The restaurant's ambiance was easily the most elaborate since she'd eaten dinner at the home of a wealthy family in Carpentras. She did her utmost to look unimpressed, to appear sophisticated.

When the Colonel offered her a cigarette from his initialed gold case, she took it, grateful to keep her hands busy. She had smoked briefly but did not care for cigarettes made from odds and ends of grains and herbs. She smiled as she leaned forward so that Von Hellmann could light it with an initialed gold lighter. She tilted back, took a puff, overcome with the sudden inhalation of smoke. She motioned with her hand like film stars did in movies she'd seen, as she stifled a cough.

"Ah, how lovely, Colonel Von Hellman," Gabrielle narrowed watering eyes as she took another draught of real tobacco.

"Let us dispense with the formalities, my dear," Von Hellman leaned toward her, smoke emerging from his nostrils. "My name is Dieterich and yours is Gabrielle, isn't it?"

She nodded and he continued, "That is such a pretty name, as most French names tend to be. You and your countrymen speak almost musically. I am jealous at times when I compare them to our language, our names such as Heinrich, Gustave, Gerthrude, Werther, Manfried. Tell me, did you like the poem that I gave you? It is also so very musical when translated into French, don't you think?"

Gabrielle agreed with Dieterich's view that the French language lent itself to poetry. He described French literature that he particularly enjoyed:

Dumas' *The Count of Monte Cristo*, de Maupassant's short stories. She sat and listened, only having to smile and nod, as her companion's monologue continued with only an occasional question. They looked up to see a waiter hovering discretely nearby.

"I think that we need to decide what to eat, my dear."

Dieterich asked for a bottle of champagne while they considered their choices. Gabrielle entered into the mood of the evening as the Colonel deftly brought items to her attention and planned their dinner. The champagne was just what she needed, she decided after she finished the first glass. She had not had much appetite at lunchtime and the drink instantly calmed her. The second glass decreased the last of her tension. Gabrielle wasn't as conscious of the people around her and could concentrate on listening to Dieterich's sensual baritone.

He could not stand the modern artists that were destroying all that centuries of masters had worked to perfect. He enjoyed music by Brahms and Liszt. He described places that he'd been in France and Belgium during his year at the Sorbonne. Politics, the war, the problems of daily life never once entered their conversation. It was as if their differences did not exist. Here was this handsome, literate, educated man who obviously knew more about French culture than Gabrielle did and he delighted in her company. When she made a comment or managed a bit of humor, he smiled appreciatively.

There was a brief awkwardness when he asked about her family. She explained that her father was an olive oil producer and winemaker near Carpentras, as their ancestors had been. In answer to questions about her siblings, she said that one of her brothers was in Germany as a part of the *Service de Travail Obigatoire*, she wasn't exactly sure where. Her younger brother was in school as he was only fourteen. She mentioned that her cousin Florence's husband was from Alsace and that he spoke German. Cousin Henri taught the German language and played violin in the local chamber orchestra.

Dieterich seemed pleased, "Ahhh, how fortunate for him."

The red Burgundy with the duck à l'orange was really good, Gabrielle concluded, as she and Dieterich finished up the last of the bottle. Then came the cheese course, a Sauterne and a luscious chocolate cake with layers of raspberry jam. The meal was the best that she could remember ever eating. Dieterich, who became more and more physically attractive to her the more they chatted, insisted that they round out the dinner with Port that had come from the Duoro Valley in Portugal. A cup of real coffee topped off the evening.

Gabrielle relaxed into the Louis XVI chair, fingering the gold brocade of the seat. Music still played in the background. Shimmery lights bounced off mirrors and crystal pendants. The sight of Dieterich's lovely blue eyes made her feel like she had stepped into a fairy tale. It had been so long since she felt like the world was such a safe and beautiful place. When it was time to go, she felt like she was floating then skating on smooth ice. Dieterich helped her on with her coat and she walked among blurry faces.

Once in the car it seemed perfectly natural when Dieterich kissed her. He put his hand on her breast, his tongue in her mouth and she responded. When she fumbled with the keys to her building, he reached for them and deftly unlocked the door. She thought perhaps he waved to the chauffer. Gabrielle was neither terribly surprised nor at all unhappy when Dieterich, such a gentleman, walked her upstairs to her apartment. When he grasped her and kissed her at her doorway, she felt his hard groin up against her and reached down, instinctively, to rub it.

⚒

The next morning, Gabrielle awoke with a pounding headache, her mouth tasting of tobacco and dry as old bread. She looked around her room and there was no sign of Dieterich. She rummaged through fuzzy thoughts and vaguely remembered that, after some of the greatest sex she had ever had—which was not surprising considering how little she had experienced—her lover got up and dressed, then kissed her on the mouth. She remembered hearing him open the door and leave.

Even with her headache, even with vague regrets about not having cleaned the room the day before, Gabrielle lay back on her pillow and smiled happily.

The whole evening, the physical delight that Dieterich brought out in her willing body, brought her such tender happiness. She could hardly wait for the next time, as she was sure that there would be one.

OCTOBER:

Antoine was concerned that a collaborator might lurk in the reading room, watching for a pattern of visits. He decided that it was not safe to meet too often so sessions discussing literature were sporadic, although he still plied Florence with books from his collection. They met once a week at two o'clock in the afternoon, alternating Tuesdays and Thursdays. If a cleaning rag was draped over the edge of the trashcan next to Madame Poitiers desk, Florence was to dawdle by the stairwell. Antoine would drop packets into Florence's bag on the floor as he walked past. They continued to swap Antoine's books back and forth at the same time and conducted transactions in a matter of seconds.

He handed her instructions as he pretended to juggle his pail and mop before descending the stairs. One such was 'meet the contact at *Notre Dame d'Observance* at five o'clock tonight. Third pew on the far left. Brown gloves and a cane. He will say, '*the candles are creating a lot of smoke.*' You are to respond, '*we should put them out.*' "

Florence dropped a scarf or a sweater on top of the satchel and either waited a few minutes and left, or returned to a table where she read a book until time to leave and make contact. Once in a while the transfer occurred the next day. When she got home, she put the packages under her nightgowns far back in her armoire's shelf. She slept fitfully those nights, occasionally waking and glancing at the armoire's closed doors and then over to confirm that Henri was snoring soundly in his own bed.

In early October, Antoine tucked a piece of paper inside one of the poetry books and muttered 'read this.' Florence waited until no one was in the vicinity and opened the note. Antoine suggested that she come to the Museum the following Monday while he was cleaning, as both it and the library would be closed. They would have time to talk about poetry and review how the document transfers were working. He would leave both the entrance gate and the door unlocked. Florence could come any time that was convenient since he would be there all day. The *Kommandantur's* residence was across the street so Florence knew that she needed to be cautious.

That evening after dinner, Florence watched as Henri muttered over news in his evening paper. She was surprised to feel empowered instead of frightened. She had begun to acknowledge that she disliked her husband almost as much as she now realized that she loathed the Nazis. Over the years she had become adept at repressing feelings of resentment, sure that she was at fault.

Years before she had confessed to a priest her confusion and unhappiness in the marriage. It was difficult to talk about the lack of closeness between her and her husband. Outwardly everything seemed normal, a young couple with a baby, each occupied with new duties: a husband anxious to do well and advance in a career, a wife absorbed in managing a home. There were times when Henri did not touch her other than proffering kisses on the cheek when he greeted her in public, only then referring to her as '*cherie.*'

The priest listened to Florence's halting, apologetic confession and told her that she was expecting too much of marriage. He was he oldest of the three who ministered to the flock at Saint Siffrein and replied in unctuous tones that, as man's helpmate, she was to obey her husband. The *curé* did not sense any grave problem. It was an adjustment period in the usual peaks and valleys of marriage. He advised her to pray about it and recite several *Hail Mary's* in penance for her negative thoughts. Florence never again expressed concern over her marriage to a priest.

The first indication that Henri might not love her came shortly after she announced that she was expecting, three years after their wedding. Henri's reaction was mild anger and obvious disappointment that the pregnancy interfered with a trip that he had planned to Berlin.

"You realize that now we can't go?" he had frowned, backing up a step.

When Florence bowed her head and said nothing, Henri paused then grudgingly continued, "Never mind. We can plan the trip after the child arrives."

Florence observed that Henri basked in the attention of other women. He often complimented someone on a stylish hat or dress. Well-meaning ladies in the church and even in shops would ask about Henri. They commented 'what a charming husband you have!' or 'your Henri is such a nice man.' Florence suspected that he had found someone else and felt heartsick to think that she might not only be unloved, but also humiliated publicly. But he was discrete, as he never came home smelling of perfume or with lipstick on his collar.

A husband having an affair or a mistress was something that many French women faced. Most rose above it and were not judged. Catholicism provided certitude for the legitimate wife and children. So Florence stopped looking for someone specific. It was highly unlikely that any of their friends would be so gauche as to tell her about an affair.

She never questioned Henri's evening rehearsals for chamber group performances or 'practicing' with a member who needed help. She didn't probe when he said that he had a meeting to attend. She never asked about his occasional two or three day trips to Aix-en-Provence or Paris for conferences, in which she was never included. Florence rationalized that this was probably typical of a long-married couple with eleven years difference in age.

So the realization of how angry she felt was a new sensation. And the fact that she could direct this anger in absolute opposition to Henri's conservative, critical, fascist points of view was affirming and enervating. She managed a genuine smile when Henri turned toward his favorite chair.

"How was your day,...dear?" she said, as she took a seat opposite him and picked up her knitting.

OCTOBER:

In between training young charges, imposing discipline on boys raring for a fight, René Char found time to sit at a simple desk, surrounded by favorite art on the walls and shelves of books. He scribbled random poems, thoughts and artistic doodles in his journal. Exchanging correspondence and prose with good friends, he wrote to Gilbert Lily: 'Poetry represents freedom, it is what I hold as an intense prisoner in my arms.'

The autumn of 1943, a team of Gestapo and Milice descended on Cereste looking for *Lazare,* the leader of a group of Maquis reported to be in the area. Six of them arrived by truck, posing as members of a youth camp wanting to join the Resistance. After chatting with a few locals, they went to a café where villagers stopped for a glass or two while waiting for the erratic bus to Marseille. They ordered drinks and observed the comings and goings of local residents.

The sudden interest by such a large group seemed suspicious. A man at the bar finished his drink, left the café and immediately went to see *Captain Alexandre* at his command center. René asked Vincent, a young Maquis from the Bastidon farm, to check things out. As soon as Vincent entered the café two of the strangers asked to see his papers. One of them questioned his work, listed as 'woodcutter.' The young man assured him that his job was removing timber in the forest to be made into the charcoal.

Identifying himself as a member of the Milice, the man grabbed his arm, "These aren't the hands of a woodcutter."

Another collaborator threatened, "We're looking for Lazare and you're going to tell us where to find him. We know how to make you talk."

He was pulled out the door and pushed down the street with a gun at his back.

A villager reported that Vincent being taken to Digne on the other side of Mont Ventoux. René grabbed his pistol and two automatic rifles then chose three men to help, including Irénée Pons. By luck, the chief of a neighboring Maquis unit was in Cereste and had a car. The five men stuffed themselves into the man's Simca and headed for the *route national* going toward Forcalquier. They were out of town before the Germans and the police, with their prisoner, had arranged themselves in their vehicle.

Char placed the Simca at a bend in the road, blocking the route. The *Maquisards* clambered into the woods, hiding behind rocks and fallen trees. They attacked as the Germans slowed down, shots echoing off the ridges. The soldiers fired a few volleys in return. Vincent escaped in the confusion, running over a hill and into the woods. Surprisingly the Germans did not counterattack. Instead they grabbed their wounded and turned back down the main road.

No one in Char's group was harmed and, miraculously, the Simca also survived. They returned to Cereste and faded into secure hiding places.

The next day a company of field soldiers swept into town and went directly to the grocery store. They took the owners, Monsieur and Madame Christol, to the police station. The grocer's wife asked to return to the shop to lock it in case of thieves. She entered the store then slammed the door in the face of the soldiers following her. She locked the door and escaped out a back window.

Furious, the soldiers placed a charge of dynamite against the front door and lit the fuse. The explosion blew off the storefront causing part of the second floor to collapse. The soldiers released the grocer, considering their vengeance complete, telling him to look for his wife in the ruins. As soon as they left, Christol raced to his shop and home. When he stepped past the debris on the street he discovered his mother sitting up in her bed in the middle of the floor. She had fallen from above, unharmed but frightened and shaking.

Vincent was given false papers and Char sent him to stay with friends in Paris. He assured the young man that they would meet again to continue discussions on the poetry of Rimbaud.

Between successes there were bitter moments. When a known collaborator caused the arrest or death of a member of their group, he was to be killed. René and the other section chiefs handled this themselves as they felt that it was wrong to ask a young man, someone barely into adulthood, to do a task that could leave a lasting, horrific memory. It was one thing to shoot in self-defense; another to murder a fellow Frenchman, even if he was a traitor.

Captain Alexandre's steady hand guided his partisans with a combination of discipline and encouragement. He wrote in his journal: *At every meal taken together, we invite Liberty to sit down. The seat remains empty but the dish and utensils stay in place.*

COUNTRY WALKS - 1978

The bus to Pernes-les-Fontaines left right on time and trundled down Avenue Victor Hugo. I was one of only three passengers. The deluge of workers, students and tourists going back and forth between villages would not flood the seats until later in the afternoon. Chunks of limestone townhouses became broad expanses of fields interlaced with ancient stone bridges and clots of dark trees. In one recently plowed field a bevy of birds, in tandem, swooped into the sky and banked their wings into the sun, reflecting it as if they were mirrored.

Professor Claude Lapeyre was meeting me at a café by the Nesque River in Pernes. At the mention of my contact at the Sorbonne, Lapeyre said that he was delighted to talk with me about his favorite poet and dear friend, René Char.

The satchel leaning against my leg contained a tape recorder that I had purchased in town, a new composition book and several pens. I hefted the bag to my shoulder, stepped down into leafy shade then walked toward the rendezvous point. Sitting at a table under an umbrella emblazed with the name *Pernod* was a man with a dark beard and glasses, wearing a rumpled plaid shirt. Even from a distance he looked like someone who smiled easily and loved life.

"Professor Lapeyre?" I extended my hand.

He stood and clasped mine with a hearty grip. "Professor Somerset. *Quel plaisir!*"

We ordered mineral water from a waiter wandering among a handful of other people at the terrace tables and went through the usual pleasantries.

"I must say that I am curious about why you want to know more about René. We don't see many Americans in this area, particularly anyone familiar with René Char."

"Unfortunately he is not well known in the United States except by a small group of academics." I leaned back in the chair. "I'm doing research on early twentieth century French writers who were active in the Resistance. Char is known for his involvement and for the prose that he published right after the War."

"Will you be using the information for a book?"

"A few short stories will be published in academic and popular magazines. However, I intend to use the material to make modern prose more meaningful to my students."

"I see. Well, how may I be of help?"

"I wondered if you teach literature, yourself?"

Lapeyre laughed, "No, I teach mathematics! A completely different field from that of poetry."

"How did you become interested in Char and get to know him?"

"If you can imagine, I hadn't read anything by René until about fifteen years ago. Then I picked up *Fureur et Mystere* and was struck as if by a *mistral* on the top of Mont Ventoux. There was something about the images, the emotions that he expressed and the way he sees the world that touched me. Of course I knew that he had grown up in L'Isle-sur-la-Sorgues and lived nearby, but I hadn't really paid much attention." The professor beamed. "I was so struck by what he'd written that I got directions to his house and marched up with the book in hand. I told him in person how impressed I was! What must he have thought!"

His remark tickled my sense of serendipity. "And that led to your friendship!"

"Yes, René welcomed me warmly. He was too busy that day but he invited me to come back the following week and join him on a walk. Since then, we get together several times a week. After recovering from a stroke in 1968, he has walked almost daily as part of his therapy--until his heart attack earlier his month."

"I had heard that he was ill."

"Yes, he is still recovering at his dear friend Tina Jolas' home in Le Barroux, northeast of Carpentras, but it looks like he will be home next week."

"I will be here until the middle of October so perhaps by then he might feel well enough to talk with me."

"If you'd like, I can ask him and then let you know."

I nodded agreement and Professor Lapeyre continued, "René is a private person and does not give interviews. He refuses to be on television."

"I know. His family information is difficult to find."

"What do you want to know about him?"

I retrieved the notebook and placed the recorder on the table. "Do you mind if I record the answers? It will save me from having to write everything down."

Lapeyre nodded and I started with questions about Char's early life. He recounted a history that could have been written by Kipling, Dumas or Defoe. The poet's grandfather was an abandoned child who was raised by cruel peasant families. One day, when he was about ten years old, a wolf dragged off a lamb from a flock that he was guarding. Afraid of the severe beating that he was sure to receive, he abandoned the sheep and made his way down the mountain. At a quarry, the workers gave the boy food and shelter. When asked his name, he told the quarrymen it was 'Charlemagne' after the king who united Western Europe.

He stayed with them and helped by running errands and holding tools. He became a quarryman, then a foreman. A hard worker, he was also ambitious. With support from a patron, he bought his own quarry and became a prosperous merchant of gypsum, sand and gravel. He changed his name to Char-Magne, or sometimes Magne-Char. He married and moved to

L'Isle-sur-la-Sorgue, a town with dozens of water wheels delivering power to mills that provided textiles, paper, grains and flour.

His son and René's father, Émile, reduced the name to 'Char.' Émile bought more quarries and increased the production of the plaster used to cover the rough stones of houses. The factories were called *Les Platriéres de Vaucluse* and produced fifty tons per day. Outside the island center of L'Isle-sur-la-Sorgue, Émile Char built a grand home, *Les Nevons,* named after a stream at the edge of the property.

René-Émile was born there in 1907, fifteen or so years younger than his three oldest siblings. His was a conservative and bourgeois family. His father was mayor of the town; his mother was quite religious. After their father died his brother Albert, who had always been mean to young René, became head of the family.

Claude recounted more about this poet's early years. "He was an independent and difficult child. He left the house, sometimes for days, and made friends with people his mother felt were 'the wrong kind:' uneducated workers, communists, old men who taught him Provençal and the sky's constellations."

Sent to school in Marseille, he visited bordellos, wandered the cafés and bistros of the *Canebiére* north of the old port, and learned to box. His first job was in a produce market in Cavaillon. When he came down with a virulent fever and was bedridden for weeks, he started writing poetry. A small inheritance from his grandmother made it possible to publish his first booklet, and then René left for Paris.

Claude spoke of him with pride, "There he got involved with the Surrealists, took part in anti-fascist rallies, partied wildly and was arrested more than once. He and his friends published a communist literary review whose purpose was to open people's eyes to the blind, patriotic nationalism as it was practiced at the time."

"It does amaze me," I interjected, "how these young and radical poets influenced modern writing to the extent that they have. One thinks, usually, of more mature, well-known writers making an impact. Musicians and artists of the time were doing the same."

The professor motioned to the waiter. "Would you prefer more water or wine, Madame?"

I requested a glass of rosé. He ordered then turned back to me, his hands clasped on the table.

"What is it that the Canadian fellow, Marshall McLuhan, said in his recent book about artists? They are the 'antennae of their race' or something like that."

"It is true, isn't it, that they see the world differently and often reflect that world more accurately than people of the era can accept." I leaned closer. "So what else did René do?"

"When the family business got into trouble in the middle of the Depression, he came back from Paris and took over the plaster factories. At age twenty-nine he was a manufacturer and chief administrator with fancy engraved cards." Lapeyre laughed out loud. "He readily admits that he was never meant to be a businessman."

"How long did this last?"

"Within months of his new job he became ill with another fever that left him bedridden for weeks. A friend found a house for the Chars to live in while he recovered, in a hamlet up on the mountain called Cereste. The place was, actually still is, quite rural and undeveloped. The locals herded sheep and goats or farmed. It became his center of operations during the war." Claude continued, "The Chars also spent time on the Côte d'Azur with other couples from Paris. I know that Paul Eluard and his wife Gala were there. Tristan Tzara and his wife Greta Knutson came. I believe that she did portraits of them. René published more poetry and Picasso illustrated one of these books."

Lapeyre paused. "Then all hell broke loose when Germany invaded France. Like many of his friends, René was drafted into his former regiment and sent to fight on the front lines in Alsace. He doesn't make much of it but he became brigadier of his column. Then our troops were pushed back, the Maginot line did not hold and the Germans occupied northern France."

Lapeyre sat for a moment. "Since you are interested in René's work during the Resistance, I'll tell you how he ended up there."

I checked the recorder and my pen, ready to jot down ideas.

"In December 1941, gendarmes arrived at *Les Nevons* and searched it from top to bottom trying to find subversive materials. René was suspected of being a communist although he was not a member. As they left, a policeman told René that he was to be arrested the next day. He and Georgette disappeared that night. Later they moved to Cereste where he managed parachute drops in the *basse-alpes*."

"I know that he refused to write and publish anything from 1940 until the War was over."

"Yes, he was well aware that everything would be censored and, as well, it would make him too visible. To add to his problems, his brother was a staunch *Petainist*. I believe Albert also enlisted in the *Milice*, turning in his countrymen to the Gestapo."

One sensitive subject that I wanted to explore was this poet's reputed romantic liaisons. I broached the subject of his marriage. "I understand that he met his his wife while on vacation in Nice. Did you ever meet her?"

"No. He married Georgette Goldstein in 1932 and they had been divorced years when we met."

"So he never remarried?"

"No," Lapeyre took off his glasses to wipe them with a handkerchief. "René has always attracted and been attracted to women, but he never married again. During and after the War, he was in love with a woman named Marcelle from Cereste, and he adored her daughter. He had an affair with Greta Knutson for a while. I mentioned Tina Jolas, whom he has known for years. And he has been living with a charming woman named Anne at *Les Busclats* for a long time. I'm sure there have been other liaisons as well."

"Hmmm." I waited a minute, hoping for more.

The professor's eyes crinkled, "You should be careful when you meet him. I think that you are just the type that he likes!"

I felt my cheeks flush.

"You will not leave our friend without a little gift, whether a book or a bunch of lavender from his garden. René is content to live a simple life yet is quite generous to his friends."

"What was it that impressed you in Char's poetry?"

"He believes strongly in justice and despises those who oppress others. He's a humanist and an incredible optimist, considering what he has seen in his lifetime. He believes in battling tyranny and, at the same time, he believes in love and restoration." Lapeyre's forehead crinkled, "Reading his poetry is like starting on a foot path that gradually becomes a larger route and then on to a greatly expanded point of view."

Pointing to a stack of books on his side of the table he said, "I brought several of his works. He explains his process of writing, how he evolved as he matured. Here's one of his:

"The scavengers of poetry are in general devoid of the sentiment of true poetry, unable to pierce the process of its action. One must be both a man used to storms and a child of good weather." (18)

I brushed at a crumb, saying, "Many of the best artists and writers have had difficult lives. It seems that painful emotions are sucked down inside, tiny forgotten pockets of memories, and released drop by drop in carefully crafted words or paint strokes."

He agreed, saying, "I look at things differently now, having read his works. Here, for example..." Lapeyre picked up a second book. "In the 'Lost Nude,' *Le Nu Perdu*, he describes Venasque. Have you been there?"

"No, not yet. I know that is a fortified hill town where the bishops of Carpentras fled invaders in the Middle Ages."

Claude adjusted his glasses and read aloud:

The bundled frost gathers you together,
Men more fiery than a bush;
The long winds of winter are going to hang you.
The roof of rock is the scaffold
Of a frozen church left standing. (19)

"We used to take long walks, often stopping to look over at the town, and I never viewed Venasque the same way after reading this. René knows so much about the history of this area and always had interesting stories to tell. He would point out migrating birds, snakes and lizards hiding under rocks, a wary fox almost hidden by the brush. A very observant person."

I read from a book that I'd marked, "Char also uses prose, comments, impressions that remind me of a modern version of Rochefoucauld's seventeenth century maxims. He has several in *Aromates Chasseurs* -- 'Fragrant Hunters: *'I would like my regret of times past to be like gravel in the river: all at the bottom. My present day would not then have anxiety.'* "

I turned a page, "Here's another: *'Mental house. It is necessary to occupy every room, the wholesome just as the unwholesome, and the beautiful airy parts, with the prismatic knowledge of their differences.'* "

"You may not have seen one of his most recent publications. It is called *Chants de la Balandrane* and is dedicated to me." Claude handed it to me, appearing almost shy.

"No, I have not seen this. How special! But the word *'balandrane?'* What does it mean?"

"The large cape worn by shepherds was, in olden times, called a *balandrane*. Or it could also be from an ancient farm, high on a Luberon plain. René thinks of language as supple, dynamic and likes to play with words, to challenge the reader. He leaves a great deal for you to interpret. Of course, much that he has written in here reminds me of our many long walks together."

Turning to the front page I read, "To Claude Lapeyre, who helped me build seven little houses during the frost, in order to receive my inveterate wandering through that winter."

"Well, they weren't exactly houses but simple places where we could rest on our promenades. This copy is for you, if you would like it. As my friend has aged he has become a bit more cynical, I think, yet at the same time there is an undercurrent of regeneration." Lapeyre looked at his watch. "We could continue to discuss every poem. It would be my pleasure; however, I think you mentioned earlier that you have to catch the bus."

I glanced at my watch. "Oh, my! I'm glad that you said something. It will be here in ten minutes. Thank you, Monsieur Lapeyre. I do hope that you can help arrange for a meeting with Monsieur Char. Au revoir et merci!"

Grabbing the recorder, I threw it, the pen and the notebook into my bag. Claude Lapeyre stood and bowed slightly, seeming unsure about whether or not to shake my hand. I kissed him on the cheek before hurrying up to the main road. As I climbed the stairs, I turned to wave before heading across the street. He gave me a little salute in return.

THE VAUCLUSE – 1943

NOVEMBER:

The first snowfall covered the POW camp's parade ground in sparkly winter crystals. Barrack roofs oozed water from beneath the white layer, making a constant plinking noise. A recalcitrant generator kept up a rhythmic whacka-whacka sound as it provided electricity for spotlights focused on gray buildings. Searchlights swung back and forth at points on the perimeter.

Transport trucks of shivering, emaciated workers rumbled past barbed wire encircled gates, returning from another twelve-hour workday. Guards in wool coats, heavy leather boots, hats, gloves, showed no concern or empathy for the laborers as they struggled down from the rear of the trucks, dressed in striped cotton shirts and drawstring pants, worn out shoes, motley sweaters, jackets and caps.

Some guards, Sigmund among them, used rifle butts to swat at those nearest, barking orders to 'move along, bastards.' Fellow inmates supported the weakest as they shuffled off toward the barracks and a nightly allotment of thin soup and moldy bread.

Étienne Bertolini had a hacking cough and stopped mid-way to Barrack 13-C. He bent over to catch his breath, wracked with another lung-wrenching fit. His bunkmate Jean-Paul stopped and held him as they slogged toward the steps. It was fractionally warmer inside the bunkroom, but still barely above freezing. As soon as each prisoner received his tin cup of warm water with a few vegetables of unknown origin and bread made with sawdust, he headed for the security and semi-warmth of his assigned bunk. The men huddled close, finishing the meal in a few mouthfuls.

Six workers had collapsed in the fields and their lifeless or nearly lifeless bodies had been hauled off in the bed of one of the trucks to an area outside the camp's fence. They would be tossed into a recently dug pit and covered with a layer of dirt. Usually there would be a series of gunshots to ensure that no one regained consciousness and attempted an escape. The families would be told that they had died 'of natural causes.'

Étienne pulled up the neck of the heavy wool sweater that his girlfriend Laurianne had knit for him then tugged down the cuffs under his threadbare overcoat. Wrapping his blanket around his body, he clambered to the far side of the bug-infested mattress, waiting for Jean-Paul and two others to join him in sharing what little body warmth they could exude.

In the morning, Klaus and his sidekick Hans lugged pails of watery gruel into the barrack and clanged the ladle loudly against the side, signaling the beginning of another workday. The inmates slid off the bunk beds then lined up holding cups used the night before. They sat in silence, broken only by an occasional spitting of gravel found in the porridge. Before the trucks arrived to pick them up, the prisoners straggled out, wrapped in blankets, stumbling toward rank smelling toilets.

Étienne's cough was deep and bronchial although he had slept through most of the night. Jean-Paul was developing a cough and Étienne feared the infection might spread throughout the building. He hoped to make it through one more day, digging up potato plants from an icy field.

A raspy voice called from the other end of the barrack. "Petter is dead, I think."

Hans slung the rifle across his shoulder and marched toward the rear. He confirmed the death and left to get another soldier and a stretcher. There was always the suspicion that a disease would lead to a culling of prisoners. The weakest would be selected for transfer to a 'special camp' then there would be an influx of new workers. A sense of desperation was flowing through the camps, a stealthy fog that caused the Germans to be more short-tempered than usual.

As Étienne reached the pail Klaus looked up from ladling the gruel and gruffly stated, "You are on latrine duty today. Step aside so the others can pass."

The young prisoner knew that Klaus's outward gruffness was necessary to keep from being accused of being too familiar. Latrine duty was filthy, putrid, repulsive, and probably ten degrees warmer than a wind blown, snow covered field. Étienne and another worker exchanged their clothes with some retrieved from men who had died. They were handed pails and shovels and taken to the toilets under guard.

In the latrine barrack the men lifted the long board with butt-sized holes off the cement box that supported it. They set to work scooping out urine, feces and vomit that had risen almost to the edge of the container. Once the buckets were filled, they carried them to a deep wooden cart. The filth was poured in and, when it was full, they pulled the cart out the gate accompanied by two armed soldiers. The slime was dumped into a pit used for kitchen garbage and dirty straw. In the spring, this 'compost' would be dug up and used as fertilizer for the next potato crop.

Étienne was allowed a rare shower, a bucket of cold water thrown on his head. It wasn't enough to clean up completely but he used the least dirty part of the dead man's shirt as a towel to wipe himself. He was able to wash his hands under a water faucet before putting on his own clothes. He knew that he still reeked and his bunkmates would let him know it that night.

As Klaus walked beside him, he looked at Étienne with concern.

"You don't sound good, your cough."

"It's only a cold," Étienne shrugged.

Klaus ducked his head as he marched in step with his prisoner. "I think that it is time that you go home."

Étienne looked over and laughed caustically. "Sure. Just walk out of the gate, get on a train and go home."

Klaus wiggled his head, "Yah, pretty much like that."

Étienne's first reaction was fear that this was some nasty trick.

The two marched on in silence until Klaus said slyly, "So, you don't want to go?"

Étienne stopped mid-step. "You're serious?"

The gray-haired guard shook his head, "Yah. I will need a photograph and I brought my camera with me. Let's go inside the building and get it done. I'll tell you my plan."

Étienne felt his face crinkle up for the first time in weeks. Inside the room he turned and surprised even himself by grasping Klaus's shoulders and kissing him on each cheek.

"*Mon cher* Klaus, you are a wonderful man!"

The German looked startled, blushed and said shyly, "*Nein, nein.* I realize that Germany can't win this war. It is only a matter of time, although Hitler will fight to the end. I don't like seeing a nice boy like you waste away to nothing."

Klaus put his large hand on Étienne's thin arm.

"You must not tell anyone! If you do, I will not help you. I would deny everything and turn you over to Sigmund or one of the others. This time you would not survive. Because you speak German, almost no accent, I think it will work. But I can only help you. Understand?"

Klaus stepped up close and took a quick snapshot.

"The man who is making your German identification card can fix it to look like you have more hair. You must keep your hat on so that yours can grow out. Now, this is the plan."

The guard outlined how the escape would work. It was daring, yet Klaus had thought it through in detail.

Étienne shook his hand saying, "*Dankeschön! Dankeschön!*"

Klaus opened the barrack's door, shouting back, "Dumkopf! I expect this floor to be swept clean within ten minutes."

NOVEMBER:

Moving camp further up the mountain, once more Francois and his cell cleared brush, cleaned out a dilapidated, abandoned shelter and dug holes for latrines and garbage. The possibility of an invasion was gaining momentum. The month before, *Centurion* had been notified that a man called *Achiduc* was arriving from London. General de Gaulle assigned him to organize landing and drop fields for munitions and men from north of Mont Ventoux down to the Mediterranean. There were an estimated eighty fields being considered in the *Basses-Alpes* department alone.

Their area was under the guidance of *Capitaine Alexandre*, residence unknown. He was said to be tall, imposing, generally amiable but occasionally angry to the extreme. He was as revered for his leadership and planning as for his protection and concern for those working closely with him. *Centurion's* group would assist by stacking wood in piles around a field, lighting fires or torches, retrieving cylinders, extinguishing and burying evidence of the fires. Weapons and food would be distributed; coded phrases for the next drops would be given to those assigned to listen to clandestine receivers.

The BBC broadcast coded messages three times on the day of scheduled drops, at 1:30pm, 5:15pm and 9:30pm. Key members in each network listened to concealed radios, every appointed hour of every day, listening for statements such as 'Isabelle always smiles,' or 'the library is on fire.'

One evening, when one of the underground papers was passed around, *Petrarch* was stunned to learn that his favorite poet had been arrested with twenty-two others in his Resistance cell. Missak Manouchian was the leader of fifty-some saboteurs and fighters in Paris, primarily composed of immigrants from Eastern Europe, Spain, Italy. Many were Jews. Manouchian's group was credited with derailing a train to Reims, executing two German police in Argenteuil and killing five soldiers in various parts of Paris--all in one day. Between August and November they carried out nearly thirty successful attacks on German installations and individuals. They assassinated General Ritter, an assistant to Fritz Sauckel, the German responsible for the deportation of workers to Germany under the *Service de Travail Obligatoire*.

Francois stood, listening to his friend rant. Roland was ready to head for Paris and fight to have his hero released.

"The Fritz will regret this!" Roland slammed his fist into his hand.

"They haven't shot them yet. That's a good sign."

"You can bet those bastards aren't treating them like honored guests! They're being tortured, beaten. I told you what happened to my brother and father, Francois!"

Francois picked up the newspaper with the article about Manouchian's arrest and skimmed it, as his friend sat glowering.

"It says there is to be a trial. That might mean that they'll be sentenced to prison."

Petrarch looked at him in amazement, his eyebrows raised. "Oh, sure. And I'm likely to join a convent!" He stormed off.

As Francois read more about the arrests he realized that Roland was right. These men would probably not survive. All over France the Gestapo was increasing raids against suspected anti-fascists. In September alone they had arrested one hundred and twenty-six suspects in the Vaucluse and forty of these had been deported without a trial. The week before Gaston Cat had been arrested again, once more suspected of using his van to aid 'terrorists.'

Francois walked over to his friend.

"Hey, Roland, I'm really sorry to hear about those guys in Paris. We can't afford to lose so many. How they were caught?"

"It doesn't say." Roland reached for the paper in Francois' hand. "The Gestapo rounded all of them up so they must have had a list of their names. Manouchian was arrested at a train station, but it says that his wife escaped. What a tragedy!"

"Maybe the War will be over before they go to trial."

Roland shook his head with a defeated grimace.

"Well, still, I mean, they might escape." Francois' hopes of cheering up his friend were fading.

Roland turned away without answering and walked to the far edge of the camp near one of the sentries. Francois watched him pull out a tattered book of poems and lean against the tree, reading.

Roland knew that his favorite poet, his fellow-Armenian, would never publish any more. This book would hold the last words of a man who had given him solace during the worst of times.

Before night falls, you have gone around the world,
You bring to us the echo of all the horizons of life
From all the hands used for work, the struggles and victories
Your call is similar to a light unblocking the dawn's rays
Pinched and beaten by the tempest, you are the fire that warms us
In cursed obscurity, you are the silvery flame of our oath
Eternal flame that our furious spirits
Scream at their impudent hatred in order to never extinguish you
It sometimes seems that you are going to extinguish yourself,
However each day steel intentions poke you, make you stand
You show the way by a light for a grand victory of humanity. (20)

He turned, laid his forehead against the tree, and wept.

DECEMBER:

Christmas was always more chaotic than usual. Germans were tradition bound when it came to observing their favorite holiday. Soldiers and guards were distracted by plans to celebrate. More people would be traveling. New troops replacing those sent to the front were less likely to challenge travelers and shoppers. It was as good a time as any.

Klaus volunteered to bring a Christmas tree to the guard's mess hall. He tied it to the top of his 1938 Opel and parked the car close to the latrine near the entry gate. With prisoners locked in the barracks for the night, guards were happy to have a diversion and it was received with a certain amount of fanfare. The tree was bushy and it took a phalanx of five to carry it. Klaus walked behind, beaming happily, carrying bottles of homemade schnapps. He presented one to the commandant as he passed headquarters.

Étienne went into the toilets a few minutes before the lock-up whistle blew. Waiting until the last man left, he jumped up to a rafter directly above the door. A minute later a guard opened the door, made a cursory glance around, then closed and locked it from the outside.

Étienne lowered himself to the floor. He used Klaus's key then slithered outside. He reached up, locked the door and dropped onto snow-covered ground. Waiting until a searchlight passed, he crawled around the building to the side of the Opel. He felt for the bottom of the partially open side door and eased behind the seats, groping for a blanket to cover himself.

It seemed like an eternity before he heard Klaus's off-key voice warbling a carol. There was backslapping and guffawing, a strange sound in such a place. Klaus dropped onto the seat, shaking the car. Étienne held his breath as the sputtering engine warmed up, hummed, then headed for the gate.

Klaus handed each guard a bottle of homemade fruit schnapps. He commiserated at their being on duty overnight and hoped the drink might warm them up. Étienne heard the sound of a cork being removed, then metallic clanking as the bar raised and the gates whined open, followed by the lovely sound of tires crunching over snow.

Minutes later, Klaus parked at the end of a road and reached back. Étienne sat up as best as he could in his cramped position.

"So, *mein freund,* inside the shed you'll find a bucket of water. You need to smell a lot better if you are to travel without being noticed. A coat with the pass, map and train ticket to Koblenz is hanging on a nail, with a cap. The sweater, pants and socks are on the shelf. I'm sorry there aren't any shoes; you'll have to wear what you've got. There's a rucksack with a chunk of bread, a sausage and a jar of water on top of them. I hope that you can find all these things by feeling."

Klaus lumbered out of his seat and helped Étienne emerge.

"The last train will be at 9:30 tonight and you mustn't miss it. From Koblenz you'll have to go on foot."

As Étienne returned the latrine key, he grasped Klaus's hand and tears pooled in his eyes. "I cannot ever repay you, Klaus, for what you are doing. Thank you from the bottom of my heart."

"Ach! Maybe when this war is finished I will come to Paris and you can show me around. How about that, heh?" Klaus's voice sounded more gruff than usual. "Have a merry Christmas, Étienne."

THE VENDANGE - 1978

Georges parked the Renault on the incline behind a row of cars, a truck or two, that ranged along the long driveway of *Domaine de Lauritaine*. Sophie and I clambered from the car and pulled sun hats and baskets from the trunk. A sizeable group of casually dressed harvesters was on the terrace of the *mas* in leaf-laced shadows. People recognized the Duprés and waved.

The week before, Sophie had mentioned the Laurents' harvest celebration and asked if I would like to go. I assured her that I would be interested in seeing what a grape harvest was like. The *vendange*--'the angel's wind'--had swept across the muscat vineyard, the grapes were at their peak, the flavors just right. While hired laborers would harvest, always by hand, the grenache, syrah and cinsault crop, the crush of the muscat was a time of celebration and hospitality to be shared with family and friends.

"The Laurents even invite a priest to bless the harvest. Sometimes it seems a bit much," Sophie shook her head. "Of course, he's a distant cousin so he'd be here anyway."

"It's a tradition!" frowned Georges. "Claire, you'll find that we are loathe to give up centuries-old ways of doing ordinary tasks. If you stayed until November you could go to the opening of the truffle market in Carpentras. Trumpeters in medieval costumes and representatives from nearby towns parade in colorful gowns and carry banners at this first sale."

"I love that sort of pageantry. It's an acknowledgement of the history behind what is ordinary work and daily living. The rituals that lend importance to what we do to ensure survival."

Maurice walked through the arch and greeted Sophie, then Georges, then paused a second or two longer when kissing my cheeks. I hoped no one else noticed his wink. Although we were keeping our fling a secret, in the past two weeks we had gotten together every chance that we could. When he was in town, we had lunch at my apartment; after a piece of fruit and a half-sandwich we had a little something extra in the bedroom. Twice I had stayed at the Domaine while Madame Laurent was visiting her daughter, granddaughter and first great-grandchild in Aix-en-Provence. Maurice drove me home well before anyone arrived.

Today I was to casually meet the family that I knew only through Maurice's descriptions and photographs in the downstairs rooms. There were great-grandparents in a sepia-gray, eyes-staring, stiffly posed wedding picture; grandparents and parents in scallop-edged pre-war photos taken in front of the farmhouse; Maurice and his siblings, chubby-cheeked innocents in knee-britches and laced shoes, holding tin lunch buckets. In one, his brother Francois and several other young men stood on a dirt road proudly displaying rifles and pistols, wearing berets with Resistance badges. A gold-edged frame held one of Julien and Martine at their wedding. On a shelf in the square-shaped library was a studio portrait of Maurice and his wife taken in the mid-1960s. Next to it was one of their three children taken at the same time.

My cautious evaluation of situations, first sticking in a toe then easing into water, had been fairly well dismantled. The explosion of passion we'd experienced was called '*le coup de foudre*,' the thunderbolt. It was so sudden that I thought that it would probably also end as quickly, but in the meantime I'd decided to luxuriate in kind words and good sex. I hadn't even told Sophie about our fling.

The Merciers and Grimauds, couples that I'd met at the Duprés' dinner party, came up to greet us. Cheeks were tipped and swiped amid a series of new faces and new names. The American custom of nametags had great advantages--how was I to remember so many people?

Julien, who resembled a slim Maurice, and his wife in a short skirt, glasses and a ponytail relieved us of our baskets. At the front door, Sophie introduced me to Madame Laurent. In her late seventies, she was straight and slim, with a face that radiated warmth. Her silvery hair was in a neat chignon. She wore a lilac colored suit with gray pearl earrings. I liked her instantly.

Madame Laurent shook my hand as she welcomed me to the *Domaine de Lauritaine*. She kissed Sophie and Georges then steered us to her grandson who stood by a nice looking girl his own age.

"Joseph, I am sure that our guests would enjoy something to drink. Do you prefer coffee or perhaps fruit juice?"

Joseph led us toward a table against the wall of the terrace. We chose coffee, strong and dark. No leisurely café-au-lait in bowls on this working day. Maurice stepped to the front of the terrace and tapped a spoon against a glass to get the attention of the chattering crowd. He welcomed everyone and thanked us for helping with the harvest amid humorous comments..

"On this special day the *Domaine de Lauritaine* becomes, for a brief time, the *Domaine du mal a dos,* the 'domaine of the bad back.' "

He was interrupted by remarks about the price of friendship and who would pay the doctors' bills. Maurice then introduced Father Jean-Yves, a short gray-haired man in jeans with a clerical collar jutting from a black jersey shirt. Julien handed his father a box of dewy yellow grapes. Father Jean-Yves gave an eloquent but short blessing of the vines and harvest, then sprinkled water over the grapes. Guests responded with 'amen' and signs of the cross then, cheerfully chatting, headed for a pile of baskets and cutting instruments. A number of older guests followed Madame Laurent into the house.

Maurice and Julien handed out utensils, baskets and occasionally a straw hat to their enthusiastic harvesters. After the last one moved through the arch toward the vineyard across the creek, he came and stood by me.

"I can give you a quick lesson since you've never done this before." Maurice guided me by the elbow, handed me a basket and a pair of clippers. "Did you bring gloves like I suggested?"

I reached into my bag and pulled out new garden gloves.

"Leave your purse over here with the others."

After crossing a wide stone bridge over a rivulet, pickers spread out among the rows and soon only the edges of sunhats, caps and the backs of shirts could be seen above the vines. We walked along the road in the midst of a few stragglers. Maurice's muscular arms and chest filled out a brown linen shirt. Momentarily distracted, I missed part of his explanation. He guided me to a row, knelt and motioned me to stoop down as he grabbed a bunch, turned them slightly and snipped the stem.

"You need to cup them gently in your hand," he motioned in a vaguely suggestive way, bumping against my hip. "Try to cut the stem fairly close to the top. When your basket is full, carry it to the road and dump it in the container at the row's end. Any questions?"

I nodded a 'no' and bent over to snip the first cluster. Maurice watched as I cut a few and gave me a surreptitious pat on my rear. He told me that I was doing fine then headed back to the barn, where the first grapes were already being loaded into the crusher and de-stemmer.

It was back breaking work. Although my muscles were strong from swimming and walking, this didn't prevent a dull ache from starting within half an hour of bending, cutting, and carrying. As the sun rose higher, sweat rolled down my spine, dampening my armpits and leaving dark spots on the back of the denim shirt. The hatband felt sticky and my hair hung limply. I was sure that eye make-up was decorating my cheeks. I mopped my face with a bandana.

Looking at the volunteer workers on either side, I was not alone. As the morning wore on, light-hearted smiles became grimaces, conversation stopped except for an occasional 'whew' or 'I'm ready to quit.' Yet each time that I made the trip back to the container there was satisfaction in seeing how the pile had grown.

When the truck bed was full, Julien drove it across the bridge and behind the barn where Maurice and several others unloaded the golden-green pile. The crusher whirred and whined its mechanical song, pouring forth fruit and juice that was de-stemmed then funneled down a chute into a wooden vat.

As the final truckload wound its way up the hill, dog-tired pickers stripped off gloves, wiped flushed faces, sipped paper cups of water and found places to sit. The last few arrived, signaling the end of the *vendange*.

I pulled off my gloves, poured some water and drank thirstily, then walked over to Georges and Sophie who stood by the sliding door. Conversation was almost impossible because of the noise. When the crusher was finally turned off, I noticed a burbling sound at the wooden vat. I walked toward it and leaned toward its side.

Maurice yelled over, "That's the fermentation starting."

He motioned for me to climb up to the road and then pointed down into the liquid where tiny bubbles furtively popped, creating not only a mellow sound but also an aroma that was the harvest's perfume.

"Already? That's amazing."

I darted a look toward Maurice. Sweat trickled down his temples and he looked so sexy. I bent my head, knowing that I looked damp and dust-smattered.

Maurice whispered, "Don't worry. I like you clean or dirty."

I stared at him before turning away, thinking that was one of the nicest things any man had ever said to me. Stepping down into the barn, I joined others marching toward the terrace. A garden hose was in constant use at the edge of the driveway. I waited my turn, splashed my face then headed indoors to use the bathroom.

As I walked past the stairs, a woman called out, "Excuse me, may I help you?"

I recognized Maurice's sister immediately. She was as beautiful as her photos suggested. Her wavy auburn hair was gathered in a loose clutch at her neck. Her outfit appeared very chic, probably expensive. Her expression was austere, unwelcoming.

I stammered, "I would like to use *la toilette* if I may."

"I don't believe that we have met," she said coldly. "I'm Gabrielle Laurent Thibault. Are you the Duprés' American visitor?"

I nodded as I extended my hand, "Yes. I'm Claire Somerset."

She did not offer hers and said, "Let me show you the way."

She walked past the staircase toward the back room that Maurice used as his study. She opened the water closet's door and gestured inside.

"If you need anything else, please ask one of us."

I did what I could to restore my ruddy face, put my hair into a ponytail and returned to the kitchen. Gabrielle and several other women were putting food on platters, adding spoons and forks, carrying dishes into the dining room.

"May I be of help?"

One of the women smiled but Gabrielle instantly responded, "No thank you. We are almost done."

She turned to the refrigerator. I backed out of the room, harboring the suspicion that my knowing where the toilet was might have annoyed Gabrielle. Otherwise I couldn't understand why I sensed resentment. Too strong a word, I thought.

Maurice, his sons and other helpers were placing bottles of wine on each table from cases that they balanced on their hips. Georges waved for me to join him at a table where he introduced me to another couple. The man was helping seat an elderly woman who seemed confused, her thin hands waving about as if she was falling.

"Claire, These are our friends the Bertolinis, Étienne and his mother, Anne-Marie. Where is Laurianne?"

Étienne Bertolini, slightly stooped with thinning dark hair, gestured with a toss of his head, "She is in the kitchen."

He placed a napkin under the chin of his mother, murmuring reassurances.

Georges quietly explained, "Perhaps you have been to the *Boulangerie Bertolini* in town? They are supplying the bread today."

"Yes, I've been there a few times although I usually go to one that is around the corner of my apartment."

"Étienne is Francois Laurent's brother-in-law." Soto-voce he added, "As you can tell, Madame Bertolini has suffered a stroke."

"*Excusez-moi, Madame,*" Étienne turned to shake my hand. "How nice to meet you. From America?"

Georges explained that I was visiting from California.

"A friend of mine lives in Cheecago," he beamed. "We've been there two times."

"I've never been to Chicago," I admitted. "I've lived near San Francisco most of my life."

Ah! San Francisco! I loved the film 'Eenspector Harry' with Cleent Eastwood and all the beautiful hills and the ocean."

"It is a lovely city. Do you see many American movies?" So began a recitation of those that Étienne liked.

The Merciers wandered over. Étienne and Sylvan Mercier compared their favorite American films. Jeannette Mercier and I discussed an exhibit in Avignon of Picasso's sketches. This friendly company felt welcome after the cool reception by Gabrielle.

Madame Laurent appeared at the door and announced '*à table*' to the crowd. Guests closest to the entrance went into the dining room first. They straggled back with full plates and the next table entered. After more groups paraded in and out, it was our table's turn. As I left the dining room, Maurice's group headed inside and he winked when he passed.

The Laurent family was at a table under the vine-covered *tonnelle*. Gabrielle sat on Maurice's right with her back to me. An animated woman with short, spiky red hair was on his left. I did not recognize her from the family photos. When Maurice and I stood chatting at the barn, I had noticed her watching us.

I asked Sophie, "Are all the people at the Laurent's table family members?"

She looked at the group for a time then answered, "Almost everyone. Let's see--there's his sister Gabrielle, her daughter with her husband; Maurice's son, Julien and his wife Martine; his son Joseph with his girlfriend, Cécile. At the other end Madame Laurent is next to Father Jean-Yves. Then there's his brother Francois with his wife, Amélie. Gabrielle's good friend Yvette is sitting next to Maurice. I think that Gabrielle is hoping that Maurice and she will get together."

Sophie looked at me. "Why are you so interested?"

I shrugged my shoulders. "I'm trying to figure out who I've met, who I haven't. The names and faces are all mixed up."

"Well, since you are interested," she continued with an amused look, "About four years ago Yvette's husband was killed in an automobile accident. With his mistress. She went through a difficult time but has recently opened a dress shop in town."

Étienne Bertolini interrupted us with a bottle in his hand. "*Mesdames,* would you like a bit more?"

As Sophie and I held up their glasses, she added, "You'll probably not see these people again, at least for several years. Unless, that is, you return for next year's *vendange.*"

She smiled winsomely, her dark eyes blinking at me.

I laughed, "It would be tempting. Who could resist spending half-a-day walking around stooped over in the hot sun?"

"You'll get your reward later."

"My reward?"

"You don't think that we have worked for nothing? The Laurents will give each of us a case of mixed wines from last year's vintage. That's the reason he has so many willing workers. Plus it is fun, don't you think?"

I stretched my arm back to my shoulder muscles. "I'll let you know tomorrow!"

THE PRISONER
ROBERT DESNOS

The train rumbled along clackety tracks, swaying around curves, throwing one hundred and ninety emaciated prisoners back and forth against each other's striped cotton uniforms. A dozen had fainted and were partially held up by the press of bodies; a dozen more were on the floor, balled up, the feet of those standing pushed into every crevice. It smelled of every possible body odor: vomit, feces, sweat, bad breath, urine, fear.

This was not the first prison train in which Robert had traveled. He had been on one from Paris to a camp in Poland called *Auschwitz* two months before, in March 1944. It seemed an eternity since he had arrived at that place of huge eyes in ghostly faces that had given up hope. A month later he was thrown into a line of emaciated, exhausted, gritty laborers: Poles, Roma gypsies, Jews, political activists, homosexuals, Free Masons, a mix. They were herded aboard another filthy cattle car and jostled along to another camp, *Buchenwald,* in Germany.

Such a pretty name, he thought, 'birch forest.' It was here that he and his fellow rebels, outcasts and waifs came face to face with the worst, the most vicious, evil guards and commandants. To escape his misery, Robert Desnos reflected on his charmed life growing up in the third arrondissement in Paris, near *les Halles*, the huge food market where his father sold poultry and game.

He was seventeen when his first poem was published, right before World War I ended. His teachers predicted a bright future for him. In the luminous days of 1920's Paris, Desnos joined the cacophony of intellectuals moving in overlapping circles of *avant garde* art, music, philosophy, film and literature. He became one of the first members of André Breton's group of Surrealist poets. They were so young and yet felt immortal, fully convinced of their own points of view.

Marcel Duchamps illustrated his first book of poetry. Desnos befriended an American writer named Ernest Hemingway as they shared views on Spain's political problems. He rubbed shoulders with the artists Pablo Picasso and Man Ray, Salvador Dali and Joan Miro. He toyed with being a communist, but in 1930 fell out with the Surrealists over their hard line position that sprouted from a conference in the Soviet Union.

A nineteenth-century darkly gothic prose-novel, *The Songs of Maldoror*, was a major inspiration for Surrealist ideas. Breton and his friends were enraged when Desnos proposed a new club called *Le Maldoror* for those at odds with Breton's decrees. Using this name for non-Surrealists was equal to using 'Christ' as part of a name for a club of atheists. One night René Char, Louis Aragon, Paul Eluard, Breton and other hooligans showed up at a private party of silk pajama clad guests at *Le Maldoror*. Accusations were hurled back and forth, then plates and glasses. Knives were drawn. Police arrived and arrested the intruders.

A prolific writer, Desnos continued with his poetry, became a journalist, and wrote columns and articles for Paris newspapers. He had a radio program and became a film and music critic.

In 1941 he joined the Resistance in Paris. His job was to gather information through his work at the papers, write anti-fascist tracts and articles under pseudonyms, and help make false documents. When he and his Swiss-Belgian wife Lucie, nicknamed Youki, vacationed in Normandy, they walked the beaches, sunbathing, reading books to each other. He surreptitiously collected data about troop movements and passed these on.

After three years, an informer had betrayed his network. Robert was grateful that doe-eyed, sensual Youki had not been with him when he was caught with damaging evidence in his coat pocket. He had seen her once at the prison, before he was put on the first of the trains with other beaten, broken men. Just one week before his arrest, they had attended the premier of a film that he had co-written, called *Bonsoir Mesdames, Bonsoir Messieurs.*

Desnos' imagination was able to create an altered reality that kept him going and his life often seemed luckier than most--although there was one very close call. He and other exhausted laborers were told to get into a canvas-covered truck. They knew that no one ever returned from this ride. When they arrived at buildings where acrid smoke billowed out in a constant burnt-meat stream, the guards ordered them off the truck.

As the group lined up Robert stepped up to a woman in front and began to read her palm. His loud, self-assured voice caused everyone to stop and listen.

"I see from your palm a long life line, prosperity in later life, many grandchildren, great happiness."

The poet patted her reassuringly as she stared at her splayed out hand. A man held out his arm, his palm open. Robert, again, predicted a long life full of joy and success. The other prisoners jostled for their turn at a reading. He stared carefully into each hand, telling each person that his or her life would be long and satisfying.

Perplexed at this odd behavior, the guards made no attempt to stop Desnos from making his predictions. One tentatively put a hand up then sheepishly stepped back with his colleagues. The prisoners milled about, smiled, showing each other their palms. Unexpectedly the Germans told them to get back in the truck. They were driven back to their former barracks and released.

This day in May, the train slowed as it came toward a track leading off to a series of buildings in what appeared to be a former rock quarry.

"Where are we?" a hoarse voice whispered to his neighbor as they peered through a crack in the reinforced wood. Only the creaking, squealing of the train and an occasional cough or raspy gasp of a passenger broke the long silence.

The man at the crack muttered, "It says *Flossenberg*. Where is that?"

No one answered.

The cattle car jerked and the yelling of orders, the shriek of whistles and barking of dogs were heard along with locks being unlocked and heavy doors sliding open. The sudden light caused most of the men to flinch, look down, blink, as they descended among heavily armed guards, many of them Polish *kapos* who made it their goal to kill a man a day.

A prisoner turned to a soldier and asked, "Where are we?"

The *kapo* muttered "On the border of Czechoslovakia, now move on. Faster."

Desnos was assigned to an outside camp called Floha where he worked in a factory that produced fuselages for Messerschmitt airplanes. The most hazardous part was the exposure to poisonous chemicals and metals, and wounds that did not heal.

The weather in late summer 1944 was beautiful. Each day dawned with deep blue skies interrupted by the sight and drone of planes passing overhead and gunfire eliminating workers. Bird song could be heard at a distance. Warm breezes wafted between buildings. The heavens valiantly tried to ignore the atrocities in the war-torn countryside. Men worked, men struggled, men died.

Fall arrived, summer warmth replaced by a chilling rain that eased into snow piled up against the barracks, oozing into ice on the inside. Desnos was grateful that the factory was warmer than his sleeping quarters. His flesh seemed to have melted, his collarbone, elbows, knees, hips jutted out. Yet he persevered, knowing that the Allies were gradually winning against the Germans.

Spring 1945 arrived and with it came more prisoners, more illness, less food, more deaths, more trains to extermination camps. But hope. Desnos dreamt of Youki and summer at a beach and a meal at Café Procope.

In mid-April the Nazis became frantic. Convoys of trucks and cars started carrying hundreds to Dachau, as trains were no longer available. Then, days later, large groups were sent on foot toward Dachau and Buchenwald. Desnos was in a group that was forced to march ten miles to *Theresianstadt*, across the border in Czechoslovakia. He was pulled aside by a young Parisian named André and asked if he had heard the news that the Russians were coming from the east.

"*La liberté* !"

Robert was motivated that, somehow, he had to survive with liberation so close at hand. He guarded his strength, and wrote a poem to Youki as he crouched on the edge of his bunk, his thin hands shaking.

> *I have dreamed so deeply of you that you lose reality.*
> *Is there still time to reach that living body and kiss*
> *On those lips the birth of the voice so dear to me?*
> > *I have dreamed so deeply of you that my arms so used*
> > *While embracing your shade to cross themselves on my chest*
> > *Would not shape themselves perhaps to the lines of your body. (22)*

Then in May 1945 Russian troops arrived with news that Western Europe was free. German and Polish guards were confined in the same barracks in which they had ruled over their walking corpses. Disorganization reigned. Rumors circulated that prisoners were going to be sent home 'tomorrow' then that they were not to be released for a month.

The fever and stomach ache began one evening. Robert's hope was that it was due to excitement that the war was over and he was going to be released. By morning, he was clearly sick. A Jewish doctor came to examine him and his expression was grim.

"Typhoid," he said.

The Epitaph (1943)

I lived in those times. For a thousand years
I have been dead. Not fallen, but hunted;
When all human decency was imprisoned,
I was free amongst the masked slaves.
  I lived in those times, yet I was free.
  I watched the river, the earth, the sky,
  Turning around me, keeping their balance,
  The seasons provided their birds and their honey.
You who live, what have you made of your luck?
Do you regret the time when I struggled?
Have you cultivated for the common harvest?
Have you enriched the town I lived in?
  Living men, think nothing of me. I am dead.
  Nothing survives of my spirit or my body. (23)

Robert Desnos   1900 – 1945

THE VAUCLUSE - 1944

JANUARY:

The steam engine of the passenger train snorted out a plume like a spray of feathers near the southwestern frontier of Rhineland Germany. Inside were an assortment of Nazi soldiers splayed in sleeping positions, surrounded by packs and rifles, along with a handful of citizens guarding baskets and bags and one extremely tense, recently escaped prisoner of war.

The conductor had examined Étienne Bertolini's German ID and travel permit carefully, glancing from the photo to his face and back for several seconds. He asked how far he was traveling. Étienne stated 'Koblentz.' When the official moved on, Étienne pulled his cap over his forehead, tucked his chin to his chest, folded his arms and pretended to sleep.

At the station where his map said to transfer trains, guards with rifles stood on the platform. Soldiers with aggressive dogs patrolled the tracks. Outside lights were blue and dim. Inside, shades were drawn. Passengers huddled near an iron stove. After an hour's wait, Étienne got on a second train, his cards and ticket checked once more. He settled into a corner and dozed as the locomotive wound its slow way southwest. With black paint covering the windows one could only imagine the scenery as the passenger cars wound through a series of villages, farms and forests dusted in snow.

Suddenly the train screeched to a halt, pale lights inside were turned on and a man in a Gestapo uniform entered the car, accompanied by two soldiers. The Nazi took his time, shining a flashlight in the face of each person, verifying each picture on the identification cards. When the SS officer stood directly in front of Étienne there was a sudden burst of gunfire outside. The three men leapt to the back vestibule and, as the door opened, pale light poured into the passenger car. Étienne scratched a corner of the paint off the glass, wincing at the glare as he peered out at train cars curved around a low hill.

Clumps of uniforms ran toward two bodies lying in the snow. One was a young woman with her legs splayed apart, her arms outstretched and a halo of bright red forming in the brilliant white that cushioned her head. Étienne leaned back against his seat. Passengers in the coach, including the soldiers at the other end, stayed completely still. To the left of Étienne, a shabbily dressed man with sunken cheeks checked the packages in a bag between his knees. He leaned back and sighed.

"Well at least now we can be on our way."

Very few passengers were left when Étienne got off at the stop that Klaus's map indicated. A few buildings still stood, but bombing raids had left this town in ruins. Rubble and dirty snow piled up against remnants of buildings, fragments of walls. Almost no one was in the streets except for a few hunched-over passengers, arriving for unimaginable reasons in the desolate place.

Étienne put his hands in his jacket pocket and plodded through ice-encrusted snow onto a road that had not been used for days. Heading into a wooded area, he stopped once to break off tree bark to plug the holes in the soles of his shoes. For over two weeks he trudged on, avoiding villages except to buy food, following creeks and windbreaks, the edges of gnarled vineyards. Hiding until after dusk, he used constellations as his guide when the sky was clear and walked until he could go no further. One snowfall delayed him two days. He stayed in the corner of a mildewed hayloft at a burned farmhouse, drinking only water but getting needed rest.

If he shared space with a goat or cow, usually as skinny and as hungry as he, Étienne relieved her of a bit of milk. Chickens tucked into a barn for the winter provided occasional eggs. Once he broke a window to steal bread placed on a kitchen counter. He stumbled upon a cache of wine, a broken barrel covered with debris in a bombed vineyard. It tasted bad, but he slept well that night.

As he walked, he often repeated a favorite segment of a poem by Robert Desnos that Laurianne had sent him:

> *The track I'm running on*
> *Won't be the same when I turn back*
> *It's useless to follow it straight*
> *I'll return to another place (21)*

When he realized that he was past the German-French border, Étienne approached a cloister attached to a church surrounded by a dozen decrepit buildings. He knocked on the cloister's door. A wrinkled nun with missing teeth looked at him suspiciously. He asked if she could tell him the best way to get to Provence. She crossed herself then told him that he would have to pray for God's help. He should light a candle in the chapel and recite his rosary. It seemed odd, but he was cold and tired; the shelter of a chapel was appealing. He did as she directed and nothing happened.

As Étienne started to leave, a priest entered from the side and said that he was there to hear Étienne's confession. Inside the booth, after being questioned rigorously, he was told to look for the town blacksmith on the main road and tell him that he 'needed to repair a wagon axel.' The blacksmith motioned to a boy of eight or nine and told Étienne to follow him. Within a few minutes he was in a house, eating hot soup. The boy's father looked over his ID card and pass and said that he thought it would be safe for him to get on a bus heading south. He gave Étienne some money, a chunk of bread and cheese, directions to the bus stop and the coded names of men who could help him along the way.

Four days later, with help from other Resistance members, Étienne arrived in Orange. The town was awash with uniforms and vehicles, damaged buildings, broken windows, sandbags piled against shops, doors with 'closed' signs. People walked with heads down, thoughts elsewhere.

He decided to go to Beaumes-de-Venise where Laurianne lived. From there he would find out if he could safely return to Carpentras. He found refuge in a small café occupied by men with hunched shoulders and eyes that looked sideways at him as they sipped on coffee cups and glasses of brownish liquid. When the bus finally arrived, the engine strained and banged as it jerked along frosted roads, stopped for passengers, then lurched onward with gears whining resentfully.

As Étienne stepped onto a frozen road in Beaume-de-Venise, he looked at familiar sights: the jagged peaks of the Dentelles de Montmirail, the Romanesque church's square bell tower sticking up from the main square, the olive mill spritzed with hoarfrost.

At Laurianne's home, high up the hillside near the town's prehistoric caves, her mother looked at Étienne for a full thirty seconds before she recognized him. She pulled him inside and slammed the door.

"*Mon dieu!*" she exclaimed. "How did you...oh, my!"

She looked frightened. Laurianne entered the room, wiping her hands on an apron then shrieked aloud, waved her hands and threw herself into Étienne's outstretched arms as she covered his face with kisses.

JANUARY:

Amélie Bertolini carefully balanced a silver tray of pastries as she entered the top-floor salon of the commandant's residence. She removed an empty tray and put the full one down on the desserts table. Her parents had started early that morning baking the *mille feuilles, tartes, éclairs* and other sweets.

Kommandantur Schneider had spared no expense for the reception welcoming the Brandenburg Division contingent. The specially trained troops, many bi-lingual, had appeared in the Vaucluse a few days before. Everyone knew that they were part of an intelligence gathering corps, the *Abwher*. They were in Provence to find and exterminate the *terrorists* that were damaging roads and communication lines. Local officials, the mayor and a few business owners were also attending, with well-dressed wives and girlfriends.

As Amélie repositioned pastry pieces, the commandant motioned for her to come over. His limp brown hair had a tendency to flop onto his forehead reminding Amélie of Hitler himself, but he had no mustache and an enlarged chin. The officer looked the girl up and down as if she were a recruit under inspection. He knew that her brother was in a German prison camp doing forced labor. Her parents reluctantly reported on suspicious activities in town. Their reticent daughter was a decorative addition for his occasional parties, with brown hair coifed in a 'pageboy' style and hazel-colored eyes.

His bad French was heavily accented, guttural. "Tell Gustave to replace the beef is cold. Is necessary enough horseradish sauce."

In the kitchen, activity was frenetic. A fat, balding man in a chef's hat was slicing up a ham, yelling orders to others in the room. He glared at the girl interrupting him.

"Monsieur, I have been asked to tell you that *Kommandantur Schneider* would like the beef platter refreshed."

He nodded and barked an order in German to a man in a white apron who turned, took a large roast out of the oven and started slicing it.

"Amélie, I need you to serve more champagne," the owner of a local wine shop commanded. "Please take this tray of flutes upstairs. Careful!"

In the salon Amélie offered the champagne but most guests already held a glass. The tray remained half full as Amélie stopped at one group after another. She glanced at the orchestra tucked in a corner next to an enormous fireplace. The music was barely audible over the cacophony of voices echoing in the large room. Francois' Uncle Xavier played his clarinet in a lack-luster fashion. She recognized austere Obersleutnant Ziegler at the piano, Professor Gilles-Martin and two other civilians playing violins and a cello, with a uniformed musician playing a flute.

Amélie wandered apathetically among the arrogant new guests, amid raucous, unintelligible talk, black and red swastikas ever present. Although the war was not going well for the Germans, the laughter of women blended with grandiose pronouncements.

Moving closer to the orchestra Amélie smiled at Monsieur Chevalier as he glanced her way. She paused and listened to the familiar 'Bring a torch, Jeanette, Isabella,' a well-known Provençal melody. For one golden instant she reflected on a childhood that was full of warm memories. The reverie ended as a uniformed man put his arm across her shoulders and leaned in to pick up a glass. His eyes were bloodshot and he had trouble standing.

In poorly pronounced French he snorted, "*Bonne Année!* Here's to a happy New Year. And what's your name, darling?"

A woman with dyed blond hair in a tight red dress stepped in front of the man, sliding between him and Amélie. "Heinrich, *mein liebchen!*" She kissed him and linked her arm in his, speaking more broken German. Amélie recognized her as a *coiffeuse* from a shop in town and stared as she guided the man to a couch where he sat with a thud. The woman glanced back at her and winked.

A Mozart piece abruptly changed to the German national anthem, *Deutschlandlied.* At the end, the Germans erupted in a Nazi salute. The commandant stepped onto a square box with side handles, one that his aide carried around for moments when his superior addressed a crowd. Schneider gave a brief speech, gesturing now and then to the severe-looking Brandenburg delegation.

After the guests departed well before the eleven o'clock curfew, the commandant sequestered himself in his office with four of the *Abwher* officers. The kitchen staff started clearing the dishes and silverware. Monsieur Chevalier and other members of the music group packed up their instruments. He limped to where Amélie stood holding a tray of dishes, smiling his quixotic smile. He peered through round wire-rimmed glasses, gray-white hair sloping onto the jacket collar.

"I need to talk to you, Amélie, but can't do it here. Can you join me at the *Café du 19ᵉᵐᵉ Siècle* as soon as you are finished?"

She was instantly fearful as well as curious, "Yes, though I need to work for another twenty minutes."

"I'll look for you upstairs in one of the meeting rooms."

⸺

Xavier Chevalier scanned through smoke clouding the café, walked to the bar and ordered two glasses of wine, handing over some ration coupons. He continued toward the rooms on the second floor. Walking stiffly up the stairs, past a bulletin board with schedules and notices, Chevalier knocked at a door that had a taped paper: 'poetry and fiction.'

Two girls in fur-collared jackets and three men in workmen's clothes sat around a table. The fellows stood to greet Xavier with quick handshakes. The girls stood to kiss him and appeared pleased to see their poetry instructor.

"Are you here to critique our writing this evening?" One joked as she turned over a piece of paper.

Chevalier shook his head. "I am meeting a friend."

A short, serious girl with a short, serious haircut moved from the table. "We're finished for the evening, aren't we, guys? It's almost curfew."

As they gathered up their papers, Chevalier avoided looking too closely in case they had illegal tracts that circulated in town. After they left, he hooked his cane over a hat rack's hook, put his black beret on top and placed the clarinet case on the table. A waiter appeared and put two glasses next to the case.

Xavier pulled out a chair, sipping his wine, lost in thought. He stretched and ran his left hand along the thigh where shrapnel had sliced the muscles in the 1914 Battle of Ypres. Ten million young men had died on those battlefields, accomplishing nothing. Horrified by what he had seen, Chevalier became and remained a pacifist. He avoided taking political sides, focusing instead on the virtues of Provençal life. His military disability pension, supplemented by writing for the papers, made it possible to live adequately; leading the poetry club gave his life purpose. This particular errand was apolitical, he reassured himself.

He heard Amélie's rapid footfall coming up the steps and stood to greet her. Her expression was terrified.

"Dear Amélie, do not fear. I actually have good news! Sit down, my dear as what I'll tell you may come as a shock." He paused, "Your brother Étienne has escaped from the POW camp."

Amélie's hand flew to her mouth as she shrieked. "Étienne! Where is he? Is he all right?"

The elderly man placed his hand over hers as he leaned in, whispering. "Étienne is hiding but not in Carpentras. He wanted you to know that he has no injuries, although my source said that he is quite thin."

"How did you find this out?" She looked with wide eyes. "Are you in the Resistance, Monsieur? Don't worry, I won't tell."

Xavier stammered that he was a pacifist; he was not involved in any opposition to the Germans. "Oppressive as their presence is. But, no, a former poetry club member gave me the message."

Amélie clasped Monsieur Chevalier's hand, "Monsieur, how wonderful! My parents will be so relieved to hear this news."

"Perhaps you should not say anything to them. If they are questioned it would be better if they could truthfully say that they didn't know. Don't be surprised if your apartment and bakery are searched."

"Right. I should act as if nothing unusual has happened. But I am so glad to know that he is safe."

"I thought that we could have a little toast on this occasion." Chevalier cleared his throat and offered the wine glass. "May the future bring more good news, a cessation of violence, and peace throughout our precious land."

Their glass rims ticked and Amélie restrained herself from swallowing the liquid in two gulps. They sat for a moment then Amélie leaned over, put her hands on Chevalier's arm and kissed his cheek, her eyelashes glistening with tears.

"Merci, Monsieur Chevalier. Can you get a message to Étienne?"

Chevalier shook his head. "No, but he may contact you later. I think that we should leave before curfew starts."

He stood and reached for his cane as the young girl bolted from the room after blowing him a kiss. Amélie bounced down the steps of the café. She hummed a tune to herself as she rushed home. Her mother looked up as she came in the door, pleased to see her looking happier than usual.

"Did you have a good time at the party?"

Amélie stepped across the kitchen and gave her mother a warm hug and heaved a relieved sigh. "Everyone loved the desserts, *Maman*. I didn't have any problems."

She stepped back and looked at her mother. "Those men, the ones who arrived from Germany to get rid of the Resistance? They look dangerous and seem very powerful. You and Papa, you need to be very careful!"

FEBRUARY:

The passing of documents and illegal newspapers, such as *Combat* and *Liberation,* became routine. Florence got into the habit of carefully checking her surroundings before making a 'drop.' Being aware of people and sounds became second nature. She hadn't realized how much she had ignored her environment until she trained herself to observe. Colors, noises, facial expressions, body language, seemed sharper. Her journal, too, reflected more keen observations.

Henri's friendliness with the Germans provided such a safe cover that sometimes Florence carried information when they were at a café with one of the officers or musicians whom Henri knew, often his friend Obersleutnant Ziegler, the pianist. She would go to the toilet after signaling her contact and the person would line up behind her. The packet would be retrieved from under the trash container. So far there had been no trouble.

Newspapers and posters announced rewards for information on terrorists and indicated that Resistance activities had increased substantially. One article reported that on January 10 a group attacked a German Patrol in the town of Murs. They took several prisoners, left two dead and four Maquis were wounded. Then members of the *Groupes Francs* and the *Maquis Ventoux* attacked another German Patrol in early February.

On February 22, *La Provence* announced that a major SS success had occurred at a camp near the town of Izon-les-Bruisse when three networks of the *Maquis Ventoux* arrived to pick up pigs for a special feast before Lent. Two-hundred-and-sixty motorized German soldiers, aided by French militia, blocked roads in and out of the area and attacked in force. Thirty-five men had been killed.

When Antoine and Florence discussed this he offered to terminate her involvement. She said 'no,' vehemently. She didn't tell him that she felt more alive than ever before. She looked forward to sidling into the Museum when it was closed and he was cleaning the floors. They would talk out loud, laugh, at ease in one of the upper rooms as they pored over the latest book.

Florence was devouring prose written by Rene Char, fascinated since he was well known locally due to the family's plaster business. His ability to capture both atmosphere and emotions in a different yet understandable way pleased her. Pierre Reverdy's writing was contemplative and poignant. Paul Eluard tended to be a romantic.

She liked Antoine's suggestion on how to interpret modern writing. He squinted as if the sun was in his eyes. "It's sort of like describing a leaf, then a twig, maybe a bit of bark. Then it is up to you to make it a tree. If that's what you want to envision."

This blustery March day Florence had fed her husband and daughter well. Two days before, she had biked over to the Laurent's farm for a winter squash, some wine, and a jar of wild mushrooms that Juliette had pickled. At the time, Florence was surprised to be entertained in the front room rather than the kitchen. Her cousin did not seem welcoming and even Jean-Pierre seemed nervous. Florence became suspicious that they might be hiding someone. She did not want to know.

After lunch was over and Henri and Gigi went on their way, Florence pulled two slim volumes from under her chair cushion and put them into her purse. She tucked a scarf around her neck and smeared on pink lipstick that she obtained from one of her contacts, through the 'black market.' It had cost her two knit scarves. Considering the fact that she had been given some wool and spun it herself, the exchange was a bargain.

Florence, as always, checked her surroundings before sliding into the Museum's gated entry and behind a tall bush on the right. The mistral and Monday had kept sensible people indoors. She watched a repair in progress at the German headquarters across the street, as a carpenter sawed a board next to the front steps. Two guards stood chatting by the door, leaning on rifles, their jackets puffed by the wind. No one looked her way.

The oak door was open no more than half an inch, indiscernible unless one was close enough to touch it. Antoine had oiled it so it no longer squeaked. Florence slipped inside and closed the door. The reception area was dim and she felt for the iron railing, climbing past landscapes and portraits arranged haphazardly on the wall. At the top she opened one of the doors leading to a gallery. She called out Antoine's name.

His silhouette appeared in the archway. "I was watching out a window to make sure that you weren't followed. All looks fine. Let's go into the next room and sit down."

He wanted to hear about the transfers and if she suspected she was under surveillance. Florence reported that she didn't think so. She had left the hollowed out hymnbook with identity cards in the corner of a pew where Sister Monique sat saying her rosary. Florence lit a candle in a nearby chapel to check that the nun was not followed. At the post office she handed a box labeled 'cloth diapers' filled with copies of *Combat* to a young mother in a red blouse who answered Florence's coded question correctly. The woman put the box next to her sleeping child in its baby carriage and walked away.

Antoine held out a small packet for delivery. This was to be left at the 19th Century Café on Tuesday. Florence was to put it in the morning paper and appear to be reading the front page at the bar while waiting for a coffee. She would leave it for *Maxmillian* to pick up with her cup and saucer.

Florence sighed and smiled. "I'm amazed that we have been able to keep this up this long, without anyone being suspicious."

"Thank your husband, as he is our perfect cover without knowing it!" Antoine chuckled.

"You can't know how satisfying it is for me to do this under his nose. At least I counter-balance his activities."

"You must be careful, Florence! The director of the town's Judicial Council was just arrested. There are a number of secret agents in town trying to ferret out anyone who might be helping the Resistance." It was Antoine's turn to sigh. "If you ever think that you're in danger..."

Florence looked over, relaxed. "I'll be fine. The war must come to an end sometime, and hopefully soon."

Antoine reached for her hand, "Then what will you do?"

Florence was slightly startled. "I don't know."

"You deserve more in life." Antoine's voice was soft.

Florence blushed, shook her head. "Thank you. You will never know how much knowing you has changed my thinking."

Antoine pursed his mouth, "That can be both good and bad."

"It's good, believe me. But we haven't talked about poetry today."

Antoine looked at her, "How diligent you have become. So, tell me, what have you learned this week?"

Florence pulled a book out of her bag and turned to a marked page. "I compared one of Eluard's early poems with one that was more recent. He married his first wife Gala during World War I. The early poems were much more abstract compared to the ones he writes about his second wife Nusch, whom he married a few years ago." She looked at him shyly, "He comes across as rather starry-eyed."

Antoine waited. Florence opened the book and read:

"The world is blue as an orange
No error the words do not lie
They no longer allow you to sing
In the tower of kisses agreement
The madness the love
She her mouth of alliance
All the secrets all the smiles
Or what dress of indulgence
To believe in quite naked.
The wasps flourish greenly

Dawn goes by round her neck
A necklace of windows
You are all the solar joys
All the sun of this earth
On the roads of your beauty. (24)

Then she took a paper from the back and read the second poem, one that she had copied. "This one is titled *Nusch*."

The sentiments apparent
The lightness of approach
The tresses of caresses.
   Without worry or suspicion
   Your eyes confide in what they see
   Seen by what they gaze at.
Confidence of crystal
Between two mirrors
At night your eyes are lost
To fuse waking to desire. (25)

"So, how do you analyze the difference between the two?"

Florence fiddled with the book and opened to the first poem. "The woman in the first poem comes across as flirtatious, unpredictable. He uses the word 'wasp,' indicating something stinging about her. He uses other words, such as *madness, secrets, indulgence.* Yet she apparently entranced him."

"Ah, I see," murmured Antoine. "And the second?"

"Well, she sounds more loyal. I think that Eluard sees her as someone whom he can trust, someone who is steadfast and closer to him."

Antoine looked puzzled when he gazed into her eyes. "I am impressed. I mean, you have grasped the intent of the words, found underlying meanings and seen beyond the surface. That is admirable, considering the short time that you have analyzed poetry."

She felt his hand over hers as she peered at her wristwatch. "I think that I need to go now."

"Yes, perhaps you should," Antoine stood up, releasing her hand. "I'll walk you to the door. I can shake out the dust mop and make sure it is safe to leave."

They slipped down stairs, sliding hands along the bannister in the dim light. At the door, Florence turned to give her usual farewell kiss and felt Antoine's lips on hers as he pulled her toward him with firm hands. She closed her eyes and relaxed into him, snuggling her head on his shoulder.

"I think that you are one of the most courageous women I have ever known," he murmured.

She turned her face and returned his kisses with fervor. They began a gentle exploration of each other, touching fingers to cheeks, tongue to tongue. His ardor was intense, surprising Florence, and her physical restraint released, her body sprang to life, shivering, receptive.

Backed up against the ornate gold and marble 18th century console, Florence pulled up her skirt and pulled down her panties as Antoine unzipped his trousers. He lifted her up on the table and thrust into her with a low groan as she guided him with her hand. They were beyond rational thinking and dispersed into rhythmic pleasure. She was the first to cry out in gasps as she clutched his shoulders and swung her head from side to side. Seconds later he made one last thrust and collapsed around her still form. They stayed that way for several minutes; she barely aware of the cold stone beneath her, he not conscious of cool air on his buttocks.

When he withdrew Florence looked down at his withered cock. She thought that he had felt different when she first touched him and now saw why. She put one hand on her lips, her eyes wide, and looked up. He returned her stare and tipped his head as he buttoned his pants.

"I guess that you can tell that I'm Jewish," he murmured, as he tucked in his shirt.

She didn't answer.

"I hope that doesn't make any difference," he finally said.

"No, no. Of course not. It is just that I...you...I mean, I didn't even guess. Your name and all."

"Antoine Dupont isn't my real name. I'm Benjamin Landau."

"Benjamin?" she repeated. "Benjamin. I like the name."

"But maybe not the Landau?" Antoine looked concerned.

"A rose is a rose is a rose, isn't that what the American woman in Paris said? It doesn't change you." Florence accepted Antoine's handkerchief as she slid to the floor. "I must look a complete mess..."

Antoine reached over and pulled her face toward him, "Your appearance doesn't matter. It's the 'you' that I like."

Florence looked up and grinned, "And I like you so very much, Jewish or not, Benjamin or Antoine or *L'imprimeur* or whatever you want to call yourself."

"This changes things, I'm afraid," Antoine said. "But at least now you know who I am and how I feel about you. Are you all right with this?"

"Although I know that I have sinned, it was a wonderful feeling." She leaned into him, "I hope we can do this again."

Antoine laughed, "We have to! I don't think I can bear not loving you. Somehow we will find time to be together. We can meet here every Monday and maybe even in between."

They stood, holding each other closely. Florence looked up at him. "Are there very many other Jews still in the area? I never see any, although I don't know any of the families well."

Antoine laughed aloud. "Several of your contacts in the Resistance are Jewish, as you might imagine. '*Anatole?*' He's a Jew from Paris who started our network. Good people in this town and the farms around it are hiding many of us. I understand that there are tunnels near the old Jewish ghetto, so that it is possible to move around between buildings."

"I've not heard, even from Henri, of any Jews from Carpentras being captured or imprisoned here and I think he would know about it."

"Several people from Belgium were turned in to the Gestapo in the summer of 1942 but, so far, none of us French citizens have been arrested. Our own *collabos* and the *Milice* realize that they may soon be prisoners of the Allies and aren't as quick to condemn someone who might testify against them. You watch, suddenly most of the people in Carpentras and everywhere else in France will be magically transformed into de Gaullists!"

"I think that my cousins are hiding someone," Florence spoke very softly, then added. "I didn't see or hear anything when I was there but since their farmhouse is isolated, it would not surprise me."

"Does Henri suspect?"

"Henri and my cousins have never gotten along well. They used to argue about politics then at some point we were no longer invited to Sunday dinners. Of course, when the Germans invaded everything changed. Having family gatherings, especially with an outspoken fascist, isn't particularly comfortable."

"But you still see them." Antoine hugged her. "That's good."

She twisted her wedding ring. "I'm thinking of asking Juliette and Jean-Pierre if they will let Gigi live with them through the summer. I'm worried about what will happen when the Americans and British arrive."

"With de Gaulle in North Africa and the Allies moving up through Italy, an invasion could happen at anytime. She would be a lot safer in the country in case we are bombed. Marseille and Avignon are the likely targets but airplanes sometimes get off target."

"Enough of this," Florence leaned up and kissed his lips. They stood entwined, ignoring the mistral whistling through the door, content with the warmth of each other's bodies. With a sigh Florence pulled away and stepped back.

"Time for me to go," she murmured.

Antoine nodded, walked to where his mop leaned against the wall. He opened the door enough to step out and shake off a smattering of dust. He nodded to Florence and she slipped out, hearing the click of the doors lock behind her. Neither noticed the face looking out from a window on the third floor of the German headquarters across the street.

PART TWO

A PLATEFUL OF PROBLEMS - 1978

I stood before the bathroom mirror and applied lipstick bought days before. Blotting it, I leaned over, squinted, re-applied it then blotted again. My armpits felt damp although the late September weather drifting in from the balcony door was pleasantly cool. Using a hand towel, I dabbed under each arm then re-applied deodorant.

A two-year old colt gearing up for its first race could not have been more jumpy. I chided myself for acting like it was my first prom date. I had defended research papers to grim-faced committees, dealt with an occasional contentious student, handled attorneys anxious to rush through the divorce. Having lunch with Maurice's family should not be a time to go all twiddly and jittery.

The zipper slid up smoothly and the new dress fit comfortably. The coiffeuse had done a nice job of curling my hair. I wrapped a multi-colored scarf around my neck, put on new sling pumps and was ready, with Sophie's borrowed purse in hand.

Mincing down the cobbled street, I saw Maurice standing next to the deux-chevaux looking like he might be going to a funeral. He wore a black suit with a necktie of blue and orange stripes that stood out from his white shirt. I waved a hand in what was meant to be a jaunty gesture.

We kissed cheeks then he kissed me on the lips. He said that he'd had a glass of wine before he left. Baguettes perfumed the car. I could also tell that he'd been smoking. Maurice gripped the steering wheel with one hand, staring straight ahead as he pulled at his tie knot with the other.

"Do you always dress up for Sunday dinner?" I inquired.

"Not usually but almost everyone will be there today, which isn't unusual. We're sentimental about being together during harvests." Maurice cleared his throat. "I asked everyone to dress nicely because an American professor was coming. A few may expect a man."

"What in the world have you told them about me?"

He looked completely serious. "I've said that I met a hot *Americaine* who can't get enough of me."

I reached over and rubbed his crotch. Maurice's 'whew' made us both snicker.

When Maurice opened the front door, I was introduced to his mother simply as 'their guest.' Madame Laurent offered her cheek as well as warmly grasping my hand.

"How nice to see you again."

Maurice led me toward the salon and stated, "I would like you to meet our guest, Professor Claire Somerset."

I smiled at everyone, "Please, call me Claire."

The Laurent family lounged on the couches or stood by open windows. Cigarette smoke wafted in white arcs as heads swiveled toward the doorway. There was a general murmur of voices blending in *enchanté, quel plaisir.* A couple of them looked surprised. Julien stepped forward to shake my hand and asked if I would like an *aperitif.* I chose champagne and gripped the stem of the glass.

Maurice named names as he gestured: his daughter-in-law Martine; his brother Francois and wife Amélie; his sister Gabrielle, her daughter Audrey with her husband Pierre and their baby, Jeanne; Gabrielle's son Gerard; Francois and Amélie's son Thierry and his wife Suzanne. There was another series of *enchanté, bienvenue,* a flurry of handshakes. (Where were those nametags!)

Joseph, a university student, remarked, "You're a professor?"

As I responded there was a knock at the front door. Maurice leapt into the hall and effusively greeted the Duprés. Sophie and Georges slid in amid kisses and handshakes and a litany of 'how pleased to see you, delighted to be here.'

Dear friend that she was, Sophie stood next to me and launched into an amusing story. At Friday's market an English tourist requested 'pasta' and the vendor thought she said 'pesto,' as the French word for 'pasta' is *pâte*. She had us all laughing as she imitated their dialogue of continued misunderstanding.

Joseph asked if I had ever met a movie star. I said that I had spoken with George Lucas, the director of *Star Wars* several years before. We happened to be in a bookstore in San Rafael after the release of the movie and chatted about a book on display, although I didn't acknowledge that I recognized him. An audience of wide eyes smiled and commented. Lucas and *Star Wars* had been wildly popular.

There was a lot of talk about the harvest and wine as Sophie guided me around. We chatted with Francois and Amélie, then Julien and Martine. Audrey disappeared to nurse her baby then reappeared with the child asleep in her arms. Maurice's sister sat in a chair behind the far couch, smoking and talking with her family, deliberately isolated.

When Elodie the cook appeared, Madame Laurent stood and stated '*à table*.' A blur of faces spun before me in the bustle of entering the dining room. Because there were sixteen of us, a game table was placed at one end. Maurice's chair was almost at the door to the hall. I sat a full table length away at his mother's right, across from Julien and next to his brother.

Madame Laurent asked how I was enjoying my visit and I thanked her for including me in the opening harvest. Then Julien asked about the wine industry in California. I told him that there had been wineries there for over a hundred years and launched into the story of two brothers who ran a family winery. The younger one came to France to learn better production methods. The older insisted that what was good enough for their father was good enough for them. They physically fought over the idea of making better wine, so Robert Mondavi left and opened his own winery in 1966. He'd been very successful, which led to many new vineyards springing up in Napa Valley.

Julien agreed whole-heartedly that there was much that Americans could learn from French vintners. "But where is this Napa Valley?"

"It is north of San Francisco." I didn't mention the Paris tasting.

When Madame Laurent asked what I taught, I once again explained that I was gathering information about Surrealist authors and poets, active anti-fascists during World War II. I said that I hoped to meet Réne Char.

Francois wiped his mouth with a napkin. "I met him toward the end of the War, just before the liberation of Provence. Of course I have read many of his works, especially the reflections about his experiences in the Resistance."

" I have read excerpts from his *Leaflets from Hypnos*. What an interesting title he chose, citing the Greek god of sleep."

Madame Laurent added, "I believe that he was referring to both his writing and our country slumbering during that time."

"I know that Char does not give many interviews, although a friend is trying to arrange one for me before I leave."

Francois commented. "A man I know in our town, Claude Lapeyre, is passionate about the man's work."

"What a coincidence. He's the one I'm talking about."

"Really? Well, if anyone can get you a meeting, it will be him. I think that Monsieur Char would welcome the chance to talk with an American professor. He has a tender spot for those who teach." Francois continued in a soft, rumbling voice. "Did you know that the word 'char' in French also means 'tank.' You will find that this family name fits him well."

"Would you be willing to tell me about some of your experiences in the Resistance? If it's not difficult for you."

Francois paused. "As I've grown older, I realize that what we did should not be lost to history. Yet old memories may not always be completely accurate."

"I'll give you my phone number before I leave."

Francois whispered, "I believe that my brother has it."

I felt my typical flush, "Oh. Yes, ummm."

Elodie removed our plates and Gabrielle rose to help. The main dish of sliced *sanglier*, wild boar, was served next, topped with a sauce of rippled chanterelle mushrooms. Madame Laurent explained that a friend of Francois' traded game for a case or two of wine every year. Julien and Maurice opened bottles of their recent blends. Once filled, our glasses were raised in a toast. The Laurents enjoyed laughing—jokes at the expense of Belgians, gentle teasing, anecdotes about their work, animated talk about politics. There were times when speech was fast or the punch lines so idiomatic that I did not understand. Although everyone spoke at a subdued level that was typical in France, conversation never lagged.

As Gabrielle and Elodie cleared the dishes, Gabrielle made a point of coming to my side of the table. I smiled and she smiled back. As she lifted my plate, it tipped and a stream of meat juice dribbled onto my hair and down the left sleeve.

Gabrielle apologized profusely. Madame Laurent patted my hand and suggested that I might want to wash it off in *la toilette*. "Elodie can direct you there."

Gabrielle muttered, "She already knows where it is."

When I returned, my hair was limp and damp on one side. The dress sleeve was spotted a darker color. Gabrielle looked up and apologized again, insincerely it seemed to me. I said that I was fine and went to my seat feeling as if I had swallowed a rock.

Elodie brought in plates with slices of *tarte aux pommes*. Maurice passed chilled decanters of their *muscat*. Madame Laurent then served espresso. I did my best to not show discomfort over my damp dress and sticky hair. Conversation veered to chitchat about people they knew, updates on small town gossip. By four o'clock the family started kissing and leaving. I thanked Madame Laurent and told Francois that I hoped to see him again.

As we got up from our chairs Francois planted a kiss on my hand. "What a pleasure to meet you. I look forward to another time."

I thanked him, twice.

When I passed Gabrielle, she glanced up with a bland look then turned back to Pierre. At the doorway Audrey, holding the baby, marched unfalteringly past me toward her mother.

I sidled up to Sophie and said, "Would you take me home? I'm not feeling well...,"

She frowned then tugged at her husbands' sleeve. "We're taking Claire home."

Georges looked startled but he knew not to resist when his wife spoke firmly. When Maurice saw me with the Duprés, he started to speak.

I blurted out, "I'm not feeling well, Maurice. I think that it would be best if I went with Sophie and Georges."

He reached for my hand. "If it's your dress, you needn't worry. I'll pay the cleaning bill."

I didn't blink or tears would have tumbled out. "Maurice, don't worry about the dress. It's just….between the big meal and meeting everyone, I'm feeling overwhelmed."

Sophie looked from one to the other of us with mild disgust. "Come, Claire. We need to get you home so you can take something for your headache."

Outside I pulled a handkerchief from the purse and dabbed at my eyes. On the way to town I did breathing exercises and practiced a smile. Sophie and I agreed to have coffee the following week. I let myself out of the car and waved back as I walked up the street. As soon as I closed the apartment building's oak door behind me I looked down at the oily sleeve.

This time I muttered 'fuck!' as I ran up the staircase.

THE REFUGEE
MISSAK MANOUCHIAN

Missak thought of his days living with the Kurds with great fondness. He was nine years old at the time, skinny, traumatized, introspective and quiet, overwhelmed by the noise and activity in the sun-washed stone village.

The smell of wood smoke and spices hovered over flat-topped roofs. The colorful robes of the women, their bangles and beads, startled him. The men seemed like giants on skittish desert horses, mustached and turbaned, brandishing spears and rifles. Children played gaily in the streets and alleys, always in motion except at the hottest time of day.

The family with whom he and his brother Karabet lived showed them unexpected kindness, plying them with delicious foods and the warmth of lumpy beds filled with children of various ages. He no longer remembered their names; perhaps one of the boys was *Karzan* but he wasn't sure. He simply remembered his wonder at feeling uneasily safe after the horror of seeing his father shot and his mother becoming so thin and ill that she faded quietly into death.

Scooped up from his Kurdish home by a Christian organization, he, Karabet and other Armenian children were sent to an orphanage in Syria. There they stayed until Karabet reached the age of eighteen and was legally on his own. In 1924, the two brothers reached the coast of Beirut where they scrounged, worked, begged for enough money to pay for passage to France, the destination of many other Armenian refugees.

Life was still not easy. Karabet died two years after they arrived. Missak had to learn a new language and a trade. He became a wood worker and, for two years, worked as a lathe operator for the Citroen car company until he lost his job during the Depression. He then found work as a model for artists making sculptures.

Missak was determined to get an education. First he studied in what were called 'worker universities' created by the General Confederation of Labor. Later he audited classes at the University of Paris, the *Sorbonne*, where he learned about great literature, wrote poetry and translated French poems into his native language. He soon became known as a 'literary figure' in Armenian circles. By his late twenties he had founded two magazines: *Tchank* (Effort) and *Machagouyt* (Culture) and had become editor of a third.

In 1934, as with most workers and artists of the time, he became a communist. His wife Mélinée had also been born in Turkey and escaped to France after the massacre of her family. She was close to the Aznavourian family that owned a local restaurant. Their son, Charles Aznavour, was becoming a popular singer and actor. Missak remembered well when Mélinée rode with one of the Aznavourian boys on a bicycle out to visit him in 1941, when he was arrested the first time. Now she was condemned to death 'in absentia' and this family was hiding and protecting her.

Sitting in the prison cell, the poet sat with his head bowed, tapping the table with his fingers, thinking of the other twenty-two in his *reseau*. It was a rag-tag group, refugees from a variety of countries or citizens on the run. Each was a patriot, a freedom fighter determined to do whatever he could to free their adopted land. They had zigzagged in and out of the narrow streets and alleys of Paris, singly, in pairs, in small groups, disrupting and damaging German transports and communications whenever they could. They stole, they murdered, they created mayhem, striking fast, running faster, and furtively hiding in abandoned apartments, murky cellars, frigid attics, rotting barges.

They were proud of what they'd inflicted on the Germans in Paris, with over thirty successful attacks, far beyond what should have been expected. They had even assassinated General Julius Ritter, the assistant to Fritz Sauckel who had been responsible for the deportation of French citizens through the obligatory work service.

Missak sat with a pen in his hand, a blank piece of paper on the table in front of him. He was in the process of writing a letter to his wife. It would be the last that she would ever receive. For months he and his comrades had endured torture, deprivation and--eventually--a three-day 'trial' where they were condemned to death. Today he and his male compatriots were to be shot. Olga, the Romanian Jew and sole female member, was being sent to Germany for beheading. He wrote:

My dear Melinée, my beloved little orphan,

In a few hours I will no longer be of this world. We are going to be executed today at 3:00. This is happening to me like an accident in my life; I don't believe it, but I nevertheless know that I will never see you again.

The sound of the pen scratching on the paper signaled the speed at which his life was passing by.

I'm sure that the French people and all those who fight for freedom will honor our memory with dignity. At the moment of death I proclaim that I have no hatred for the German people or for anyone at all; everyone will receive his due, as punishment and as reward. The German people, and all other people, will live in peace and brotherhood after the war, which will not last much longer.

Missak ran his fingers through his thick black hair. Melinée must not be made to feel sad at his death. He owed her so much:

I have one profound regret, and that's of not having made you happy. I would so much have liked to have a child with you, as you always wished. So I would absolutely love for you to marry after the war and, for my happiness,

that you have a child and, in fulfillment of my last wish, that you marry some-
one who will make you happy.

A guard knocked on the cell door. His rough accent made 'hurry up' sound coarse, slicing through Missak's concentration on carefully selected words. He skimmed through what he had written and added that she was entitled to his military pension.

With the help of friends who'd like to honor me, you should publish those of my
poems and writings that are worth being read.

The poet wrote a few more phrases then paused and looked up at the barred window:

It's sunny out today. It's gazing at the sun and the beauties of nature that
I loved so much that I will say farewell to life and to all of you, my beloved
wife and friends.

The knocking was more aggressive this time, the voice more strident. "Are you finished?"

Manouchian shouted back his answer, dipped his pen in the ink and continued, then added a heartfelt ending:

I embrace you fervently, along with your sister and all those who know
me, near and far; I hold you all against my heart. Farewell. Your friend, your
comrade, your husband.
Manouchian, Missak
P.S. I have 15,000 francs in the valise on the rue de Plaisance. If you
can get it, pay off all my debts and give the rest to Arméne. MM (26)

The Nazis publicized the trial and execution of the Manouchian Group by putting pictures of ten of them on a poster with a red background and posting fifteen thousand copies throughout France. Missak Manouchian's photo,

as leader of the group, was placed below an arrow at the bottom. They presumed that it would show that terrorist groups were composed of outcasts and
criminals. Instead, the idea backfired and the men were considered martyrs, immigrants fighting for France's freedom from German domination. Scribbled over
most of them by passers-by were the words 'they died for France.'

The Red Poster

You demanded neither glory nor tears
Nor organ music, nor last rites
Eleven years already, how quickly eleven years go by
You made use simply of your weapons
Death does not dazzle the eyes of partisans.
    You had your pictures on the walls of our cities
    Black with beard and night, hirsute, threatening
    The poster, that seemed like a bloodstain,
    Using your names that are hard to pronounce,
    Sought to sow fear in the passers-by.
No one seemed to see you French by choice
People went by all day without seeing you,
But at curfew wandering fingers
Wrote under your photos "Fallen for France"
And it made the dismal mornings different.
    Everything had the unvarying color of frost
    In late February for your last moments
    And that's when one of you said calmly:
    "Happiness to all, happiness to those who survive,
    I die with no hate in me for the German people.
Goodbye to pain, goodbye to pleasure.
Farewell the roses, Farewell life, the light and the wind.
Marry, be happy and think of me often

You who will remain in the beauty of things
When it will be all over one day in Erevan.
    A broad winter sun lights up the hill
    How nature is beautiful and how my heart breaks
    Justice will come on our triumphant footsteps,
    My Mélinée, o my love, my orphan girl,
    And I tell you to live and to have a child."
There were twenty-three of them when the guns flowered
Twenty-three who gave their hearts before it was time,
Twenty-three foreigners and yet our brothers
Twenty-three in love with life to the point of losing it
Twenty-three who cried "France!" as they fell.

* *Composed in 1956 by Louis Aragon for the inauguration of a street in Paris named for the Manouchian Group (27)*

Missak Manouchian   1906 – 1944

THE VAUCLUSE – 1944

FEBRUARY:

F rancois arrived at *Domaine de Lauritaine* after midnight, walking through a low fog. As he stepped across frosty ground toward the back terrace, Primo greeted him with a snarl and yap then jumped up, his tail flapping wildly. The young Maquis used a key under a stone in the garden to get into the house. Footsteps pounded downstairs and his father yelled, "Who's there?"

"It's only me, *Papa*. I'm back for awhile."

Jean-Pierre lumbered into the room, lunged at his son and enclosed him in his arms. "*Mon cher* Francois! You scared me terribly. Are you all right? Has anything happened?" He squinted in the dark, looking his son up and down.

"*Non, non,* everything is fine! I'm sorry I couldn't let you know ahead that I was coming. I'm here for a day and then I have a mission, near Avignon."

Juliette and Maurice ran down the stairs and into the kitchen, Juliette holding a lantern. Jean-Pierre checked the windows to be sure blackout curtains were in place and they embraced amid reassurances. Sitting at the kitchen table, after his father stoked the stove's fire, Francois described in thin sketches his life in the Resistance. The closet was cleaned out and Francois trekked down to his hiding place, grateful for the soft mattress and down comforter tucked into a recess at the back of the *cave*.

The next morning he ate breakfast in the kitchen with his parents. As a precaution Maurice stood at slightly open shutters in his bedroom with binoculars focused on the road. Primo lay under an olive tree along the driveway.

Francois revealed details about the drops of armaments, radios, money and men on Mont Ventoux. He had no idea how many there had been but it seemed like a lot of planes had arrived. He sensed that an Allied invasion could happen anytime within the next few months. He did not disclose the contents of his rucksack, sitting on the top step of the cellar stairs, or the purpose of his visit to the plains along the Rhone.

The day passed slowly, the family content to spend time indoors avoiding the winter cold. A hearty stew lunch took an hour longer than usual. Afterwards a disgruntled Maurice was sent down to the olive grove to move around, imitating work. Francois and his parents sat at the table drinking another glass of wine, reliving happy pre-war times.

There were rumors that Étienne Bertolini had escaped from the POW camp. Jean-Pierre said that he'd heard that Gaston Cat had also recently escaped from a prison in Cherbourg and was hiding out near Carpentras. Amélie was fine and still worked at the commandant's house on occasion. Cousin Florence was interested in poetry but Henri was not to know about this. He seemed even closer to the Germans, spending a lot of time at their headquarters or in Nazi officers' apartments.

Francois brought out his fake identity pass. Jean-Pierre showed his son the document they had purchased from a counterfeiter verifying his STO participation, that had fortunately confused then convinced the gendarmes. Francois carefully wrote down the dates, the name of the German town, his supposed job on an assembly line making parts for tanks.

Supper that evening was dried sausages, fried potatoes and applesauce. To Francois it tasted of home, his grandfather's secret recipe for *saucissons*, winter evenings permeated with the scent of a fire. For his parents, the taste was powdery, a tidge of fear, at the thought of their son leaving for the unknown once more.

Before midnight Francois headed toward the Carpentras Canal, following it to a point not far from Pernes-les-Fontaines. Roland's uncle's farmhouse was southwest of the river *La Nesque* that ran through the village. Francois used skills developed as a hunter, keenly aware of sounds wafting in his direction, stopping to confirm that he was neither followed nor coming upon a patrol lying in wait.

The distance was probably no more that twelve or thirteen miles, yet according to his watch he had traveled for over five hours. When he was where the map said the house would be, Francois left the bank of a stream, crossed a road and walked down a gravel driveway. He recognized the Najarian farmhouse from Roland's description. On top of each stone pillar that supported a locked iron gate was a round ball. He felt in between hedges splayed against the wall for an iron ring connected by wire to a bell inside the house. He pulled it several times and waited. When his compatriot loudly whispered *'Androcles,'* he jumped, rattling the branches of the hedge.

"Sheesh, Roland, you scared me."

Roland chuckled as he stepped past a pillar and inserted a key in the lock. "I have been known to profit from my stealth when pilfering items from unguarded pockets. Welcome to Chateau Najarian."

They grabbed bread from the kitchen, checked their explosive filled rucksacks and left the house before the family awoke. An intermittent fog hung low, giving cover. They cut across a field dusted with ice and walked along a path until they came to the ruins of a shed. Parked behind the building was a battered *deux chevaux* with Michel at the wheel, his arms folded, his head on his chest. Awakened, he shook hands then started the car. Using gas that was only available at a huge price on the black market meant that this mission was very important.

Michel drove without lights from dirt roads to gravel ones, on narrow paved ones and across ancient stone bridges. Once or twice they pulled off to let a German vehicle pass. On the outskirts of Avignon the car turned down a street lined with three and four story homes, braced shoulder to shoulder, none appearing well tended, tile roofs at different heights, pocked walls, evidence of medieval windows and doorways now filled with rocks. As Michel pulled up next to one he explained that it belonged to a man in Carpentras who was letting them use it for this meeting. Roland, using a code, rapped on a wide double door that swung open. Michel backed up the car and swung it into the garage. Two men closed the door; a light in the ceiling went on.

Francois and Roland were introduced to Michel's father who had been reassigned as a dispatcher in Avignon and two uncles employed at the depot and switchyards by the *societé national de chemin de fer (SNCF)*. After introductions, the arrivals were taken up to the kitchen-dining area. Given hot drinks and cheese, augmenting the bread that Roland brought, they learned about the purpose of the explosives Francois had in his rucksack.

Josef Perrin explained, "In late 1942 trustworthy engineers, machinists, repairmen and conductors organized into groups willing to do sabotage. Those working at the *Rotonde*, a roundabout where trains are repaired and re-directed, began a campaign of passive resistance. Since trains are the German Army's primary source for transporting machinery, goods and troops, disruptions are costly to them."

Uncle Sebastian, possibly in his late forties, muscular, sporting a thick mustache, continued, "At first we simply slowed down, tools got lost, replacements went to wrong addresses, orders were delayed, acetylene gas tanks were found empty. We also gathered information on troop movements and materials which we sent to the *Maquis*."

Michel's youngest uncle, Grégoire, interjected, "Then we got leaflets dropped from planes encouraging us to damage or destroy engines and engine parts. Last year explosions ruined a number of the old workhorse engines, called *Pacifics*. Of course the Bosch retaliate. Every month co-workers are arrested or shot for sabotage."

Josef Perrin added, "The Germans have started bringing in their own people to take over running and repairing the trains because SNCF employees cannot not be trusted. We call them *Bahnhofs*. Some are fairly competent but the majority are railroad men only due to the uniforms that they wear. As often as not, they aren't even German but conscripts from conquered countries forced to work for the fascists."

Michel's father, a taller, thinner version of his brother but without a mustache, pointed out that since the Germans were mounting a new offensive in Italy against the Allies, Hitler had ordered that airbases in North Italy be defended at all costs.

"French trains transport supplies that the Germans desperately need to halt the Brits and Yanks, and most of them have to be shipped through Southern France. To prevent these supplies from arriving, the SNCF Resistance has to cause as much damage as possible and as soon as possible."

"We received two hundred pounds of plastic explosives yesterday from a group up north," grinned Uncle Sebastian. "The guys in the Jockey Network hid boxes under the seats of a bus from Montelimar to Avignon. But we also needed detonators and dynamite in case the other cache is discovered, so that is why we contacted Michel."

"Do you need us to help plant the explosives?" Roland looked eager.

"*Non, non*, only employees have access to the *Rotonde*." Josef Perrin lit his cigarette from his son's. "We try to pace our sabotage. If a *Bahnhof* does a good repair job, sometimes we can loosen a wire or a bolt enough so the machine doesn't pass inspection. But to effectively install the explosives, we have to schedule a time when most of our people are working the same shift, preferably at night. This time we are targeting the control systems which take much longer to fix."

"We have messages for you to take to *Anatole* and *Colonel Bayard*. Ah, here's one for *Maxmillian* in Carpentras, too." Uncle Sebastian handed several letters to Michel who put them in a secret compartment in his rucksack.

"Our letterbox is in a grocery store in Avignon," Grégoire explained. "The place is always busy, people in and out all the time, so it's a good place to pass notes."

"Here are three fake ration books as thanks for your help." Monsieur Perrin handed them out. "You might want to fill your knapsacks with food before heading back to Mont Ventoux. I'll need the car key, Michel. Give your *Maman* and Nicole my love, when you see them. Let them know that I'm fine."

Uncle Sebastian added, "It might be wise for you to split up when you leave. Use the bus, if it's running. And Arnaud's horse-drawn stagecoach, the *patache*, goes a couple of times a day between Avignon and Carpentras. Be safe!"

Over a week later *Centurion* brought a copy of an underground paper into the camp and read aloud that, on February 19th and 20th, seventeen of the twenty-two engines in the *Rotonde* in Avignon had been badly damaged by explosions. Several *Pacifics* were pulled to a nearby field in order to remove unexploded bombs. Two SNCF workers were killed when one detonated. Suspects were being rounded up.

Michel spoke up, "I found out this morning that Uncle Sebastian was hit in the leg by shrapnel and he can't work for awhile, but Papa and Uncle Grégoire are all right."

Francois, Michel and Roland were slapped on the back and congratulated on the success of the mission. Then Roland grabbed the paper and stared at another article on the front page. He looked stricken and murmured, "Oh no, please no."

Francois looked puzzled. "Hey, what's wrong?"

Roland dropped onto a log, letting the paper fall to the ground, and put his head in his hands. Francois picked it up and looked at another article: '*Terrorists Responsible for Paris Attacks Executed.*' A copy of a poster with pictures of ten men covered a corner of the page. Below photos of derailed trains, a bullet-riddled body and an arms cache, was: "*Liberation! By the army of crime.*" Each photo identified members of the group and their crimes. 'Alfonso--Spanish Red--7 attacks,' 'Grzywacz--Polish Jew--2 Attacks,' 'Rayman--Polish Jew--13 Attacks.' At the bottom was: 'Manouchian—Armenian--Chief of the Group--56 Attacks 150 dead 800 Wounded.

MARCH:

Gabrielle Laurent sat at her desk, chewing on the end of her fountain pen, contemplating what to say to her parents. She had managed to write short notes about boring work typing up letters and filling out forms, or a film that she'd seen. She tried to make her situation sound as humdrum as possible. However this last letter from her father, not her mother, required her to be more specific as well as more thoughtful.

She was usually able to coax her *papa*, who had tended to dote on her, into letting her have her way. Her response to his very direct questions, his insistence that she come home for a visit, was a problem. At least she wasn't pregnant; she rolled her eyes at the thought. However explaining the weight that she had put on might be tricky considering the food shortages.

As she anticipated, Dieterich and she continued their relationship much the way it started. Twice a week he took her to dinner, often giving her a gift ranging from extra ration stamps to something to wear. Her wardrobe sported lacey underwear, a silk nightgown, a sweater, two more scarves and an expensive leather purse. Dinner was followed with sex at her apartment. Cash left on her dresser now partially subsidized her rent.

Gabrielle occasionally felt a vague feeling of guilt at the idea of the gifts and money. Then she gazed into Dieterich's eyes or listened to his voice whisper amorous phrases and felt that they were truly in love. There was enough deprivation in these few precious years of her diminishing youth. She rationalized that the luxuries that she enjoyed were fair compensation. Besides, who knew how much longer the Occupation would last?

Her lover, as she thought of him, was adventurous when it came to intercourse. She was learning a lot about her body and about his. What she learned was far different from the farm animals that had been her basic sex education and one clumsy and disappointing scrambling and thrusting with a friend of Francois.

She started the letter with a warm, flowery greeting to her 'precious, darling Papa,' and wrote a paragraph on memories of favorite things that they had done together. She hoped they would soon have a chance to go fishing at *Lac du Paty* and hike up on the mountain, collecting wild mushrooms that he had taught her to identify. She expounded on how she missed helping with the olive and grape harvests. She pointed out the difficulty of getting from Cavaillon to Carpentras. The erratic buses were so loaded with passengers that it was horribly uncomfortable. She ended her letter with a promise to try to visit soon, followed by endearments for her 'most understanding Papa.'

Gabrielle thought of including the photo that Dieterich had taken one wintry Sunday when they had hiked to *La Colline Saint Jacques* above the town. But the leather gloves and fur jacket, with the owner's name torn out, would require an explanation. With relief that her letter was satisfactory she put it in an envelope, licked the flap and sealed it.

Glancing at the clock she realized that the chauffeur would arrive to pick her up in a few minutes. Gabrielle had noticed that the food was not as good as during the previous fall, and not as generous. However, she and Dieterich were more focused on the 'dessert' to be served horizontally. Their conversations had become full of sexual innuendos. When they faced each other, Gabrielle became adept at using her foot to rub up and down Dieterich's pant leg. Sometimes she would sit beside him and they would fondle each other's crotches beneath a long tablecloth. As they maintained public images of indifference, the sub-rosa verbal and physical foreplay was almost as much fun as the romp later.

This Sunday evening Dieterich had returned after two weeks away. Gabrielle was surprised that he had picked a country bistro several kilometers from Cavaillon. The restaurant was small, traditional, with a fire helping ease the wintry chill. A worried owner greeted them as they entered, wiping his hands nervously on his apron. He showed them to a spot far from two tables where other guests looked warily at the newcomers. Dieterich appeared distant and did not interact with his usual charm.

The fare was simple: a pumpkin soup followed by thin slices of pork, in a sauce containing a smattering of mushrooms, and boiled rutabagas. Dessert was a cheese plate, a *chevre*, served with dark bread. The wine was a definite *vin ordinaire*. Gabrielle enjoyed the humble dinner and felt relaxed. Dieterich acted unusually restrained during the meal. He asked about Gabrielle's week.

She described the plot of the film that she'd seen, called *Bonsoir Mesdames, Bonsoir Messieurs*, a light-hearted farce about a radio singer who falls in love with a young dancer. She did not mention the rude noises many in the audience made during the newsreels, shuffling their feet, blowing noses loudly, boys farting and giggling—she could imagine Maurice behaving like this. Yet Dieterich's gaze did not change and Gabrielle stopped speaking.

"*Mon cher*, is something bothering you? You seem…like your thoughts are far away."

Dieterich paused, touching his napkin to his lips. "Well, my sweet one, I'm sure that you know that our…my country has recently suffered a major defeat in our battle with those communists in Russia. And with the Allies in Italy, it means that we have had to send many more resources down south. We are constantly dealing with the sabotage of trains and tracks. Trying to round up the terrorists takes up a great deal of manpower and time. So right now I have a lot on my mind."

Gabrielle was well aware of long lines of undernourished people fumbling with books of ration stamps since she joined them on many days. The weekly market was a madhouse of people trying to scrounge for a rare potato or onion. The caloric limit, she had read, was now down to about 1300 calories per person. But she really did not want to talk about how bad things were.

"Is your brother still working in Germany? Is he safe?"

"There has been no news in the last couple of letters so I think that he must be fine." Gabrielle twisted the napkin in her lap and frowned.

"Hmmm, I hope for your family's sake that he will be all right. So many of our German cities and factories are being bombed. Civilians are being killed due to this." He looked tearful, "In fact, I just received word that a dear uncle and his wife died in a bombing raid. Uncle Fritz and Aunt Trudy were good people, supportive of the Reich. Their oldest son is flying with the Luftwaffe. Uncle Fritz taught me to play chess when I was eight years old."

Gabrielle nodded, her lips turned down in sympathy. She said that she was sorry for his loss.

"Well, my job is here in Provence and I am more concerned about the enemy around us. Occasionally, though, we are successful at eliminating the terrorists, many of them hiding up around your Mont Ventoux." Dieterich's smile appeared thin, severe. "This past week a Gestapo unit, with the help of several *Milice*, were able to get rid of thirty-five saboteurs, all at the same time."

He looked across the table at Gabrielle, waiting for a reaction. Her eyes widened but she did not move.

"It happened close to a nearly deserted town called Izon-la-Bruisse, north-east of Sault. A few more raids like this and those terrorists will think twice about destroying the railroads and telephone lines." Dieterich sipped from his fourth glass of wine, taking Gabrielle's silence as affirmation of her interest. "A couple of their so-called comrades tipped us off. The idiots from three different terrorist camps were planning to celebrate Mardi Gras with a pig roast! Can you imagine? One man did manage to escape when our soldiers machine-gunned his buddies. I'll bet he went back with his tail between his legs, scaring others from joining up."

He paused, stubbing out a cigarette. "We even got rid of the informers. Who knows what men like that will do for more money? I tell you, a few more successes like this and terrorism will not be a problem!"

Gabrielle's intake of breath and wide-eyed stare caused her companion to frown and narrow his eyes. "Does this bother you?"

Gabrielle looked off to the side. "Dieterich, I thought that we weren't going to talk about things like this, the war part. Of course it bothers me. It's bad enough when I see people suffering daily but to hear about killing young men, whoever they might be, the battles being fought. I don't like it. I want it to end."

"Don't you ever read the papers?" Dieterich barked at her.

"Not if I can help it." Gabrielle straightened up and stared directly back at him. "You know that you have inspired me to read literature so I am trying to focus on books and poetry. I much prefer to discuss these with you."

Dieterich looked at her with a bland expression and Gabrielle detected an underlying irritation when he stated, "I will try to be more discrete in the future, *ma cherie*, and confine our talks to topics of more general interest. Still, you need to understand that I am under a great deal of stress. And it is due to this 'war' that you so delicately want to avoid."

Gabrielle seized the opportunity, "I will be glad to help relieve your stress but it won't be at a table in public." She tipped her head and smiled coquettishly, trying to coax him out of his mood.

He laughed and the lover that she knew began to emerge again. "Thus, dear student of the great classics, what have you been reading this past week."

Gabrielle put down her fork and leaned forwards, concentrating on lines that she had worked hard to memorize:

"The anemone and columbine
bloomed in the garden
where melancholy sleeps
between love and disdain.
Our shadows also are there
which the night disperses as
The sun that darkens
Disappears with them
The deities of living waters
Let their tresses flow
It happens that you must follow
This lovely shadow that you desire." (28)

Dieterich pursed his mouth, smiled and nodded, "Well done, *ma petit choux.* I don't believe that I am familiar with that particular poem but it was lovely, especially coming from your lips."

Gabrielle smiled broadly, her green eyes wide as she brushed back her hair on one side, like a child who has been awarded a good grade for a recitation.

"I'm glad that you liked it." Gabrielle told her unintentional tutor that it was a poem by Guillaume Apollinaire called *Clotilde,* which happened to be the name of the family horse on which she had learned to ride.

"Apollinaire? I think that he associated with eccentrics and degenerate intellectuals that I consider disgraced the world of art." Dieterich tapped his spoon lightly on the tablecloth. "However, that was a sweet poem and you spoke it very well."

Gabrielle was apologetic, "I think it was one of his early poems, written about... I didn't realize...," her voice trailed off.

"Non, non," Dieterich reassured her while looking off in the distance. "I commend you for taking the time to learn it. It was lovely hearing you repeat it."

Gabrielle lowered her eyes, not sure if she had been slighted. Her companion's detached attitude seemed somewhere between terse and melancholy. Conversation resumed with a discussion about the weather, the bone-chilling frost of the previous week when Dietrich was in Northern France.

The chauffeur had eaten in the kitchen under the anxious eye of the chef. He had the car running as the couple emerged. Gabrielle chatted about the weather, the extra tasks being assigned to her now that one woman had not shown up for work.

At her apartment she was startled when Dieterich roughly undressed her and shoved her onto the bed. He entered her as soon as he had rolled on a condom. His needs were consummated within a matter of minutes. He rolled over, propped himself up on a pillow and lit a cigarette. He offered Gabrielle one as she raised herself up next to his shoulder. They sat in silence for a few minutes, then Dieterich leaned over and patted her pubic hair. He got up from the bed and dressed.

After he buttoned his beribboned jacket and adjusted his jodhpurs at the top of highly polished black boots, he leaned over and kissed her saying, "Thank you, *cherie,* I will see you next Thursday."

For the first time Gabrielle felt glad to see Dieterich leave. The evening had ended up being awkward and she puzzled over what felt wrong. She thought that quoting a poem would impress him and keep conversation from current problems. Then she shrugged her shoulders, slipped off the bed and put on her robe. She checked the empty hallway before tiptoeing down to the bathroom. Putting money in the meter to heat the water, Gabrielle stood and watched the liquid creep up the side of the tub. Maybe if she did go home for a weekend, she'd feel sorted out.

APRIL:

When Étienne first arrived at Laurianne's home it was not difficult to stay inside. Exhausted and undernourished, he reveled in the chance to sleep as long as he wanted, to read, to hold hands, to make love. It was wintertime and being outdoors was no great pleasure. Wrapping up in a warm sweater and reading in a comfortable, cushioned chair suited him. Since both Laurianne and her mother worked during the week, he took advantage of the dark quiet days to recover from the brutal years at the POW camp. Gradually he put on weight and his thin frame became more muscular. He let his hair grow out and grew a moustache.

As the days lengthened, he and Laurianne occasionally ventured out after dark, before curfew, to walk on the town's upper lanes past the prehistoric caves from which the town got its name—*baumas* was Occitan for 'cave;' *venise* was from the Papal State's *Comtat Venaissin*.

By April the weather became sunny and full of promise. News in the underground papers announced a successful bombing raid on Berlin as the British sent a steady stream of planes to ravage German cities. The Soviets were making steady advances, pushing the German Army further west. The Allies were inching up through Italy, although Vesuvius' eruption the month before had slowed their progress.

Étienne's confinement in Laurianne's home had finally become a form of self-imposed imprisonment--and he'd had it. He convinced her to go with him to a café up the street from the Romanesque chapel. He wore her deceased father's best jacket, a fraction too large, and put his fake STO identification card in one pocket and his French identification card in the other. A neatly brushed beret and one of Laurianne's knitted scarves made him feel smartly dressed for his first normal public outing in four years. She wore her best winter suit and a hat with a jaunty feather. They strolled down the lanes to the square, lighthearted and happy.

When villagers in the café greeted Laurianne, she introduced her escort as Paul, no last name. They picked a table by the front window in order to watch people coming and going. Ordering a carafe of wine and something to eat, the couple basked in ordinariness that was so unordinary.

Étienne's eyes followed a woman who walked directly past the window toward the entry. "Isn't that Madame Laurent?"

Juliette Laurent walked into the café, spoke to the owner and then turned to look for a vacant table. She noticed Laurianne and waved at her, then headed toward the couple.

"*Bonjour*, Laurianne," she leaned down for a brush on the cheeks. "How nice to see you here."

Laurianne stiffened. "Madame Laurent, what a surprise. We don't often see you in town anymore."

"I drove over to pick up cases of our late harvest olive oil. Jean-Pierre meant to do it last month, but nothing seems to get done on time. You know how it is these days. They're loading up the wagon so I thought I'd have a coffee before going home."

Juliette glanced at the man shrouded in a scarf with a beret shading half his face. He looked vaguely familiar yet he did not acknowledge her and continued to stare out the window. Then she looked more closely as he glanced toward her. She covered her mouth in amazement, dropped rigidly into a chair, whispering 'mon dieu.'

Laurianne pulled on Juliette's arm and whispered, "Madame, don't say anything. We'll explain."

Étienne couldn't keep from grinning slightly, "It is good to see you again, Madame Laurent."

"We didn't expect to see anyone who would recognize Étienne," Laurianne looked worried.

"I had heard that you escaped from the POW camp," Juliette leaned over and patted Étienne's hand. "But I didn't expect to see you here!"

"I suppose *Maman* told you after I sent them the letter in February."

"Yes, but they have no idea that you are so close. We all presumed that you would be up in one of the Resistance camps." Juliette looked around then spoke softly. "Francois has been with the *Maquis Ventoux* for exactly a year. We have to be so careful, as those new troops are in the area specifically hunting for partisans. You are...."

Her voice trailed off as a man in a hat and trench coat slammed open the front door. He marched into the café followed by two soldiers and announced, "Present your identification papers. Have them open and ready for inspection."

The rustle of clothing and papers filled the room. Laurianne and Juliette opened their purses and withdrew their cards, holding them so the photos and signatures could be seen. Juliette looked at Étienne with eyes wide, lips pinched.

Étienne turned in his chair and casually reached into his jacket's inside pocket and withdrew the German STO card. One soldier checked the papers of the people at the next table, then those of the two women. When he opened Étienne's, he looked at his face, clicked his heels and said "*Dankeshon, mein herr.*"

Étienne nodded, retrieved his card and murmured, "*Bitte, sehr gut.*"

The soldier moved on to another table and the three turned toward the window, not speaking, waiting for whatever was coming next. After a few more minutes, the Germans left the café and crossed the curved street to another bistro. A single audible sigh was heard from those in the café then muted conversation resumed.

Juliette was so pale that the skin around her mouth looked blue. "I was terribly afraid for you, Étienne. How did you manage that?"

"This is the forged identification card that got me out of Germany. I wasn't sure if it would work but thankfully it did."

"And you spoke German with that man."

"I'm considered fluent, I suppose, after more than three years there. One guard was pretty decent and we would talk whenever we could. Other men in the camp also spoke it well."

Juliette tapped her fingers on the table. She looked at Laurianne and then at Étienne. She asked in a whisper, "I don't suppose that you might be able to come to the *Domaine* for a visit? I think that you could be of help to people that we know.

MEETING THE CAPTAIN - 1978

Claude Lepeyre called to say that René Char had agreed to my request for an interview but could only spare a few hours one afternoon. He was busy compiling an anthology of poetry by famous writers from other countries. I assured Claude that I would not stay long and would limit my questions to poetry and his activities during the war.

Parking the Duprés' car at the end of a gravel driveway outside the entrance to Char's home, I walked from there. The house was a tiny bucolic Provençal place, more of a cabin, on a plot of land with a garden near a meandering creek. A mottled dog with floppy ears and a white chest greeted me, followed by the writer who introduced his pet as 'Tigron.' Glancing at the house, I noticed the face of a woman peering from behind a curtain.

Although he was eighty-one years old, Char stood erect, with a full head of neatly trimmed dark hair above a long face and high forehead. Tall and thin, he showed almost no sign of having suffered a stroke a decade before or of the recent heart problem. He kissed my hand, his smile flirtatious as he guided me by the elbow to chairs under a Sycamore tree.

A carafe of coffee, cups and saucers and a plate of pastries were waiting on a chipped green metal table between the chairs. My charming host poured the coffee, offering cubes of sugar and we shared pleasantries about the weather, the beautiful garden and setting.

It became clear that René Char genuinely liked Americans, or perhaps it was that he simply liked women. While his eyes concentrated on me, he had the practiced behavior of one who listens while at the same time is keenly aware of his effect on others. He combined gentleness and inner strength, an independent soulfulness that meshed with his style of prose.

After the usual introductory exchange, I asked, "Is there a particular poet who inspired you?"

"Rimbaud!" Char was firm. "He was the first to use language to meld fantasy and symbols into descriptive prose. Paul Valery said, *'all known literature is written in the language of common sense—except Rimbaud's.'* Yes, he was slightly mad and led a wild life before dying at thirty-seven but he opened our minds to possibilities of expression never before considered."

I watched Char's face, his gestures, as he enthusiastically talked about André Breton, Pierre Reverdy, Philippe Soupault, Louis Aragon and other Surrealists who were his friends and colleagues in Paris. His enthusiasm, unabashed and childlike, was refreshing. He was delighted at his acceptance into this circle. He told me about a famous journalist and Parisian critic who had dedicated one of his poems to 'the reclusive young artilleryman of Nimes' when he was barely in his twenties.

Char shared an amusing story on how an early triumph came to be. André Breton and Paul Eluard came to visit him at *Les Nevons*, the family home in L'Isle-sur-la-Sorgue. André had been dumped by a sensual blonde and Paul was deeply depressed because his wife Gala was living with Salvador Dali. Char talked them into publishing a book together called 'Slowing Down Work,' *Ralentir Travaux*, that gave an outlet to their misery and depression.

"I understand that this led to many other successes throughout the twenties and thirties. Yet you waited until after the war to print *Feuillets d'Hypnos*, your wartime journal."

It was a matter of principle and the difficulty of censorship." Char paused. "I was also quite busy."

He raised his eyebrows as he said this.

"I imagine that you were! I'd like to ask about the stories behind some of your prose in '*Feuillets*,' if that is permissible."

I read excerpts from the book that I brought with me. The writer was very open as he told background stories that inspired each one. There was the contrast of sadness and pride as he sketched the men and women with whom he worked in the Resistance.

When I asked about 'My Fox,' René looked off in the distance, contemplating. "Marcelle was an amazing person, a very special part of my life during a difficult time. We were together for almost a decade. Her daughter Mireille was especially precious to me."

He paused, I waited, then he shrugged his shoulders. "It was not meant to last."

I noticed that Monsieur Char was looking tired so I closed my notebook and said that I had the information that I needed.

"*Merci monsieur.* Talking with you has been such a pleasure and I'm deeply appreciative of your time."

The former *Captain Alexandre* stood and clasped my hand in both of his. "Before you leave, let me show you inside *ma petite cabine* where I am working on the latest project."

He walked slowly and with dignity to the front door. There was no sign of the woman whom I had seen earlier.

On the walls, propped on bookcases and tables, was a hodge-podge gallery of sketches and paintings by Pablo Picasso, Max Ernst, Wilfred Lam, Alberto Giacometti, Joan Miro, Georges Braques, Fernand Leger, Nicolas de Stael, Maria Elena Viereira da Silva and Michel Brauner. And others. I was stunned at this collection yet not surprised. The community of artists and writers in Paris of the early twentieth century traded or gave away their drawings and their books to close friends. The little house was a monument to those years.

When I looked at René Char in astonishment, he smiled.

"It was quite a remarkable time," he murmured.

I could only nod in agreement. I could have happily spent hours with this man, hearing his philosophies, learning about his passions—from anger about nuclear proliferation to adoration of nature's splendor—and his exquisite way of framing phrases.

Instead, seeing how fatigued he seemed, I thanked him profusely once more and was not surprised when he kissed my cheeks three times. Then he reached for a small *potiron*, among other winter squashes placed on a counter.

"*Un petit memento*," he said, as he placed it in my hand. "From my garden. It makes a lovely soup."

The following day, I copied one of his printed statements onto a three-by-five card:

"*Why did I become a writer? A bird's feather on my windowpane in winter and all at once there arose in my heart a battle of embers never to subside again.*" Poetry was "*Hell in our heads... Spring at our fingertips.*" *(29)*

THE VAUCLUSE - 1944

'MY FOX:'

G eorgette Char had been right about her husband.

Not long after she and René settled in Cereste in the spring of 1941, René noticed an attractive young woman getting water at the public well. Asking around, he learned that she was Marcelle Pons-Sedoine, the wife of a prisoner of war, and that she was raising her nine-year-old daughter Mireille at her mother's home. She came to the well every morning to draw water for the day.

One morning René arrived as Marcelle filled her pitchers. He helped pump the water and they spoke briefly. He pretended to pick up a handkerchief folded in quarters, placed it in her hand and said, "I believe that you dropped this."

When Marcelle undid the cloth, there was a note inside asking her to meet him later that day in a secluded spot.

A dozen years younger than Char, Madame Pons-Sedoine was a woman of the mountains, courageous, hardy, humorous. She made her living, along with her mother, as a seamstress. Her brothers lived and worked in the village. Char was struck by her natural confidence, her connection to her surroundings and her knowledge of the area. This erudite, imposing man, who clearly was attracted to her, melted her inclination to resist him.

"What about your husband, Madame?" Char inquired. "I understand that he is in a prison camp."

Marcelle was honest. "I married him when I was eighteen, a boy I'd known all my life. He was captured over two years ago. He begs me to come to Germany and live near the camp but Louis does not understand that it is impossible for me when there is so much at stake here. And I won't leave my daughter."

She let Char interpret what she meant. Within a short time they started an affair that they took great pains to conceal. The lovers managed to behave discretely in a village that put its nose in everyone else's window, two partisans coping in wartime.

He called her '*ma renarde,*' my fox, and described his feelings about her in his journal, remembering a time when she put her head on his knees. Although he was not happy, she made his life bearable, 'whether as a candle flame or meteor.'

He compared her, in the twilight, 'to the murmur of mint and rosemary, a blending between the red shades of autumn and her own light dress, the soul of the mountain from its depths to the rocky slate of its height.' When he was with her, he felt enclosed in a private, wooded copse. He vowed 'to the stars, the frost and the wind' that she gave him hope for a swift victory out of what appeared to be dangerous isolation.

Marcelle's family, all socialists and deeply anti-fascist, welcomed Char into their midst. Marie Pons was prepared to dislike this intruder yet within minutes she succumbed to his charisma. Marcelle's brother, Irenée, arranged for René to use his rented room as one of his hideouts and drove him on missions. Marcelle's daughter, Mireille, was captivated by this fatherly man's kindness and interest in her schoolwork. Soon René spent most of his time in their home and was treated like a member of the family.

Other leaders of the Maquis came to confer and coordinate with *Capitaine Alexandre.* They were welcomed at the Pons home, given meals and places to sleep. One special friend who often stopped was Jean Garcin, *Colonel Bayard,* leader of the *Group Franc,* who had grown up in Fontaine-de-Vaucluse. Jean and René had played on the same rugby team. Garcin's and Char's fathers had been mayors of neighboring towns.

René also worked closely with Camille Rayon: '*Archiduc confided to me that he discovered his truth when he got hitched to the Resistance. Until then he was an actor in his fault finding and suspicious life. Insincerity had poisoned him. A sterile sadness bit by bit overlapped him. Today he loves, he gives of himself, he is engaged, he is vulnerable, he provokes. I greatly appreciate this alchemist.*' (30)

Gathering up and inventorying the explosives and arms that began to filter down from the night sky, organizing and disseminating them, took up significant time. Thanks to Char's adept management, his teams ended up with an enormous amount of armaments secreted around Mont Ventoux. However, at one point, he offended Maxime Fischer when he declined to share the largesse with another network.

APRIL 30:

Amélie Bertolini nodded at the sentries on duty at the gate as she strode through the courtyard of the commandant's *hotel particulier*. She walked past another guard at the door to the kitchen, then down the steps into a scene of mild chaos. The chef banged a metal spoon against a chopping block, berating a young assistant. Two other cooks stirred pots, tasting, adding ingredients. A kitchen helper swept the floor. The chef broke off his tirade when he saw her.

"Amélie! Finally! Take the tablecloth and napkins in the pantry, on the bottom shelf, up to the dining room. We have twenty people for dinner in three hours. It's *Walpurgisnacht*--a special celebration."

Unknown even to the chef, the dinner's purpose was to review the damage being done by Allied bombers up and down the Normandy coast and speculate on where an invasion might take place. Two of the four army divisions based in Provence were to be routed to the west coast.

The girl hung her purse on a hook and put on an apron. She found the linens, neatly ironed, and napkins with the original owner's initials. Her arms loaded, she walked past the cooks and up the stone steps. At the street level, she paused and noticed, through a crack in the slightly open doorway, another group of guards in the entry hall. Then she continued up the staircase to the dining room's service entrance.

Amélie was fully aware of the increase in Resistance attacks. Retaliations were becoming severe, impacting people whom she knew. On May 6, the *Petit Vauclusian* announced the arrest of Monsieur Leyris, president of the Carpentras civil courts. He was suspected of helping in the sabotage of the trains in February, as explosives similar to those used were found in his apartment in Avignon. Other arrests were expected to follow.

She smoothed out the tablecloth, placed napkins at each seat and replaced the three silver candelabra that ranged down the middle. The table looked majestic. The paneling around the room was painted in shades of ivory, the palest rose and apricot, with touches of green. Above every doorway paintings of cornucopia with fruits, flowers, or vegetables were framed in gilded moldings. Heavy satin drapes in faded pink and apricot stripes, lined in white silk, dressed each tall window. She imagined how elegant it must be to enjoy one of the meals being prepared below.

As she stood by the closed door leading into a dainty salon next to the dining room, she thought that she heard music. The *petit salon* had once been a parlor for ladies who were expected to leave the dining room while their gentlemen enjoyed cigars and brandy. It was now filled with file cabinets, easels with maps or charts and boxes. She opened the door a crack and listened. Across the narrow room, double doors led to what had been the music room, now the office of that rude Obersleutnant Ziegler. It sounded like the chamber music group was practicing in the officer's private room. Amélie opened the door wider and listened more closely. She couldn't tell if it was the small orchestra or a recording.

She tiptoed across a plush oriental rug up to the double doors and put her ear to the crack. She could tell that the music was clearly a recording. The Obersleutnant was working in his office, she thought, and she turned back to the dining room. Then she heard strange grunts and the murmur of voices. Was he discussing war plans? Or did he have some woman with him? Could it be someone she knew?

Amélie stood still and listened for a few more seconds. Someone was groaning but the voice did not sound afraid. It wasn't likely to be torture—the

Germans did that elsewhere. As the moans continued, Amélie concluded that the German was entertaining his mistress or one of the *putains* from a nearby brothel. She knew the risk of being in the wrong place at the wrong time, of being accused of spying, and was about to turn away. Then, with only a second's hesitation, she slid down on her knees to the rug and looked through the keyhole.

At first she couldn't see much, then her eye focused and she saw the Obersleutnant leaning against his desk. With a start, Amélie saw that he had on his jacket but no pants. Another person was in front of him, on his knees, wearing black socks and shoes, a loose beige shirt but also bare-bottomed, his hands gripping the German's thighs. She couldn't see him clearly.

She blinked, her vision cleared, and she saw the features of Henri Gilles-Martin as he moved back from the officer's groin and looked up. Ziegler was making the moaning sound, his right hand gripping the edge of the desk. His head was back and his hips were thrusting. Amélie held her breath and watched for a few seconds until it was clear that the Obersleutnant was getting close to a climax. Both he and the professor were grunting in rhythm as the crescendo of a loud symphony came from the record player.

Moving slowly, Amélie stood, turned and tiptoed back across the carpet to the dining room. She stepped inside and with the greatest care she shut the door, releasing the handle so that the latch did not click. She glided across the Aubusson rug to the service entrance and down the circular staircase to the kitchen, stopping only to make sure that no one was looking in when she passed the street level door.

In the kitchen the chef was instructing two helpers, the sous-chef was basting a large ham and the sweeper was gone. The chef turned and barked at Amélie.

"Go polish the silverware. We're using the Christofle tonight. Mind that you set the table with the fish knives, too."

Monsieur Blondine, the wine merchant, walked into the kitchen from the outside door with a box of bottles, followed by his son with another box. "Here are your wines, as you requested."

THE BITTEREST WINE

The chef pointed with his knife to the side room and the two men carried the boxes to a counter and set them down then started sorting out champagne and white wines to be put in the refrigerator. The reds were ranged along the counter.

"Did you get all the wines I ordered?" snapped the harried cook.

"Of course, monsieur," the younger man replied. "We select only the best for *Herr Kommandantur.*"

Amélie thought that she detected the father and son exchange a slight smile as she stepped into the butler's pantry. She loaded silverware onto a towel-covered tray with shaking hands and took it to a corner sink with the silver polish and a hand full of rags. As she rubbed the antique silver spoons she thought of her mother's friend, Florence. Did she suspect that her husband was a homosexual, involved with a German? Didn't they realize it was against the law? The scene of the two men flashed in her mind and she breathed deeply, collecting her thoughts.

A chill caused her to stop, motionless except for a slight shake of the coffee spoon in her left hand. She had been walking on a tightrope far too long, overhearing secrets, knowing that her brother was somewhere in the vicinity. She knew of several families with sons in the Resistance and was suspicious that Francois Laurent was one. All it would take would be the slightest hint that she had information and she could be interrogated.

The hour that it took to polish, wash and dry the Christofle seemed like five. Amélie's armpits and back were perspiring and she felt like she had been running a race. The thought of going back up to the dining room again was terrifying. When the chef started yelling over at her in his accented-French that was all it took.

Amélia looked at the overweight German, his purple face, a huge cleaver in his hand. She burst into tears, ran to the stairs leading out of hell's kitchen, grabbing her purse from its hook. She opened the back door, walked at a near run past the guard then between staff cars parked in what had once been a garden. She started running until she reached the bakery. The shop was closed and her parents were gone. She raced up the back stairs to the apartment and headed for her room.

225

Within minutes she had crammed a dress, pants, her hiking boots and several pairs of socks in an old book bag and a carryall. She grabbed items from the bathroom—toothbrush, a brush, a lipstick. Throwing in sweaters and a blouse, underwear, Amélie turned around and around in her bedroom trying to focus on what else she might need. In the corner of her armoire she grabbed another pair of socks, put them on and laced up an old pair of school shoes. From the top of the armoire she grabbed a felt hat and slapped it on her head. The last item was her wool coat, a bit short in the arms, but it would do and she put it on over the cardigan she'd been wearing.

Tearing a page from a composition book, Amélie wrote a note to her parents saying that she was fine but needed to hide out. They were to tell people that an aunt in Lyon was sick and she was taking care of her.

Racing downstairs, she stepped to her bicycle leaning against the entry hall's wall. The carryall went into the straw basket in the front. The bag was slung over her back as she used the bike's front tire to edge the door open. She eased out onto the street, turned toward the Porte d'Orange, jumped on the seat and pedaled as fast as she could.

Amélie headed down the hill in the direction of Aubignan. Soldiers huddled around a machine gun overlooking the bridge by the Notre Dame de Santé chapel. She slowed until she was directly on the bridge over the river then sped up, fearing a sudden burst of gunfire. The sound of tires chafing against the road brought a feeling of relief. The steady pumping of her legs calmed her mind. Almost automatically, she turned onto one of the farm roads heading toward *Domaine de Lauritaine*. Looking back she watched a column of German trucks roar up the road toward Beaumes-de-Venise.

At the gravel road leading to the Laurent's farmhouse she dismounted and pushed the bicycle up the incline. She heard a door closing, then Primo barked inside the house. Amélie shoved the bike through the ruined archway. Madame Laurent appeared at the door, looking alarmed. Amélie dropped the bicycle, stepped forward, wrapped her arms around the woman's shoulders and began sobbing.

Through hiccups, Amélie told Juliette Laurent that she had seen something at the commandant's house that frightened her. She feared that she was in danger. Juliette led her into their kitchen, sat her on a chair then poured a glass of water. The gasps and tears slowly diminished and Amélie breathed deeply, then stuttered out a *'merci, madame.'*

"All right, my dear," Juliette said as she clasped one of Amélie's hands, "What happened? Are your parents all right?"

Amélie nodded, wiped her face with her other hand. "I saw something and if the Germans knew, they might arrest me."

"You poor dear," responded Juliette, pausing and waiting for the girl to control herself, to continue. Silence was often the best interrogator.

"Monsieur Gilles-Martin.....," she trailed off. "I'm sorry, Madame, I can't tell you exactly what happened but I am afraid to stay in town!"

"I understand, *ma chérie.* We are aware that Henri Gilles-Martin is, as one might say, allied with the Germans. You didn't see him physically harm anyone, did you?" Juliette bent closer and touched Amélie's hand.

"*Non, non.* Poor Florence....," She sighed.

"Florence? Do you think that she is in danger?"

Amélie shook her head.

"No." She paused. "But you need to be careful. I don't think that Monsieur Gilles-Martin should be trusted."

Juliette could not help but smile at the innocence of the remark. Henri had not been considered trustworthy for many years, not just for his fascist-leaning politics but also his arrogance and attitude of superiority.

"Amélie, have you told anyone else about this?"

She shook her head 'no.'

"You may be right about being in danger if you learned something that the *Abwher* would consider 'sensitive." Juliette paused. "Unfortunately, we think that our place is under surveillance."

"Oh, Madame, I hoped that maybe I could hide here for a day or two. I told my parents to say that I went to Lyon to help an aunt who was sick. I want to find Étienne."

Juliette patted Amélie's hand. "I actually saw Étienne not long ago. He looks well."

"Madame! How wonderful!" She grasped Juliette's hand hard. "Do you think I could stay where he is?"

"No, but you can stay with us until we figure out what to do. We have a secret cellar. It is cold and hasn't much light but there is a sink with running water and mattresses with coverlets. When it is safe to be in the main house you can come upstairs but you'll have to spend most of the time down there."

Amélie watched as Madame Laurent walked to the closet door at the entrance to the kitchen and began to pull out her vacuum cleaner, mop, pail, suitcases.

She turned once, "Go put your *velo* in a corner of the barn with the other bicycles, then hurry back.

MAY 15:

As dusk fell, Étienne walked from Laurianne's house to the Laurent's home by circuitous paths through the garrigue, vineyards and orchards. Primo the dog did not hear him and did not bark any warning. He entered quietly through the kitchen door as Juliette had told him to do, and caught a startled Amélie at the kitchen sink. She dropped the dish she was washing, splashing water on her apron as she grabbed the edge of the sink.

She turned and walked slowly to her brother. She reached up and put her hands on either side of his face, then leaned her forehead onto his chest as she reached around his neck. Étienne felt her sobs as he clasped her to him. They stood without speaking for a full minute. Gradually Amélie stopped shaking and tipped her head back.

"I thought that I would never see you again."

"This shouldn't be such a shock. You've known for months that I was no longer in prison."

"Dear Étienne, I never really believed it in my soul until this minute, until I could feel and touch you." She stepped back and looked him up and down. "You look so much older. And you're terribly thin."

"You should have seen me when I arrived. I'm almost fat in comparison." He looked with amazement at his sister, who had been fourteen when he was imprisoned. "*Sacre bleu*, you're so grown up. You are even prettier than I imagined."

"It's been a rough few years." His sister let out a huge sigh and leaned against him once more. "Our parents, what they have gone through. Somehow you need to see them, to let them see you."

"How are they?" Étienne stepped back. "I've gotten reports from time to time and it sounds like they are all right."

"Overall, yes, considering how bad things are. The commandant has had them under surveillance ever since I left town. They barely get any flour and are only open three mornings a week. I think that their friendship with the Gilles-Martins may be the only thing protecting them."

"Amélie, this Occupation isn't going to last much longer. We know that the Allies are going to be here soon, possibly within weeks." Her brother pulled out two chairs by the kitchen table. "I'm here to find out if I can help with translations of German documents or radio transmissions."

"Madame Laurent told me that you now speak German fluently."

"Yes, and using what I've learned is the least that I can do. Tell me, *ma petite soeur*, what's been happening to you? Are you engaged yet?"

Amélie tapped her brother's hand. "Silly! I'm hardly an old *celibetaire*, I'm barely eighteen. Besides, no one has asked me."

"You wrote something about Francois Laurent a couple of times. I thought perhaps….."

At that point Maurice Laurent walked in from the front room, having heard voices. He greeted Étienne with a handshake, then a quick kiss on his cheeks and a slap on his back.

"Welcome back, Étienne! *Maman* told me that you would be coming for a visit. We've fixed up a really comfortable place for you, in the cellar with your sister. It's becoming our preferred guestroom."

"Wow, you've grown, too, Maurice. I can't believe the changes in everyone since I left. That's been the hardest adjustment, knowing that I've missed almost four years of everyone's life here."

"You've missed four of yours, don't forget." Amélie said bitterly.

Jean-Pierre and Juliette appeared and, once again, Étienne was exclaimed upon, examined, welcomed. Jean-Pierre pulled out chairs, motioning to the others to sit.

"We need to decide on strategies to stay safe until we contact the Maquis for you, Étienne. We're not worried about Amélie staying, as everyone believes that she left town to care for your aunt in Lyon."

"Our aunt in Lyon?" Étienne looked amused.

"I couldn't take working for the Germans any longer. The things that I learned about the Brandenburg Division, the fear that I felt every time that I was around them--it was too much."

Jean-Pierre turned to Maurice, "Sorry, son, but we need for you to go up to the attic and watch the roads with binoculars. Primo warns us when someone gets close to the house, but that's not enough."

Maurice didn't mind being the lookout. It seemed better than sitting around talking about what might happen. He took the stairs two at a time, imagining himself guarding a Resistance camp, the sole person who could save their lives.

COFFEE WITH SOPHIE - 1978

During the next few days, I alternated between angst over my attraction to Maurice, fear of causing friction within his family and a creeping suspicion that I was setting myself up for a big disappointment. We met for lunch and passionate, effusive, silky-sweaty, visceral sex. Words were unnecessary as our bodies communicated with lust.

Maurice assured me that his sister was 'just that way,' explaining that she had an unhappy marriage. Her much older husband had a series of mistresses. He was a busy attorney, practicing in both Avignon and Marseille, and rarely attended Laurent family functions at the Domaine. Maurice alluded to an incident when the American Army liberated Provence.

On the day of our coffee date, Sophie waited for me at a *patisserie*. She looked up from the table. Her slightly almond-shaped eyes, thick lashed and penetrating, looked directly and suspiciously into mine. She'd known for a couple of weeks about my summer affair.

"OK, Claire. What's going on?"

"Let's get our coffee first," I said.

Minutes later we were waiting for espressos and pastries to arrive.

Sophie again looked at me intently, "Well…?"

I puffed out my cheeks, "I think that I'm *dans les choux*, in a big mess. I've made a mistake getting involved with Maurice."

"Well, how 'involved' are you? Is this a diversion, a summer romance, or are you serious?"

I looked at the table, unable to face her. Tears welled up in my eyes.

"It doesn't matter. We have very different lives, our cultures are different and I live far away." I looked up and blurted, "His sister hates me!"

Sophie sat back and burst out laughing. The server interrupted, balancing a tray with our order. We waited while he placed cups, saucers, plates, forks and napkins on the metal table.

"I don't think it's that funny, Sophie." I narrowed my eyes and briskly stirred sugar cubes into the coffee.

"His sister! I bet it's because of her friend Yvette. Now I see why you were interested in her at the *fete de la vendange!*" Sophie bent forward and put her hand on mine. "Ma chérie, Yvette has thrown herself at Maurice over the past few months. He mentioned to Georges that his sister's efforts to put them together have had the opposite effect. Maurice says that Yvette is a nice person but there are no…how do you say?…fireworks."

My thoughts jumped to the previous afternoon when Maurice and I had been together.

"Claire?" She smiled pleasantly, "How serious are you two?"

"I find him extremely attractive and we get along well. It's fun. Yet I have a life not only an ocean away but a continent beyond that. His roots are deep in the Vaucluse. I think that we'll kiss good-bye when I leave and that will be that."

I stopped to chew a bite of the *mille-feuille*.

Sophie nodded. "Don't fret. My dear Claire, Maurice is not the kind to treat a woman shabbily. If he indicates that he cares for you, you can be sure that he is sincere. Why not let things progress as they will?"

"Thanks, Sophie. And you are right, *que sera, sera.* In the meantime I have my work to occupy me. Every day I find something new about the Resistance. I'm writing articles about the poets, sending them out for publication. They might make a good subject for a doctoral dissertation." I twisted a paper napkin into a knot. "Besides, in three weeks I'll go home."

"Can you change your tickets and stay longer?"

"It would be difficult and expensive, although I am checking with your travel agent."

"Wonderful!" Sophie exclaimed. "I have a good idea. Why don't you and Maurice come for dinner this Saturday? We can spend time together and I can check out how serious this romance is becoming."

I knew that Maurice could come. We had talked about seeing a film but dinner with friends sounded better.

Sophie whispered soothingly in my ear as we parted, "It will all work out, you'll see."

I wasn't so sure, but how nice of her to reassure me.

As I walked down *rue de la Republique*, I noticed Yvette standing in the doorway of her boutique with her arms crossed. I could see her watching me by the reflections in the windows that I passed and wondered what she was thinking.

THE INMATE
PAUL ELUARD

The asylum of Saint-Alban-sur-Limagnole, on a plateau below ragged slopes in the Cevennes mountain range, was surrounded by snow and buffeted by icy winds. Built as a chateau in the 13th century, the songs of troubadours and festive parties had given way in the 19th century to the cries and wails of inmates that echoed down the stone halls. Tortured mutterings of the demented were interspersed with calm mutterings of nuns and nurses attending them. Urine, antiseptics and mildew perfumed the cold air.

In one of the cells a man held a fountain pen in a hand encased in a mitten that did not fully cover his fingers. A bottle of ink and sheets of paper were scattered over the table where he sat by a window that let in fragile winter sunlight. Since his arrival, words had poured out of him, inspired not only by the tragic conditions of fellow inhabitants but by the grim circumstances that surrounded them all. His sense of isolation, perhaps from being hospitalized twice for tuberculosis, was reinforced by confinement in this institution.

The Gestapo had been on his trail for many months. As a member of the French Communist Party and a poet of the Resistance, he was one of many on a list of 'those most wanted.' Confinement in the asylum provided protection for him as well as others evading capture. The asylum director had managed to mask his special residents in such a way that the Germans had not penetrated the ruse.

In June 1917, Paul Eluard had been sent to a military evacuation hospital ten kilometers from the front line. His job was to write letters to the families of the dead and the wounded. He wrote more than one hundred and fifty letters a day and, at night, he dug graves to bury the mutilated bodies. Shaken by these horrors, Paul started writing poetry to express his emotions.

At the end of World War I, Eluard and two of his closest friends, André Breton and Philippe Soupault, turned the literary world upside down with what they termed 'surrealism.' They were involved in the 'Dada' movement that decried following traditional principles and authorities that so often led to wars. His wife at the time, a Russian beauty named Gala, encouraged this as her Communist ideology supported anything that flew in the face of rampant capitalism and western establishments.

Performances that he, Breton, Louis Aragon and Tristan Tzara concocted were meant to shock and confuse audiences. Sometimes their poetry was devised by cutting out words from an article, putting them in a bag then pulling out the slips, one at a time, and gluing them on a piece of paper. Reading this aloud to a group of paying patrons often ended up with both insults and eggs thrown at the 'poets.'

One of Paul's closest friends at the time was the German-Jewish artist Max Ernst. Max, in contrast to Paul, was tall, blue eyed, light haired, handsome and athletic. In the 1920's they had collaborated on two books of Eluard's poetry, with sketches by Ernst. They and their wives spent time together in both Germany and Paris. Soon it was obvious to Paul that Gala and Max were having an affair.

In 1924, after a dinner with literary comrades, Paul disappeared without a word. Many feared that he had died. Without telling anyone he boarded a ship in Marseille and spent seven months travelling around the world: Australia, New Zealand, the Antilles, Panama, Malaysia, Java, Sumatra, Ceylon, and India. Paul met Max and Gala in Saigon, Indochina, and Paul was the one who went back to Paris with Gala. The three never talked about what happened on this trip.

To the relief of his friends, the resurrected poet continued in the Surrealist movement. However, within months, exotic, temperamental Gala divorced Paul and moved in with Salvador Dali, her companion for the rest of her life.

Now forty-eight years old, Eluard had matured along with his contemporaries. They still clung to their youthful idealism but with the threat of losing their lives instead of ducking eggs. He thought of his second wife who inspired many of his poems. Nusch, the name she chose rather than her given name of Maria, came into his life with a showgirl body and the attitude of one who knew how to cope with the unpredictable.

One evening while walking around Paris, he and René Char encountered this beautiful young girl, incredibly thin and apparently lost. Eluard invited her to join them for a meal. She was a comedian, a trapeze artist, had modeled for post cards, acted in a Strindberg play in Germany, worked with a troupe of puppeteers and was twenty-three years old. And she was absolutely destitute.

Paul, ten years her senior, offered their place. It took some convincing before she acquiesced. They fell in love and had been together ever since. Her existence made the difference between his being a true inhabitant of this mad house or that of being a slinger of words thrown in defiance.

Eluard closed the fountain pen and stared at the bleak sky, remembering those youthful, exciting, wild times. André Breton's home on *rue fontaine* was their gathering place where they read each other's prose out loud. He reflected on their joy as they discussed politics, revealed strange dreams, told ribald stories and rubbed elbows with the intelligentsia of 1930's Paris.

A knock on the door startled Paul out of his reverie.

"Monsieur?"

He pushed back his chair and opened the heavy door. A nun with a starched cowl surrounding a wrinkled, cherubic face said, "Father Mathieu is ready to take you to Saint-Flour, if you wish. It appears to be safe to leave."

Paul took an overcoat and hat from a hook and accompanied the nun along an interior balcony and down a staircase to enormous wooden doors dotted with metal rivets. Outside, a priest waved from a car and Paul got in.

The priest drove several miles then circled a square in a village, the passenger checking to see if they were followed.

The car pulled into an alley and up to the back door of a building with barred windows. Near the street corner a man lounged, bundled up against the cold, smoking a cigarette. He appeared to be checking the alleyway then gave a signal. The passenger stepped out and the priest drove off as Paul knocked out a code. The door opened and he stepped into the relative warmth of a print shop.

Eluard set to work editing and correcting texts for a weekly underground paper, *Lettres Françaises.* He also ran a clandestine publishing house called *The French Library* from here. To the printers, he was known as Jean du Hault, one of several pseudonyms. The shop owner's son worked nervously at the front presses, vigilant for the appearance of Germans or the dreaded French militia. Paul handed articles to the printer who pulled typeface from drawers, arranging them in wooden forms. When the last article was done and the first copy printed, Paul stood by the typesetter with the paper in his hand.

"This looks fine. We need to get it out of here quickly."

"Monsieur, we will print it right away and the distributors will pick it up tonight."

"*Merci beaucoup, mon ami,*" Paul spoke sincerely. "I am full of hope that France will soon be free. There are many signs that our days under the Occupation are coming to an end. *Bon courage!*"

Eluard waved to the young man in the front, stepped to the rear door and opened it a crack. Another member of the *Maquis* stood with a dog on a leash at the alley's end. Paul put his hat through the crack and the sentry looked in both directions, gave a nod of his head then walked his dog around the corner. Paul stepped out into freezing air, crunched across a patch of snow and followed in the same direction, meeting Father Mathieu at the car. He wrapped a muffler around his jaw as the car made its way past ancient buildings. The only Germans on the main road were in a canvas-covered truck going in the opposite direction, followed by a motorcycle with an intense young man brandishing a rifle in the sidecar.

At Saint-Albans Paul met others in the dining room for a supper of thin soup, men from the Free French of the Interior recovering from wounds, less-volatile inmates and the staff. A fire in an enormous fireplace reduced the chill. Bottles of wine did the rest. Paul found conversation among other intellectuals-on-the-run muted but stimulating. Once the Dadaist poet Tristan Tzara and his son, Christophe, had stayed for a few weeks.

General de Gaulle had achieved his goal of unity and inclusion in the disparate groups in the Resistance. It was becoming clear that no one group on either the 'right' or the 'left' would be governing France in the years to come; all would have a part. The hope was that the French motto 'liberty, equality, fraternity' would become a reality. Paul now viewed his role as a messenger, wielding a pen instead of a sword, to encourage all those he could reach that there was hope. France would be free again.

Liberty (Abbreviated version) (6)

On my schoolboy's notebooks
On my desk and on the trees
On sand on snow
I write your name

On all pages read
On all blank pages
Stone blood paper or ash
I write your name

On jungle and desert
On nests on gorse
On the echo of my childhood
I write your name

On all my rags of azure
On the pool musty sun
On the lake living moon
I write your name

On fields on the horizon
On the wings of birds
And on the mill of shadows
I write your name

On the wonders of nights
On the white bread of day
On betrothed season
I write your name

And by the power of a word
I start my life again
I was born to know you
To name you *Liberty.*

Paul Eluard   1895 – 1952

THE VAUCLUSE – 1944

MAY 27:

At 10:45 Saturday morning the sun ricocheted off the fuselages of dozens of silver-winged bombers, accompanied by fighter planes, as they followed the Durance River valley toward Avignon. In Cavaillon the wail of air raid alarms warned of the approaching planes minutes before the roar of their motors. British-made Lancasters, known as 'flying fortresses,' flew in four formations of twenty planes, pregnant with 1400 five-hundred-pound bombs, on a mission to pulverize the railroad system of the ancient city of the French Popes.

Instead of scurrying to the basement with the other tenants, Gabrielle Laurent wrapped herself in an old robe and curled up on a chair. Although Cavaillon was a dozen miles from Avignon, Gabrielle could see puffs of white, spirals of black smoke and hear vague thumps of explosions. Viewed from her fourth floor apartment's open window, anti-aircraft guns' arcs of fire were dots of orange peppering the perfect blue sky. When a plane was hit there was the smear of a flame against the western horizon.

She shivered as much from the realization that actual war--fighting, shooting and killing--was on its way as from the fresh morning air. She faced the fact that her respite from the Occupation, her escape through her affair with Dieterich, was going to end. There were rumors that the Americans could arrive soon and Gabrielle dreaded having her world up-ended again.

During the past six weeks Dieterich had taken her out only twice. His apologies seemed genuine when he cancelled their dates due to being out of town or working long hours. Their rendezvous were much shorter, banal conversation over two course dinners followed by tempestuous but shorter sex. Her requests to get a pass to visit her home were denied and Dieterich chided her for wanting to leave at such a time.

Gabrielle was surprised that she missed him, feeling abandoned if only for a few days. She mused that he might ask her to go with him if he left for Germany, but she had seen the photo of his wife and three blond children behind his desk. Once, when delivering papers to his building, she had snuck up to his office with the packet instead of leaving it downstairs. An inattentive guard had rushed in, his hand on his pistol, grabbed her arm and sternly said that she was not allowed up there. He marched her down to the street, cautioning her to speak to the receptionist first.

The news that she read in Vichy-approved papers made it sound like Germany was winning. She hesitated picking up *Combat* or other underground journals. If caught, she could be imprisoned. As she stared at the roiling panorama, tears came to her eyes and rolled down her cheeks. She mopped at them with the sleeve of her robe. She missed Dieterich. She missed her home. She missed feeling safe.

A group of planes spun east toward Cavaillon and she saw their shapes clearly as they swung over the town and south above the Durance plain. Within forty-five minutes the flashing silver and roar of the last of the bombers was far in the distance, heading toward the coast.

On Monday the town hall was a scene of chaos. City council members showed up for an emergency meeting with the mayor. The head of the *Milice*, the chief of police and a representative from the gendarmerie arrived minutes apart. Dieterich appeared with two other officers and took the steps two-at-a-time, not glancing in Gabrielle's direction. Soon townspeople and district wardens began to gather outside the building, a few arguing with the guards and demanding to speak to the mayor. The clamber of voices grew louder.

Gabrielle filled out reports sitting on her desk, hitting the typewriter keys with unsteady fingers. At noon the meetings dispersed and a string of solemn men filed downstairs. Gabrielle was given three hand-written pages and was instructed to type them up after lunch. The notices were to be printed, posted around the town and placed in local papers.

One statement, "to loyal citizens and patriots of France," said that during "possible enemy attacks and future bombing raids" they were to seek shelter immediately. Curfew hours were two hours earlier, anyone careless with blackout curtains would be fined double and suspicious activities were to be reported. It ended with the reassurance that the German Army and the local *Milice* would 'do their utmost to protect the townspeople from the enemy.'

A second one was to alert the city that the next day, May 30, was declared a day of mourning throughout Avignon. The caskets of those who had been killed in the bombing raid were to be placed along the main street. Cinemas and restaurants in the region would be closed for a week as a sign of respect to those who died.

Gabrielle placed the notices in her drawer. She dawdled, expecting to see Dieterich emerge. Instead, a truck pulled up and two soldiers carried in covered trays up to the remaining dignitaries. Picking up her purse, she walked out into a crowded street.

She walked two blocks to a family café where she had not eaten in several months. It was a quiet spot where she could sit alone and perhaps write a note to her parents. At the café, a middle-aged woman with a tight face and stiff lips told her that there were no tables available. Gabrielle looked inside and saw three vacant ones.

When she objected, the woman blocked the doorway with her arms crossed and repeated, "Mademoiselle, there are no tables available for you. Please leave."

A chill spritzed down her spine and she turned and walked away. At the corner she looked back and watched two couples--a man and a woman and two women--enter the café and not emerge. With her head tipped low, her scarf fluffed up around her chin, Gabrielle walked home.

In her apartment she found a few limp strawberries, a bit of leftover cheese and a stale piece of bread. The first thing that she did was open the bottle of Bordeaux wine that Dieterich had given her a week before. After two glasses, she lay on her bed and muffled her sobs into her pillow.

JUNE 2:

When Charles de Gaulle was told that two British passenger planes were at the airfield in Algeria, ready to take him to England to 'discuss some important recent developments' with Prime Minister Winston Churchill, he was highly suspicious and refused to step aboard. He told the British representative that he would not budge until he was assured that his new provisional government was recognized as legitimate. The General slammed his fist on his desk and stood to his full height of six feet, five inches, not including another two inches due to his oak-leaf encrusted *kepi*.

De Gaulle understood that President Franklin D. Roosevelt was extremely displeased, livid in fact, that he had established the Provisional Government of the French Republic (GPRF) less than a year before, with the support of the Resistance and pre-war political figures. During this time he also organized an army—the Free French Forces--with the Cross of Lorraine, a cross with two bars, as their symbol. One of his greatest concerns, as liberation looked imminent, was the possibility of a political vacuum when the Germans left France. A communist takeover was possible if the Americans tried to govern a country already in civil turmoil.

After two days of negotiating and placating, the General agreed to meet with the Prime Minister in London on June 4. He was then told that the Allied invasion was imminent--Churchill and Roosevelt had not trusted him enough to let him know beforehand. He was asked to speak once again to his countrymen and handed a prepared script. It instructed the French to obey Allied military authorities until elections could be held, instead of recognizing the GPRF.

De Gaulle exploded! He called Churchill a gangster. Churchill accused him of treason. The Frenchman demanded that he be flown back to Algiers. Due to the Normandy landing scheduled within forty-eight hours, Churchill and Roosevelt gave in. The General composed his own speech.

Although his troops were significantly smaller in number, in comparison to the staggering amount of Allied forces, de Gaulle also insisted that the Free French be included in the invasion: on four of their own warships and destroyers, as paratroopers, as bombadiers, and as foot soldiers slogging onto Sword beach. General de Gaulle remained in London, waiting for news of the successful liberation France.

JUNE 6:

The pounding on the door woke the Gilles-Martins at seven in the morning. Henri leaped up, grabbing a robe as he muttered sleepily. Florence followed him more slowly, wrapping a housecoat around her as she stood by a wide-eyed Gigi. The two stood back as Henri opened the door. Florence recognized the son of one of the town's Council members.

Still buttoning a shirt, the young member of the Milice spoke agitatedly, "Monsieur Gilles-Martin, I'm bringing bad news. The defenses in Normandy are under siege. My father wants to know if you want to join us to listen to *Radio Paris.*"

"*Mon Dieu.* Normandy? Hmmphf. I wouldn't have expected it there, even with the recent bombing." Henri's shoulders slumped, "Yes, I'll come right away. Thank you for letting me know."

The young man bounded down the stairs as Henri shut the door. He turned, his face strained, fearful. "My dears, don't worry. Our defenders will soon push these invaders back to England."

He rushed back to the bedroom and began to dress. "I'll find out what is happening and then come back."

Florence and Gigi stood with their arms around each other, speechless. What had been feared, hoped for, dreaded, anticipated, had finally arrived. Florence's first thought was that life as they knew it, as difficult as it had been, was going to get worse.

Within seconds, the carillons of Saint Siffrein began clanging.

———

Jean-Pierre and Maurice Laurent had been up for over an hour and were at work in their olive grove when the sound of bells came from Aubignan. Then they heard faint clangs from Beaumes-de-Venise and Serres. They looked at each other, puzzled. It wasn't Sunday. There was no mass that they knew about; it wasn't a holiday.

Juliette appeared at the kitchen door wiping her hands on a towel, and walked toward the vineyard. "What do you suppose is happening?"

The father and son met her at the road. Jean-Pierre took a puff on his cigarette.

"Maurice, ride into Aubignan to find out what's going on. It must be something important. Perhaps a bad fire?"

Maurice raced off to the barn for his *velo*. His parents watched as he swerved through the gravel on the drive, his expression grim, standing up on the pedals, riding as hard as he could.

Juliette bit her lips, "Jean-Pierre, this can't be good."

"How much worse can it get?" Her husband shook his head and shrugged. "We might as well let the Bertolini kids sleep until Maurice gets back and we know what is going on, then we'll open up the cellar.

———

The sudden loud noise of bells banging steadfastly startled Gabrielle Laurent. She looked over at the alarm clock on her bedside table and pushed aside a scarf in order to see it. It was not yet eight o'clock. What was going on now? Not another damned bombing, she hoped. This was getting beyond tiresome.

She padded in bare feet to the wood shutters and opened one a crack, squinting at the bright light bouncing off the wall across the street. She could hear a cacophony of voices below, muffled by the constant ringing. Waiting a few seconds for her eyes to adjust, she opened the window fully and leaned out over the ledge between two pots of red geraniums that she had been coaxing into bloom.

"What's going on? Is it another evacuation?" she yelled at no one in particular.

A boy of fifteen saw her, looked up and smiled. Even disheveled, Gabrielle's pretty face raised feelings in his adolescent groin. He shouted over the clamor, "The Americans have attacked the German Army in Normandy."

"What?"

"The Americans are coming!" He threw his cap in the air and ran to join other boys near his age who were jumping up and down and whooping.

Gabrielle withdrew from the window and frowned. She raised a hand to her cheek and sighed, her eyes closed. Then the bells stopped as suddenly as they had started.

She might as well get dressed and go to work, she thought. At least there she would be able to find out the details. The attack had happened far away and she hoped that the fighting would not reach Provence. Surely this kerfuffle would dissipate soon. She wondered how Dietrich was reacting to this news. Where was he? Damned war.

⁂

The Bertolinis rose up in unison at the first bong of the cathedral's bells. They looked at each other then got out of bed. They opened the windows to the inner courtyard and saw a neighbor across the way, as startled as they. A young voice from an attic apartment above yelled down, "The Americans and Brits have attacked. They're in Normandy. Yahoo!"

Stepping back inside, the baker turned to his wife, "Well, Anne-Marie, I think it is time."

The couple had discussed leaving Carpentras ever since Amélie had disappeared and their bakery could no longer get adequate supplies. Not being able to contact their children, fearing reprisals themselves, the Bertolinis were constantly on edge.

Anne-Marie had written a distant cousin with a goat farm on the other side of Mont Ventoux, asking if they could stay with his family. She had received a letter from Nicholas, assuring them that Germans were few and far between in their tiny hamlet. He and his wife would be happy to have their help even though few goats were left and times were difficult. The Bertolini's suitcases had been packed for two weeks and now final items were tossed in. Émile's second suitcase contained sacks of grain, yeast and salt. Anne-Marie carried a bottle of olive oil in her purse.

"We can walk to Mazan in about an hour and hope the bus to Sault will arrive later today. From there we may have to walk or hitch rides, but we'll get there."

"I'm leaving a letter with Florence to give to Amélie at the Laurents. We can drop it by as we leave."

Within minutes, the clanging of bells in all the villages and towns had been stilled. As the Milice beat on the front doors, priests and their helpers dropped ropes and disappeared into recesses of the churches or out the back doors. News of the invasion continued to spread, person to person.

DINNER AT THE DUPRÉS - 1978

M aurice and I walked hand-in-hand to the front door of the Dupré's farmhouse. A Mistral wind had blown for two days and the trees around the *mas* thrashed back and forth as if in a childish battle for dominance. My fluttering scarf looked like an escorting butterfly. Maurice held his beret to his head with his left hand.

Georges stood behind the door, holding it from snapping open. We swished in, laughing, re-arranging clothing and hair. Maurice commented that he hoped this would be a three-day Mistral, not a five-day one. Legend was that the wind lasted for odd-numbered days.

The three curses of Provence," observed Georges, "the Durance for its floods, the mistral for its winds…"

Maurice continued "…and Parliament for its idiocy!"

Sophie arrived from the kitchen wiping her hands on her apron, bubbling a greeting. She ushered us into the kitchen where the table was set for supper. She stirred *ratatouille* on the stove while Georges poured the wine. The men lit up cigarettes and sighed as they exhaled. I mused at the difference between France where it seemed everyone smoked, while in California there was a movement against it, except the 'non-smoking movement' in Marin County apparently didn't include marijuana.

Maurice inquired about the Duprés' children. Both parents spoke alternately, all but finishing each other's sentences as they sketched the latest news from the oldest to the youngest. My dear friends were so in tune with each other that they did not realize that they spoke as if in a duet.

As the meal progressed I sat back and basked in the wonderful normalcy of being part of a couple, if only for an evening. The comfortable badinage of neither exclusively male conversation nor female points of view was something that I missed. Leaning forward, clasping my hands, I listened to Maurice and Georges discuss the spring's election. A high percent of communists and socialists had won under Valery Giscard d'Estaing's new administration.

"After all, Claire," expostulated Maurice, "You know that, at the end of the war, different groups wanted to control the government. The Americans had picked out General Giraud who would be likely to follow their suggestions. The communists were determined to steer our country to the left. But because de Gaulle had broadcast constantly from London, most Frenchmen looked to him as our future leader.

Georges added, "Remember him saying 'how can you govern a country that has two hundred and forty-six varieties of cheese?' Yet he was probably the only one who could have made the government inclusive, to allow all voices to be heard."

Maurice frowned. "Now we have this new Front National Party that Jean-Marie Le Pen is organizing. I don't think this is a good sign."

Puzzled, I asked, "What is this all about?"

Georges explained, "It is a very conservative, nationalistic group, fortunately very small, that is openly against communism as well as capitalism. This party blames immigrants for our problems with unemployment. However, I don't think that it will ever be much of a player in politics."

Maurice disagreed and the debate went on, swerving into philosophical references. "Think of what Voltaire said, *'Those who can make you believe absurdities, can make you commit atrocities.'* We've lived through this and we shouldn't fall for it again!"

"Ah yes, and Rousseau's comment, *'man was born free but everywhere lives in chains.'* Too often of our own devising. One thinks that one has gained one's freedom then too easily slips into another sort of bondage."

I mentioned that the topic reminded me of Albert Camus' wartime essays, 'Letters to a German Friend.' "Do you remember reading these?" Everyone at the table nodded. I continued, "He was so eloquent in his defense of his country, its ability to bide its time and regroup, to not succumb to Nazi control. His statement regarding existentialism comes to mind, about believing that the world had no ultimate meaning but something in it has meaning and that is man, that the concept of justice was only something that man could conceive."

"Yes," Maurice joined in. "Even when 'absolute power corrupts absolutely,' man's determination to survive and overcome eventually triumphs.'

"One hopes!" said Sophie.

Conversation was interspersed with many Provençal-toned *"mmm-bah oui's"* and, so French, a series of opposing thoughts as well. Maurice glanced toward me with a wink as the banter continued, hands gesturing, mouths occasionally breathing out the expressive "poufgh" showing disgust and resignation in one single breath.

Georges turned to me, "And how is our American professor doing with all her investigations into our Resistance stories?"

"*Ca va*, it's progressing. Most of the material is organized and I've written several articles. Right now I am concentrating on André Malraux, one of France's more colorful characters from that period."

"Colorful, yes! A bit of a chameleon, as well," interjected Maurice. "He always tried to hitch his chariot to the fastest horse."

Sophie spoke up, "Considering his personal tragedies, the man surmounted a number of obstacles to achieve what he did. His mistress Josette tripped and fell under a train at the end of the war, then both of their sons were killed in a horrible automobile accident when they were university students. How does one ever recover from something like that?"

I agreed, "That was awful. But what is surprising is that Malraux did not capitalize on his war experiences by writing an autobiography. Instead he turned to one of his main interests and wrote 'The Psychology of Art.' "

Maurice added. "Still, when he became Minister of Culture, discord followed him as he re-organized cultural groups or appointed controversial directors to museum positions. He certainly made his mark on our history, though."

We rehashed more politics, talked about wine--of course—and spent a lot of time laughing over inconsequential things. It was nearly midnight when we wrapped up to brave the buffeting on the way to the car. Masses of tiny dots, swathes of the Milky Way and constellations with scarcely remembered names, were scattered across the dark blue-suede sky.

As we drove, Maurice hummed a tune under his breath, his hand on my knee. Leaning closer, I realized that it was '*J'attendrais*,' a song popular during World War II. It was a song of parting and promise, the sentimental 'I will wait.'

Remembering the words, I sang along: "*J'attendrais, le jour et le nuit, j'attendrais toujour, ton retour.* 'I will wait, day and night, I will always wait for your return.' "

When the song ended I couldn't speak or my voice would have cracked. If Maurice intended this as a message all it did was make me sad.

THE VAUCLUSE – 1944

JUNE 9:

The Gilles-Martins agreed that it was too dangerous for Gigi to stay in town. School was almost finished; besides, who could concentrate on studies at times like these? The Allied raid on May 27 had been terrifying. Aircraft swooped and rumbled through the skies followed by the faint whomp of exploding bombs in Avignon and along the Rhone. Air raid sirens mixed their mournful whines with anti-aircraft guns tat-tat-tatting. Occasionally a plane at a distance would burst into flames and trail like a comet on its way to oblivion. Black and gray smoke billowed in immense clouds, wafting across the fields for days.

Afterwards the Gilles-Martins read the newspapers, saw the photographs and talked with those who had radios to learn of the damage. Railway systems, depots and buildings had been reduced to piles of stones, shattered roof tiles and twisted metal. The Ports of Marseille and Toulon were cluttered with useless battleships. Submarine station structures along the coast were bent into what looked like coat hangers.

Parts of cities existing prior to the Romans were reduced to remnants of walls amid scattered chunks of rock. In Marseille, bodies were still being recovered and the count was edging up toward 1700. In Avignon, just fifteen miles from the Gilles-Martin apartment, over five hundred residents had lost their lives. Their coffins had been publicly displayed along a broad avenue during a day of mourning.

After the Allies landed on the Normandy beaches, the Maquis became brazen and clearly more skilled in sabotage. French Forces of the Interior were parachuting in and joining the Resistance, blowing up bridges and cutting telephone and telegraph lines. *Les pianists,* radiomen, relayed information back to London and down to Algeria. Allied successes were published in more easily available underground papers.

In retaliation Nazi brutality increased. The day before, on June 8th, German troops and a handful of Maquis had encountered each other in Beaumes-de-Venise, five miles north of Carpentras. At the end of the fighting, eight men were dead and a dozen wounded.

At breakfast Florence informed her daughter that she was going to the *Domaine de Lauritaine* and would stay until it was safe to return home. Gigi hugged and thanked her mother as she had been having nightmares since the day the planes had attacked. She didn't want to be bombed. Florence held her tightly, smoothed her hair and murmured, "Then we need to get going."

"*Maman*, are you coming, too?" Gigi's eyes were imploring.

"*Non, chérie.* But I will join you if it looks like there will be fighting here. And then there's your father...." Florence let the sentence linger.

Two battered suitcases, a few books and a favorite doll were strapped on the backs of their bicycles. Edging their way through German military vehicles and other refugees, they soon branched off onto a rural road. Well before noon Primo greeted them with vicious sounding barks until Gigi called out. He quieted and padded up to the house in front of them.

A tense Juliette met them at the door and showed them up to Gabrielle's room. While Gigi unpacked her few things, the cousins walked down to the kitchen. Juliette shook the coffee pot on the stove and lit the burner underneath. She put cups and saucers on the table then she and Florence sat across from each other.

"I brought a letter for Amélie from Anne-Marie. Her parents have also left town."

"I knew that she had written to them saying that she was here. Who else knows?"

"If you mean 'Henri,' he still thinks that she is with her aunt in Lyon. Now that her parents have left I doubt anyone will even be curious."

"If Gigi mentions Amélie being here, he may want to know why."

Florence thought for a minute. "Why not say that her aunt died and she's staying with you since her parents are gone?"

Juliette closed her eyes, "So tangled a web we weave…"

Florence swallowed and said, "Juliette, my sympathies are not with the Germans. I want you to know that. Even though Henri is very close to them I have tried hard to remain…neutral."

"I realize that, dear Florence. Our families have been through too much together. I know that we can trust each other."

Suddenly Gigi came running down the front stairs and into the kitchen. Juliette brightened and motioned to her. "Gigi, ma chérie, would you like a piece of my bread? I just took these loaves out of the oven."

She got up to cut a slice for the girl at her side. As they sat down Juliette reached around the child's shoulders. "I'm so glad that you are staying with us. It is nice having another girl around the house with Gabrielle gone. However, Gigi, I expect you to work. There's a lot of gardening that needs to be done in the *potager* and we will soon need to start canning tomatoes and beans for winter."

Gigi brightened, "I can help do that! You know that I love working in the garden."

"Speaking of that," Juliette suggested, "why don't we take some bread out to Uncle Jean-Pierre and Maurice then we can pick something for dinner. You won't mind our leaving for a minute, Florence? Help yourself to more coffee."

Juliette tore a thin multi-colored loaf in half and wrapped it in one of her kitchen towels. Gigi was out the door in seconds carrying a flat straw basket as Juliette followed, saying over her shoulder, "She's growing up so fast!"

Florence sat quietly, toying with the cup, when she heard a sound from the hallway. Amélie was about to turn back.

Florence called out, "Amélie! It's all right. I have a letter from your mother for you."

Amélie's face was pale, her green cotton dress hung on her as desolately as her expression. She edged into the room, looking around suspiciously.

"I thought that everyone was outside. You are alone?"

"Come over and sit down." She retrieved the pot on the stove, "There's a bit of coffee left."

Easing into a chair, Amélie picked up the envelope as Florence poured her a cup. Suddenly her expression relaxed and she looked up. "They have left town and are staying with one of *maman's* cousins on the other side of the mountain. I'm so relieved. If we can only remain safe for another few weeks…"

Florence then asked, "Have you heard anything from Étienne?"

"No, we haven't heard anything," she fibbed. Amélie visibly swallowed, her eyes lowered. "I don't think that it's safe for me to stay here, now that you and Gigi know."

"Juliette and I have already decided to say that you are here because your aunt died and your parents had left. My husband realizes the danger of being in town."

"How are you and Monsieur Gilles-Martin?"

The question caused Florence to pause. "Like everyone, we are concerned about bombing raids coming further inland. I know that Henri worries about retaliations if the Germans leave and the Free French Army is in charge. However, appreciating German culture and playing in the commandant's orchestra is no reason for him to be harmed."

Amélie sipped her coffee not looking at Florence. "Do you suspect that he could have been mixed up in any espionage or is…especially close to those German officers?''

Florence sat back, surprised at her question. Amélie's cup bumped against the saucer but she did not say anything. Florence toyed with the napkin on the table.

"I never thought of Henri as someone who would risk anything dangerous. He does spend a lot of time with the Germans because he enjoys speaking their language." Florence babbled with a forced laugh, "Are you saying that I should suspect him of spying? Or that he has been turning in people to the Milice? Did you hear anything when you were working at Kommandantur Schneider's headquarters?"

Amélie paused to sip the last liquid in her cup. "I did learn something about your husband that I think...perhaps you should know. I don't like being the one to tell you but...", she covered her mouth with her hand, then lowered it. "I feel that you should know, just in case..."

At the alarmed expression on Florence's face, Amélie blurted out, "Henri is involved sexually with a German."

"Sexually?" Florence looked puzzled. "What are you talking about? How could you think this...? There aren't any German women in town. What are you saying?"

Amélie's face blushed pink. "I saw them."

"What do you mean? How could you 'see them'?" Florence sounded irritated.

Amélie's voice grew higher pitched. "I was...in a place in the Germans' headquarters where I should not have been. I looked through a keyhole, spying...sort of....and saw Monsieur Gilles-Martin. And that officer named Ziegler, undressed and...doing it."

Florence sank back into her chair and looked into the distance. Her eyebrows furrowed, the color drained from her face. The room was silent.

"That was why I left. I was afraid they would find out that I knew."

"Oh, *mon dieu!*" Florence turned to Amélie. "I can't believe this. Who else knows?"

"I've not told anyone and I'm not going to. With Nazis sending people to those awful camps for any reason, including being a homosexual, he could be killed. You could also be in danger."

Florence sat immobilized.

Amélie continued, "And Gigi shouldn't be faced with her father's perversity. What if it became public?"

"Oh my God!" Florence was ashen. "How will I explain this to her?"

Amélie leaned close to Florence and grasped her hand tightly. "She must not be told. What if she said something to her father? Perhaps when she is older and more mature."

"Of course, of course. I must talk with Henri about how best to handle this."

"Madame, don't be stupid!" Amélie's voice was sharp. "You mustn't mention this to him. He and that German still have influence. They could concoct all sorts of stories about you, call you a liar, a subversive, have you arrested and shot. You mustn't say a word! Do you understand?"

Florence covered her face with her hands. "I can't believe this."

"You can't tell anyone else. But at least...you know the truth in case something happens." Amélie added, "Maybe Henri will leave with the Germans when the Americans arrive."

Florence bitterly interjected, "I just have to hope that he won't get arrested or be accused of being a spy."

"Monsieur Gilles-Martin will probably be careful. I wanted you to know enough to protect yourself, in case...I mean...," Amélie's voice faded.

"Amélie, it's hard news to hear yet I'm glad that you told me. I'll be very cautious." Florence looked toward the back kitchen door. "Please, please promise me that you won't ever tell anyone. Not a soul. Gigi must never know. My family must never know. Promise me."

Amélie quickly responded, "I promise that I will never tell anyone, especially not Gigi. Ever. It will be up to you to decide how to handle this. Also, please, don't do anything that would put either of us in danger."

Florence latest thoughts were not about danger. The news eased the guilt that had weighed her down about deceiving her husband. Her Catholic conscience was already in the process of forming an absolution. Amélie was more than a little surprised to see Florence's face relax, followed by a faint smile.

They both turned to see Juliette and Gigi coming toward the house, carrying the basket of vegetables.

"I'm going upstairs. I don't want Gigi to know that I am here until Madame Laurent tells her." Amélie stood, patted Florence's hand and ran into the hallway as Juliette and Gigi entered.

Florence stared at her daughter and a defensive instinct took over. She needed time to figure out what to do. She got up and touched Gigi's hand. She spoke, her heart heavy but her voice lilting. "What a wonderful harvest! Think of the things that you can do to help your *Tante Julliette?*"

JUNE 10:

Early the next morning, a highly-strung, sleep-deprived Florence left the apartment as soon as an oblivious Henri went out to meet one of his friends. She walked west then turned right on *rue des Frères Laurents*, past the opening to *rue du Refuge* and its brothels where smirking soldiers sauntered into the doglegged street.

She had spent much of the night debating whether to share her trauma with Antoine. She trusted that he would give her sound, rational advice. Her fear was that he might report what she disclosed and Henri and the officer would be arrested, sent to a camp or killed outright. Her husband's involvement with the Nazis also could be significant enough that he would be in danger if anti-fascists and communists took over. Henri had alienated several townspeople.

Overriding every thought, every idea: how would this affect Gigi?

As she came down the long steps toward the boulevard above the north wall, a squat black Simca with a dented bumper and a shattered back window sped past her. The car wove back and forth then slowed, a driver slumped over the steering wheel. It headed straight toward *La Pyramid,* the obelisk built in 1712 as part of a promenade. Florence gasped as the car swerved, hit a curb, bounced then stopped, blocking the road.

A young man in his early twenties was one of several on the sidewalk and the only one who reacted. As he ran toward the car, Florence turned and quickly walked away with others who didn't want to get involved.

The man inside the car was either dead or close to it. A stack of rifles lay on the back seat. Georges Blanchard, known as *Mekan* in his Resistance cell, tore off his coat, opened the door and wrapped the garment around the armaments. He heard the sound of German vehicles and gunfire as he dashed west into a section of narrow lanes. Wending his way, breathless, the young man carried the goods as casually as one could half a dozen rifles inside a coat. Within minutes he was at his building, up the stairs and inside his room with the door locked. He laid the cache on his bed.

"Not a bad haul!" the young *Maquis* spoke out loud. "Poor guy, to lose your life over this. But at least the Germans didn't get them. Thanks, whoever you were!"

Florence walked east along the street with her head bent low, not paying attention to the commotion that she heard on the boulevard: the squeal of brakes, the pounding of boots, shouting, gunshots. As distraught as she felt, as shocked by what Amélie had told her, she was so grateful that Gigi was no longer in town.

She had also made her decision. As much as she loved and trusted Antoine, she did not dare tell him or anyone else.

JUNE 12:

Valreas, a peaceful village eighteen miles north of Vaison-la-Romaine, was part of the Vaucluse, although encircled by the Department of the Drome. With fewer than five thousand people and far from the main highways, it didn't anticipate being in the middle of a conflict.

Two days after the Normandy invasion, the *Maquis Vasio* and Free French of the Interior forces took over the town. They cut telephone and telegraph lines, blocked roads and occupied the gendarmerie and post office. A number of the gendarmes not only willingly handed over their munitions but joined the opposition. When word came that a contingent of the *Abwher* was on its way to arrest the 'terrorists,' the Maquisards left to avoid reprisals against the town.

At one o'clock twelve hundred German troops arrived, surrounded and entered Valreas. A General Unger told the mayor to assemble everyone in the main square or the town would be destroyed. Residents crammed themselves into the main square. Several FFI who had been arrested at a barricade stood with hands tied. The General selected a group of citizens to be killed with the FFI men unless the Maquis were turned in—an impossible task. The mayor negotiated, pleading for the lives of the townspeople. He managed to reduce the number from fifty-five to fifty-three.

Forced to stand on a low wall, the men were machine-gunned and fell into the square. The General stated that the bodies were not to be touched for twenty-four hours. During the night, four wounded men were replaced with corpses from the mortuary to keep the count at fifty-three.

The following evening the dead were placed in coffins and escorted to the cemetery. Only the families and the mayor were allowed to attend the burials, with a contingent of Germans surrounding them.

CONFLICT OF INTERESTS - 1978

At nine o'clock in the morning the sun sifted through lace curtains and chirps drifted through the window-paned doors. Birdsong signaled the end of the Mistral and I rose to look out. The tops of trees barely moved. Provence was tranquil again.

I turned to Maurice, memorizing his face. I wondered how long I would be able to recall its details: the white wrinkle lines around his dark eyes, unruly curls that felt luxurious as my fingers stroked them during love-making. His body was like a man twenty years younger due to working outdoors, carrying wine casks and cases, constantly in motion. Beyond the pheromones or musk, the strong physical attraction, I felt safe when we were together.

Maurice smiled as he awoke. I knew that I intrigued him and brought him pleasure. Perhaps he found my American accent and idiosyncrasies appealing. Certainly my body responded to his willingly, imaginatively, and I felt more alive than I had in years. He pulled me close and we lay together, dozing.

A half hour later we walked to my bathroom with our arms around each other's naked waists. I ran water in an old enameled tub. When it finally filled to one-third full, we stepped in and sat at opposite ends, legs tucked between legs. Giggling and splashing, we leaned forward for a kiss and a soapy rub.

Maurice sat back with a grin on his face. "Madame, you are full of surprises. I didn't know what I was getting into when I invited you to taste my wines."

Maurice reached under the water for my hand and pulled me toward him. "I think that we could have a future together. Is it possible that you think so, too?"

He smiled but I saw apprehension in his eyes.

"Oh, Maurice," I whispered a response. "I do like being with you."

"Is that a 'yes'?" His eyebrows went up a fraction.

I slid my legs under me and swept into his arms. Our noses and chins slapped together as we glided down in the water then came up, hair dripping at the edges, eyelashes sparkling with water droplets.

I spoke with my cheek against his neck, "I don't know. I'm divorced, you're Catholic, I work in academia, you work on a farm. We live a world apart. There are our families to consider. It's complicated."

Maurice's voice rumbled against my hair. "We'll figure it out, my love. As long you feel the same as I do."

He turned my face toward him and kissed me then levered himself up and stepped out. Turning back he helped me out. We managed a slippery embrace and it was clear that breakfast would be delayed. Later we sat at the table by the balcony window drinking café-au-lait, I in a short robe, Maurice in a towel and a partially buttoned flannel shirt.

"I'd like for you to come for lunch again today," Maurice put his hand on mine. "My family might as well get used to seeing more of you."

"But they aren't expecting me. Are you sure there's enough food?"

Maurice laughed, "There's usually enough food for a small army on Sundays. Elodie made a simple *cassoulet* to reheat so it won't be a gourmet dinner. *Maman* and Gabrielle are driving back from Aix-en-Provence before noon. Martine and Julien are the only others coming today. Joseph is at university and the others have plans."

"We could go to the patisserie and pick up something for dessert."

"And we'll need bread, too. *Alors, ma chérie,* time to get dressed." Maurice stood up, kissed the top of my head, pulled on his jeans and buttoned his shirt. I picked out some jeans and a navy blue pullover, my favorite loafers. Tying my hair into a ponytail with a scarf, I added lipstick, turned and grabbed a cardigan and purse.

On the drive to *Domaine de Lauritaine*, it felt as if we were in a Hollywood film. It wasn't just that my body was flooded with endorphins. The aftermath of the Mistral was purity, dust swept away, colors concentrated, air oxygenated, the population calmed. Vineyards were turning from summer green to chartreuse and shades of orange. The sky was an intense blue. Every crevice in the *Dentelles de Montmirail's* jagged peaks was crisp, detailed.

At the house Maurice pranced around the front of the car, opened my door with a flourish, offered his left arm while holding two baguettes in his other hand. I exited with a pastry box. As we walked through the arch, Simon rose from his spot on the terrace, wagging his tail.

Maurice opened the door and called out *"Maman*, we have a guest."

His mother came from the kitchen into the hall, a towel in one hand. When she saw me her reaction was hesitant then she strode forward with a gracious, "Welcome, Madame Somerset."

Maurice apologized for not calling her, explaining that we had been at the Duprés for dinner the night before. Lingering in the pause, open for speculation, was the time between the dinner and the morning invitation. After all, I mused, this was France. It was the 1970's. I proffered the pastry.

"How thoughtful! Thank you very much. We're in the kitchen since there are so few of us," Madame Laurent turned and motioned to us. "Julien and Martine aren't here yet."

Maurice paused and reached for an envelope that was sitting on the table in the hall. "I forgot to tell you that a letter came here for you. It's from Francois."

I opened the envelope, "He and Amélie will be in Carpentras on Wednesday and he can talk with me then."

Maurice beamed, "I'm glad that you will have a chance to hear some of his adventures. Is it all right if I come, too?"

I poked him with my elbow. As he strode ahead toward the kitchen, I followed closely behind while re-reading the note. When Maurice suddenly stopped at the doorway, I bumped into him and looked up quizzically. He looked stunned, then smiled and entered the room.

"Bonjour, Gabrielle," he said. "Bonjour, Yvette."

Over Maurice's shoulder two equally startled women stared at us. My mood changed like a deflating balloon. My eyes narrowed as I followed him into the room, saying with fake bonhomie, "*Bonjour!*"

Madame Laurent rescued the situation gracefully, "Yvette, I don't believe that you have met Claire Somerset who is visiting from California. Madame Somerset, this is our friend, Yvette LaPierre."

I greeted Yvette with an '*enchanté*' and extended my hand which she grasped and, equally politely, said '*enchanté.*' The redhead then greeted Maurice with kisses on his cheeks and started chattering brightly. Gabrielle coolly acknowledged me and we shook hands. Her expression reminded me of a chess player who has cornered her opponent's queen.

"I do hope that the little accident last weekend did not spoil your lovely dress."

"The dress will be fine but thank you for your concern." I put on my most diplomatic smile. "May I help?"

Gabrielle, as I expected, said '*non.*' Madame Laurent asked that me to cut up the baguettes that Maurice held. I reached for them with one eyebrow slightly lifted. Maurice, the lone male surrounded by three combatants on high alert, looked like he was about to be offered his last cigarette. I did not feel sympathetic, watching Yvette in a form-fitting olive green sweater that matched her eyes. A skin-tight skirt barely reached her knees above high-heeled boots.

Yvette cocked her head to one side as she thanked Maurice profusely for loaning her a book about wine. She planned to immerse herself in learning as much as she could. Someday she hoped that, with his help, she would be able to develop a sophisticated palate.

I vigorously sliced the bread, placing the pieces into a napkin-lined basket. As I put it on the table I noticed that there were places set for six. I would make a seventh, which would crowd those on one side together. Julien and Martine's appearance amid '*bonjours*' from the hall momentarily attracted everyone's attention. Martine had brought an apple and custard tarte that needed refrigeration. There was a sashay of bodies within the space. Maurice sidled toward me.

I whispered, "There's not enough room at the table."

Julien greeted me as Maurice moved the silverware, glasses and plates to make room for another place. He asked Julien to bring in a chair from the side room. He opened a drawer and a couple of cupboards, gathering up what was needed.

Great, I thought to myself, now there are two desserts. Extra flowers can always be used. But two desserts! I sighed out loud and Maurice glanced at me. He looked relieved when I flashed a falsely cheerful smile.

Madame Laurent announced suggested that we move to the front room for an aperitif while the cassoulet heated up in the black-enameled Lacanche stove. Yvette removed cold radishes from the refrigerator, placing them on a tray with a dish of butter and a saltcellar. Gabrielle picked up a plate of melon slices wrapped in thin *jambon cru,* speared by a toothpick through a sprig of mint.

Family and guests winnowed themselves onto two couches and assorted side chairs. As Maurice took a chair next to the fireplace Yvette pulled up one next to him. I retreated to the farthest corner of a couch. Martine inched past the table to sit beside me. Julien sat down on the opposite couch and regaled his Aunt Gabrielle with stories of cycling from Barroux to Malaucene with friends the day before. Madame Laurent sipped rosé in a favorite chair off to the side. I observed Yvette coquettishly tipping her head as she and Maurice conversed.

Then I turned to Martine who asked me about American education. I explained the difference between the US and French systems. She had countless questions and I was grateful for her focus on a topic of mutual interest.

Occasionally one of the family included Madame Laurent but for the most part she sat contentedly, basking in the ambiance surrounding her. At the sound of a buzzer from the kitchen she stood and announced that it was time to eat.

Maurice took his place at the far end of the table. Yvette followed and took the chair to his right. He courteously helped push Yvette's seat forward.

"Claire, this place is for you," he pointed as Gabrielle headed for the chair on his left.

She glared at her brother then moved down to sit next to her mother. Julien took the seat between Gabrielle and me. Madame Laurent folded her hands and the others followed suit as Maurice intoned the blessing. Everyone, including non-Catholic me, made the sign of the cross then placed napkins in our laps. At Madame Laurent's request, Julien got up and brought the steaming *cassoulet* from the oven, placing it on a metal trivet at his grandmother's place. Maurice uncorked a bottle of red wine. As his mother served the Provençal stew, he poured some into my glass then Yvette's, then his own, before passing the bottle down to Julien.

Julien raised his glass and looked to me on his left.

"I propose a toast to our American guest. May she find everything that she is looking for during her sojourn in Provence."

There was some hesitancy in raising their glasses on the part of Gabrielle and Yvette, but this was hardly noticeable during the litany of 'bon chance,' 'cin cin,' 'santé.' I caught the *double-entendre* immediately and decided to brave a reply.

"*Merci*, Julien. In addition to learning a great deal about your fascinating cultural heritage, I have been welcomed by many kind and gracious people whom I hope will remain friends long after I leave, including your wonderful family."

I raised my glass and smiled at each person, including the two women who in olden times might have added something lethal to my wine glass. Everyone murmured a response such as 'lovely,' 'we hope so,' 'of course.' The last comment was from a beaming Maurice who placed his left leg by mine and squeezed my knee.

Yvette's gaze across the table toward me did not match her honeyed tone. "Madame, what is that you are looking for?"

Once more I reviewed the purpose of this sabbatical.

Yvette chewed for a moment. "That must be so very interesting," she purred. "But there are some secrets that are better left unearthed."

"Secrets?" I was puzzled.

"Well, what I mean is that since 1945 we French have been trying to get our country back to a stable, traditional way of life. Even with the recent election, I can't imagine France ever becoming so radical or divided again."

Julien took exception with her statement and a rousing discussion ensued. There were hand gestures, 'poufs' indicating agreement and disagreement. Then the subject switched to wine, a subject that caused no friction.

Madame Laurent and Martine tactfully placed both desserts on the table and everyone took a slice of each. After coffee and conversation centering on the weather and the vineyard, family and guests began their exodus. Julien and Martine gathered up jackets, kissed family members, shook Yvette's and my hands and left. Madame Laurent thanked all for coming and excused herself to go to her apartment, which she traditionally did after the Sunday meal. An awkward moment arose as the remaining four of us stood in the hall.

Yvette broke the silence. "Claire, I would be happy to give you a ride into Carpentras since Gabrielle and I are going that way."

"That is very kind of you."

Maurice spoke up, "I wanted to show Madame Somerset some books in the library as there may be a couple that she could use." He stepped closer to me, touching her elbow. "Would you be interested?"

I kept my face totally straight, "Of course, how thoughtful," and almost added 'Monsieur Laurent.'

Yvette looked at us then offered to stay and wash the dishes. Maurice and I walked to the library at the end of the main salon. Once up the steps Maurice pulled me into a corner and we kissed hungrily.

"Ummm, that really was a good *gateau au chocolat!* It's even better second-hand."

Maurice held me to him, his hand clasping the back of my head as he murmured, "*Je t'adore, ma chérie.*"

I reluctantly pulled back, "I think that we'd better look at some of your books. I'm sure that there are etchings in them that I would enjoy."

"Etchings? I didn't know you were interested in etchings, too?"

I chuckled and explained, "It's an old pick-up line that a man would use to entice a woman to his apartment and his bed."

Maurice nodded, "Ah, but closets with secrets have a better effect on you...."

I stifled a laugh into his shirt and punched him on the shoulder. We stopped and listened and did not hear voices coming from the hall. I spoke up loudly, "I see, Maurice, this book does look promising."

Maurice walked over to an opposite corner near a battered violin case propped up by the bookcase. He looked up and down the shelves, edging out one or two books then pushing them back.

"Ah! Here it is," he exclaimed. He blew at some dust and brushed the book lightly with his hand. "It's an old edition by an author named René Carnat, *Le Parnasse, La Littérature Française au XIXe Siècle.* It belonged to my wife's family."

I looked at the table of contents then thumbed through the pages. "Actually this does look like something that I could use. The writing style of the Parnassian poets later led to Symbolism, the precursor to the Surrealists. They were beginning to look at writing as 'art for art's sake.' Are you familiar with these poets?"

"You're not the only one who can do research. I spent an hour looking through our library trying to find something that would appeal to you. I'd never even noticed it before." Moving away he called to me from the next bookcase. "Here's René Char's *Feuillets d'Hypnos.* It was a Christmas gift to Brigitte from Francois and Amélie... in 1954."

He offered the book and I took it with a sense of reverence as I opened the first few pages. "Albert Camus was instrumental in getting this published and the two writers became good friends after that. I've never seen an actual copy of it. Only parts of the book are in an anthology that I brought with me from California. This must be very special to you."

Maurice shrugged, "It has sentimental importance. However, books are meant to be shared. I'm happy to loan it to you while you're here."

I clasped the books to my chest, "I will take good care of them. Thank you."

From the hallway came Yvette's sharp soprano, "Madame, if you're ready we can give you a lift."

I raised my eyebrows, shrugged my shoulders and said to Maurice, "I might as well go. It will save you a trip not to mention your reputation."

"Are you sure?" He reached for my hand and kissed it.

"Yes, I think that it would be…practical."

This was the first time in several weeks that the idea of being practical had entered my mind. I smiled at Maurice and whispered. "I'll see you next Tuesday."

I poked my head past the library's arch. "I'll be right there."

On the ride home I sat in the back of Yvette's *Fiat*, a sleek yellow convertible with a black cloth top. Yvette and Gabrielle talked about an event in Avignon and ignored me. My mind wandered as I looked at the now familiar scenery, the substantial *platane* trees shedding leaves the size of saucers, a few narrow cypress pointing accusations at the sky. Within minutes, the car wound its way down the street on the west side of town.

Yvette slowed, pulled to the side and stopped. "I hope that you don't mind if I let you off here. It's easier if we turn right at the next intersection instead of having to drive all the way around again."

Gabrielle opened the door, stepped out and bent the seat back frontward so I could get out. I pulled myself up from the low-slung back, my chin almost touching my knees as I struggled to exit, clasping the two books and my handbag. Gabrielle stood by the door, not offering to help.

Yvette peered back, "We're blocking traffic, please hurry up."

I grabbed the side of the front seat and made a lunge, got some leverage then twisted to the right and got a foot out on the street. Unwinding as I emerged, I smacked my head on the metal frame of the cloth top.

"Ouch!'

Gabrielle slid back into the car. "Oh, I hope that didn't hurt. By the way, Claire, when are you planning to leave for the United States?"

I rubbed my head, "I'm, uh, I'm leaving in three weeks.

"Well, I hope that you have a safe trip home. Bon voyage."

Gabrielle pulled the door closed and Yvette merged into the traffic. The chic sports car careened around the corner and sped west. I rubbed my forehead, re-arranged the books and purse, rotated my clothes and started the long walk to the apartment on the opposite side of *Centre Ville*.

THE PACIFIST
JEAN GIONO

Jean Giono's experiences as a soldier on the front during World War I ingrained in him a passionate distaste for the idiocy of war. In 1939, because of his pacifist beliefs, he was arrested for being a Nazi sympathizer. He was imprisoned for several weeks then released without a trial.

When Germany invaded France, Giono was grateful--along with the majority of his fellow Frenchmen--that Marechal Petain managed to avert what would have been further devastation of their homeland. Well before the Germans imposed their inhumane, racist policies on French life he had commented, 'I'd rather be a live German than a dead Frenchman.'

During the first months of the Occupation Jean contributed to a clandestine journal put together by *The National Committee of Writers*. Although a periodical of the Communist Party it included authors with many political points of view. Now, however, German censors subjected all stories to scrutiny before allowing publication and the journal was defunct.

Giono's writing had always been about capturing the personality of his beloved region in southern Provence, emphasizing the virtues of a simple, rural life. The Vichy government promoted his essays and articles because they were in keeping with Petain's goal of returning France to a more 'pure' way of living: women as mothers and helpmates; men attuned to the outdoors and sports. As someone used to this simpler existence, Giono concurred with a number of the objectives. That it was now overlaid by hypocrisy and violence did not deter his appreciation for an unadorned existence.

Since 1939 only two books of his had been published: a sequel to his original translation of Melville's 'Moby Dick,' called 'A Salute to Melville,' and a bland novel titled 'The Living Water.' The Gallimard Company in Paris had re-published three earlier plays that were acceptable to the Third Reich.

Anticipating possible shortages when the war started, Giono had purchased nearby farms so that his family and neighbors might have a ready supply of food. He rarely left Manosque, hibernating in his native village tucked in the south side of Mont Ventoux. He avoided being drawn into political discussions—except for promoting peace.

In January 1943 a bomb was thrown against the front door of their home. The heavy oak portal was obliterated. The incident threatened the family's neutrality and Elise, especially, resented it each time that she opened the re-constructed doors.

This June day he sat at his desk in his upstairs office, looking out the window to a view of Manosque on one side, the Durance valley and the Valensole plateau on the other. Jean ran his hand through his thatch of blond-tinted hair. He riffled through the pages of a play that had been rejected. It was a favorite of his but apparently the theme had been too radical for the censors. Putting his pipe in the ashtray he picked up a pencil and made a note in the margin.

Elise knocked softly, "There's someone here to see you."

Giono walked to the door, opening his arms as he did so.

"Roger, mon ami!" He greeted a robust man in his early twenties with a kiss on each cheek. "What a grand surprise to see you. Have you brought me one of your poems to review?"

Roger Bernard smiled, his handsome face reddening slightly.

"I might have one or two in my pocket if you'd like to read them. I haven't had much time to write. Since the Allies landed I've been busy."

"As you know, we are remaining neutral. Certainly we are aware of the bombing of Avignon and Marseille. It probably means the German Occupation will end even though many more lives will be lost."

The young poet stood, looking downward, twisting his cap in his hands. "I have to ask a favor of you. Our friend Monsieur Char said that you might let me stay here with you or at a farm overnight. I'm on the way to take him a message. I'd rather rest up and travel early in the morning."

"As long as you won't stay more than one night. And I don't want to know if you are involved with anything subversive, Roger."

He nodded, "I'm grateful to you. Are you writing something new?"

"A play called 'A Voyage in a Carriage.' The censors have rejected it so obviously it won't be staged until after the war ends."

He picked up his pipe by its curled stem and dug out the burnt pseudo-tobacco, then tamped in dried leaves. "So, what have you written?"

Bernard reached into his back pants' pocket and took out a notebook wrapped in a type of oilcloth. "I'm putting down thoughts, not trying to publish. Here's one of my poems if you'd like to read it and make suggestions."

Giono took the notebook and his face softened as he read a tribute to the end of summer that ended strangely with the phrase '*I am living--upon eternal joy--living to die.*'

"Ah, you must continue to write, Roger. You are very talented."

They reminisced about happier times, their love of prose and their hopes for a better future. He enjoyed the young man, not much older than his own daughters, who had a bright future ahead of him. Giono congratulated Roger on the birth of his first child, a boy named Alexandre. It would be no problem to give him a place to sleep for one night. After supper with the Gionos, Roger was given a note to take to one of their farmhouses where he could stay.

In the morning, Jean went up to his study to write in the journal that he had started the previous year. He kept notes on family events, friends who were betrayed, the STO *refactaires* that he and the family fed, those whom he felt obliged to shelter for a short time. As a pacifist he tried not to take sides but he was, after all, French.

Elise stood at the door, "Are you busy, darling?"

Giono motioned for her to come in as he slipped the journal into a hiding place in back of a drawer.

"I'm going to walk into town with Aline and wondered if you would go with us?"

"Certainly, *ma puce.* I need to make an appointment to have my hair bleached and we might as well stop at the bank."

His wife was frowning.

"Elise, you aren't still frightened, surely?"

"Jean, you know that I feel safer when we all stay together. Especially after harboring a fugitive overnight."

"Ma chérie, young Bernard is a fellow writer. What do we know about what he does the rest of time? We talked about his poems and my play. The collaborators think that I sympathize with them to a degree."

"It's not just that!" Elise was upset. "I'm sure that the communists, the terrorists, were responsible for our door. Today I heard that a family at a farm up the mountain was slaughtered because they turned in some neighbors to the Germans. Trying to balance between two such violent beliefs is dangerous!"

Giono sighed, deeply. "War is a terrible thing, Elise. A terrible thing. I will never cease to be shocked by what man is capable of doing."

—∞—

Song of the World

(excerpt from the novel, published in 1934)

*Spring in the south was climbing from the forests and the waters. It had already
conquered evening and night. It was the master of the length of hours. Tall
mountains of ice were tearing up the north; a covering of clouds leaned upon
their sides. But one no longer was feeling the cold. The fish were jumping. A
male fox was calling in a plaintive, soft voice. Gray turtledoves flew against
the sun with the edges of their wings illuminated. Kingfishers raced along the
water. Some cranes threw themselves toward the north like passing arrows while
crying aloud. Clouds of ducks crushed the reeds. A pig-backed sturgeon swam in
the water as the sun sparkled on its scales. A cloud of mud followed the wavering
of its tail. An immense orchard of pussywillow bushes, clumps of trees, flowering
trees, sharp like beards of wheat and covered in blooms, barred the lower stream.
Water bathed them up to the shoulders. Eddies balanced in the branches. Pollen
wafted at eventide like sand under the feet of dancing athletes.   (31)*

Jean Giono   1895 – 1970

VAUCLUSE - 1944

JUNE 13:

X avier Chevalier sat without moving. The news shocked him to the point that his body froze, his mind could not grasp what he had read. He blinked and reread the first few sentences and then could go no further.

War was obscene in any sense but what had happened in a village one hundred fifty miles due west of Carpentras on June 10th was beyond obscene, beyond comprehension. It was even worse than what had taken place the day before in Valreas. Tears rolled down his cheeks and he wiped them with balled-up fists.

Chevalier had stayed neutral throughout the short 'phony' war and the Nazi Occupation of half of France in 1940. He had optimistically supported Marechal Petain's taking the helm of Vichy-controlled Southern France. Even after the Nazis took over Southern France, in spite of harsh laws and controls, Xavier innately believed that pacifism would be the best way to negotiate through the morass of conflict.

Now he felt completely betrayed.

His mental state alternated between a deep sorrow and an intense anger. Sitting stiffly in a chair, Xavier stared at the wall. This incident was something that he could neither rationalize nor ignore.

He pushed himself up, favoring his damaged leg, and stumbled through blurred vision to his desk. He sat, turned on the light, opened an inkbottle and filled his fountain pen.

'There are those of us who have stood passively by for far too long. Now we must take action! The recent massacre of 642 innocents in the town of Oradour-sur-Glane is of a nature so barbaric that it is hard to conceive. The cries and screams of grandmothers, mothers and babies, little boys and girls, as they burned to death in a holy sanctuary, their own church, must ring in our ears as we take up arms against an invader that has no humanity.'

Xavier got up to retrieve the page with facts about the massacre that had been slipped under his door. Smudged with blue ink, clearly it was written hurriedly but the story appeared incontrovertible. He took it to his desk and wrote more, stopping only to fill a glass with the last of his wine.

A regiment of the 2nd SS Panzer Division, on the way to Normandy, learned from the *Milice* that the Resistance had captured one of their Waffen-SS officers in a town called Oradour-sur-Vayres. The regiment commander ordered that thirty hostages be rounded up to exchange for the prisoner. When the commander learned that the officer had been executed he ordered the townspeople in Oradour-sur-Glane, a neighboring village with no connection to the kidnapping, to gather in their town square.

One hundred ninety men were taken into barns, machine-gunned in the legs and then set on fire. The elderly, the women and children were herded into their church and burned alive. The buildings were then destroyed. Six hundred forty two people were incinerated to avenge an act that they did not cause.

Chevalier used details furnished by the anonymous writer with his own impassioned views added. He moved to his typewriter and pecked out, with his forefingers, a final copy. When it was done he put on his jacket and hat, put the article in his pocket and headed for the newspaper office.

The editor of *La Provence* looked surprised to see him. "Xavier, *bonjour*. Do you have some poems for us?"

Chevalier placed his article on the editor's desk.

After reading it, the man looked up, "I'd heard about the...tragedy. But you must realize that we can't print anything so inflammatory. The commandant and his SS troops are looking for any excuse to arrest people."

He handed the page back.

"My advice to you is to save this for much later. And don't show it to anyone else! *Mon dieu*, do you want to be shot?"

Chevalier nodded, put the paper in his pocket and left. At the bar of the Grand Café of the 19th Century, he ordered the strongest drink available, a low quality Armagnac. He drank a second one, then ordered a third, giving up his last ration coupon.

René Dulfour watched in surprise as Xavier grabbed the glass and stumbled to a table far from a group of Germans surveying the café. Antoine Dupont, sitting alone at an adjacent table, nodded his head and tipped a wine glass in greeting. Chevalier saluted with his own and hunched his shoulders, staring at the amber liquid. He looked up to see Dupont standing beside him.

"May I join you?"

Xavier had occasionally spoken with the janitor as he cleaned the library. He seemed pleasant if not communicative. Perhaps he shared his own pacifist philosophy.

"*Bien sur*," he motioned to the empty chair.

The two men sat in silence for a minute or two. Antoine Dupont finally said softly, "Well, it does seem like the Occupation may soon end."

Chevalier turned to Antoine, his eyes unfocused, "D'ya mean 'cause the Americans are in Normandy? This jus' means many more deaths, more hardships. What we've suffered and will suffer seems un'maginable."

Dupont nodded. "I certainly agree with you. Many more sacrifices, I'm afraid."

"Di'ya hear about wha' happened in Valreas and Oradour-sur-Glane?" Chevalier squinted as if he was having trouble seeing.

"Yes, such horrible tragedies! So many innocent lives taken," Antoine Dupont sighed. "And for what?"

Chevalier sensed a kindred soul. He fumbled and held up his article.

"I wrote a' editorial but the paper won' prin' it."

Dupont picked the paper up and looked it over.

"Well done, monsieur. One can understand why our newspaper would hesitate to print this; however, I think that it deserves to be read. If you don't mind I may be able to pass it on to another journal."

Chevalier blinked and stammered, "Only if ish anonymous."

"I can assure you of that."

Dupont folded the paper and tucked it into a pocket in his overalls. Xavier finished his drink. He got up unsteadily and shook hands with Antoine. "*Merci, merci*, and good luck."

His limp was apparent as he wobbled toward the exit, grappling with the idea that what he needed now was a gun.

Bumbling attempts to obtain a firearm resulted in friends shushing him, acquaintances backing away. People began to avoid him. The wine from the Laurent's farm was gone. Since alcoholic beverages could only be served every other day, there were a number of dry ones. On the 'wet' days, Dulfour would only serve what Xavier's coupons allowed and these were quickly used up. The elderly man often sat sipping flavored water, staring at nothing.

JUNE 14 :

After the successful June 6th invasion, Churchill hesitantly authorized General Charles de Gaulle and two of his aides to make a brief visit to Normandy, France, to meet with General Bernard 'Monty' Montgomery. De Gaulle arrived at the coast on the French destroyer, *La Combattante*, with a large entourage and significant amounts of luggage.

After greeting Montgomery, de Gaulle marched through the nearly destroyed coastal town of Isigny surrounded by tumultuous crowds. He continued into Bayeux to the accompaniment of more enthusiastic supporters and announced that the town was now the temporary capital of France's new provisional government. Putting his staff in charge of removing the Vichy administrators and setting up a preliminary Fourth Republic governance system, he returned that night to the UK as agreed.

Churchill had already grudgingly conceded that this French General embodied the spirit of the fighting French and, as the first high-ranking officer to reject Nazi rule in France, had earned his place in history. President Roosevelt and his Allied commanders were increasingly furious at his impertinence.

JUNE 19:

As soon as Florence slipped into the dim museum entrance Benjamin clasped her to him and started kissing her. She unbuttoned her blouse and he unhooked her bra as she dropped her hands to below his waistband and rubbed his protrusion. He lifted her up and carried her to a stack of packing quilts that he had placed up against the stair wall.

They moaned and panted as they stroked and rolled their way to almost mutual climaxes. Then Florence lay, depleted, with her head tucked between his arm and shoulder, and let out a full sigh. How was it possible that their lovemaking got better each new time? She placed her right hand on Benjamin's chest, absorbed in his heartbeat and slowing breath. They lay together, not moving or talking, as if suspending time and refusing to let reality interfere with perfection.

"I suppose that we should get up?' He finally murmured.

"Do you think anyone would get suspicious if we barred the museum doors and lived here until the war was over?"

His chest puffed, heaved as he spoke a slight 'haha.' "We could say that we were quarantined due to a new disease—'*amorosa romantica*.' Very contagious. Affects the mind."

"It definitely affects the mind!" Florence said, as she pushed up to a sitting position and began rearranging her garments.

Benjamin looked up at her, with his arms crossed behind his head. "You're...umm...not running into any problems with the exchanges of information, are you?"

Florence felt as if a bubble in which she was poised had burst, dropping her to the stone floor. "No, not at all. There's something to be said for being ordinary, almost invisible, a quiet introvert who's not expected to say much."

"And you have Henri," he said, "your inadvertent protector."

There was no response from Florence. She tucked her head as she finished fastening the last button on her blouse, a sour taste in her mouth.

Benjamin rose up, put on his pants and looked around for his shoes. "Let's go on upstairs. I have some fake *cartes d'identités* for you to deliver, for the new recruits in the *Maquis Ventoux*. Also, I thought that you might like to read some poetry that was in the latest *L'Humanité*, by Louis Aragon."

He paused, "I'll tell you a bit about this 'poet of the Resistance.' He has some friends in Avignon and used to visit now and then. I understand that he is now using fake names and hiding from the Gestapo."

JUNE 22:

René had developed an especially close bond with Roger Bernard, the twenty-three year old poet. They would often share their prose, to discuss words and images. Char encouraged him to keep writing.

"After the war is over," he said, "I will help you contact the right people in Paris."

The birth of Roger's first child, a boy, was an occasion for a celebratory drink. As they clicked glasses, René clapped him on his shoulder, congratulating him with *felicitations!*

René had told his men that they were never to carry firearms with them when going about daily business. If captured, they were to delay giving out information for as long as possible so that others could be warned and hidden. In case of arrest no extreme measures would be taken in order to save them, especially if it meant jeopardizing the lives of many.

Every *Maquisard* was aware of these ironclad policies.

No one ever fully understood why the young *Maquisard* decided that he needed a leather holster for his pistol. He could have taken measurements with him but he didn't. Instead he carried the gun as he walked toward the town of Viens, not far from Cereste, where he planned to order the pouch from a *cordonnier*, a shoemaker.

The trees along the road gave off the scent of summer, their leafy protection easing the heat radiating from a dusty path. Roger turned at the sound of a car coming up the road and was startled to see a German staff car. He ducked into the woods. A man yelled for him to stop and two armed soldiers ran after him. After being questioned he was searched, arrested, put in the back of the car and driven into town.

As soon as René Char learned of his friend's capture he sent Irénée Pons to alert fellow *Maquisards* who had any connection to Roger. Those in nearby camps and cabins were told to scatter. When Pons was done he stopped at a farmhouse and asked one of the farmer's daughters if she would walk with him into Viens, as if they were lovers, to see what had happened.

Irénée came back to Cereste and told Capitaine Alexandre. René asked Marcelle Pons-Sedoine to bicycle over and find out where Bernard was being held. Near Viens, she watched a truck come down the road with the young poet in the back, surrounded by soldiers. Marcelle moved into the woods as the truck passed and saw his bruised, bloody, terrified face. The truck stopped at the highway then went west toward the town of Apt. Racing far behind, she watched as it turned toward an unused railroad depot a short distance from the road. Within minutes she heard gunfire.

A few days later, Capitaine Alexander wrote in his journal:

Roger was completely happy to be valued as the husband-who-is-hiding-god in the mind of his young wife.
I spent today at the edge of a field of sunflowers from which the view was inspirational. The drought caused the heads of these admirable, colorless flowers to sag. It was a few steps from there that his blood pooled, at the foot of an old Mulberry tree, heavy from all the thickness of its bark." (32)

Another entry described the day that Char and his compatriots stood helplessly on a high ridge above the town as the Germans executed 'B,' a villager.

He called it *'Horrible day!'* He and his Maquisards were hidden from sight on a ridge about three hundred feet above Cereste, sufficiently well armed and equal in number to the SS. His men waited for a signal; all he had to do was press the trigger of the machine gun. He shook his head *'non'* at eyes imploring him to open fire and felt a polar chill glide down his bones. The man fell as if he did not see his exccutioners and so lightly, it seemed to Char, that the least whisper of wind could have raised him from the ground.

Capitaine Alexander noted that he did not give the signal because the village, the inhabitants, had to be spared regardless of the cost of one life. *'What was the importance of this village, similar to so many others? Perhaps 'B' knew himself at that final moment.'* (33)

VERLAINE'S SURPRISE - 1978

On Wednesday afternoon I wandered among the library's stacks. The section on biographies held a number of tattered and faded bindings of mid-twentieth century books. One was unusual, a leather-bound book with the title *Paul Verlaine* in dim gold leaf. This was not the sort of book usually purchased with public funds but more like one from a private library.

Curious, I pulled the book off the shelf and checked the table of contents, divided into periods of the author's life. A blank bookplate was glued to the front page. Gathering this up with two other biographies I went to a table tucked in a corner of the room. Besides a sketch of the poet, the book contained etchings with transparent protective covers that coordinated with selections of poetry. I skimmed a few of the verses, amused by certain Victorian affectations although Verlaine was a precursor to modern verse.

A folded piece of paper torn from a school notebook slipped out onto the tabletop as I turned a page. Inside was a tightly penned poem in faded blue ink, the letters so tiny that I had to adjust my glasses to make them out. It was titled '*Apparition.*'

The one beloved unknown until now
Is cloaked in fog, undulating into memories.
If my tears were acid, I'd be hollow inside
Yet no scar would appear on my skin
As I watch and dare not speak.
Waiting. (34)

In a corner were the initials 'F. G-M.' and the date 'July 1944.' I turned the paper over but there was no other reference. Folding it, I was about to insert it back into the book when I paused. Perhaps the author was someone known in town, as locally published volumes were a tradition in the early to mid-part of the century. The date coincided with the Allies gathering forces in North Africa and the Resistance movement becoming active. Perhaps there was a story behind it, if I asked around.

I put the paper in my wallet then turned to another book, reading it and making a few notes. After an hour I returned the books to a box on a cart then walked back to my apartment. Madame Charpentier met me as I opened the front and we exchanged greetings. As she turned away I thought of the poem.

"Madame, I have a question. Do you know any group in Carpentras who might have published poetry during the War? I found a poem and would like to know more about the author."

She pursed her lips and thought for a minute, jiggling her keys. "I don't recall any in particular. There were teachers at the *Lycée* who taught writing and I think that there was a club that printed booklets. Someone at the office of *La Provence* might know. I suppose that the mayor's office could tell you if there is a poetry club among all the associations here."

I thanked Madame Charpentier and walked upstairs. Once inside I made phone calls using an *annuaire* dated the previous year. A clerk at the school told me that there was no poetry group anymore. The mayor's office confirmed this. A woman at the newspaper turned the phone over to a Hervé Leblanc, who said that he been in a poetry and writing club during the war when he was a student. He didn't recognize the author's initials but could look for a list of members among his mementos.

"How nice of you. If you find it, would you call me back?"

Three days later Leblanc did call; he had found his list. We met at a café near the paper's office and he seemed genuinely interested in my research. An angular fellow with thin graying hair and wire-rimmed glasses, Hervé was only missing a green eyeshade in order to be the archetypical newspaperman. He frowned as he read the poem then checked the initials against his list. After several minutes, he shook his head.

"Sorry, but it doesn't look like this person was one of us." He looked as disappointed as I felt. "If you don't mind, come to the office and I'll make a copy of it and ask around. Someone in town might recognize the writing or the initials."

THE VAUCLUSE – 1944

JUNE 25:

One hundred and fifty *B24 Liberators* made another raid on Avignon. This time their targets included the industrial area north of town, the Pontet train depot and the viaduct over the Rhone.

More than four hundred railway cars were destroyed. Among them were hoppers used to transport coal to the Nazis fighting in Normandy as well as a number of carriages carrying Cotes-du-Rhone fine wines destined for the Rhine Valley in Germany. These wagons burned for two days despite the efforts of firefighters.

Michel Perrin received a letter sent by courier from his Uncle Sebastian that his youngest uncle, Grégoire, had been one of fifteen people killed. On that Sunday he had been assigned to work in Le Pontet moving trains loaded with coal from mines in southern Provence to western France.

JULY 1:

A copy of *Combat*, the journal that Albert Camus edited, was thrust under Xavier Chevalier's apartment door before he woke up. His article was featured on the front page under the title '*A Call to Action.*' The author was identified as 'a patriot and former pacifist.' The elderly man reread the editorial that he knew by memory, noting a few changes in wording. He felt taller, his chest expanded and he smiled as his head bobbed up and down.

At the café, hoping to wheedle an illegal swig, Xavier showed René Dulfour the article and mumbled that he had written it. René grabbed the paper and thrust it under the bar. He quietly whispered that it was dangerous to openly show the paper let alone talk about it. He called his son-in-law René Alibert over and said that Monsieur Chevalier needed help returning home.

JULY 6:

When Charles de Gaulle stepped off his plane at the recently constructed National Airport in Arlington, Virginia he was greeted with a seventeen-gun salute for a senior military officer, not the twenty-one-gun salute for a visiting head of state. However, President Franklin Roosevelt publicly greeted him as if they had always been the best of friends, all smiles and warm phrases of welcome.

De Gaulle reciprocated with the utmost civility and charm, seducing even his worst wartime detractors. It became clear to many Americans in contact with de Gaulle that he passionately believed in his mission as a latter-day 'Joan of Arc' who would save France, his *Marianne*.

After an effusive welcome in New York de Gaulle wrote to Roosevelt, thanking him for his hospitality and emphasizing that he and the French people were 'unanimous in friendship and determined to continue fighting and working beside our Allies for victory and peace.'

Without consulting his closest ally Winston Churchill, Roosevelt publically announced that he accepted the FCNL as the de facto administration of France although he did not go so far as to accept de Gaulle's provisional government, the GPRF, quite yet. The British Prime Minister rolled his eyes as he chewed his cigar, stating to his aide that he was not surprised. This maneuver would help Roosevelt in the November election.

JULY 7:

Antoine Dupont adjusted his suspenders, dusted his rolled-up sleeves and walked from the museum to meet his daughter at the *rue des Halles*. After greeting each other they headed for a café by the city hall, near a fountain with a gold angel on top. Suddenly someone reached between them, grabbed their arms and pulled them into a narrow alley.

"Don't say a word and come with me," muttered Madame Michaud, co-owner of a nearby butcher shop.

Antoine and Sylvie marched with her to a double door in a wall. Delphine Michaud reached into her coat pocket and took out a ring of keys. Shakily she turned a key in the lock, opened half the door and pushed the two into a small alleyway smelling of garbage.

A finger to her lips, she whispered, "A German staff car is parked in front of the cafés on the square. My husband and I think it is the Gestapo looking for communists, Jews, the Maquis. You are to stay here until we know what is happening."

Antoine shook his head. "But...why us?"

"We have mutual friends," the woman replied. "We knew that you often eat at Café de l'Angel and were told there might be trouble today."

She pulled Antoine and Sylvie into the back of the shop and closed the door. Antoine watched her husband through thin chains that served as a screen between the front and back rooms.

Sylvestre Michaud was closing the door under the disgruntled stares of shoppers still in line. He locked it and turned a sign in the window to *'fermé,'* lowered the window shades and walked back to the three standing in the darkened room. After shaking Antoine's hand, he removed his apron.

Antoine stammered out, "What is this all about?"

Sylvestre leaned against the door jam. "*Maxmillian* alerted us that the Brandenburg Division was raiding cafés and rounding up suspects today. He didn't want anything to happen to you and Sylvie, so Delphine went looking for you."

"Are you part of the Resistance?" Antoine blurted out.

"Not officially but we try to prevent the Germans from harming others, when we can."

A commotion at the door was followed by several knocks. The shadows of two men could be seen through the shade. The butcher shoved Antoine downward.

"The safest place for you to hide is behind the counter, under the butcher block by the cash register. Try to curl up between the legs."

Antoine dropped to the sawdust floor then scooted backwards. With the butcher's help he stuffed himself between thick wooden legs, his knees up around his face. Madame Michaud removed a gold chain with a cross from her neck and placed it around Sylvie's.

"Put on one of the aprons over there. If anyone asks, you are my grand-daughter visiting from Le Thor."

Sylvie did as the woman said as the knocks intensified. A gruff voice spoke in accented French, 'open up!'

Michaud called out, "It's lunchtime and we open in two hours."

"Open up immediately!"

The butcher moved slowly toward the front door noisily jangling his keys, "*J'arrive*, I'm coming, I'm coming."

Fussing with the keys and muttering under his breath, Sylvestre wasted several seconds before he opened the door a crack.

"What do you want?"

A fair-haired thin German officer, accompanied by a burly soldier carry-ing a rifle, stared at Michaud with squinty eyes. The heavy-set man pushed on the door so that the butcher was forced to step back. Both Germans muscled themselves inside. The officer abruptly closed the door, the sign bouncing and slapping between the window and the shade.

"You are the owner?"

"*Oui*," Michaud replied.

"How many people are here?" He looked toward the open doorway to the backroom where Madame Michaud and Sylvie stood.

"Only my family, monsieur."

Delphine walked into the room, pulling the girl's hand. "I am Madame Michaud. This is my granddaughter Sylvie."

The officer looked at Sylvie as he began to remove a glove, "And your family, Mademoiselle? Do they live in Carpentras?"

"No," she remained calm as she lied. "My parents live in Avignon and my father works for your Army."

"Ah, I see." The Nazi seemed suspicious. "Is he fulfilling his obligation with the *Service de Travaille Obligatoire?*"

The young girl replied without missing a beat, "He is helping repair train tracks that were bombed."

The officer looked at the girl, waited a second or two then replied, "The Reich is appreciative of his service."

He and his henchman marched into the back of the shop and could be heard moving boxes and opening the refrigerator door. In a few minutes they reappeared.

"You have a nice piece of lamb in your refrigerator, yes?"

The butcher nodded.

"Wrap it up for me as I am entertaining a guest tonight."

Michaud paused to put on his apron then went to the back room, brought out the meat and did as requested. Without a word he handed the wrapped shanks over the butcher block. The officer took it without offering to pay, tucked it under his arm then smoothed on his gloves as he looked around. He snapped his right arm in the air with a 'Heil Hitler,' turned and left, his companion trailing behind.

Sylvestre once again locked the door then turned to help Antoine unfold from the butcher block. Delphine Michaud took Sylvie's hand.

"Stay in the back. I will see if Monsieur Devereaux at the café knows what is happening."

She removed her apron, took her purse and walked out the front door. Skirting a crowd gathered at a corner of the city hall, she slowed as if checking her purse as she looked toward the Café de l'Angel. A German staff car was parked in front with a canvas-covered truck behind it. Several people huddled inside, guarded by Germans with pistols. Two Milice stood by the car with arms crossed. She saw at least three *Abwehr* members inside the café. Hurrying to the far corner of the city building Delphine turned left then walked back through the arcades of Les Halles. Sylvestre opened the door as she knocked.

"*Maxmillian* was right. People have been rounded up and are under guard in a truck."

"You saved our lives!" Antoine kissed the woman on either cheek. "But what about you? Is your shop under surveillance?"

"We are restricted to being open only three days a week and can barely get anything to sell. Madame Michaud and I think that it is time that we took an early vacation and visited her parents in Cucuron. Between the bombing along the Rhone and the Allies moving toward Paris, we would feel safer there."

Antoine stated, "There is a *hotel particulier* where Sylvie and I were told to go if we were in danger."

"Let's eat lunch upstairs then you can leave when it's safe."

Precisely at two o'clock the butcher came downstairs, put on his stained apron, washed his hands at a stone sink then moved to the front of the shop. He turned the sign on the door around and pulled up a shade behind the window marked in gold with '*Michaud et Fils - Bouchers.*' Half a dozen customers pushed their way inside, looking with disappointment at the meager choices in the case—a chicken cut into pieces, half-inch-square bits of what might be mutton. A dozen more stood in line behind them.

Madame Michaud went out the rear door and walked to the square. She came back to report that the car and truck were gone. It would be safe for the Duponts to leave. Antoine held Sylvie's hand and led her down the alley and toward the address that he'd been given. Several blocks further south he pulled a metal ring at the imposing doorway of a town mansion and heard, distantly, the sound of a bell.

They waited. Once again he pulled on the ring. The grating of a key in an ancient oversized lock came before the squeak of the heavy door as it opened a crack. A woman of advanced years peered at them.

"Monsieur?" she inquired. "What do you want?"

Antoine parroted the phrase memorized from a piece of paper that he'd been given months before. The door swung open and closed quickly.

"Come, *monsieur, mademoiselle*. Follow me, please."

They entered a paneled reception room with sun pouring through a stained glass window above marble steps to the left of the door.

Dressed in black, a long skirt over serviceable shoes, gray-white hair pulled into a bun, the Dupont's benefactress walked briskly across the elegant hall below an immense crystal chandelier dangling from an encrusted circle in the ceiling. She unlocked double doors leading into a second reception area with pillars and a view of a neglected courtyard. She fumbled with another lock at a second set of double doors then stepped into a garden of overgrown shrubs, tangled vines, weeds and clots of untrimmed trees, Antoine and Sylvie following her.

"The entrance to the *cave* is behind those trees, in front of a large wall fountain. The trapdoor has a bench attached to it. Pull up on the handle under the front edge to raise it. A ladder leads to a tunnel then to the cellars of the old Jewish ghetto. Someone down there will help you."

As Antoine turned to thank her, the *grande dame* was already relocking the door and hurrying back toward the first room. Sophie and he walked between mounds of earth with thickets of thin trees and unkempt shrubs, barely aware of the magnificent three-story mansion that curved around them.

A WARTIME REMEMBRANCE - 1978

I spent much of the week going through notes and typing up articles and ideas for lectures. A vase of roses and daisies from the Domaine's garden brightened the room. A cassette tape of Louis Aragon's poems set to music and recorded by the singer Jean Ferrat provided a mellow background to the tap-tap-tap of typewriter and the *ka-ding* of the return carriage. I hummed part of a melody, written about his wife Else.

What would I be without you....la la lee la,
What would I be....hmmm...la la, la la,
La la...an hour stopped on a watch...hmm...mmm,
What would I hmm...hmm...but this stammering word.

The phone rang and an unknown voice inquired, "Claire Somerset?"

"*Hallo*," I responded.

"My name is Nathalie Prevette. I was contacted by Hervé Leblanc who gave me your number."

I responded with "*Oui.*"

"Hervé told me that you were looking for information about someone who wrote a poem during the war."

"Yes. Have you found out something about him?"

"I'm not sure. After my parents died ten years ago, I found a box with all sorts of memorabilia from the Occupation. Among this stuff was a school composition book. The initials on it are the same as on the poem's."

"That's exciting! What can you tell about him?"

"It's actually written by a woman and, unfortunately, I have no idea who she was. She only used codes and initials and they aren't familiar."

"Oh? But your parents had possession? Do you know why?" My curiosity was mounting.

"They were pack-rats and collectors. My mother worked at the hospital, the *Hotel Dieu,* during the war. I think that this stuff was either given to her or simply left behind. The box is a treasure trove of World War II mementos that I'm saving for my children: photographs, ration books, posters, postcards, letters, real and fake ID cards, a couple of STO passes, empty shell casings, military insignias, some German badges and medals, even an American soldier's cap."

"And the journal?"

"It might have been left behind by a patient. The author describes daily life during the Occupation, the hardships, and her interest in poetry." Madame Prevette lowered her voice slightly. "Although she never mentions anyone by name, people living here might be harmed if some of the incidents were known."

"I would like to take a look at it, if that is possible."

"Can you meet me tomorrow at four o'clock, at the bistro on the *Place du General de Gaulle.*"

Agreeing, I gave a quick description of myself. As I was about to ask more questions the caller abruptly stated, "I'll be wearing a light green suit. I'll see you tomorrow."

I arrived early and sat at a table across from the *Palais de Justice.* The square was busy with shoppers, students lounging with friends, workers taking an afternoon coffee and even a few tourists. A plump woman about my age, wearing a green suit, crossed the square. Her short hair was gray-flecked, reddish-blonde. I stood up and waved. Nathalie Prevette smiled and extended her hand as she arrived. We exchanged quick greetings then ordered glasses of rosé.

"This journal sounds like it could be an interesting perspective from someone who both lived here in wartime and wrote poetry. I appreciate being able to see it."

"I must admit that I was curious when Hervé, our neighbor and close friend, mentioned over dinner that someone had discovered a poem written during the war with the initials 'F.G-M.' He knew about my box of mementos as he'd looked through them before. I remembered the diary and, voila, the initials were the same."

I reached for the paper in my purse. "Here's the poem that I found."

There was a moment of silence as Madame Prevette skimmed it. "The handwriting looks identical. But this doesn't answer, who was she?"

"So there's no indication in the journal?" I inquired.

"No. I checked and the hyphenated initials of the last name don't match anyone in our phone book. She uses initials and what might be a code. Even though she doesn't name anyone specifically, except for famous poets, some people might be identifiable and certain events are sensitive and possibly inflammatory." Nathalie seemed nervous as she sipped then cradled the cup. "In general, she writes about problems faced during the war. She was fascinated by poetry and someone with the initial 'A' was tutoring her, so there's a lot about this. Then she ends up in the Resistance and has an affair with this man. However, her husband was a collaborator."

"That's a fascinating combination. Do you think that she is still here?'

"I don't know. The journal stops before the Liberation so it's hard to know exactly how things turned out." Nathalie paused, "How would you use the information?"

I repeated my standard explanation, adding, "Her comments could reinforce how people coped and the importance of wartime prose."

Her face relaxed, her eyes looked less tense. "So it would be used for academic purposes, in California. You would not reveal it to anyone in the Vaucluse, or publish it, or anything like that?"

"No. The reason for my research isn't of interest to the French. You already know about your war experiences, the poets, the various literary movements. Why do you think the information might be harmful?"

"Among other things, it appears that a family member was murdered by another. It's been many years since this happened but who knows what this could stir up. It's best that it not be made public."

Madame Prevette reached across the table and placed her hand over mine.

"You must promise me that you won't tell anyone here about it. I've often thought that I should just burn it." She sighed and looked directly at me. "We French have worked to unify over the past decades. It's not that we wanted to cover up incidences and histories from the war but our country needed to come together, to mend estrangements. This woman's stories could cause a rift in a family as well as the town, if this information was published."

I reassured my companion, "I leave in less than a week and I promise that I won't mention to anyone that I have it. If I do use any of the compromising details I'll be sure that they are disguised as fiction or are very general remarks."

Nathalie Prevette reached into the handbag at her feet and pulled out the composition book, yellowed at the edges and tied with a twist of blue yarn. She handed it to me but when I started to open it, she frowned. "Madame, please do not read it in public."

Looking around as if someone might be watching, I slipped it into my black bag on the back of the chair and asked, "Do you know much about the Resistance here?"

"Only what I learned after the war ended. Our family tried to stay out of politics at the time. My father had a shoe store that almost went out of business; my mother's job at the Hotel Dieu meant that we could get necessities. I remember always being hungry, then frightened when the bombing started." Nathalie toyed with her espresso cup. "We knew people who hid Jewish families. I suppose that our country's saving grace is that about seventy-two percent of the Jewish citizens in France survived, while the majority in other countries were killed."

"Yes, I had heard that statistic."

A half-hour passed as we talked about the war years and her childhood memories. As we finished up and shook hands, I thanked her profusely.

Nathalie Prevette again said, "You will be sure not to share the journal with anyone here in the Vaucluse?"

Once more I stated, "I promise."

Back in my room I took out the notebook. 'March 1943' was written in faded ink and the first few short lines were innocuous. The author jotted down events of the day: the problems getting food, her daughter 'G's' progress at school. Her husband was 'H.' She was learning about poetry from a man named 'A.' The notebook had terse comments about poetic phrases, ideas on what certain poems meant. Further on I found a poem called *'Temporal'* that appeared to be another one that the author had written:

> *History is written in smoke*
> > *Power is sung in stone*
> *While the sun embroiders bitterness*
> > *across a granite plain,*
> *Man considers his importance.*
> > *In fields of swords and bayonets*
> *Poppies sow their seeds and await another day.* (35)

There was an 'F' who worked in Germany and a 'G2' who worked in Cavaillon. There was mention of visiting her cousins 'J and J' in the country. When I read 'M is helping farm,' I realized that many of the initials fit people in Maurice's family. Was it possible that the 'F' was for Francois, the 'G2' for Gabrielle, the 'M' for Maurice? But the author's hyphenated initials and the 'G,' apparently her daughter, weren't any that I had heard a family member mention. Francois had been in the Resistance, not an STO labor camp. And who was 'A?' I settled down in a comfortable chair by the window and began to read the memoire from start to finish.

THE IRISHMAN
SAMUEL BECKETT

T he man with the hoe moved steadfastly, rhythmically, down a row of cabbages, chopping at pubescent weeds, up-ending worms that thrashed themselves back into the rich red-orange earth. A scrunched straw hat was pulled down almost to his ears. A faded yellow linen shirt's sleeves were rolled back to show well-muscled arms, lightly tanned. The narrow face was sharp in features: a straight nose, sunken cheek bones, furrowed brows and slim lips that turned down more in melancholy than anger. The face and posture were of an age hard to determine, possible mid-thirties, more likely early forties. His focus on his work was robotic, mechanical, as if his mind rambled far afield.

At the clanging of a bell from the clock tower in Roussillon, the man paused, leaned on the hoe's handle, removed a crumpled handkerchief from his pocket and wiped his brow. He counted the peals, cleaned his glasses and placed the hoe on his shoulder. After making his way down the row toward a garden shack he stowed the utensil and, latching the door shut, he sighed and stretched.

Walking north along the edge of the field by a copse of spindly pines, the laborer seemed to be looking for something. He stopped and snapped a head of cabbage from its stem then picked a second one. Clenching the green balls, he meandered down a road. The country lane was roughed from wheels of wagons and automobiles, splatted with manure at intervals, and varied from pale shades of ochre to throaty deep iron-reds. A short distance later he turned up another lane toward a stone farmhouse. A kind-faced woman appeared at the door, wiping her hands on her apron and came toward him.

He offered her a cabbage, softly saying only "Bonjour, Madame Aube, here's one for supper."

She nodded and went back into the house. She handed him a basket with carrots, rutabagas, an onion, and several eggs neatly tucked into a wad of moss on the bottom. He gently placed the second cabbage in it, adding a "*merci, Madame.*"

"Say *bonjour* to Madame Suzanne," she said as she turned.

"*M'bah, oui,*" he replied, as he barely doffed the brim of his hat and re-turned to march in measured cadence down the road toward the rosy tinted walls and houses that staggered up and down the curly lanes of Roussillon. By the time he entered the Hotel Escoffier bar, the workman had rolled down his shirtsleeves and combed his damp hair behind his ears. The straw hat was rolled and tucked under the handle of the basket.

"*Monsieur…,*" said amiable Madame Escoffier, proprietor and overseer of her highly respected restaurant and inn.

A nod of the head, a mumbled "*Bon soir, Madame*" trailed behind the man as he headed for a corner table where his friend Henri Hayden sat contemplating a chessboard.

Hayden looked up, "Ah, Samuel. *Bon soir.*" He looked to the side. "White or black?"

He held out clenched fists. Sam pointed to the left and a black pawn lay on Hayden's open palm. The men settled into their chairs, arranged the chessboard and were soon engrossed, with only occasional grimaces and rubbings of chins. The room filled with customers: a few old men, some couples, a family of five.

The door opened and a teen-aged boy stood silhouetted against the ripe pink of the sunset's rays against far cliffs. He looked around the room hesitantly, a battered beret in his hands, then spoke to the server behind the bar. She pointed toward the men in the corner. The young man brightened as he walked between customers to the chess table.

"Monsieur Beckett?" he inquired.

Sam looked up, frowned, annoyed at the interruption.

The boy squirmed and whispered, "I have a message from *d'Artagnan*."

Sam recognized the name of the Resistance leader, a former colonel in the French Army. Silence hung pendulum-like as he leaned back and heaved a huge sigh. The boy dug into his pocket and handed him an envelope then bowed slightly and backed away. He muttered *'Messieurs'* as he turned to leave.

Beckett slid the envelope into the pocket of his shirt then propped his elbows on the table, back to concentrating on the pieces on the board.

Henri Hayden raised his eyebrows. He knew that his friend had barely escaped capture by the Gestapo in Paris. Dozens of people in his Resistance cell had been arrested, tortured, executed or sent to concentration camps. A coded telegram from the wife of one of Sam's compatriots had alerted him and Suzanne in time for them to grab a few meager belongings and leave, three hours before the Nazis arrived. The two spent weeks moving from cheap hotels to friends' apartments. Finally Sam decided that they should leave for Provence. They made their way by train to Lyon then trudged the one hundred fifty miles to Roussillon, hiding by day, walking by night.

During the past year Samuel Beckett had tried to adapt to the measured way of life and rural viewpoints of this isolated *village perchée*, sticking its colorful head up out of verdant, gray-green foliage that surrounded it like a fox collar. He was relieved to find a friend like Hayden who provided adequate competition in chess and was interested in learning English. Miss Beamish, a plump, outspoken, erudite British spinster, discussed literature with him on occasion although her single-mindedness regarding Shakespeare had begun to rub. The Aube family's farm provided not only fresh food for his and Suzanne's table but a physical way to release his frustrations. Still, he missed the stimulating collection of the creative, passionate, intellectual companions that he had known in Paris such as Alberto Giacommetti, Salvadore Dali, Marcel Duchamps, James Joyce, Jean-Paul Sartre.

Beckett had stated that 'he preferred France in the time of war to his native Ireland in the time of peace.' Yet Hayden sensed that Sam's patience and acceptance of the situation in France was starting to wear as thin as the old shirt he currently wore. His silences betrayed the bouts of depression to which he was prone.

At the end of the game Beckett accepted Hayden's congratulations with a nod of his head.

"Another day then, Sam. My regards to Suzanne." Henri was pleased that he managed to reduce Beckett's chessmen to a few even though he lost the game.

"Sam, this is too dangerous!" Suzanne's normally mild demeanor was gone. She stared down at the letter he had handed her. "You can't consider being involved again."

"Ma chérie, they are simply asking if we will hide some munitions and weapons. Men and arms are being parachuted in constantly in preparation for the Allies arrival."

"We barely escaped once and you promised that you would not join the Resistance again." She looked on the verge of tears. "The Gestapo has stepped up raids on the *Maquis*."

Sam relied on Suzanne's common sense, her stable nature, her quiet ways. He had been attracted to her from their first meeting, when she stopped at the hospital while he was recuperating from being stabbed by a deranged Parisian pimp. That she was several years older, mature, reliable, had cemented their bond. He took the letter and returned it to his pocket.

"The Germans are losing the war and we have a chance to help, even in a small way. Let's think about this over supper." He reached over and pulled her athletic, petite body into the crook of his shoulder. "Don't get upset, don't worry."

"I was hoping that you'd finish writing *Watt.* You've made a lot of progress on the novel. Getting involved in the war...." Her voice trailed off.

Suzanne looked into the craggy face of her lover, her poetic genius, her beloved friend. She sighed, hugged him briefly, then set about putting the bowls of stew on their pine table.

The evening of June 6th, a group gathered around a radio in the back of Café Escoffier to listen to a fuzzy BBC broadcast, *Ici La France*. Cheers erupted as villagers leaned close to hear details of the Normandy invasion and General Charles de Gaulle encourage the French to fight whenever and wherever they could.

Days later a stranger knocked and asked to speak with 'a Monsieur Sam.' Suzanne shrugged her shoulders in resignation as Sam quietly said, "I will be back in a few hours."

He grabbed his jacket and followed the young *Maquisard* who called himself *Androcles*. A second man, *Petrarch*, sat in the rear of a gaz-o-gene refitted Citroen with the metal furnace partially blocking the back window. The car coughed, jerked, then gained momentum as the group settled in for the drive to St-Saturnin-les-Apt. As they drove, *Androcles* explained that a *Captain Alexandre* and his network expected a drop on the plateau. The Resistance appreciated Sam's willingness to help out since the amount of arms and munitions within the past few months had exceeded the hiding places.

Androcles and *Petrarch* talked about many successful drops and a few amazing escapes and recovered blunders.

"There was an awful accident last week, though," *Petrarch* leaned forward.

Sam looked back with a nod, encouraging him to continue.

"One of the Wellingtons bombing Avignon had been hit but was still flying. It came east toward one of our landing fields. We had dozens of men out, signaling and trying to guide it to a safe landing. Suddenly it went into a tailspin and crashed near *l'abatteur* drop site. When we got there the plane was on fire and all five aviators were dead."

Androcles, driving the car, looked over, "*Captain Alexandre* wanted everything covered up and hidden. Once the fire was out, we pulled the bodies from the wreckage and wrapped them in whatever cloth we could find. The Captain insisted that we bury the remains with military honors, so we held a whispered ceremony as we stood around the graves."

His voice trailed off. Stillness resumed. A moment later Petrarch added, "It took several days to retrieve the plane's parts and conceal them. They're under haystacks, behind woodpiles, down in basements, wherever we could find hiding places. There is no trace of wreckage at the site."

"*C'est horrible,*" Beckett murmured.

Sam was to be a lookout on a road leading to the evening's drop site. Androcles showed him how to use the rifle, how to steady it against a felled tree trunk. Had Beckett not been anticipating the trauma of shooting or being shot at, the writer would have sat contentedly on the soft grass and dead leaves for hours. Yet his ears were tuned to any odd noise: the distant rumble of a German truck, a whine from a motorcycle, any number of easily imagined horrors that might emerge from the rutted road.

The noise that he did finally hear was the hum of a plane making an incredibly slow trajectory toward the field of a farmer who had been encouraged to plow but not plant. Sam saw the airplane sweep low in the sky and circle once, then jellyfish-like items descended from below its belly. It was over within a matter of minutes. The plane's noise evaporated and silence settled.

Sam heard a low whistle and moved his stiff, damp body up the incline. Petrarch offered him a cigarette. The three men talked quietly. Within minutes a flatbed truck jostled its way toward them. Petrarch and Androcles climbed up on the back, perching on four wood boxes with black lettering. Sam swung up onto a worn leather passenger seat. At a cluster of farm buildings on a side road, the young men unloaded two of the boxes and carried them toward a barn. The truck immediately continued toward the main road.

The driver finally spoke in a dusty, guttural twang. "I've been told to drop you and your boxes at Les Cordiers. Another contact will take you home."

"My boxes, you said?"

"M'bah oui, the grenades that you're hiding for us." The driver spat out the window.

Sam thought that he might be asked to hide some rifles or handguns. He wasn't sure how to store grenades. His activities translating German troop movements from French to English when he was in Paris seemed pallid in contrast to surrounding himself and Suzanne with explosives.

He shook his head and grinned at the absurdity of the situation.

Watt *(an excerpt)*

As there seemed no measure between what Watt could understand, and what he could not, so there seemed none between what he deemed certain, and what he deemed doubtful.

"Personally of course I regret everything.
Not a word, not a deed, not a thought, not a need,
not a grief, not a joy, not a girl, not a boy,
not a doubt, not a trust, not a scorn, not a lust,
not a hope, not a fear, not a smile, not a tear,
not a name, not a face, no time, no place...that I do not regret, exceedingly.
An ordure, from beginning to end." (36)

Samuel Becket 1906 – 1989

THE VAUCLUSE - 1944

JULY 12:

Increased chatter on the radio over the previous week made it clear that the next *parachutage* was special.

"An important guest is arriving," *Centurion* told his crew.

Francois, Roland and several members of their camp had come down from camp via separate routes to the Roux's farm southwest of Sault, the 'Spitfire' drop zone. Sentries were posted nearby and on roads leading to the area—two of them were members of the local *gendarmerie,* appearing very official as they diverted cars to a lower road due to an 'accident.'

The presence of *Capitaine Alexandre* and Camille Rayon, *Archiduc,* confirmed that this was more than the usual drop of armaments.

Francois and his companions remained in the shadow of the trees as Centurion and the men greeted each other and shook hands. The three-quarter moon provided light that emphasized the shadow of every hillock. Periodically a puff of wind wafted up the fresh scent of blossoms that had dropped on an adjacent field after the recent lavender harvest. Their chief walked back to his men and pointed to their large flashlights that had arrived in a recent container.

"Be sure the lights are shining upward when the airplane is overhead. I'll give the signal with mine—three quick blinks. Then keep your lights steady as the plane comes in."

The *Maquisards* scattered around the field, swatting at insects, talking in whispers. Reacting to the sudden blinking of the flashlight, Roland and Francois turned theirs on. The reliable little Lysander swooped, banked, circled and then, instead of parachuting its cargo, dropped down to land. As it rolled up near the end of the field, Camille Rayon and René Char raced out to greet the man who jumped out. They led him to the safety of shadows at the edge of a copse of trees as the flashlights flickered off.

"Welcome, mon ami," *Archiduc* greeted de Gaulle's emissary, Commander Gonzague Corbin de la Mangoux. "We are looking forward to working with you as we prepare for our liberation."

Corbin de la Mangoux shook their hands. "It won't be long. Another group arrives in four or five days to work with the Free French and the *Maquis Ventoux*."

"Another field will be used for that plane," *Capitaine Alexandre* stated. "So far our parachute sites have never been compromised. The Germans have not been able to track where we will be next."

"Ah, *Capitaine*, I understand that General de Gaulle is very impressed with your coordination of the drops in this area. Apparently that is why he wants to talk with you about directing the final delivery of arms and men from his headquarters in Corsica."

When Char had been informed a few days before that he was to leave, he was not happy. He complained to Camille Rayon that he wanted to be with the Maquisards when troops arrived to liberate Provence.

"I must stay with my men!" he repeated to his friend.

Archiduc tried to reassure him that the exact date of the Allied arrival could be weeks away. It was possible that he would be back before then. Char designated a second in command, doubtful that he'd return in time.

In the moonlight the poet looked sullen as he said, "*D'Artagnan* is anxious to find out how the Maquisards can help. The Commander needs to leave immediately and I shouldn't make the pilot wait any longer."

Archiduc shook his hand, patted him on his shoulder. "René, have a safe trip. I'm sure that we will see each other again soon."

Francois and Roland hunkered down and watched the shadowy figures in conversation near the wing of the plane. As *Capitaine Alexandre* moved toward the open door Francois muttered to his companion.

"Why do you suppose Monsieur Char is leaving?"

Roland squinted as he followed the plane's bumpy progress across the field. "Maybe de Gaulle can't invade without his help. We just do as we're told. Hey! There's the signal!"

Flashlights went on once again as the *Lizzie* turned and roared its way across the uneven plain, rolled abruptly into the sky, wiggled its wings and began to climb.

Capitaine Alexandre looked down to see a line of bright lights waving at distances along a mountain path. His comrades, his friends were signaling their goodbye and good wishes. He added to his journal:

> *Refractaires, my comrades,*
> *Today you are numerous and each day you increase in numbers.*
> *All the forests in France where you conceal yourselves will soon be opening to let you through, you and your victorious army of free men! The enemy fears you. You must not disappoint him. However, do not be imprudent in offering yourselves to him. We must be the last to live and fight against him to the end.*
> *Refractaires, I am not anxious about anything. I have confidence in you. (37)*

JULY 16:

Gabrielle Laurent began to see the handwriting 'writ large on the wall' since the Normandy invasion. Dietrich hadn't been around for three weeks. Madame Moreau told her that he was directing raids on terrorist groups up on the mountain. Gabrielle almost sent him a note but thought that he might not like something in writing between the two of them.

One minute, tears piled on her eyelids. The next, she spoke sharply to a shopkeeper, angry with anyone who contributed to her world falling apart. The atmosphere at the town hall and mayor's office was so full of tension that the air fairly crackled. One difficult day Gabrielle came very close to telling Madame Moreau that she was 'a nasty old cow.'

She did go to the guard at the door and said in a hushed voice, "If you ever leer at me or make another snide remark again I'll send a letter to the Gestapo denouncing you for every charge I can think up."

From then on he and the other two men who sniggered at his side ignored her.

In early June, after the invasion, a lonely Gabrielle had gone to mass at the Romanesque cathedral in the center of town. The ritual calmed her and she kept returning. On the previous Sunday almost every seat was filled, the majority by a subdued congregation, only a few by Germans. A hollow-eyed priest with gray-white hair repeated in a strained voice a message from Psalms on 'hope.' Each person could interpret it to suit their own situation: *I will not fear the tens of thousands drawn up against me on every side.*

When she opened the psalm book, a folded, well-worn copy of *Combat* glided into her hand and she slipped it into her purse. When she read it later, the news was very different than that in the Vichy newspapers. It appeared that the Allies were doing well. Reports on reprisals by Germans stunned Gabrielle; she had trouble believing that they could possibly be true. With a sinking feeling, she remembered Dietrich's story about catching 'terrorists.' She had recently overheard someone at the weekly market state that a woman had been shot in front of her young children and her mother for giving food to a man thought to be in the Maquis.

She wrote a long letter to her parents, finally admitting that her situation was precarious. She wanted to come home but Madame Moreau needed her to purge files and rewrite documents incriminating the city administration. She longed for *maman's* understanding, *papa's* protectiveness. Gabrielle read over the letter then set it aside. She knew that censors would delete any mention of destroying records let alone her desire to leave.

Instead, her second letter was reassuring: her health was fine; during bombing raids she stayed in a shelter; she was going to mass; she couldn't come home because the city hall was 'very busy.' She missed them all. How were Clotilde and Primo? Had Francois been given time off from his STO work? How tall was Maurice?

The sound of the air raid siren began wailing its mournful song and Gabrielle folded the second letter and put it inside an envelope. Tucking it in her purse, she grabbed a sweater and headed down the stairs toward the apartment's cellar. Subjected to the glares and mutters of her co-dwellers she muttered back 'jealous old cats' then turned around and went back upstairs. Throwing her purse angrily into a corner, she dropped into the chair near the window.

Gabrielle picked up the book of Guillaume Apollinaire's poetry that she had found in the desk of her room. Over the past months she had read then reread the poems in the well-worn, cream-colored paperback book. She had to agree that his images were sometimes strange, yet somehow the words became soothing and made sense at a deeper level. Her cheeks felt hot and her vision blurred as she tried to focus on one titled 'One Evening' that seemed to fit her situation.

An eagle descended from this heaven, white from archangels
And you sustain me
Will you let all these lamps shake a long time
Pray, pray for me
The town is metallic and it is the single star
Drowning in your blue eyes
As the tramways roll gushing from pale fires
Upon mangy, dirty birds... (38)

First came the roar and vibration of rows of planes, then distant 'whumps' amid gunfire. The targets seemed to be along the Durance River, south of the town, or behind the rock hill that served as a natural fortification for Cavaillon. They all would be sorry, she snuffled, if this house was hit, and she fantasized how she might be mourned.

JULY 20:

For over a month Florence stifled her feelings of betrayal and shock. She forced herself to act as if she'd never learned about Henri's 'indiscretion.' She swallowed her anger, becoming even more reticent, methodically plodding through daily routines. Not showing emotions, she realized, was how she had survived in the marriage for as long as she had. Life went on as before: breakfast, lunch, supper, cleaning the house, standing for hours in lines, knitting, listening to Henri's tirades without reacting. Henri's temperament appeared to be fraying at the edges, his comments were sharper, his criticisms more barbed. He continued his pattern of going to meetings and rehearsals, Florence as acquiescent and silent as usual.

She had last seen Antoine on July 3 and couldn't understand why he hadn't sent her a message. They had met at the museum that Monday morning while Henri and his friends in the Milice sat in a cafe, reassuring each other that the Allied invasion would fail. She had left at eleven then waited in line for bread and prepared lunch as usual. The following week the building was locked tightly. Again this past week, it was closed. Antoine had not contacted her and neither had Sister Monique.

The Milice and Brandenburg Division's attacks on *Maquis* in the Vaucluse were happening on an almost daily basis. Several groups of two or four and as many as eight, had been shot in the vicinity around Carpentras during the past week. Everyone knew about the massacres at Valreas and Oradour-sur-Glane. Most also knew of the successes of the Resistance in attacking German convoys and individual patrols. Although the Allies had not yet arrived, the Vaucluse was already a war zone.

On Tuesday Florence went to the almost deserted library. As she walked by Madame Poitier, the woman was wringing her hands, tapping her fingers. Florence risked asking if the janitor had cleaned the room as it seemed dustier than usual.

The librarian went wide-eyed and stammered in a whisper, "Oh, Madame! Last week the Milice ransacked my house because Monsieur Dupont was my tenant. They didn't find anything incriminating, but he hasn't been seen since. Both he and his daughter have disappeared."

She looked around and leaned forward. "I was terrified that I would be arrested! I think that I would have been if Monsieur Caillet, the library director, hadn't convinced them that I was a pacifist and would never do anything unprofessional!"

"How awful for you!" She stood for a moment, a book in her hand.

"Do you want to check that out, Madame?"

"*Non, non, merci.* I'll put it in the box to be re-shelved."

Florence walked out slowly then all but ran to the Café of the 19th Century. The front square crawled with Germans, appearing to Florence like dull green maggots rummaging in rotting meat. *Maxmillian* was wiping the bar. The room was smoky, hot and zapped with tension. Florence stepped up and ordered a coffee. As he placed it in front of her, she looked through her purse for coins and mumbled, "*L'Imprimeur,* has he been arrested?"

René Dulfour gathered the coins and seemed to be checking them, then whispered. "No. He has gone underground." More loudly he said, "*Merci, Madame.* Have a nice day."

AUGUST 5:

A second Allied invasion of France along the Mediterranean coast was expected within days. Commander Corbin de la Mangoux told Colonel Philippe Beyne to contact the Maquis Ventoux groups and instruct them to attack German troops, destroy their weapons, block escape routes and eliminate the enemy wherever possible. The Maquis were to find safe positions, hit hard and disappear quickly. No action was to take place with three miles of a town for fear of reprisals against innocent citizens.

Germans still controlled the strategic town of Sault where six roads formed a junction leading up into the lower Alps and down toward the Durance Valley. Part of the German 19th armored division, also called Group Kniess, patrolled the D543 and D542 attempting to keep the roads clear so that, if needed, troops could retreat and regroup in the northeast.

Colonel Beyne contacted the *Maquis Vasio* in Vaison-la-Romaine for reinforcements. On August 4 a dozen Maquisards under the direction of a Capitaine

Bourcart attacked a patrol near St.-Saturnin-les-Apt, a few miles north of Apt. They positioned a machine gun on a point overlooking a narrow pass, killed two men, wounded five and took four as prisoners. No Maquisards were hurt.

Further up that route, close to the 15th century fortified Chateau de Javon, five *Maquis Ventoux* members attacked a German patrol on bicycles. Two officers were killed and four were taken prisoner. When interrogated, one of the prisoners confessed that a division of three hundred soldiers would arrive from Sault within the next two days, specifically to eliminate terrorists.

On August 5 Centurion selected Androcles, Petrarch, Baptiste, Pedro--a Spanish Republican--and Rougie--a Jewish merchant from Toulon--for a special mission. They left their camp in a forested area on the Albion Plateau and drove west in a gazogène car that had been requisitioned from the owner, who was happy with the amount of francs that he'd received. They parked three miles from Saint Christol and made their way to a rendezvous point. After midnight they met *Robert* and a Russian code-named *Ivan* from the *Maquis Vasio*. A ninth man, *Le Gris*, knew the terrain well and led without hesitation in the near dark, crossing fields, avoiding houses, following goat paths and climbing rocky trails. The trek was fifteen circuitous miles, with each man carrying a heavy weapon and sacks of grenades.

A shepherd familiar with the area had recommended an ambush site above a road that zigzagged between two rocky precipices four miles west of St.-Saturnin-les Apt. At the south end, the twisting road crossed two damaged bridges in the deep gorge. At the other end, a promontory overlooked the canyon.

Arriving the morning of August 6, Centurion placed himself, Androcles and Rougie at the north end where the gorge narrowed and started its convoluted route. One hundred feet further down the ridge were Petrarch, Baptiste and Pedro. Le Gris, Ivan and Robert settled above the bridges. Robert reviewed instructions: as little movement as possible, no talking above a whisper and don't let sun reflect off the guns.

Androcles and Rougie slept a few hours while Centurion kept watch. Then the two younger men stood guard while their chief snoozed. As it became hotter the men hunkered under shrubs, trees or a rock outcrop. They pulled food from backpacks, crept into the forest to relieve themselves, kept conversation muted and sporadic. Several had paperback books.

Androcles had borrowed a well-thumbed book from Rougie, the novel 'Nadja' by André Breton, illustrated with artistic photographs. It had been published in 1928 and filled the time, even if it caused him to pause and try to figure out exactly what the author meant. The story was about a poor but beautiful young woman with whom the writer becomes obsessed during the ten days that he meets with her. The author compared perceived reality, memory, dreams and the meaning of life, along with detailed descriptions of Paris. Francois didn't understand it all but it removed him from the boredom of waiting for a battle:

> 'In order to create a diversion I ask her 'where does she eat.'
> And suddenly there is this lightness that I have only seen in her,
> this seemingly virtual freedom, "Where (her finger points) but there,
> or there (the two closest restaurants), where I am, you see.
> It's always thus."
> At the point of my taking leave of her, I want to ask her a question that sums
> up all the others, a question that only I can ask, without any doubt:
> "Who are you?"
> And she, without hesitating, says, "I am the wandering soul." ' (39)

At five o'clock that evening the enemy finally appeared. A large open-topped Mercedes with four officers and a driver rode at the head of a column of trucks covered by gray-green tarps.

The Maquisards slid to the edge of the cliffs. As soon as the Mercedes was directly under their position, Centurion's group tossed grenades into it, twenty-five feet below. Others threw grenades on the trucks. Explosions vibrated off the canyon walls, bevies of birds shot into the sky, bodies tumbled onto the road. As soldiers poured from the vehicles and pointed rifles toward the assailants, machine gun fire stopped them before they could focus. When some tried to escape toward the front, Le Gris, Ivan and Robert herded them back into the canyon with bursts of bullets. Centurion, Androcles and Rougie did the same at the other end. Several Germans lay under the trucks; others hid behind rocks and trees and shot blindly toward the cliff tops.

Shooting continued off and on for an hour then diminished. The Maquis moved their positions to make it look like there were more men. For a time there was no movement, then four soldiers jumped up and sprayed bullets into the shrubbery where they'd last seen gunfire. The *Maquis* leapt forward and rained grenades once more into the ravine.

Quiet returned and no one moved for at least thirty minutes then several Nazis crept behind the trucks toward the burnt Mercedes and fired up at the promontory where Centurion and his companions crouched. Grenades tossed over the edge killed them. Two other Germans suddenly stood up behind a large rock and shot toward the ridge.

As Francois scrambled away, a bullet cut through his left leg. He groaned and rolled over, grabbing his knee. Rougie pointed his machine gun downwards and held the trigger, keeping his head low. Centurion wriggled toward Francois and pulled him back from the edge. He took a cloth from a backpack and wrapped a tourniquet above the knee, then handed it to Francois to grip. Centurion crawled over and joined Rougie in a rapid spray of gunfire. Once again quiet returned except for the squawks of birds wheeling off to safer perches.

Fighting went on sporadically until sunset. The Maquis constantly herded their prey back into the canyon when they tried to escape. The trapped dodged about, looking for shelter, less and less inclined to fight. At dusk Centurion crouch-walked to where Roland and Michel were lying near the edge of the ridge, saying that it was time to go.

Roland crawled over to Francois. "How bad is it?"

Francois was surprised that, after the initial intense pain, the wound seemed almost numb. The tourniquet had stopped the hemorrhaging; the blood on his pant leg was dry around the edges.

"I can't feel much, Roland, and it's not bleeding anymore."

Roland pulled a knife from the scabbard on his belt.

"Let me take a look. We'll bandage it before we start back."

He hacked at the pants leg as Francois grimaced. Below the kneecap was a hole with torn flesh where the bullet had exited.

"Turn over so I can see if there's more damage." Roland helped his friend onto his side and looked closely. "It's a clean wound, but I think that the bullet nicked your bone. I'll get the first-aid kit and bandage it."

A sudden burst of machine gun fire from Rougie's position lit up the bushes around him. Return fire came very close and he backed off with a resounding, "Whew!"

"Hey! Use a grenade, jerk!" Roland snapped. "They can pinpoint us if we use guns in the dark."

Roland took a kit from one of the backpacks, swabbed Francois' knee with iodine and wrapped gauze arund the wound. He used branches from a shrub as splints and wound them with torn cloth. Francois moaned as his leg was straightened.

Robert appeared a few feet away, barely visible in the dusk. "Let's go, guys. Toss a couple and then leave."

Rougie popped two pins and threw the grenades. He grabbed his gun, ducked and ran to Roland and Francois. Roland handed Francois' gun and backpack to Rougie.

"Put your arm over my shoulder, come on."

Francois groaned as he put weight on his leg. *Le Gris* walked over and grabbed him under his other arm as he whispered, "*Zut alors*, let's get going."

The fighters made their way down to a creek curving around a hill. Francois with his two human crutches did not hinder the retreat at first but when they reached a steep path it was clear that he could not keep up.

"Our friend at the Chateau de Javon helps Colonel Beyne and will hide you until we can take you someplace safe," Centurion murmured to Francois.

The friend, Claude Pissaro-Bonin, was the grandson of the painter Camille Pissaro and conservator of the nearly empty chateau that was miraculously ignored by the Germans. Although the main rooms appeared poorly furnished, art works from the Louvre Museum in Paris and the Calvet Museum in Avignon were hidden in deep cellars.

Baptiste replaced Le Gris as a crutch. The Maquis Vasio group--Robert, Le Gris, Ivan--along with Pedro and Rougie were to head back and send someone with the car. Centurion arranged to meet them one kilometer from the castle. The men parted after shaking hands, expressing gratitude for each having made the mission successful.

After an hour of hobbling along with frequent stops, the enormous hulk of the chateau was a welcome sight. It loomed large in the dark with its turrets and corner towers, its neatly cut, austere stones. Leaving the others, Centurion checked to see if Germans were in the vicinity. He slid along a wall up to an arch with the bust of a smiling lady above it, opened an iron gate leading into a neglected garden and headed for a narrow door. He pulled on a ring jutting from a stone and waited until a wood covering behind a tiny grated square moved.

A voice whispered, "Who is it?"

"A woodpecker with acorns for the squirrels."

"How many?" the voice retorted.

"One, with a damaged shell. I need to retrieve it."

Francois was carried the last hundred feet then hopped through a door to a low tunnel. He was introduced to a man in his twenties, stocky, dark curly hair and a wide smile.

"*Androcles,*" Centurion gestured, "*Monsieur le Prince.*"

Claude Bonin-Pissarro peered at him in the dim light of a single candle placed in a metal holder on the wall. "*Enchanté.* Can you walk at all?"

Francois took a step, cried out and grabbed his companions.

Centurion sighed. "Where do you want him to wait?"

"Probably the storeroom down the hallway is the best spot. I don't anticipate problems but you never know."

"Baptiste and I will get the car and be back in an hour. Petrarch, you stay and help."

Bonin-Pissaro said, "The sooner you return, the better."

Centurion and Petrarch walk-hopped Francois to another doorway that their host unlocked. They helped him lie prone on a row of wood boxes inside the nearly empty storeroom.

"Does your leg need medical attention?" Their host looked closely at Francois. "You seem to be in pain."

Francois nodded, his lips pinched, his eyes squinting.

"It's been wiped with iodine and bandaged with a makeshift splint, but it should be bandaged professionally." Petrarch spoke.

"I have a kit with some morphine that I can give him." Bonin-Pissaro turned to Centurion, "There is a patrol that comes by at midnight. They snoop around but don't bother me. I've told the officers in Sault that I live in the back turret and can't hear anything. But please, do hurry up!"

Centurion and Baptiste backed the car cautiously through the garden gate, narrowly missing the pillars on either side. Francois stood at the castle's open door, supported by Roland and Claude.

"Hi, guys," Francois mumbled.

"Hi yourself. How are you feeling?"

"Pretty good, pretty good." He looked unfocused.

"Um-hmm. All right then, let's get you to the car."

"Where we going?" Francois slurred.

"We've decided to take you home."

A crooked smile formed on his lips. "Yeah, that's a good idea."

His friends knew of the secret cellar at the *Domaine* and agreed that this would be the best place for him. Francois was helped into the car's rear foot well, his back against the door, his leg propped on a sack of charcoal. Baptiste sat with his machine gun out the side window. Petrarch crouched in the back, his gun pointing between the cylinders of the gaz-o-gene engine.

Centurion eased out of the gate, lights off, then drove slowly to a turn-off. It took two hours of winding through the *Forets de Lambert*, around the desolate hamlet of Methamis and almost haltingly on farm paths to the Laurent's. Primo greeted them with ferocious barking, following the car as it crunched to the house. A pale light from the front door silhouetted Jean-Pierre. Baptiste jumped and ran through the arch and the light went off. Juliette appeared, wrapping a housecoat around her. When she heard the news she ran in bare feet to a haggard, unshaven, thin replica of the young man she had last seen.

Maurice was the last to arrive, whispering loudly, "Is Francois all right? Is he all right?"

Centurion, Petrarch and Maurice eased Francois out of the back and carried him into the house. Juliette and Jean-Pierre pulled out the items on the cellar's trap door and raised it up. Francois cried out as he was carried down and placed on the mattress at the back of the cave, his mother hovering over him. The two Maquis disappeared up the cellar steps, raced to the car and headed toward a safe house in Malaucene.

Jean-Pierre was closing the front door when Amélie arrived in the kitchen. "What's wrong?"

"Francois has been shot and is in the cellar."

Amélie ran to the door and called his name, starting down the steps.

Juliette spoke sharply, "Amélie! Francois is wounded and I need for you to take care of him. Get dressed. Bring some of his clothes as well as changes for yourself. You may have to stay down here for several days. Be quiet! I don't want Gigi to wake up and know that he is here!"

AUGUST 6:

One-hundred-and-eighty Allied bombers arrived, coming in six successive waves, targeting Avignon then areas to the north and east. Once again, the roar of four-engine B-24 *Liberators* and the piercing wails of air raid alarms melded with the rat-tat-tatting of anti-aircraft. Townspeople and country folk raced to cellars and shelters. Ancient walls shook and tumbled; dust and smoke filled the air. Frightened animals--cattle, horses, goats, sheep, dogs, cats--ran in panic as the earth exploded around them. Many did not survive.

Objectives were the railroad lines south of the City of the Popes, the viaduct over the Rhone, then the Gauloise and Saint-Gobain factories to the north, a gasoline refinery near Sorgues, the airfields and hangers between Orange and Carpentras. One bomb was dropped off course in a wooded, slightly hilly area southeast of Carpentras' *Centre Ville* where it left a large hole.

The following day, another wave hammered strategic facilities in the same areas. Sure that the worst was over, people ventured forth cautiously on August 8 only to be greeted once again with the shriek of alarms, the sounds of explosions. Forty-seven civilians were killed and ninety-three were wounded in Avignon and Orange.

A LITTLE KNOWLEDGE - 1978

As much as I was attracted to Maurice it was clear that our relationship was a minefield of problems. His sister's coldness was causing an
uncomfortable rift. Gabrielle's friend Yvette was a much better match. My
family and career obligations were in California. And I'd discovered a family
secret that could unlock a Pandora's box of trouble.

From what I'd deduced so far, 'B1, B2, B3 and B4' possibly referred to the
Bertolini family, as they had a bakery and B3 was in a POW camp. B4 had told
'F' that her husband was gay. The daughter referred to as 'G' in the journal
might be a nickname for Maurice's wife, Brigitte. Had Brigitte's mother managed to keep both her activities in the Resistance and her affair a secret? Did
anyone in the family know about the murder? I alternated between curiosity
and unease at the possibility of learning more about the Laurents and putting
together the puzzle.

Maurice and I spoke several times after the awkward Sunday lunch but
avoided mentioning it. He was preoccupied by the harvest and monitoring the
wine; I listened and didn't say much, constantly flashing on what I'd learned
from the journal.

After Madame Laurent left to spend the weekend at Gabrielle's on Friday
evening, I biked out to the farm. As we ate supper, I made a point of chattering about a film that Sophie and I had seen, rehashed a bit of our nice time
at the Dupré's, commented on the weather. I gave a rundown on what his

brother Francois told me about his experience in the *Maquis Ventoux*, when we had met mid-week. Maurice had not been able to come, due to supervising the winemaking.

As we sat together on the salon's couch after dinner, Maurice asked how my project was going. I reached into my bag and brought out a copy of the poem with F. G-M's initials, my heart beat accelerating.

"It's going well. I'm uncovering more examples of wartime poetry. I found an anonymous poem written during the war by someone who evidently was from Carpentras. It's nice, don't you think?"

I handed a copy of it to him and stared as he read it over in a desultory way. At the end, his eyes widened and he exclaimed, "*Mon dieu!* These are the initials of my wife's mother!"

Ka-ching! The knot in my stomach was not from the *potiron* squash soup and croque-monsieurs that we'd eaten.

"Oh, really? You never mentioned that she was a poet."

"I never knew. Where did you find this?"

"It was inside a book that I found in the library."

"My memories of her aren't particularly vivid. She was quiet and rarely offered an opinion. We were all very upset and sad when she died but, you know, it was wartime. There were a lot of other things going on."

"So, as far as you know, she didn't publish her works?"

'No, I had no idea that she even wrote poems." He shook his head in amazement. "I'm sure that my children would like to have this as a memento of their grandmother. Would you mind?"

"You're welcome to it, Maurice. So, what was her name?" I pointed to the 'F.G-M.'

"Florence Gilles-Martin. How amazing! There's an album with a picture of her somewhere. I think it's in a trunk in the attic. Would you like to see it?"

"Sure!"

Maurice ran up the stairs and was back within fifteen minutes, carrying a small well-worn album. He sat on the couch and squinted at the tattered, disintegrating cover. 'Gigi' was handwritten in black ink on brown suede.

"Gigi?" I asked innocently.

"That was Brigitte's nickname when she was little." Maurice seemed pensive. "This album was special to her since she didn't have many pictures of her parents. I hadn't thought of it for years."

The scallop-edged faded photos mounted on black paper showed a chubby-cheeked toddler in a lacy bonnet and crocheted sweater, then a child with long braids and a sweet oval face, up to a mid-teenaged girl in a school uniform. I told Maurice that I thought that she was pretty. He looked sad when he nodded and said 'yes.'

There were several photos of Gigi-Brigitte with her mother, a dark-haired, petite and wide-eyed woman. Her mother's expression came across as someone constantly surprised or frightened. Her father was much taller than his wife, slim, well dressed, mustached, stiff, usually with a hat on his head or in hand. Handwritten notes in white ink indicated dates, places and *'Maman et Gigi,'* or *'Papa et Gigi.'*

"What was her father's name?"

"Henri Gilles-Martin. He was from the Alsace-Lorraine region."

He put the album on the shelf then sat down and hugged my stiff shoulders. "Who knew what your research on poets would turn up! What an amazing coincidence."

What I'd just confirmed knocked me sideways. I could barely stretch my lips into a semblance of a smile. After a brief kiss, Maurice turned back to reading the newspaper, still smiling. I reached for a book on the table in front of me. *French Gardens of the Late 19th Century* was full of tiny print and unfocused photographs and I stared at it, unseeing.

The romantic afterglow under which I'd basked was fading as I faced the fact that I did not really know Maurice well. I'd never met his daughter. His sister and her family clearly were not welcoming. This euphoric interlude had been just that, and it was time that I acknowledge that our affair had been delightful but would not last beyond this fall.

When I looked at him I thought, 'Did you know about the murder? That your uncle was a homosexual! That your mother-in-law's lover was a Jew?

What would you say if you knew that I knew all this? What other secrets is your family hiding?'

Maurice folded the paper and stretched out his arms. His eyes looked tired although he smiled as he said, "*Ma chérie*, I think that it's time for bed. I'm going to have to take you home before noon tomorrow with all that's going on."

We held hands and silently walked upstairs.

THE VAUCLUSE – 1944

AUGUST 8, TUESDAY:

The Maquis under Commanders Grangeon and Beyne constantly blocked the roads toward the Alps that German troops wanted to use as escape routes if an Allied invasion along the Mediterranean coast was successful. Grangeon reported back to de Gaulle that, under Beyne's guidance, the *Maquis Ventoux* was among the best trained and well equipped of all the Resistance groups.

On August 8th a cyclist in civilian clothes suspected of being a *Milicien* was stopped, interrogated and imprisoned in a tower of the Chateau de Javon. He finally admitted that another German column stationed in Apt was leaving that night in an attempt to reinforce the troops in Sault. Members of the Maquis Ventoux, joined by a number of FFI soldiers, once again lay in wait on a hill above a deep ravine four miles south of the chateau, not far from the successful attack on August 5th.

Lying on their stomachs, camouflaged by wispy bushes and piles of rocks, the sweaty partisans patiently lounged at the edge of spindly pines and oaks in the *Foret de Lambert*. Exhaustion from long treks and earlier assaults showed on their faces. They had twenty machine guns and rucksacks full of grenades, received from nearly continuous drops of arms around the mountain.

A doctor from Sault took first watch. At one o'clock in the morning, he alerted the group that a German column was arriving, preceded by six combat groups. As soon as the column reached the south end of the ravine, the Maquis and FFI bombarded the trucks and staff cars below them. Twelve minutes later they retreated, leaving a reported two hundred and fifty dead Germans. Six of their men were wounded and all survived.

AUGUST 10, THURSDAY:

Bombing raids to the west of town during the previous three days had been terrifying. Florence flinched each time she heard the sound of low flying planes passing overhead. When an air raid siren sounded she and Henri joined their neighbors and rushed down to the apartment building's cellars. They huddled in sweaters, surrounded by cold stone and the dim light of candles and oil lamps, speculating on what was happening. Florence tried to find a spot as far from Henri as she could, and took her knitting to keep her hands busy and her mind occupied.

Knowing of Henri's involvement with Erik Ziegler and not finding Antoine made her stomach clench, her appetite diminish, her desire for wine increase. Had there been an unlimited supply she would have drowned her emptiness in bottle after bottle. She began drinking an extra glass as she worked in the kitchen, then watering what she served to her husband.

Standing in queues for food became a welcome pastime instead of a chore. She ironed and then re-ironed clothing at a board set up in Gigi's empty room. She began reading, or simply holding, books with tiny print that had lain dustily on Henri's bookshelf. A raised eyebrow was his only reaction. He didn't want to talk either and left after supper almost every night, trailing a criticism of something she'd done before closing the door.

Their one joint effort was making the trip every week or ten days to see Gigi. The first Sunday the Laurents invited them for lunch. Jean-Pierre and Henri had been cool but polite and the visit delighted Gigi. However, since then Juliette had asked that they meet in the nearby village of Aubignon. Henri was irritated, but Florence reminded him that Jean-Pierre and Maurice had to work harder due to Francois being in Germany. They were probably in the fields every day, including Sundays. Henri's mustache twitched.

On August 4 she and Juliette met at Friday morning's very reduced weekly market. Juliette suggested that they come to the farm sometime after lunch the following Sunday. However, the morning of August 6ᵗʰ was the first of a series of six successive and massive bombing raids targeting the triangular area between Avignon, Orange and Carpentras. The Gilles-Martins retreated to the apartment's cellar and did not feel safe the rest of the day. Then again, on Monday and Tuesday, the region was under attack. At the end of the raids, forty-seven civilians had been killed; niney-three wounded. Several planes were shot down. Florence mentioned that perhaps they should go stay at the Domaine but Henri said 'no,' there was no need.

When Thursday appeared eerily calm Florence sent a message by courier that they would come for a brief visit in the afternoon. Henri looked smug when he announced that his friend Obersleutnant Ziegler, the pianist, had arranged for a driver and car to take them, upon learning that they were visiting their daughter and relatives. Florence bit her lips, her head dipped, her stomach tightened. She did not respond to the driver's greeting and remained silent as the car sped along, Henri chattering away in German.

After being deposited at the pillared entrance, Henri took off his jacket and fanned himself with his hat. Striding up the driveway, he snapped at Florence, "Hurry up! We can't keep Gigi waiting."

Florence, two steps behind and keeping pace, gritted her teeth. Gigi stood under an apricot tree near the house, her face pink from the heat.

She ran to them, calling, "*Maman! Papa!*"

She hugged and kissed each of them. "I'm so glad that you are safe. You must be awfully hot and tired. Cousin Juliette has some cold cider and I made some *petites tartes*. You'll love them."

Both Florence and Henri showed relief at her youthful joy. She looked healthier and plumper after two months with her cousins. They held hands, with Gigi bouncing happily between them. Florence was amazed at how well her pubescent daughter handled her father's questions as he basked in her attention. She talked about farm life: collecting eggs from the chickens, watching chicks as they hatched, riding Clotilde around the pasture, helping Cousin Juliette with canning.

Jean-Pierre and Juliette met them at the archway and guided them toward a table and chairs that were placed under a fig tree on the road to the wine barn. Florence was somewhat surprised as it would have been cooler inside the house. She saw Henri frown and start to say something but he shrugged and walked over to the table, fanning himself dramatically.

Neither Juliette nor Jean-Pierre looked good. Their eyes were bloodshot, squinty, fatigued; their mouths looked strained. Florence thought that it was probably the extra work and Henri's presence didn't help.

A farmyard cat had had kittens and Gigi was anxious to show them to her mother and father. She grabbed their hands and they followed her quick stride toward the barn.

"You're not bringing home a kitten," Henri admonished as they walked away, although he was smiling.

Juliette turned to Jean-Pierre. "I still think that we should have either told them not to come or met them at the village."

"We've discussed this, Juliette. Henri might have become suspicious if we did that, but we need to encourage them to leave as soon as possible. I'll emphasize that I have to work in the fields today."

"I hope that they don't ask to stay because of the raids, let alone come inside."

Jean-Pierre ran his fingers up both sides of his head. "They can use the toilet downstairs but if Henri starts nosing around, we'll have to keep him from leaving, tie him up and put him in the old animal shelter. You can work something out with Florence."

"You're right, dear." Juliette looked grim. "I'll go get Gigi's burnt tarts. Maurice also needs to join us and talk about the work that you have to do."

"Fine. I'll use a 'wine thief' and let them do some tasting of the recent vintage. This is one time that I won't mind if Henri has too much to drink."

AUGUST 11, FRIDAY:

A Wehrmacht group on patrol near Sault heard an Allied plane circling and circling, apparently looking for one of the drop zones. London had not sent the coded message in time and no beacons had lit up 'spitfire,' the field where René Char's plane had landed when flying him to Corsica. Using tracking devices, the Germans were able to determine the exact area and, at dawn on August 11, they arrived at the farm of Gustave Roux.

Awakened by trucks roaring down their road, Roux and four other Maquis fled the farmhouse for the woods. They were gunned down and died as they reached the tangled vines of the underbrush. The house and outbuildings were set afire.

When the message was relayed to Corsica, the poet slammed his fist against a wall and swore. It was the first time that any of the drop zones under *Capitaine Alexandre* had been compromised.

AUGUST 13, SUNDAY:

Jean-Pierre Laurent emerged from a cloudy, ambiguous half dream and opened eyes that registered total blackness. He blinked. It wasn't a dream after all. He heard Primo barking and whining downstairs. Juliette bolted upright next to him.

"*Mon dieu*," she whispered. "What now?"

Simultaneously they jumped up, shoved feet into slippers, grabbed wraps and raced for the bedroom door. As they reached the landing, pounding began on the front door and they could hear men running and shouting on the kitchen terrace behind the house. Juliette looked out the back window.

"*Sacre bleu*, Jean-Pierre. It's the Milice!"

Gigi stood at the door, terrified. "*Tante Juliette*, what is happening?"

Juliette walked over to her, hugging her closely. "We don't know, dear. Jean-Pierre is going to find out."

The pounding increased and an angry voice shouted, "Open up! Open up! Now!"

Jean-Pierre switched on the downstairs light and strode to the front door, holding Primo's collar. He turned the iron key in the old lock and twisted a knob on a modern bolt. "*J'arrive! J'arrive!*"

The door opened abruptly as three Milice and a German officer barged in, pistols in hand. One man turned his gun to Primo, who snarled in a crouch as Jean-Pierre held his collar. Two shots rang out and the dog's body fell to the floor. Behind the four men already inside, half-a-dozen others stood outside brandishing rifles and waiting for orders.

"Jean-Pierre Laurent, I arrest you on behalf of the Third Reich for treason against the state," the Milice chief pointed a pistol directly in his face.

One of his aides took out handcuffs. He shoved Jean-Pierre against the wall and told him to place his hands at his back. The German motioned to the rest of the men and directed them to start searching the house. He turned to Jean-Pierre.

"Who else is here?"

"My wife and our cousin. That's all!"

The officer strode to the staircase. "Come down immediately!"

Juliette and Gigi walked slowly down, arm in arm. When one of the Milice started toward them with a rifle they stepped more quickly to the hall. At the sight of Primo, Juliette sighed 'oh, non.' Gigi turned her head.

The troops turned on lights in the other rooms and four of them pounded up the stairs, turning on more lights, slamming doors. The family could hear the sounds of cupboards opening and contents being dumped onto floors.

"Take the women into the kitchen and guard them!"

Juliette recognized the son of the optician in town. A few years back he had assisted his father when Juliette was fitted with reading glasses. He seemed uncomfortable, awkward, as he motioned with his rifle and mumbled, "Get into the kitchen," with an added, "Madame."

Another man, older, a scar on his cheek, followed and pointed his rifle directly at Juliette then Gigi. "If you move, you'll be shot!"

Clinging to each other, the women backed up against a wall facing the sink. Gigi shook, tears streaming down her cheeks, sobbing so quietly that Juliette was keenly aware of the running, pounding, dumping going on.

The young *Milicien* kept his gun pointed at the women as the older one began to ransack the kitchen. He opened the closet door and stepped inside, looking through the contents of the cupboards. A bag of salt used for pickling splattered on the floor, glass jars of vegetables and fruits broke as they dropped off the shelf. The German emerged with two jars of peaches and took them to the kitchen table. He opened one and used his fingers to retrieve slices and slurp them into his mouth.

In the pitch dark of the cellar Francois and Amélie clung to each other in a corner of the mattress, listening to the sound of boots pounding back and forth, muffled sharp commands, then gunshots.

"*Non!*" exclaimed Francois, "*Mais non!*"

"Shush, shush," Amélie placed her hand on his lips.

Within a minute came the crash of glassware on the trap door, the mingling of odors and liquids plopping on stone echoing in the dark. There was nothing that they could do but remain quiet. If they were found, it would mean death for the men; prison for the women. They could only guess at what was occurring and expect the worst.

Jean-Pierre stood with his body and right cheek pressed to the wall of the hallway. His nose was up against the edge of a portrait of his great-grandmother, tilted at such an angle that it looked like she was frowning at the men guarding him. He gazed down at a reddish-brown liquid gliding slowly around his left foot. He had raised Primo from the age of two months. He did not move.

Juliette tried to inventory what she and Amélie had left up on the top floor when they had cleaned. They had made sure that the one room with a bed in it had been stripped bare. She couldn't think of anything important, simply unwanted furniture, trunks of ancestral outfits, a box of toys passed through generations.

The intruders' descent down the stairs sounded like rocks being rolled down a board. With his minions gathering behind him, the German raised something in his hand and pulled Jean-Pierre around to face him.

"We know that you're hiding someone! You'd better tell us where or you and your women will be sorry!"

He brandished a burnt, partial cigarette within inches of Jean-Pierre's eyes. "Where is he?"

Jean-Pierre frowned, "What do you mean? An old cigarette butt? Why would that mean someone else was here?"

"Up in the attic? Under a bed? I suppose you sleep there sometimes?" He turned, "Bring in the women!"

The man with the scar shoved Juliette and Gigi out of the kitchen, back into the hall.

"I'm in no mood for playing games, Madame Laurent. Unless you want to see your husband cut up in pieces before your eyes you had better tell me where you are hiding the person that smoked this...cigarette!"

He brandished the crunched item as if it was a flag at a parade.

Juliette stepped away from Gigi toward the officer, looking more closely at the crumpled object. She felt the girl's hand grab the back of her sweater. She squinted.

"Is that real tobacco?"

The officer looked surprised, brought it closer to his face, sniffed at it and snapped. "Yes! You have been hiding someone from the Resistance, haven't you? Where is he?"

Juliette stepped closer, feeling her sweater stretch further.

"This bit of cigarette has probably been under that bed since before the war. My son, who is now working in Germany, probably snuck up there years ago to smoke it." She looked calmly at the officer and spoke with sincerity, "We haven't had access to real tobacco for years. Check the ashtrays in the house. Look at my husband's tobacco pouch. All he smokes are the grains and herbs that he mixes himself."

The German considered this, looking doubtful. One of the Milice, standing at his side, leaned and whispered to him.

"Where is your other son, the one who is supposed to be still here?" He put both his gloved hands on his hips.

"Maurice?" Juliette wet her lips. "He's helping one of our neighbors. A beekeeper. They are in the process of moving the hives so Maurice is staying there for a couple of days."

The officer looked skeptical. "We haven't finished our search. I warn you that if we do find someone and you've lied, it will much worse."

He waited expectantly. The men around him looked at each other then back to the German.

"All right, men. Search every inch of this place including the barns, every out-building, every bit of the property. I want this to be thorough even if we have to stay here all day. Our informant assured us that they are hiding someone!"

After three hours Juliette and Gigi were allowed to sit down. Gigi had to use the toilet and the optician's son took her to the back bathroom. Jean-Pierre, lying on the floor of the hall, had two black eyes, blood oozing from the edge of his lip, bruises forming on his wrists from the handcuffs.

Juliette looked through the open front door at sunlight slowly pushing the shadow of the roof closer to the house. Typically, the electricity was intermittent and gas lamps and candles were insufficient lighting. Resorting to flash lights the Germans had seemed to deliberately knock things over or bang into picture frames on walls. The search of the outbuildings and farmland had gone on well past dawn. She smelled smoke from something burning yet dared not ask. She knew that their old mare was still alive as she heard her whinny, probably wondering why she had not been fed.

She guessed that it must be around seven o'clock. Their one rooster had crowed his last cock-a-doodle hours before and his dark-red feathered body hung limply from the side of the staff car parked on the terrace, along with a cluster of dead hens. Primo had been dragged to the terrace where flies circled his body.

The Milice had helped themselves to food in the kitchen and fixed a breakfast of eggs, canned fruits and bread baked the day before. Neither Juliette nor Gigi had not been permitted anything, including water, and had been forced to stand by the stairwell, unsupported. Now sitting on the bottom stair Juliette closed her eyes and breathed deeply.

The officer marched into view. Behind him three men carried a wine barrel that they placed on the staff car's back seat. Entering the hallway, brushing at something on his shoulder, the German barked to three Milice standing guard.

"Get that piece of baggage up and put him in the truck."

Jean-Pierre was pulled up by his armpits and groaned as he leaned on the men. Juliette wanted to reach out, to say something, but she did not dare. Gigi arrived, gaping, her eyes pink and watery.

"Madame, although we did not find anything except the cigarette butt, I know that testimony against your husband will result in swift justice. I warn you, do not make any attempt to contact him or do anything rash."

Gigi walked around the stairs and sat next to Juliette, clasping her left hand with both of hers.

The German paused, slapping an empty glove against his gloved palm. "You can be grateful that you are not going with him, in consideration of your young cousin or niece or whatever she is. I have a daughter about the same age and as a display of compassion I am letting you stay with her."

The man turned, clicked his heels, thrust out his hand and snapped out a 'Heil Hitler.' The Miliciens around him did the same then scattered for their vehicles and roared off in a spray of gravel and dust. Juliette buried her face in one hand, Gigi still clinging to the other. She looked over at the girl.

"Let's drink some water and then I need to contact your mother."

"But why would they arrest Cousin Jean-Pierre?" She looked around. "What's going on?"

Juliette hesitated. "Francois is back home because he has been hurt. Amélie is taking care of him and they are in a special, hidden cellar. We will signal them when it is safe to come out."

Gigi's eyes widened then she whispered, "I thought that was strange when you told me that Amélie had gone back to Lyon."

"I'll tell you more in a minute." Juliette stiffly moved toward the kitchen. At the open closet door she knelt in the sticky, salty crust that had formed and called, "Amélie?"

A muffled 'oui' could be heard.

"Jean-Pierre is alive but he has been taken to town. You must stay in the *cave* with Francois for several more days."

"Of course!" Amélie answered.

Francois shouted from the back, "Why did they take *Papa?*"

"Apparently they were told that we were hiding someone. I'm going to talk with Florence to see if Henri will help get him out." Juliette looked over at Gigi then reached for her hand. "You won't betray us, will you?"

Gigi looked even more shocked and wide-eyed than before. "Why would you think that?"

"Of course you wouldn't, darling." She spoke closer to the closet floor. "Gigi will be here. If you need anything, ask her to get it for you."

"We heard shots. Was anyone hurt?" Amélie's voice came from directly under the trap door.

Juliette paused. "We've lost Primo. I'm grateful that it wasn't Jean-Pierre."

She heard fading footsteps going down the staircase. She rose and headed for the sink, stepping carefully through broken crockery and scattered utensils, looking for a container that she and Gigi could use for water. Then she and Gigi needed to have a long talk.

CROSSROADS - 1978

Underneath the pencil holder at the top of the desk, dated a few days away, was my return plane ticket. The train ticket to Paris was waiting at the SNCF office in town. A box of books and reference materials lay on a table, ready to be mailed. My suitcase gaped open on a bedroom chair, stuffed with clothes and gifts. The diary of Florence Gilles-Martin was wrapped in a sweater, tucked in the bottom.

I planned to stay overnight at the Dupré's then Sophie would drive me to the train in Orange. A travel agent had arranged for a hotel in Paris until the flight from Orly Airport to New York two days later. After visiting JP at Yale I would fly home to San Francisco and return to my normal life.

Maurice and I had talked once about my delaying my return a week or two, before my latest tangle with his sister and the journal's appearance. Now, clearly, our affair was getting too complicated. Cycling out to the Domaine de Lauritaine when Maurice was on lunch break, I would return the two books and say 'goodbye.'

This would be a far different ride than the one that I had made three weeks before when Gabrielle and Madame Laurent, Audrey's family, and Julien and Martine had gone to the coast to escape the heat. Maurice gave some excuse about needing to organize things at the winery. On that lovely September afternoon as I pushed the bike up the drive toward the house, Maurice was walking down with a thick blanket over each arm and a loppy grin on his face. When he reached me, we kissed and he handed me the blankets. He took the bike and hefted it down an incline into the orchard. I followed, puzzled at first, surprised that we were going to have an early picnic. He reached back for my hands and hugged me to him.

"Darling, how I have been looking forward to this time together!"

"Me, too! Not to be rushed, to do whatever we want!"

I handed the blankets over as Maurice gestured for them. He shook one and placed it on the ground under leafy branches hanging close to the stone retaining wall. He shook out the second one and flopped it on top. He turned, took my hand and urged me to sit down. As soon as my knees touched the blanket Maurice pulled his zipper down and yanked his pants to his knees. He then lay me gently on the padding, reaching up under my skirt in anticipation of pulling down panties. When all he found was bare skin and pubic hair he looked slightly startled. I could not help but chuckle at his expression.

"You...*petite diablotine*," Maurice looked amused as he straddled then thrust into me with a groan.

The bike ride was my foreplay. Maurice had no need. The sensual feeling of velvet, satin inside me, the smell of his skin and hair, was more erotic than anything invented in my imagination. I was aware of all-over sensory surroundings, sun filtering through green leaves, bits of the sky, scratchy wool against my hips, jeans against my legs, the sounds of birds, our moans of delight. The exalted, slippery, overwhelming, quivering joy of sex.

The memory of that day was bittersweet. This time the visit would end differently. I took the last of my cheese and bread, hoping that we might drink a glass of wine and part on good terms, promising to 'stay in touch, send Christmas cards and remain friends.'

In addition to returning Maurice's two books I added a copy of Char's latest, *Le Nu Perdu*, 'The Lost Nude.' There was one poem that I marked as a way to remember our time together, one typical of the Surrealist wave and vague enough not to promise much. I turned back the corner of the page and added a note on the book's front page about how my research had led to our special friendship. I wrapped it in gift paper, plopped it into the bag with the other books, the cheese and a roll. The weather had turned cool, so I shrugged on a cardigan sweater.

The day was one of those magnificent Provençal fall displays with swipes of clouds across the sky, a gentle breeze, the odor of crushed leaves and smoke from brush burning somewhere. Murmurs of workers eating lunch came from the barn as I walked the bike up the driveway. Simon coughed a whoofy bark as he roused from his spot by the door. He came toward me, his tail wagging. I pushed the bike through the arch, propped it against the stones and strode, bag in hand, to the entry.

Maurice came to the door, shirtless, wiping water from his face. Peering at me in the bright sunlight, he frowned questioningly. "Claire?"

"Hello, Maurice."

He reached for my hand, drawing me to him.

"What a nice surprise!"

I pulled back, "Do you have time to talk right now?"

Maurice shrugged his shoulders, "Sure, darling. I'll bring out a bottle and some glasses."

He returned in a few minutes wearing an unbuttoned blue and white plaid shirt, carrying a dishcloth, two wine glasses and an open bottle. He kissed me on the lips. "The *vendange* will be over this weekend and then we can spend more time together."

We sat at the rusted green table. I drew out the cheese, bread, and a kitchen knife while he poured the wine

"Are you all right, Claire?" Maurice reached to hold my hand.

I chewed my lip. "I'm...busy. I wanted to return your books before I leave...tomorrow."

Maurice's brows narrowed into a scowl.

"It has been wonderful knowing you and we've had such fun. I hope that we'll stay in touch." I had rehearsed these phrases and, as I said them, they sounded like lines in a second-rate play.

"I thought that you were staying for another week or two?"

"I tried arranging to stay longer but ran into too many conflicts."

"Why didn't you tell me sooner?"

I grabbed the glass and swallowed the wine like it was water.

"Maurice, these past weeks have been very special, a memory that I will think of with...with fondness." My voice cracked. "It has been very romantic but I have to be realistic. My life is on the other side of the world. Here are the books you loaned me, and I brought you something as a remembrance." I fumbled with the bag sitting on the ground,

Maurice put the package on the table without looking. "I hope that you realize that this has not been what you Americans call a fling."

Chopping at the dried-out Comté cheese I handed a piece with a bit of roll to Maurice, who held it without moving. I looked down, feeling awkward. I felt my nose start to run.

"Maurice, saying goodbye is hard enough. Don't make it worse. I just wanted to leave knowing that...." I choked out,"...that we are still friends."

Maurice took both of my hands. "Claire, I thought that we were more than that."

He took a corner of his open shirt and used it to wipe my face. When he pulled me toward him I felt the warmth of his chest, the softness of the graying hairs that I loved to touch. I pulled back, breathed deeply, breathed again.

"I'll come in tonight to see you," Maurice sounded hopeful as he gripped me, both of us leaning in awkwardly from our chairs.

I pulled back. "I have to finish packing and cleaning up, since I'm going to the Dupré's tomorrow. It's best that we say goodbye now."

"But you'll be home tonight?"

I stood up. "It's been...very special but I'm leaving. I'll call you from Paris."

I picked up my purse, kissed him quickly on the cheek and ran to the bicycle. Moving through an impressionist landscape, I went down the slippery hill and soon was back on the road toward Carpentras, tears sliding off each side of my face.

I did not call. Three days later I left France knowing that this was the only option. I had big projects ahead of me, the possibility of turning my research into a doctoral dissertation, a need to map out my future. Sleepless nights and soggy pillows would be my atonement for doing the right thing.

THE VAUCLUSE 1944

AUGUST 14, MONDAY:

At noon Florence knew that Henri would leave the café where he and his friends met in the mornings. She planned to confront him in public so that he would not react for fear of embarrassment. She strode along the cobbled street, sweat trickling under her arms, her right foot beginning to blister from the too-tight sandal that she'd thrown on. A green felt feathered hat sat at a rakish angle on her uncombed hair. When she walked into the square Henri stood up from a café table and rushed over.

"Is something wrong with Gigi?"

"No. But I need to talk with you. Now!"

Florence pulled him by his right arm toward a side street, out of hearing. The two men who had been sitting at the table with Henri glanced over in curiosity then motioned for a waiter to take their lunch order.

"This is not the time or place, Florence. We'll discuss it at home."

Florence tightened her grip. When she spoke, her voice was low, "If you move away from me I will shout out to everyone within hearing distance that you are a homosexual and having an affair with a German officer."

Henri's eyes looked like blue stones floating in pudding as they widened in shock and fear.

"Shhhh. What in God's name are you saying?" He pushed Florence up against the wall and muttered, "You haven't any idea what you are talking about! How dare you!"

"I mean it, Henri. I will tell everyone within hearing unless you listen to what I have to say."

Henri came closer, his nostrils flaring. He whispered, his breath hot on her forehead. "How dare you make such a slanderous insult."

"This 'insult' came from a witness willing to go to the Gestapo about you and your lover." Florence figured that stretching the truth at this point was merely another step on the stairs toward justice. "Now listen! The Milice arrested Jean-Pierre this morning. You are going to do whatever is necessary to get him out of prison or I am going to let everyone know your ugly secret."

Florence stayed close to Henri, whose face was ashen.

"You have the contacts and I know that you can do it. What would the Commandant think of his *Obersleutnant*, if he knew?"

Henri stepped back and his shoulders sagged, "Florence, you mustn't do this. You don't understand."

The couple faced each other, not moving, expressions strained.

"Is everything all right?" A voice came from a few yards away as a teacher from Henri's school looked at them inquiringly.

"Yes, yes. Nothing at all," Henri managed a stiff smile. "Just deciding where to eat."

He grabbed Florence's elbow and forced her across the square past pedestrians walking purposefully in different directions. Henri pushed her into an indentation between buildings but stopped when Florence began to struggle.

She whispered loudly, "I warn you…"

"Shhh! What do you expect me to do? If Jean-Pierre was arrested it's because he has done something wrong. I can't help him."

"Oh, but I think that you can, Henri." Florence's face tightened. "I think that you are the reason that he was arrested."

Henri rolled his eyes. "What is this? Some crazy, imagined paranoia? I didn't have anything to do with his arrest."

"Juliette said that he was picked up because he was suspected of harboring a fugitive. The only person who could possibly have thought this nonsense, who was recently at their home, was you." Florence poked Henri in the chest with a finger. "Regardless, you are going to get him out of the prison or you will find yourself and the other sterling example of the Aryan race in there as well."

Henri gripped Florence's arm tightly, muttering angrily, "You bitch! I can have the Gestapo arrest you!"

That Henri rarely ever said 'damn' reinforced Florence's impression that he was terrified by her threat and losing confidence. She dared poke once more at Henri's chest.

"If I don't see Jean-Pierre walk out of the *Cour de Justice* today a letter will be on its way to the Commandant's office, to Father Gerard at the Cathedral and to your daughter about your....your affair. They have already been written and are being held by a friend. If anything happens to me they are to be hand delivered."

This part was true. Florence had scribbled information on three pages, put them in three envelopes and handed them to Madame Dulfour at the café on the way to find Henri.

Henri stepped back, "I can't believe this! You fool."

He clenched her hand so tightly that Florence winced.

"Do it, Henri!" She glared back at him. "Go talk with Captain Dumaine and tell him that you guarantee that our cousin would not hide anyone. You have spent enough time with his family to know that they are law-abiding, cooperative citizens. Their son is working in Germany. We have entrusted them with our daughter. Whatever you told them, you'll have to recant it."

He snarled quietly, "You must realize that this is a tense time for everyone. With the Americans and British on our soil I don't know how the authorities will react."

"Actually that is in your favor," Florence stared into Henri's eyes. "If the Allies win, which is very possible, remind Captain Dumaine that his collaboration with the Nazis won't be overlooked. Nor will yours. His releasing Jean-Pierre would go a long way to showing his, shall we say, neutrality?"

Henri frowned malevolently at his wife, shocked that her timid nature could turn so vituperative. He adjusted his fedora, straightened his lapels, turned and wobbled toward the post office.

Leaning against the wall, sighing unevenly, Florence smoothed her hair, adjusted her hat and walked down toward the cathedral. Her stomach was empty and she was desperate for a drink. She knew that the best place to watch for Henri and Jean-Pierre would be in one of the cafés opposite the Court of Justice. She walked briskly down a street behind the cathedral and past the Jewish Door. Stepping cautiously across the steps of the church, she peeked around a corner of the former Episcopal Palace. At virtually the same time she saw Henri striding south at the other end of the square, his expression furious, his fists swinging.

After he entered the immense carved doors of the *palais de justice*, Florence tucked her head and walked into a café across the square. The waiter directed her to a small table in a humid, airless corner by a window. She ordered wine and a carafe of water, anticipating that her wait might be a long one. She was relieved when Henri and the Captain, on apparently amiable terms, stepped out together.

Le dejeuner! One of the most sacred hours of the day and, of course, no business would be conducted until after lunch was over. When the two men turned to their right, up the *rue de l'Éveché*, Florence deduced that Henri had invited the Captain to the town's nicest restaurant near the *Passage Boyer*. She hoped that he would insist on a bottle of their best wine. In the meantime she planned to order whatever would take the longest to prepare.

Florence took time puréeing each mouthful of her three course meal. She was not aware of tastes, mechanically consuming whatever was on each plate. The lunchroom thinned as people returned to work or to stand in queues. Florence stayed at the table, grateful that she had one of Antoine's books of poetry. She read without understanding, flipped a page, glanced up, read from the beginning again, glanced up now and then, dawdled over a second cup of coffee.

Shortly after two o'clock she saw Henri meander back with an almost jovial Captain Dumaine. As they entered the reopened doors she signaled the waiter for her bill. She slumped against the café chair, nauseated from the four courses that she had consumed. The queasiness that she had noticed became more pronounced.

As soon as she paid *l'addition*, Florence hurried to the washroom. She dropped to her knees, the costly lunch landed in the toilet's bowl and her stomach cramped as she retched. She dragged herself over to the washstand, cupped water into her mouth with her hand, spit, rinsed again. She leaned over the spigot and smoothed water over her face. Wiping her face and hands on a towel, she looked in the dimly lit mirror. Her dark eyes stood out like symbols on an Egyptian cartouche.

Florence rubbed her stomach, hoping that the sudden illness was not from food poisoning, the fish in the *quenelles* perhaps, or the beginning of the flu. Most likely it was from anxiety. She swiped her hair with a comb, replaced her hat, picked up her purse from the floor and smeared on lipstick. After pinching her cheeks she hobbled outside into oppressive heat.

At the *maison de la presse* she bought faux cigarettes. It had been years since she had smoked, and then only for a few months. Henri despised women with cigarettes dangling from their mouths even though he was addicted to his own. With her heart beating a tattoo, her knees about to collapse, she tottered to the north end of the square and found a table behind a potted plant. She ordered mineral water and was relieved that each sip seemed to subdue the upset stomach. She puffed on icky-tasting cigarettes and swallowed the water as slowly as possible.

Florence shook her head at the irony of the message in Reverdy's book, a poem called *The Dry Tongue:*

There is a nail
    Holding up the slope
The bright tatter of twisting wind blows and anyone
who understands
    The whole road is naked
the pavement the sidewalks the distance the railings are white
    Not a drop of rain
    Not a leaf of a tree
    Not the shadow of a garment
        I wait
        the station is a long way off

The river still flows as you go up along the embankments
  the earth is dried out
        everything is naked and white.
With only the movement of a clock out of order
      the noise of the train passed
        I wait.   (40)

Twice friends stopped to say hello: two with whom she rolled bandages at the hospital, another the mother of one of Gigi's friends. Conversations were perfunctory. An elderly woman from church asked if she could join Florence. She placed her cane on the chair's back and ordered a coffee. Madame Valois launched into a litany of complaints about her health and the possibility of the town being embroiled in fighting. She fumed at the idiocy of the mayor, the air raid drills and airplanes that interrupted her naps, the difficulty of managing the shelter stairs, electricity that was intermittent and the horrible bread.

Florence nodded and sympathized from time to time as she peered past the woman's bobbing white head and watched for Jean-Pierre. She glanced at her wristwatch and saw that it was past four o'clock. Her hips were numb from sitting and her anxiety was mounting. What was going on? Why hadn't Henri and Jean-Pierre come out?

The elderly lady stopped to sip at her espresso then glanced at Florence. "My dear, you look very pale. Are you all right?"

Her mottled hand patted Florence's as she squinted.

"I'm not feeling well. The heat, you know. Do you feel that you will be...," her voice faded as she saw Henri emerge from the Palais de Justice.

Madame Valois seemed oblivious to the unfinished sentence and railed on. Florence watched Henri walk unsteadily in the direction of their home. He stumbled as he turned a corner. No Jean-Pierre. Her heart sank and she felt a wave of vertigo. She used her hat as a fan to cool a surge of heat.

Madame Valois peered more closely and remarked, "Madame Gilles-Martin, you truly do not look well."

"No, I'm feeling quite ill. It could be something that I ate at lunch. I'm sorry, but I need to go home." She leaned over and added, insincerely, "I hope to see you at church."

"Of course, my dear, do take care of yourself."

Her scheme had not worked. She walked toward the Cathedral. A few moments in the cool, serene nave with its soaring pillars and fragrance of incense would give her time to recover enough to make her way home, to figure out how to get a message to Juliette. Her fervent prayers that day had been answered with an apparent resounding 'no.'

⸺

René Char confided to Marcelle before he flew to the African coast to listen for a coded message stating *Nancy has a stiff neck.*' It meant that the invasion of Southern France was imminent. When she heard it, on August 13, she told her family. Her brother alerted others in the *reseau* to be ready.

The following day, another coded message arrived and was repeated a second time: *'The hunter is starved.'* This signaled that the invasion would take place the following day.

Although they were deeply in love, who knew what the future would bring? That evening Marcelle Pons-Sedoine sat by her kitchen fireplace and, as René had instructed, burned all the letters that they had exchanged.

⸺

Florence walked to the chapel of the Holy Virgin in the Cathedral and tucked herself into a corner of the pew. With bowed head, she spent an hour reciting silent 'Hail Mary's,' fingering her rosary, trying to still the self-recrimination for failing to rescue Jean-Pierre. She lit a candle at the chapel of St. Anthony of Padua, the saint of lost things and people.

The walk to the apartment seemed to take hours as Florence slogged along in the heat. *Cigales* provided a white-noise accompaniment to the tap-tap of her sandals on the cobblestones, her blistered foot beyond complaining. In some upper apartment an accordionist played a melancholy melody. Bells chimed, announcing that it was six o'clock. Once inside the entry hall of their building Florence sat on the curved stone bench tucked into the staircase, fanning herself with her hat. She decided to rest in front of the electric fan for a few minutes then take a note to the messenger service office where a boy would take it to Juliette.

The stair steps felt longer than usual as Florence counted all eighteen of them. She unlocked the door and hung up her hat and purse, adjusting to the dimness of the shuttered room. Henri slumped in his chair, holding a glass balanced on the arm. A bottle of cognac was on top of the newspaper on the table in front of him, a bottle saved for a special celebration that never came. His ashtray overflowed with butts and smoke fogged the ceiling. Florence felt momentary sympathy for him, embalming his mind after the day's events. She felt like doing the same.

"Well, if it ishn't the high and mighty queen of the cash'le."

Henri's eyes were unfocused, his right hand wobbled in the air, the index finger bobbed toward Florence.

"You wanna hear some good news! They hung the bassards who tried to kill the Fuehrer. By meat hooks. Serves'em right. Your cousin should'a been on one of'em."

Florence glanced at him but didn't respond. Walking past the dining table she went into the kitchen for a glass of water. When finished, she dampened her hand and robbed it on the back of her neck then walked to her chair. She sank onto the seat with a huge sigh, closed her eyes and let her head plop back on the upholstery, savoring the fan's ruffling of the air.

Neither spoke. The only sound was an occasional clink as Henri refilled his glass, a slight slurping and the fan's low hum.

Florence was jerked from her dozing by Henri's low rumble. "I never shu' have married you, you...bitch. You made my life hell!"

Her lips tightened but Florence still did not respond. Henri sat forward in his chair.

"I shu' have reported you to the Gestapo, long time ago. They would ha' believt me, anything I told them, they would ha' believt. And maybe ish not too late."

He swallowed the last liquid in his glass. Florence saw that the Cognac bottle was almost empty, barely half an inch was left. His rant was alcohol inspired she assumed, and closed her eyes.

"Don' you dare ignore me! I'm talking to you, Florensh." Henri slammed the glass down on the table. "When I'm talking to you, pay attention, you bitch."

Florence looked up, startled. She had never in all their years seen Henri completely drunk let alone spouting profanity. Annoyed, embarrassed for him, still she could not blame him. Their world balanced on the tip of a toothpick and no one could predict which way it would fall.

"Henri, can we talk about this later? I'm exhausted and heartsick. I'm sure that you tried your best to get Jean-Pierre released but it didn't work. We must hope that he won't be sent to one of those awful camps."

She closed her eyes once more.

"Dush he know that dishgusting story about me? You are all liars, you know."

Her husband pulled himself forward in the chair as if he wanted to stand up but couldn't. "Who told you there was anything between Ziegler and me? We're jush good friends and you don' know what ish like to have a friend. You would'n unnerstan'."

Florence shook her head and sighed. She knew better but said it anyway, "Henri, learning this should not have surprised me. Now I know why our marriage never worked and at least I'm grateful for that. Your being a homosexual has...."

Henri pushed himself out of the chair and yelled, "I'm not a homosexual! I jush have a close friendship with a man who cares for me. We have a, a, a fraternal relationship, thash all. "

Florence's irritation bubbled up, "I don't care what you call it, Henri. We'll deal with it later. Let's not argue, please."

She rubbed her forehead and closed her eyes. Henri stood, lurched over and leaned above her.

"Who told you this nonsense? Who elsh knows?"

His hands clenched, spittle sidled to the edge of his lips as he croaked, "Who hash those letters?"

Florence started to push herself up straight in the chair.

"We'll talk later, when you're sober."

His sudden slap across her face twist her head to the side. She barely managed to say, 'Wha....?'

Henri lunged one knee between her thighs and grabbed her throat with his hands. As inebriated as he was, his grip was strong. Florence pulled at his fingers, trying to loosen them, and managed an intake of air before he clamped tighter.

She beat at him with her fists and he leaned back out of her reach, his face contorted. She pulled at his fingers, feeling the light fading, her lungs aching for air. In flailing around she felt one of the wooden needles she was using for Gigi's sweater and grabbed the metal knob. She stabbed its pointed end at Henri's face. She heard him yell 'ouch' and jerk to his right, loosening his grip enough for her to gasp another breath. He let go with one hand and punched her on the side of the head. She heard the knitting needle fall on the floor.

Her neck and throat throbbed from the pressure of Henri's fingers and she reached for them again, pulling, kicking her heels on the floorboards, trying to loosen them as her own hands became weaker and weaker. The room grew darker with flashes of bright lights until all was black and silent.

PART THREE

ADJUSTING TO REALITY - 1979

Ater arriving back in the USA I postponed organizing the class syllabus for over two months. The visit with JT on the way home took a week and helped distance the emotional ache of leaving Provence. Tucked around Thanksgiving and the Christmas holidays were 'welcome back' dinners and parties, trips into San Francisco to shop for gifts and a weekend in Napa Valley with good friends Katy and Andrew Franchini. JT arrived for Christmas and we decorated a tree, wrapped gifts and fed his high school buddies, who paraded through chattering about college. Dealing with my aging father and his perky second wife Roselyn, my brothers, their wives and children, was a welcome, time-consuming diversion when JT spent time with his father.

In answer to questions about my sojourn in France, I said, 'fine, of value, interesting.' The enquirer usually accepted the statement and turned to a subject that they preferred. Only Katy and Andrew heard an edited version of my affair with a winemaker in Provence.

Maurice wrote an imploring letter to my office; I had asked Sophie to not give him my home address. On the back of his Christmas card Maurice copied what Pierre Reverdy had written for Coco Chanel:

'Dear ~~Coco~~ Claire,
Here it is
The best of my hand

And the best of me
I offer it to you
With my heart
With my hand
Before heading toward
The dark road's end
If condemned
If pardoned
Know that you are loved.
   Maurice (with help from Pierre Reverdy) (41)

I blotted tears into a kitchen towel as I thought of the time that he took to do this but did not respond. After the second note I wrote back, recounting my visit with JT at his school, the weather, the pressure I was under to organize the research information.

A surge of practicality inspired a visit to a Kinko's copy shop in Santa Rosa where I wandered around, watching customers at Xerox machines and three harried clerks who wrote up or handed out orders. It did seem to be successful. I wrote to UC Berkeley for information on requirements for a PhD but hadn't yet read the booklet.

Rain, steady and comforting, beat a muted tattoo on the roof of my condominium as I mimicked its thrum with my fingers, looking from one pile of papers to another on my large Formica desk. It was decorated with bookmarks jutting from a stack of books like straws to be drawn in a contest, copies of poems, sticky notes with short phrases randomly arrayed. Grabbing a three-by-five card, I wrote: *ART: get copies of paintings by Miro, Dali.* I waved it around then taped it to the edge of the desk lamp's shade. Mulling over 'where to start first,' I was gratefully distracted by the American poet Frank O'Hara's 'Lunch Poems' and flipped through the book. *Adieu to Norman, Bon Jour to Joan and Jean-Paul* that had become one of my favorites:

 .....I wish I were reeling around Paris
 instead of reeling around New York

I wish I weren't reeling at all
it is Spring the ice has melted the Ricard
                              is being poured
we are all happy and young and toothless
it is the same as old age
the only thing to do is simply continue
is that simple
yes, it is simple because it is the only thing to do
can you do it
yes, you can because it is the only thing to do
blue light over the Bois de Boulogne it continues
the Seine continues
the Louvre stays open it continues it hardly closes at all
the Bar Americain continues to be French
de Gaulle continues to be Algerian as does Camus
Shirley Goldfarb continues to be Shirley Goldfarb
and Jane Hazan continues to be Jane Freilicher (I think !)
and Irving Sandler continues to be the balayeur
                              des artistes
and so do I (sometimes I think I'm "in love" with painting)
and surely the Piscine Deligny continues to have water in it
and the Flore continues to have tables and newspapers
and surely we shall not continue to be unhappy
we shall be happy
but we shall continue to be ourselves everything
                              continues to be possible
René Char, Pierre Reverdy, Samuel Beckett it is possible isn't it
I love Reverdy for saying yes, though I don't believe it.   (42)

The exciting upheaval of what was later referred to as both the 'beat generation' and the 'San Francisco Renaissance' had not caught my attention at the
time that it was happening, although I was almost in the thick of it. Somehow,
as a 1955 graduate from an all-women's college then working on a masters

degree at Stanford, where I met Ted and fell in love, it had wafted by me without much impact.

Ted and I, out on a date during out courtship, wandered into Lawrence Ferlinghetti's 'City Lights Bookstore' in the North Beach area of the city around the time of an obscenity lawsuit against Alan Ginsberg for *Howl*, the book that Ferlinghetti had published. Both of us were intrigued by the ramifications of the court case that would determine 'free speech' and 'freedom of the press;' however, I was fixated on planning our wedding and Ted had his mind on his dissertation. I remembered speaking French with the owner of the shop and lightly touching on writers such as Rimbaud and Melarmé but not much else. O'Hara's *Lunch Poems* had been published by City Lights in 1964 when I was engrossed with John-Theodore and volunteering at his preschool. Two years later I started teaching French and 19th century comparative literature. It wasn't until I chose the Surrealists in the Resistance as the subject of my sabbatical that I had focused on this period.

Staring at what seemed to be an overwhelming amount of work, I thought about what would appeal to the students. Many could relate to these early writers, with the war in Vietnam having followed their growing years like a kite attached to their rompers. Certainly those aware of the humanistic psychology movements, the drug culture and the protests of the nineteen-seventies in the Bay Area would understand their rebellious lives.

The ringing of the telephone swooshed me from far away thoughts into the present. "Hello?"

"Claire? It's Karen Beauchamp. How are you?

I responded with 'fine,' wondering who was Karen Beauchamp? I stammered out, "How are you?"

"Not anxious to go back to school but you know how that is."

It suddenly clicked. Karen taught American History at the community college. Ted and I had once joined her and her husband, a stockbroker, for dinner in Santa Rosa.

"I'm fine, Karen. I got back from a sabbatical in France in October and am putting the material together for a new class."

"Lucky you," Karen extolled, "I'm not due for a sabbatical for another three years. How is it going?"

Another 'fine' and Karen chattered on. I remembered more about the Beauchamps, including that our husbands had polarized views on several topics and there was only that one dinner date.

Karen cleared her throat.

"I imagine you're surprised that I'm calling but I have a favor to ask. Bob and I have a dear friend who was recently divorced. We always enjoyed your company and I thought you would understand what it is like, you know, getting back into the social scene."

I said that I knew. It wasn't easy.

"I'm not trying to make a match…" Karen's laugh was a little forced, "but we're having a dinner party with several couples and it would be nice to keep a round number at the table. Would you be free next Saturday?"

I almost declined then blurted out, "That would be lovely."

My practical inner voice agreed. It would divert me from thinking about the past. "Who is he, exactly?"

Karen described Harlan as tall, a tennis player and a professor of mathematics at her school. I jotted down the time, address and his name on the desk calendar. Karen and I exchanged a few more pleasantries.

"How nice of you to think of me. I looked forward to seeing you and Bob, and meeting your friend."

As the phone clicked, I spoke out loud to the mug. "Harlan, I hope that you turn out to be 'mister wonderful!' "

THE HOLY MAN
PIERRE REVERDY

The bells from Romanesque-styled Abbaye Saint-Pierre reverberated around the village of Solesmes, calling the faithful as the sun cast afternoon shadows across fields. For most of the past eighteen years a quiet man had attended mass and vespers in the Benedictine monastery, although disillusionment with his religion had become more apparent over time. His individualism was well known, as was his tendency to be abrupt and unsociable. His wife shouldered day-to-day interactions with tradesmen and townspeople so that he could garden, care for his rabbits, wander the hills and write.

Two decades before Pierre Reverdy had chosen a contemplative life, that of a lay monk, far from the boisterous city where his poetry was acclaimed. His departure was a significant event in the Surrealist movement. He had been an integral part of the chaotic and creative world centered at the *Le Bateau Lavoir* in Montmarte. Pablo Picasso, Juan Gris and Georges Braques illustrated his publications. André Breton said that he was 'the greatest poet of the era' and Louis Aragon called him 'their elder and exemplary poet.' Philippe Soupault said that he was one of the purest writers of their time.

The search for more meaning in life had led Reverdy from exploration of abstract thought and expression to a re-birth of his Catholic faith. At the end of a five-year affair with a woman that he still adored, he publicly burned his poems and prose in a ritual emphasizing this rededication. He and his wife Henriette, a seamstress, left Paris for the tranquility of a village centered around a monastery famous for Gregorian music.

When the Germans descended on Solesmes in 1942, they seized the Reverdy's home and forced Henriette and Pierre to move into a small house at the lower end of their garden. Outraged, Reverdy sold their main house. His resentment also simmered from the tragic loss of so many of the monks from the Abbey with whom he had fought against the Germans in 1939, during the 'phony war.' Once the Germans invaded his country he refused to publish anything.

Periodically he returned to Paris where he would spend time discussing poetry, the arts and events of the day with friends. And, always, he spent time with Coco Chanel. Sometimes they remained in Paris, sometimes they traveled to her villa *La Pausa*, the seaside property given to her by England's Duke of Westminster, another of her lovers.

He and Coco had met at a dinner party in 1921 hosted by a wealthy and eccentric friend. Each came from humble backgrounds and had suffered from childhood traumas. Pierre was introspective and pensive, dark and brooding. Coco was charming, pretty, gregarious and determined to succeed. They admired each other's talents and understood each other's dedication. She provided money to publish his poems and encouraged him to write. Coco had often told Pierre that he was 'her first real love.' For over twenty-five years the two had remained devoted friends and occasional lovers, regardless of his marriage vows, her numerous affairs or their opposing political views.

As appalled as Reverdy might be by her Nazi friends, at her affair with a German baron, at her anti-Semitic attitude, he could not help but forgive Coco when he looked into her eyes. He felt that most women were weak in spirit and easily confused, and wanted to believe that she was manipulated by the more devious. She had done what she had to do, to survive.

As the Allied Forces drew closer to Paris, Pierre received a phone call. Chanel's current lover 'Spatzy,' a high-level officer in German Intelligence, had fled Paris for Switzerland. She had moved from their suite in the Hotel Ritz back to the apartment over her shop. And she needed Pierre's help.

A few days later he left for the capital. His close friend Pablo Picasso had also asked him to come for a group picture of those who had performed in Pablo's Surrealist farce, *Desire Caught by the Tail*, the previous March. Brassai took a photo of a dozen of them in Picasso's apartment, including Jean-Paul Sartre, Simone de Bouvoir, Albert Camus (the play's director) and, of course, the artist himself. Camus, as editor of *Combat*, provided up-to-date news on the Nazis' brutal reprisals against the French and the progress of the Americans and the Free French forces as they slogged eastward. Paul Eluard was still hiding in an asylum. Soupault and Breton were in the United States. Although he could not exhibit, Picasso had painted a series of 'still lifes' with anti-fascist allegorical symbols and made a few bronzes from metal smuggled to him by members of the Resistance.

Then Pierre left for *rue Cambon.*

Although sixty years old, Chanel could have passed for someone in her late forties. When Pierre embraced her, she seemed as nervous and frightened as he had ever seen her. Her thin fingers twisted a pearl necklace as she explained that a Baron Louis de Vaufreland was likely to name her as a collaborator with the Nazis. She was, as Pierre expected, extremely vulnerable and dependent upon him to rescue her. She implored Pierre to find de Vaufreland before the Allies arrived and prevent him from informing on her.

He assured her, "Coco, I will do everything in my power to locate and remove this man. Now, tell me what you know about him."

At age fifty-five Reverdy was among the most experienced of the Partisans in Paris and he soon convinced several young Maquis to join him on his mission. He got the names and addresses of the Baron's family and close friends. It was not long before de Vaufreland was tracked to the apartment of a Count Jean-René de Gaigneron. With *Maquisards* stationed around the elegant *hotel particulier* and standing on the steps of the marble staircase, Pierre knocked on the carved door. The Count answered and pointed to an interior room where the Baron hid in a closet. De Gaigneron, relieved that the men had not come for him, was glad to see his now quite unwelcome guest forcibly escorted away while he continued burning papers in his fireplace.

Pierre went with the group to an interview room where the offended and defiant collaborator was questioned. After Reverdy spoke with, then threatened him, he eventually agreed to not disclose Coco's involvement to the Allies. The nobleman was thrown in with a group of other *collabos* and trucked out to a prison built by the Resistance.

"De Vaufreland will probably be taken on to Drancy where Jews were kept before being sent on to the camps," reported a young Maquisard. "It's a fitting place for a French traitor!"

The quiet man could only nod. His faith made it hard to rationalize the actions of people that he loved yet who made poor choices. When the war was over, after the Nazis were driven out of France, he would return to his Abbey, to his quiet existence, and pray that those who had done wrong would be forgiven. Somehow, he knew that Coco would survive.

In a Lower Voice

The hunt is decided in the tympanum of wings
The macabre concern of keeping the secret
When it's as cold as snow in your breast
Clear and limpid like an ornament of summer
Your eyes laden with dead leaves
of red lists of the condemned
All along the bank without prison
Without a glint of windows
At the sinister sunset against the parapet
The shadow drifts at the base of the walls fills the town
In a sticky flood against the blood
Wings overladen with insults and murmurs
Deaf wings
Wings flying low

Then in order the knaw of dragging death
Peace in the breast
Gloved hand of earth dried up
At the heart's last undertown in the ruins
The last word of faith
Holy log of the hearth (43)

Pierre Reverdy   1   1889 – 1960

THE VAUCLUSE - 1944

AUGUST 14, MONDAY:

There was a burning sensation in her throat, searing pain, and the strong smell of Cognac from a glass being pressed against her lips. Florence swallowed, gasped and pushed away the hand holding the liquor. Every breath she inhaled caused more pain in her throat. Her lungs felt seared. She touched her neck and tried to see where she was but couldn't focus.

The blur finally shifted from side to side and settled into a recognizable face. What was Gigi doing here? Why did her throat hurt so?

"*Maman! Maman!* Oh, thank the Blessed Virgin."

Gigi's damp cheek was pressed against Florence's amid a series of soft kisses. "I thought you were dead! I was so scared..."

Florence's answer was a raspy, raw bleat. She lay in her chair, gazing toward the ceiling, her legs splayed out in front. With effort and help from Gigi, she shoved herself up and sat back. A surge of fear caused her to recoil and stiffen. The terror before she blacked out pounced ferociously. Florence reached for Gigi's hand; she tried to ask what happened but could only gasp.

"*Non, non,* don't try to talk." Gigi stroked her mother's hand and then sobbed, "I've knocked Papa unconscious."

She moved slightly to the side and Florence saw Henri lying between the windows, looking vaguely like he had decided to take a nap on the floor. Next to his head was the marble statue of David. Nearby, Florence's porcelain reading lamp lay shattered, the ruffled shade twisted to one side.

Florence pulled Gigi's face toward her, smoothing her cheek, then her hair with her hand, kissing her on her forehead. She managed to mouth 'thank you.'

"Should I get the doctor? I didn't mean to hurt Papa." Gigi looked stricken, her eyes brimming.

Florence mouthed again, "Let me check."

She slid down, dizzy from the effort, and crawled over to Henri. She noticed a thin gash, barely bleeding, behind his right temple. She reached to check for a pulse on his neck but did not feel one. She lifted his limp hand and felt his wrist. Then she shakily, tentatively, raised his eyelid. A bloodshot blue orb stared out like a dead fish's eye. Florence sat back on her ankles and signaled 'no.'

Her daughter put her head in her hands and began to wail. Florence waddled on her knees over to her and held her tightly. She pushed Gigi's head back and again had to mouth, "You saved my life, my darling. You saved my life."

Gigi sobbed out, "Why was Papa hurting you? I tried to pull him off of you but he wouldn't let go. I didn't know what to do!"

Florence held her closely, murmuring, 'shhh, shhh.'

"What are we going to do?" Gigi reared up, her eyes wide with fear.

Florence pulled her closer and whispered, "Let me think."

Then she was struck by the fact that Gigi was in town, not at the Laurent's farm. She pulled at her daughter's elbow as she forced herself to stand and mouthed, "Why...you...here?"

"Cousin Juliette got word from Jean-Pierre that he was out of prison and to come get him. I came along because I wanted to see you and *Papa*." She stared at the body on the floor, her face constricted and pale. "We need to get a doctor."

Her mother steered her to the dining table, grabbed paper and a pencil and wrote that Henri was dead and what would happen if they did call a doctor. Then Florence scribbled what they had to do. Gigi looked horrified when she read the note and wailed again.

"But I didn't mean to, I didn't mean to hurt him."

Florence held her daughter's shaking body as she convulsed once more into sobs. She let her cry and cling, until she could tell that Gigi was spent.

Then she whispered hoarsely in her ear, "My sweet child, my love. This was an accident. You never meant to hurt your father. No one else need know what really happened. This is what we must do."

Florence wondered later how the two of them found the strength to do what they did. They turned Henri over and pulled him up to a semi-sitting position, put on his jacket, smoothed his shirt and straightened his tie. Florence used her fingers to comb his hair back from his face. The two of them raised him up by crouching under his shoulders, propping him up between them and dragging him, his legs and shoes trailing behind, to a dining room chair by the front door. Leaving his body slouched in an awkward position they turned back to the sitting area.

They swept up shards and chunks of the broken lamp then put them under trash in the kitchen garbage can. The lampshade, metal parts and cord were wrapped in a pillowslip and hidden behind blankets in the guest bedroom's armoire. The table was tidied, the bottle and glass arranged neatly. Henri's paper was folded and placed on the floor beside it. The ashtray was left as it had been. 'David' had been wiped clean and put back on his stand.

Florence went into the bathroom and checked her throat. After applying liniment, she wrapped a cotton scarf around her neck, put on her nightgown and robe and pulled the bedcovers down. Gigi, her tormented face damp with tears, gently helped her dress and followed her mother as if afraid of losing her.

Once again, the two held each other tightly. Florence was able to brush through her lips a soft, "That's all right, that's all right. There's money and a coupon for a roll in my purse. Don't tell anyone that you came inside! Say that I was too sick and Papa was on his way to a rehearsal."

Checking to make sure that the one neighbor still living in the building was not by the stairwell or entry hall, Florence placed Henri's violin case and hat at the top of the stairs. She and Gigi struggled to raise the man's heavy body between them, his limp arms stretched across their shoulders. They pulled Henri across the landing to the bannister, the tips of his shoes scuffing along the marble floor.

Placing his back alongside the wood railing, Florence pushed against his pelvis with her body and on his chin with her hand to hold him semi-upright while Gigi skittered down the stairs, unlocked the door, closed it and re locked it.

Florence waited a few minutes in a gruesome death embrace with the man who had tried to kill her. Reaching around and under his waist, she used every ounce of strength she had to get behind him and, with a heave, pushed him forward. Panting from exertion she watched as Henri bounced heavily on the steps below, rolled over, thudded to the right and slid down to within six steps of the entry's tiled floor. She gave the violin case a shove with her foot and it, too, bounced its way downstairs, sliding against Henri's foot. She tossed his hat and it flopped upside down next to the violin.

Florence ran back into the apartment, locked the door, removed her robe and slipped under the covers. She lay still, feeling both gratitude and fear. She could have been the one to die yet she and her daughter now had this terrible secret to keep.

She hoped that the accident would appear to have happened because Henri was inebriated. Explaining his drunkenness might be awkward but she would think up some excuse. Florence would say that she had not heard anything as she was asleep, suffering from influenza and laryngitis. If Henri's death was accepted as an accident, only she and Gigi need ever know what really happened. If there was suspicion of foul play then Florence knew that she, alone, would take the blame.

It could not have been more than fifteen minutes later that Florence heard a muffled scream.

AUGUST 15, TUESDAY:

Before dawn, a German patrol discovered a cache of arms at a farmhouse on the edge of Pertuis, a town thirty miles due north of Marseille, across the river from Aix-en-Provence.

Rounding up workers at the railway depot and civilians in houses surrounding it, the Nazis marched twenty some hostages toward *Place Mirabeau* in the center of town. In the middle of setting up their machine guns, an air raid siren growled into a soprano whine as Allied bombers approached. Everyone scattered like frightened sparrows, including the Germans and Milice.

A viaduct across the Durance was destroyed and rail yards that connected Marseille with Lyon were badly damaged. Three members of the Resistance were killed. All the hostages survived.

He'd just celebrated his nineteenth birthday six weeks before and here he was, one of 94,000 soldiers, with a pack on his back, holding a rifle, standing in a landing craft as it rolled its bucking way in the early morning light toward a coastal French town.

He'd never heard of *Cavalaire-sur-Mer* before the previous week. He wasn't even sure how to pronounce it. The generals dubbed his Third Army Division platoon's landing spot 'Alpha Beach.' It looked peaceful from this distance, Johnny Evans thought, staring through the dimming fog and haze from aerial bombardments toward a looming promontory on the right that curled around a sandy curve of land.

So far, Johnny thought, things have gone pretty smoothly. For weeks the Allies had pummeled major ports and rail lines in Southern France. Special Forces had penetrated Corsica and other islands off the southern coast to capture guns aimed toward Allied battleships so that convoys could pass safely.

Free French of the Interior divisions had been parachuted in to join Resistance groups and were waiting to assist the Allies. Intelligence from aerial photography and Resistance networks, from intercepted messages, indicated that opposition was likely to be weak. They knew that two of the four German armored divisions in Provence had moved to Normandy after June 6th. Still, the men were told to expect anything; it was anybody's guess as to what sort of opposition they'd find.

Johnny looked at his buddies: Jacob, the Jewish kid from Florida; red-haired, buck-toothed Sam from Tennessee; Vinnie 'the procurer' from Brooklyn; Stevie, a deeply religious Baptist from South Carolina. And he, fresh off his family's dairy farm in Manteca, California.

Last night they had played card games, bantered, written letters to families, without talking about war or fighting. Were the others as nervous and, he admitted, as scared as he was? Which of them would make it through the war? Who might never live to marry, have kids, grow old? These thoughts were never far from his conscience as much as he tried not to dwell on them.

Johnny tried to enjoy the boat ride that day. He watched seagulls twirl around the vessel hoping for a fisherman to throw out entrails from a catch. He had a cast-iron stomach and reveled in the roller-coaster ride toward shore. Many of the guys retched up their meager breakfast, vomiting on their shoes or into bags, even after chewing anti-seasick pills.

The men were warned that temperatures in Provence were high in August. Johnny was used to the heat of California's Central Valley and figured that, even with heavy boots and a pack, he'd withstand it pretty well. He'd toughened up in boot camp and was proud of increased muscles on his six-foot two-inch frame. Because he stood at least a couple of inches above the others in his platoon, except for Sam the kid from Tennessee, he did worry that he might make an easier target.

From the speaker came orders to prepare for landing. The craft bumped its way through surf a few yards from Alpha Beach. Johnny held his rifle above his head with both hands and followed the man in front of him into the Mediterranean Sea, along a rope with buoys. The cool water felt good as he sloshed his way onto the gritty beach. Gunfire had been going constantly for several minutes and Private Evans hunkered down behind some crossed pieces of wood. He pointed his gun toward what he thought was a flash of light. He started firing, steadying the recoil.

LIFE TIPS OVER - 1979

April in Sonoma County, California was April at its best. Fruit and flowering trees on the college's campus were in full bloom and the air smelled sweet. The weather was temperate and gentle, promising more robust heat to come but still cooled by morning fogs and an occasional splatter of rain. I thought of Provence. The temperatures of Sonoma Valley and the Vaucluse were often within degrees of each other, two regions reigned by wine and agriculture.

I sat at my desk in the second story of the faculty building and stared out a window. The comparative literature class's mid-term exams were half corrected and I mulled over going to the cafeteria for an afternoon break.

Sophie had recently written with family news and local gossip, including having seen Yvette with Maurice at a café. Maurice had written two more short letters, essentially asking why had I not written him. I put them in a drawer and did not answer.

The professor of mathematics, whom I had met at the Beauchamp's dinner party, turned out to be good company and had a nice sense of humor. However, Harlan's first relationship after his divorce had been with the ex-wife of one of his friends. This had ended badly, as Harlan was prone to discuss. I came to the conclusion I would not have made a good therapist as I longed at times to snap at him to 'get over it and move on.' Only I, myself, was having trouble doing the same. So I nodded and listened as he rehashed his distress.

We were members of the Sierra Club and went on Saturday group hikes. Every couple of weeks we had dinner and went to a movie with friends. Sometimes we'd grab a glass of wine after work. Being in the same profession meant we each understood the pressure to keep up with trends, guide the students, deal with college politics. Neither he nor I seemed anxious to get involved sexually, having gone well past the 'third date' policy. Being practical, our relationship might eventually succeed.

Sometimes as I listened to Harlan wax on about his classes or his former love life, I compared him to Maurice. He made me laugh but he didn't have that special twinkle in his eye. When we kissed, it was cardboard compared to electricity. Harlan loved to travel but preferred England where he understood the language. I once expounded enthusiastically about Surrealist poets and their wartime poetry. Harlan's perfunctory nods of the head caused me to quickly sum up the subject.

However, he seemed genuinely interested when I talked about Char organizing 'drop zones' for men and supplies. He had loved the movie 'A Bridge Too Far,' about soldiers parachuting into Holland. When we saw 'Grey Lady Down,' a submarine adventure film with Charleton Heston, Harlan thought it was terrific. When I suggested seeing 'An Unmarried Woman' with Jill Clayburgh he said that he didn't really enjoy 'chick flicks.' I went, and laughed and cried my way through it.

I didn't mind when I didn't hear from him. At this point, living an interesting life without a partner and having a series of affairs had appeal. My career could take precedence. I'd finally read about Cal's Ph.D. program. I might write a book.

The new professor of Spanish knocked on the partially open door. Susan Perez, who had met her husband when they were students in Mexico City, smiled her wide corn-fed Nebraska grin as she entered. "I hope that you are ready for a break. I'm going crazy correcting the first year Spanish papers--will they ever get it!"

"I'm more than ready."

I grabbed a shoulder bag from a hook and followed Susan down the stairs. In the cafeteria we got coffee then picked a table by a window, a chocolate brownie and two forks on a plate between us.

"How are your students reacting to the World War II stories? You mentioned last time that a couple of them seemed quite interested?"

"Typically there are always one or two who have a passion for history and other cultures. You remember the girl I mentioned, Alyssa? She plans to go on for a master's degree in comparative literature because of her exposure in my class. Her grandfather was a soldier who landed in Provence in 1944 and she wants to write his biography. You never know, do you?"

Susan toyed with a straw in her soda, "That's why we do what we do, I guess. Even with the bureaucracy and crazy policies, there's nothing quite like seeing someone else share one's passion."

Susan leaned in to relate an incident in her classroom that caused us both to laugh. Chit chat. Pleasant conversation to pass the time. Susan asked about Harlan and I told her about our last date, dinner out with friends.

I looked out the window and stopped in mid-sentence.

"What's wrong?" Susan immediately looked out as well.

"Nothing! Just an odd sensation. I saw someone walking across the lawn who reminded me of the fellow with the winery. The one in France."

I looked at a receding figure in jeans with a brown jacket as he went up the steps to the liberal arts building. It was not the first time some distant figure had reminded me of Maurice.

"So tell me more about your move...."

Susan cheerfully regaled me with the enthusiasm of the newly wed and newly mortgaged. After gathering up cups, plate and paper debris and depositing them in a plastic bin, she and I wove our way through students arriving between classes. We were crossing the lawn in the middle of the quad when I froze, as Maurice opened the front door of the building and came down the steps. Susan turned to look at me with a puzzled expression.

I whispered 'Maurice' as he turned and started striding down the walkway toward the parking lot. Then I caught my breath and yelled.

"Maurice!"

He turned and started walking toward me as I ran toward him. I couldn't even get out the question 'what are you doing here?' when I was seized in an embrace that knocked me breathless. I was wrapped in Maurice's wonderful smell, his slightly scratchy beard on my check, his curly hair tickling my nose, then his lips kissing mine. He leaned back and said 'how are you?' in English.

"I'm fine," I answered in English and we kissed again.

Susan stood a few feet away with a puzzled look. When Maurice and I took a breath and moved away from each other, I turned with what I hoped was a perfectly poised expression. "I'd like you to meet my friend, Maurice Laurent."

Susan stepped up and held out her hand, awkwardly saying, "Oh? Pleased to meet you."

Maurice let loose of my waist and shook her hand. He responded in English with 'A pleasure,' then placed his right arm around me again and looked into my moist eyes.

"What are you doing here?"

"I came to see you, of course! We need to finish the talk we didn't have time for when you left."

I felt lighter than a meringue. The tingling sensation was back, I was next to the man I loved and April was truly a beautiful month.

I turned to Susan. "I guess I'll not be going back to the office."

Susan nodded and winked. "I guess not. I'll see you later."

Maurice had driven in from the San Francisco Airport and I could tell that he was tired. I asked, "Do you have a place to stay?"

"I was hoping…unless, of course, you have someone else at your house?" Maurice looked concerned.

"Only the neighbor's cat, temporarily. You can stay with me, of course. As an old friend."

Maurice grinned and pulled me closer. I left my car with its parking permit in the lot and he drove us home in the rental car. Once inside my modest two-bedroom townhouse he put his suitcase down and hung his jacket on the hat rack. I offered him a drink of water. Conversation was brief, about his trip over, with Maurice explaining that he was 'lairning to speak Eenglish.'

"That is good."

He stepped close to me without touching.

"I came to tell you that my life without you is misery. I need to know why you left in such a hurry, why you didn't take time to talk with me first. I need to know if there is any possibility that you love me, even if only a little bit."

I was struck with a range of emotions, from shock to the thrill of being with him again. I burst into tears. He pulled me to him as I hiccupped and dampened his wrinkled shirt.

"Maurice, I don't know how to feel right now other than I'm so glad to see you. You are right, as you usually are, that we need to talk things over." I wrapped my arms around his neck and kissed him, "I have missed you."

Within minutes we were on my bed making love. It was passionate, quick and comforting. As Maurice turned on his back, I snuggled into the crook of his arm. His breathing became slow, rhythmic and he went sound asleep as I watched, hoping that I wasn't simply dreaming.

THE VAUCLUSE - 1944

AUGUST 17, THURSDAY:

It seemed odd that the Kommandantur's headquarters wanted an investigation into Henri's death, since the invasion of Provence had happened two days before. Florence was even more suspicious that he had been closely involved with them.

She was questioned twice: in the apartment while wrapped in a bathrobe, smelling of liniment, her voice a hoarse whisper; again at the police station two days later. She responded in a croaking tone to persistent probes on marital problems, financial problems, Henri's state of mind. Was anyone else in the apartment? How was her health, generally? Did her husband complain of headaches? Two edgy investigators puffed away on foul-smelling *faux* cigarettes, asking whatever came to mind.

She repeated over and over that she was asleep when Henri left. She did not realize that he had been drinking so heavily. Occasionally she coughed, apologizing for her raspy laryngitis. She hoped that she was not contagious. Finally she emphasized that Henri was very worried about what would happen when the Allies arrived in town. The *gendarmes* glanced at each other, one wiped sweat from his upper lip and the interview finished.

The day before the funeral Florence received a visit from the deputy chief of the *gendarmerie*, Guillaume Molinari. He stood in uniform at the door, with *kepi* in hand, and stated that he needed to discuss the cause of Henri's death. Florence motioned Molinari to enter and gestured to a chair at the side of the sofa. His nervousness seemed equal to hers.

"Would you like coffee?" Florence whispered.

The Deputy Chief declined and apologized for bothering her at this unfortunate time, twirling his hat in his hands.

He bluntly stated, "Due to the suspicious circumstances of Monsieur Gilles-Martin's fall down the stairs, the investigation was finished quickly."

Her knees nearly buckled and she dropped to the couch.

He, too, sat down and circumspectly asked, "Are you all right, Madame Gilles-Martin?"

Florence responded hoarsely, "I am getting better although this influenza has lingered longer than I expected."

She knew that she looked haggard and considered sucking in her cheeks. She adjusted the scarf to ensure that the bruises on her throat were covered. The man tugged at his mustache and backed away slightly.

"Ah, that is…umm…good."

He reached into his jacket pocket, pulled out an envelope, leaned forward and handed it to Florence. "Here is the final medical report, um…, from the autopsy. Of your husband."

Florence placed the envelope in her lap then realized that Molinari was waiting for her to read it. With trepidation she slid the report out, unfolded it and scanned the typed form. There was Henri's full name, birthdate, place of birth, date of his death and the 'cause of death.' The cause was written in pen: 'blunt force trauma to the head from a fall on the deceased's home stairwell, probably triggered by dizziness from inebriation and a brain embolism.'

Florence reread the sentence again and murmured 'what?'

The deputy leaned over and pointed to a diagram. "You see, Madame, ummm….apparently your husband had some sort of a thing in his brain and that may have helped cause the fall. Besides…ummm….being very drunk."

Florence frowned and asked. "A stroke? Henri was…." Her voice trailed off.

"Well, ummm," the policeman pointed, "according to the doctor, see further down the report, the left carotid artery had a slight…umm….split and separated enough so that a small blood clot got into his brain. Evidently this can happen easily, when...aahh...if a person jerks their head suddenly or... ohhh...I suppose if he bumped into...ummm...a corner of a cabinet door or something sharp. See, the coroner noted that there was a tiny bruise near the left ear. And then...of course...hitting his head on the marble stairs caused the final....ahh...blows. There were two severe ones."

The man pointed to a diagram showing an 'X' below the right ear and another on the right temple. Florence caught her breath, glancing toward the knitting basket. Could this mean that Henri was still alive when his head bounced on the edges of the steps as he fell?

"I see," she whispered.

Molinari whinnied an odd sort of laugh.

"Of course, there is always the suspicion that a person was pushed down stairs when there is a death such as Monsieur Gilles-Martin's. In your weak condition and...umm...petite size...well...it's doubtful that you could have done it. Madame Vallois testified that you...ahh...appeared extremely sick when she saw you earlier that day. Also your husband...ummm...had enough alcohol in his system to be very unbalanced and...ahhh.... the hemorrhage made it worse."

Florence reached for a handkerchief in her skirt pocket and dabbed at her eyes, dry as they were.

"Now that you mention it," she softly croaked out another lie, "he had complained of a headache. Perhaps he drank because of the pain."

"Ah, yes, well, there you are. Captain Dumaine also mentioned that your husband had a headache...earlier that day. At lunch." Molinari stopped twisting the cap for a moment. "Umm...well, Madame, we wanted you to know that the investigation...ummm... is concluded. We wanted you to know the...ahhh...tragic reason."

Florence agreed that she was relieved to have an explanation for Henri's fall. Molinari almost leapt from the couch and barely touched her fingertips as he backed out the door, stammering something sympathetic.

Her sense of reprieve caused a light-headedness followed by a wave of calm. Florence went to the dining room cabinet. At the back in a cut glass carafe was an inch of aged Port. She placed it on the dining room table, un-corked it and took out a crystal sherry glass. The aroma as she poured the dark gold liqueur carried a hint of celebration and, even as it burned going down her throat, she felt relief.

A momentary, ingrained reaction flitted in her thoughts, the obligation to confess her sin and be exculpated. Florence swallowed another painful sip then raised the glass to the ceiling and muttered "*La Chaim.*"

⸺

August 17: From *Le Ventoux*, the daily collaborationist newspaper:
Official Bulletin from German High Command:
Many attempts by the enemy to land on the south coast, between Toulon and Cannes, have been repulsed. However, the adversary has managed to step foot on some points along the coast. Heavy battles are ensuing. Enemy forces have landed behind our lines and have attacked our reserves: 23 enemy planes were destroyed by our forces along the Atlantic and Mediterranean coasts.

AUGUST 18, FRIDAY:

When the afternoon of the funeral arrived, the brief euphoria of the previous day had dissipated like the fumes of the Port. Florence and Gigi sat on wood chairs in a side altar of St. Siffrein listening to Father Benedict murmur an abbreviated Mass for the dead. There was too much going on to spend time on any one funeral, with German troops marching north and the Allies moving into Provence.

A thick veil on a black felt cloche hat did little to hide Florence's dis-traught and gaunt looks as she shakily endured the ceremony. She wore a wide black scarf around her neck in spite of the heat. Gigi clung to her mother's hand with her left hand and dabbed at her eyes with a sodden handkerchief with her right. Further down the row of chairs, Xavier Chevalier, Juliette and Maurice provided a measure of comfort.

As others accepted that Henri's fall was due to inebriation and a mild stroke, in sympathy, in amazement, in tasteless comments, Florence rationalized that this could be true. Had Henri been on the stairs of his own volition, was it possible that the outcome could have been exactly the same? She conveyed this to Gigi whose expression relaxed in relief. Only tight comments in the well-hidden journal were witness to her jabs with the knitting needle that might have caused the bleed. She had retrieved and destroyed the three envelopes and letters from the Café of the 19th Century days before.

Gigi followed her mother's admonition to say that she had not been in the apartment that day because her mother was ill and her father was leaving for a meeting. She had not gone inside and had, instead, walked down to a café and bought a pastry while waiting for her Cousin Juliette.

Only a few others sat in the chapel with the family. Two members of the chamber music orchestra, with wives in tow, sat stiffly to the side. Deputy Chief Molinari appeared in a rumpled jacket and tie. The Mayor and Officer Demaine peered with narrowed eyes at Florence as if still suspicious. She was shocked when three German officers arrived and sat stiffly in the back row. There were other friends, Florence was sure, who would have come except for the uncertainty over what might happen as the Allies came north.

Although a devastated *Maman* wanted to come for the funeral, she was unable to arrange transportation since most of the routes from Germany had been bombed. The elderly woman badgered Florence about sending the statement from the medical examiner so that she could read for herself the actual cause of death.

At the end of the Mass, the Cathedral bells tolled a melancholy minor-key homage. Florence, with Gigi behind her, stood by the chapel's exterior grate and thanked those who came. Lieutenant Ziegler stopped, arrayed in full military garb with rows of ribbons and brass medals, silver wings, swastikas, his hat under his arm. He bowed his head but did not offer his gloved hand. Florence shivered, breathed deeply and looked at her shoes. The Kommandantur and a member of the Brandenburg Division's *Abhwer* followed him. After murmuring a perfunctory word of sympathy, they departed amid clicking heels.

As soon as the coffin was carried out to the waiting hearse, Juliette spoke in low tones. "My dear Florence, you must come stay with us until we know what is likely to happen."

"You're right, Juliette. I need to get away."

"You also need to rest and recover from that flu. I don't like the fact that you have not been able to keep food down." Juliette looked at her with concern. "You don't seem at all well."

"You are so kind! I..I'm..grateful." Florence grasped her cousin's hand. "I need to meet with Henri's lawyer to sign documents tomorrow then I will come straight to the Domaine."

Maurice stood with his arm across Gigi's shoulders in a brotherly gesture, as his distraught young cousin wiped away tears. Florence reassured her daughter that she would be at the Laurents' home within a day or two.

"*Maman,* please come with us now! I am so worried."

"*Ma petite oiseau,* I will be with you as soon as I'm able but I have to talk with the *notaire* tomorrow. Think of the good times that we will have when the war is finally over. We can go to the beach next summer, some quiet spot where you can play in the ocean. Don't worry, my darling."

While she planned to contact Henri's attorney the next day, Florence also was desperate to contact Antoine. She was certain that she was pregnant and they needed to talk.

WEDDING BELLS - 1979

The Judge at the Sonoma County Court House was always happy to take a moment from listening to irritated litigants in order to perform a marriage ceremony. The couple standing in front of him was an attractive middle-aged pair, she with blonde-streaked light brown hair, blue eyes and English skin, in a simple ivory-colored dress; he with the tan of an outdoors man, brown eyes and graying curly hair, wearing a black jacket. He paused at the string of French names indicating the groom. He hoped he would be able to pronounce them reasonably well and, with an encouraging smile, opened the Bible with its typed, large-print insert and began the brief ceremony.

Maurice and I held hands until it came time for him to place a thin gold band on my finger. I handed my bouquet to Katy Franchini, my former college roommate. I looked over at Maurice who seemed touched by our vows even though he probably understood only one-tenth of what he heard. Behind Maurice was his 'best man,' JT, who had arrived six days before.

Family and friends had been caught off guard by our sudden decision to marry although to Maurice and me it made great sense. After he arrived we had spent hours sharing thoughts, emotions and histories. I told him how the divorce had affected me, the impact of the women's movement, that I wasn't sure that I wanted a doctorate or to teach for the rest of my life. I felt guilty at causing a rift between him and Gabrielle.

Maurice told me about his marriage, a relationship based on proximity as much as anything. It lacked passion but was comfortable and welcomed by his family. He and Brigitte became lovers when she was eighteen and he was twenty. They got married when she became pregnant. Julien was born the following year, in 1951.

He didn't remember his wife ever talking about the deaths of her parents. She seemed to have blocked those memories as well as wartime hardships from her mind. She was a voracious reader yet reticent and almost reclusive. She loved opera and symphonies but had a strange aversion to art museums. She had been a wonderful mother to their children. Even more I felt deeply that the memory of Brigitte, as well as her mother, should be protected; I would never disclose what I knew.

When I mentioned his sister's hostility Maurice explained that Gabrielle had married Alphonse Thibault, a much older and very wealthy man, when she was thirty years old. It was not a happy marriage. Her husband had seemed proud to show off his beautiful bride in the early years but now he lived in Marseille with his latest and much younger mistress. Gabrielle was bitter but would never divorce him. We both commented on her drinking.

Although the sex was passionate what was most important was our simple joy in being together. We teased good-naturedly and laughed often. The only possible conflict was my love of sleeping late and Maurice's ability to wake up early, full of energy.

Even our horoscopes were good. I found a book called 'Starmates' and, according to its analysis of sun, moon, Mars and Venus, Maurice and I were extremely compatible.

"That must be the reason!" He winked as he pecked my cheek.

"You don't know how important astrology is to those of us living in Sonoma. It is hard to go to any event without someone asking about your sign." I attempted to look perturbed.

"And what do you say?" He asked.

"Either 'yield' or 'soft shoulder.'"

Maurice looked puzzled and I realized that he didn't get the reference to our highway signs. Sometimes the difference in languages was an advantage as neither disclosed every thought; sometimes it ended in either misunderstandings or hilarity.

When Harlan called and invited me to a Sunday matinee followed by dinner at his house, I explained that I was involved with someone else. He was French.

"Oh? Well, you had mentioned meeting someone over there but I didn't know it was serious."

I winced. "I didn't either, I mean, it was rather sudden."

Harlan sounded annoyed and closed with 'I hope you will be happy.' I suspected that he had decided to seduce me after all these weeks of 'maybe, maybe not.'

Two weeks after Maurice's arrival we announced our engagement. My father and brothers cautioned me about being hasty, amid concerns about living so far away. JT was stunned and asked that I wait until Christmas. I told him that he'd always be my number one man but this relationship was the right one for me. He did agree to be Maurice's 'best man' and returned to talking about finals.

My ex-husband Ted was horrified that I would marry someone I hardly knew, especially from France. It was with satisfaction that I told him that it was none of his business. I was calling to inform him, not to discuss it. My colleagues were surprised; several asked about moving into my office. The department head was very irritated that she would need to find a replacement by fall and barely mouthed out 'best wishes.'

Maurice called his mother who told the rest of the family the news. When he talked with each of his three children, he was reassured by how sweetly his children approved of his remarrying. I said that they were probably thankful to be relieved of the responsibility of looking after him, as he grew old. I promised that I'd be his nurse, wipe the drool from his chin and spoon-feed him. For that I got a tap on my rear and a nice kiss.

I graded finals, cleaned out the office with Maurice and Susan's help, and completed paperwork. A long-term visa for France was in process. In between I introduced Maurice to California wine making.

We visited the Franchinis who, in 1966, had bought an orchard and pasture with a cabin in northern Napa Valley. After building a modest home on the property they had quit their jobs in the City. Katy, green-eyed, red-haired and as Irish as the Kelly clan could produce was a real estate agent in Napa while Andrew, of Jewish and Italian descent, handled the vineyard and making and selling the wine. We toured the Franchini's property, including a new cave dug into a hill behind their house. Maurice and Andrew discussed the difference between wines made in California and France. Sampling the newest crush, we clicked glasses in shared pleasure and discussed plans for the wedding reception at their home.

Maurice and I drove down old Highway 29 starting at Calistoga's Chateau Montelena in its 1880's stone structure, famous for the Chardonnay picked as the best wine at the 1976 Paris tasting. We ended up at the southern end, in an 1880's winery re-established by the Trefethens a decade before. I pointed out that the phylloxera epidemic of the 1890's and then Prohibition in the 1920's forced most of California's wine producers to close. At one time there had been almost one hundred and forty wineries in the Valley. In the early 1970's, there were fewer than twenty newly dedicated, crazy people restarting the industry.

Maurice shook his head, "To think that our region has been making wines for over two thousand years and here, an 'old' winery is maybe one hundred years old! *Sacre bleu.* These people still have a lot to learn, I think."

On the day of our wedding reception at the Franchini home, Napa was in full summer color and already hot. The sky was a fraction lighter than the blue in Provence, the orchards were heavy with young fruit and vineyards were leafed out in deep green with budding grape clusters. Bright yellow mustard wound through fields of cows and wiggled in between vines. Oak-dotted hills were still tinted chartreuse, not yet the heat-sapped golden-beige of summer.

All my family came: my father, stepmother, two brothers and sisters-in-law with their children. JT invited a girl from high school days although I was hearing a lot about a 'Martha,' a girlfriend from Boston. The Franchinis' daughter Kimberly was home from boarding school. I invited several colleagues including Susan and Allesandro Perez, as well as friends from the

Alliance Française in San Francisco. The party was as Mediterranean as Katy and I could make it. We served typical Provençal dishes, ending with our wedding cake of *profiteroles* stacked in a cone and drizzled with caramel sauce.

Maurice and I stood together as I told about the Muscat that he'd brought. He poured the gold liquid into outstretched glasses. Maurice beamed as everyone lifted their small goblets toward us, with murmurs of 'congratulations,' 'many happy years,' etc.

My father, with Roselyn in a form-fitting red sheath at his side, had warmed to the thought of visiting his other favorite country with a winemaker as part of the family. He raised his glass and toasted, "Welcome, Maurice, to the Pearson family. To you and Claire, may the best of your yesterdays be the worst of your tomorrows. May your love be modern enough to survive the current times and old-fashioned enough to last forever!" Then he repeated the phrase in still adequate French.

Maurice then stepped forward and, in heavily accented English, stated, "To Claire, who makes today the most happiest of my life."

Glasses clinked, conversation resumed and we shared an especially sweet kiss.

Two days later I stood in San Francisco International Airport and waved to Maurice as he boarded the plane for Paris. An ancient steamer trunk of my great-grandmother's was on its way to Marseille, filled with clothes, sentimental knick-knacks, a set of sterling silver, books and picture albums. Each time that I made a trip to California it was likely that more stuff would be gathered up and shipped to Provence.

The condo had sold, a few pieces of furniture were tucked into my father's five bedrooms but most had been donated to charities. Boxes of books were stored in Dad's attic, along with my notes on the writers of the Resistance and Florence Gilles-Martin's journal. Things that once were highly desired, that I had judiciously collected, had fought over in the divorce, did not seem that important.

At this point I couldn't see ahead. Life had taken an unexpected turn and seemed to be on its own trajectory without any guidance on my part. As the writer in the journal had poignantly written in her last entry, "A new life…"

Little did I realize then how true this would become.

THE ADVENTURER
ANDRÉ MALRAUX

Still in uniform, sitting in a grungy hotel room where the Gestapo had tossed him after bandaging bullet wounds in his legs, *Colonel Berger* knew the grilling would start again soon. With a hastily fabricated background yet using his real name, he had described himself as a professor, a writer and a lieutenant colonel serving de Gaulle. He hoped that the Germans would have difficulty tracing him and would treat him as a normal prisoner of war.

How quickly things can change, André Malraux thought. At times like these he reflected wistfully on those eventful months that he and Clara had spent in French Indochina right after they were married. He'd managed to get out of tight spots before; perhaps he could do it again.

In 1922 André and Clara had spent many carefree days and most of his fortune wandering among Florence's palaces and museums while avoiding the disapproval of the Goldschmidt and Malraux families. In October 1923, after his investments in Mexican mining shares became worthless, André and Clara left France for Saigon on a boat called *Angkor*. The idea of pillaging artifacts from recently discovered Indochinese temples to sell in France seemed like a wonderful solution to their financial problems.

He, Clara and his partner loaded goods into carts pulled by buffalo, hired guides with short mountain ponies, then took off from Phnom Penh for a jungle area near *Angkor Wat* that was not yet designated a 'protected area.' They chiseled and sawed off a number of bas-reliefs then returned to Saigon to book passage back to Europe.

Arrested for defacing ancient monuments, their passports were confiscated and all three spent months under house arrest, waiting for a trial. André and Clara were stunned when he was sentenced to three years in prison and five years probation. His partner was condemned to eighteen months in jail. Clara was innocent of all charges, a dutiful wife simply doing her husband's bidding.

This innocent party sailed for Paris to enlist the help of prominent friends. Max Jacob, André Breton, André Gide, Louis Aragon and others vouched that the French literary world would be bereft of one of its most valued writers if young André Malraux were imprisoned. Many of his popular publications had been mildly pornographic, 'exotic' tales that artist friends illustrated.

Funds were raised for a better legal defense and Clara returned to Saigon. This time, with a competent attorney, André was given a one year suspended sentence. In November 1924 the couple returned to France not only chastened but with a new purpose.

During the year in Indochina, Malraux' exposure to the French Colonial culture and oppression of native inhabitants, called the *Annamese*, dismayed him. He witnessed land grabs, rubber plantation workers treated as sub-humans, the takeover of local businesses, governmental control by the foreign occupants and a lack of the most basic human rights for natives. A radical communist was gaining traction among the downtrodden in the region: a former Chinese teacher named Ho Chi Minh.

Paul Monin, an attorney and activist who was on the ships to and from France with Clara, shared the same ideals and political views as Malraux. Although sympathetic to the Russian Revolution, both were too Republican at heart, more inspired by their own country's ideals of justice, fairness and equality. They decided that what was needed was an anti-Colonialist newspaper, which happened to be illegal.

Undeterred, the Malraux returned to Paris to gather support for his publication. His father provided 50,000 francs and, upon the couple's return to

Saigon, Chinese backers gave more. *L'Indochine* was launched. A free journal, it lasted barely three months before closing; yet in forty-nine published issues it became known for exposing the overreaching of monopolistic businesses, land grabs and the governor-general's corruption and racism.

André's final editorial in August 1925 reflected his own moral and political development: *"It would seem that the political idiocies of sectional interests and money are applying themselves with unusual determination to destroying what we have been able to do, and to reawakening in this old land, with memories of a great past, the muffled echoes of six hundred revolts."*

Buoyed with the enthusiasm of revolutionaries and the obstinacy of youth, André and Paul headed for Hong Kong to publish under the new name *"L'Indochine enchaînée."* It lasted less than a month. Broke, in ill health, frustrated and disillusioned, André confided to faithful Clara that 'there's nothing left for me now but to write.'

They came back to Paris in early January 1926 and a semi-autobiographical, moderately self-promoting novel about his experiences, called *"The Conquerers,"* was published.

His relationship with the Surrealist writers, the recognized literati of the day, was rocky. Arriving late to the table, he was excluded from their séances and criticized for the perceived opportunism and self-glorification in his novel. Gallimard published Breton, Char, Aragon; Bernard Grasset's firm published Malraux.

Malraux became known for his analyses of East-West relations rather than for promoting a revolution. He was recognized as an authority, a gifted writer (one of Albert Camus' favorites) and, in 1929, was hired as an editor at Gallimard. His third book, an existential analysis of characters involved in the Chinese Revolution, *'La Condition Humaine'* ('Man's Fate,'), was awarded the prestigious Goncourt Prize in 1933 and became a best seller. His and Clara's daughter was born.

In 1934 some passing information, part from T.E. Lawrence of Saudi Arabia fame, part from the French National Geographic, caught André's attention. Within weeks he was in the air over the North African-Arabian desert searching for the lost city of the Queen of Sheba, with a pilot and a mechanic in a borrowed plane. To his dismay his detailed accounts of their 'discovery,' including pictures, were discredited within a short time.

Then problems in Spain caught his attention in 1936. Here was a cause worthy of his romantic imagination. At the start of the Spanish Civil War, Malraux organized a volunteer air force to help the Loyalists, put himself in charge, collected French planes to loan to them and personally flew on sixty-five missions as a bombardier.

Attempting to raise money for this latest project, he came to the United States. He visited Ernest Hemingway in Key West, Florida where he was writing a new novel, *To Have and Have Not.* The two men were cut from the same cloth in many ways. They admired each other's books: Malraux's *La Condition Humane;* Hemingway's *A Farewell to Arms.* They were middle class, self-educated and passionate anti-fascists. Each of their fathers had committed suicide and both loved cats.

Malraux was six feet tall, with large ears, a noticeable tic, a dark forelock flopping over one eye, a cigarette often hanging from the corner of his mouth. Used to being the center of attention, he spoke authoritatively and poetically; he elucidated brilliant new concepts, mesmerizing listeners with stories of exaggerated exploits. When in Spain, Hemingway came a few times to the Hotel Florida in Madrid, a gathering spot of intellectuals and writers, but was turned off by Malraux's dramatics. Neither liked the other.

French communists considered Malraux a 'sympathetic outsider but not one of them.' This adventurer retained his own form of idealism and fraternity and, as Hitler rose to power and fascism became a true threat, history provided him an ethical platform on which he would base his personal views of man searching for dignity and his soul: 'destiny in terms of possibility.' André's persona calmed, his confidence increased, he prepared to act once again, with greater maturity.

Knowing that war with Germany was likely, André was exasperated when the French air force rejected him. However, he was eligible to serve in a tank division—as a private. Used to custom-made suits, intellectual companions and comfortable beds, his new comrades-in-arms were peasants, firemen, pimps, farmers. Captured and confined to a POW camp in 1940, he once again came up with a creative solution. Dressed in carpenter's pants, he put a plank on his shoulders and escaped by walking out of the camp's gate. While on his way to the 'free zone' he helped some *Maquisards* blow up a munitions train near Toulouse.

Separated from Clara, Malraux and his mistress Josette Clotis, with their newborn son, moved in with her disapproving parents on the Mediterranean coast. Cut off from his publishing income André was again on the brink of poverty when he encountered Varian Fry, the American heading up the Emergency Rescue Committee in Marseille. André turned down Fry's offer to help him leave the country. Instead, he asked him to contact his publishers at Random House in New York, and the editors agreed to send regular payments. Although he was asked to join a Resistance group, André decided to spend the next two years writing. Sometimes he dined with his new friend Varian and the Belgian-Russian journalist Victor Serge. He spoke with André Breton and learned that René Char was a frequent visitor. These three had a tepid relationship and avoided each other.

When the 'free zone' was occupied in late 1942, life became precarious once again. Malraux, Josette and the baby fled west to the Perigord, an area of prehistoric cave fame. The family hid out in a remote village chateau where a second son was born in 1943.

André was sure that the Allies planned to invade France and saw an opportunity to step into a leadership role. He managed through personality, contacts and *hutzpah* to become one of the chief organizers of 1,500 Maquis. He picked the name *Colonel Berger* and worked with men sent by General de Gaulle to prepare for the invasion. As the Germans stepped up their search for terrorists, Roland Malraux, André's younger half-brother who was in the Resistance, was arrested in early 1944.

Adjusting his wounded legs, Malraux mused that things had gone fairly smoothly for his Maquis group. They helped arrange the successful drop of the largest number of arms and munitions in the forests of *Causses de Quercy* on July 14th. It was right after this successful drop that he and five in his group drove toward the town of Gramat, unaware that Germans had seized the town. The Nazis opened fire at a roadblock, wounding Malraux and killing the chauffeur. Four others, including a wounded Englishman, escaped into the forest.

The only reason that Malraux had not been tortured and shot was due to a mix-up over his name. The Gestapo could not find his dossier and did not know that his birth name was Georges-André. Compulsive about records, they were still puzzling over what might be a clerical error. It was clear that they confused him with his brother, Roland, whom they knew was in the Dachau concentration camp. Who was this unidentifiable character? The Germans moved him from town to town, periodically questioning him.

On August 19th he ended up in a prison in the town of Toulouse. After yet another rough interrogation he was sent back to a cell containing ten other prisoners. In the morning the group awakened to women singing the *Marseillaise* in the courtyard. Leaning out the window they learned that the Germans had fled during the night.

Colonel Berger stayed briefly with his half-brother Roland's wife and her family, then left for Paris within days of its liberation. He was annoyed to learn that Ernest Hemingway claimed that he helped liberate the Ritz Hotel. Malraux went to Hemingway's room. There was a sarcastic and heated exchange between the two, each claiming greater heroism regarding their parts played at the war's end. Malraux stormed off. He had other projects in mind.

Amid significant controversy André had himself proposed as chief of a group of Alsatians intent on reclaiming their homeland from the Nazis. One of his friends finally convinced the military that he was not a communist; that he was a staunch ally of de Gaulle's and should be given a chance.

In mid-September 1944 Malraux stood before a mirror in his hotel room, his tic the only thing marring his image. He adjusted the belt of his uniform, straightened his black beret--the symbol of the Spanish Republicans--pleased at the high polish on his boots. He was off on another adventure, this time as commander of what was dubbed the 'Alsace-Lorraine Brigade' of the Free French of the Interior (FFI). He already imagined himself being hailed as a conquering hero when the War ended.

Excerpts from <u>La Condition Humaine</u> *(44)*

You can cheat life for a long time, but it always ends up making us into that for which we are destined. Being old is an acknowledgment, after all, and if old age is empty to so many it is that most men were vacant and hiding it. But even that is without importance. It will be necessary for man to be able to understand that nothing is real, that contemplative worlds exist—with or without opium—where all is in vain.

The great mystery is not that we should have been thrown down here at random between the profusion of matter and that of the stars; it is that from our very prison we should draw, from our own selves, images powerful enough to deny our own nothingness.

André Malraux   1901 – 1976

THE VAUCLUSE - 1944

AUGUST 20, SUNDAY:

Étienne Bertolini, the newest member of *Centurion's* Resistance cell, translated documents obtained from German bodies and listened in on German radio frequencies. Information on troop movements and plans was then relayed down to Corsica and de Gaulle's headquarters. What amazed him was the fast and precise information sent back to the Maquis from London, through Commander Corbin de la Mangoux. Bertolini was suspicious that the infamous German code system had been broken.

Étienne and Roland often sat and talked during their breaks. They found mutual interest in patriotic poems found in *Combat*, *L'Humanité* or contraband booklets, reading out loud to each other pieces by Aragon, Eluard or lesser-known writers. Étienne had received a full report on Missak Manouchian's importance shortly after meeting Roland. The young men disagreed on who should govern France at the end of the war--one a staunch communist and the other equally strong in his support of General de Gaulle; however, fervent anti-fascism provided common ground. Being 'free and independent' was most important.

Plan Vert (green plan) required nightly forays to cut communication lines along roads and up hillsides. The more agile--Roland among them--became adept at climbing telephone poles by using a rope or band wrapped around their waists and the pole. Within days of repairing, sometimes hours, wires would once again lie listlessly in dirt.

Because of broken communication lines, General Freidrich Wiese could not reach General Johannes Blaskowitz at Army Group G on the Mediterranean coast to find out about the success of that group's defense. Both Wiese and Blaskowitz had had most of their divisions diverted after the Normandy landing. The troops that were left were ill equipped and staffed by old veterans and recruits from conquered countries. On the night of August 16, Blaskowitz realized that he could not stop the Allied advance and he, too, was unable to contact or strategize with his counterpart. He decided to appeal to the German high command.

Apoplectic at the thought of abandoning his 'no step backwards' policy, Adolph Hitler resisted approving a retreat in Provence. When he finally and very reluctantly agreed, a 'strategic withdrawal' was allowed. Blocked from leaving southern France through routes into the French-Italian Alps, there was no recourse but to move troops further up the Rhone Valley, where the officers hoped to mount a defense.

AUGUST 21, MONDAY:

When Florence arrived to hear about Henri's will, the attorney and his assistant were preoccupied with sorting and destroying documents. When she was told to return on Monday, she sent a courier to inform Juliette of the delay. Arriving early that morning, she learned that one-third of all they owned had been bequeathed to Henri's mother. Henri had assured Florence that 'she and Gigi would be taken care of well.' Seething inwardly, she signed the documents. The attorney said that he would inform Henri's mother whom Florence suspected not only knew of the will's contents but was involved in setting it up.

At eleven-thirty Monday morning, sweat beading on her face, Florence shuttered each window but one. In case of an explosion or bomb, she had packed up and carried cartons of china and crystal down to the storeroom in the cellar. Boxes of books, too heavy to move, were still on the floor. Henri's clothes hung in his closet as before; his paraphernalia cluttered up drawers and tabletops.

Uncle Xavier had come by every day, seeming confused and lonely, and they spent time talking over coffee or wine. She had tried to find out about Antoine without raising suspicion. She thought that he might have joined the Maquis Ventoux and was up on the mountain somewhere. Or living in a farmhouse with a family willing to hide him and Sylvie. Or he could be in Carpentras in one of the many cellars and tunnels honeycombing the hilltop town. Trains full of people were still being sent on to camps, and this was Florence's greatest fear.

The sudden scream of a plane passing overhead caused her to gasp, then peer out as it disappeared. Sounds of gunfire came from a distance. It was time to go. She grabbed her hat and purse, locking the door behind her. A small suitcase was strapped to the back of her bicycle with a leather belt and a piece of rope. A tapestry carpetbag in the front basket held knitting materials, a few poetry books, her journal and a velvet pouch of jewelry.

She looked around as she opened the door. As she walked the bicycle down the street Florence watched a man and woman loading a wheelbarrow with belongings. Both from working as a courier and reading poetry, Florence's sense of observation had sharpened. Reluctant to suddenly turn and stare, to see if a shadow moved into a side street or behind a pillar, she acted as normally as possible. She jumped on the bicycle, gripped the handlebars tightly and pedaled as fast as she could toward the Porte d'Orange, hoping that she would not be stopped.

Flying down the hill to the east with her feet held out in front, Florence gloried in a moment of freedom, her hair blowing in the warm breeze, her blouse puffing out like a sail. Trucks, tanks and equipment vehicles further down the road slowed her pace and she walked the bike far to the side. A narrow dirt track normally used by tractors through the vineyards and olive groves seemed to be a quicker, safer route, so she took it.

As Florence cycled up a slight hill along the narrow pathway, edged by a deep irrigation ditch on the right, she heard the snarl of a motorcycle from a distance. Within seconds, she realized that the vehicle was coming toward her. Over her shoulder she saw a motorbike with a sidecar, a lone driver wearing a helmet and goggles. In a panic, she pedaled faster, heading toward a plank across the dry ditch. As she turned to see how close the vehicle was, she felt the impact.

Florence saw her legs outlined against the sky then felt the snap of her collarbone as she hit the ground. There was the stab of pain, the harsh scrape of dirt and rocks on the side of her face, the whoosh of air leaving her lungs, the twist of her hips as she rolled onto her back, on the other side of the ditch.

Florence lay for several minutes, trying to catch her breath. She waited for the motorcycle to return, sure that the German intended to kill her. Instead she heard birds singing, the lazy whirr of an insect, the distant bleat of a goat. Gradually she turned to her left and pushed up to a sitting position, gasping at the effort. Her right shoulder and side hurt with every intake of air. Holding her right arm with her left, she got onto her knees and then her feet. Her bicycle, in the ditch, was bent beyond repair, the suitcase hanging off to the side, the carpetbag lying six feet away under a tree. She walked up to the plank and crossed back to the road. A broken sandal strap slipped and flopped as she staggered along.

She saw a low stone farmhouse around a bend. It looked abandoned, but as she got closer she saw the flutter of laundry hanging behind a corner. As Florence reached the gravel driveway, defined by low cement pillars, she saw someone at the front door.

"Hello," she called. "I need help, please."

A thin woman with gray hair pulled taut at her neck stood suspiciously inside the door's shadow. "What do you want?"

"I had a bicycle accident and may have broken my shoulder."

The woman hesitated then walked toward her. As she approached, she walked faster.

"Oh, my dear, you really have hurt yourself. Let me help you." She reached for Florence's arm and was waved away.

"Don't touch me, please. It hurts every time that I move." She bent her head, "I need to sit down."

The woman pointed her toward the low pillar. "Wait here, I'll bring you some water."

She returned in minutes with a metal cup. Florence drank deeply and murmured, "Thank you so much."

"What happened? Where is your bicycle?"

"It's down the road, with my suitcase and bag. I was on my way to the *Domaine de Lauritaine*."

"The Laurents? I can get a message to them, but you need to see a doctor if you have a broken bone. My husband will arrive soon and he can take you to town. In any case, I will get your things." The wiry woman shaded her eyes and looked down the road, saying, "I'll be right back."

Florence sat still, hoping the dizziness and nausea would recede. Intense pain diminished to throbbing, the scrapes to a low burning. Soon her rescuer came up the road, an article in each hand.

"Can you walk to the house by yourself?"

"Yes, but you are right. I should see a doctor. I'm sure that my shoulder bone is broken and possibly my wrist."

Madame Perséphoné Saint-Cloud introduced herself. What a lovely name for such a simple woman, Florence thought. The house was plainly furnished, spartan except for stacks of linens neatly ironed and arranged in baskets on a large table. The aroma of soap and sun-dried cloth permeated the room. Madame Saint-Cloud explained that she did laundry for the Germans. Within minutes, Monsieur Saint-Cloud arrived and settled Florence into the passenger seat, solicitous and concerned. The laundress placed covered baskets of ironed sheets and clean towels on the truck bed, then put Florence's battered suitcase and dirt-smeared carpetbag next to them.

Florence leaned toward Perséphoné Saint-Cloud. "When you go to the Domaine Lauritaine, please reassure Madame Laurent that I'm not seriously hurt and I'll be there in a couple of days."

Monsieur Saint-Cloud wove in and out of the traffic that clogged the main road. When the truck leaned to the side, Florence moaned and he looked over in sympathy. He drove past the Hotel Dieu, hung with red and black banners. Ambulances and trucks rotated out of the entrance, evacuating wounded German soldiers from the hospital.

"Please stop at the *allée-des-platanes.* I can walk from there to the doctor's office. Thank you very much, Monsieur Saint-Cloud."

Saint-Cloud parked and helped his passenger down from the truck. He carried her suitcase and satchel as they crossed boulevard Jean Jaurés to the *cabinet* of Doctor Desjardins, and waited until the doctor came to door. Desjardins immediately took Florence into the examination room and told a woman with a little boy to go to the waiting room. He would bring out a prescription for the child's cough. Only one other person was there, an elderly man with a patch on one eye and a left hand that continually shook.

The doctor helped Florence onto the table and questioned her. She made the accident sound like it was her fault; that she had tried to avoid the traffic going north and had fallen into a drainage ditch. As he removed the scarf from Florence's neck, he spoke sharply. "Madame!"

Florence put her hand on his and shook her head. I was....attacked. But that was a week ago and the bruises aren't painful anymore."

"I am so sorry."

Without saying anything more, he gently applied an ointment, wrapped a wide swath of gauze around her throat and taped it. He listened to her heart, shone a light into her eyes and asked her to move her head to each side, up and back. He inspected her right hand and wrist, moving up her arm to the shoulder. Florence cried out as the doctor felt along the bone.

"You probably have a broken clavicle. It won't be possible to get it x-rayed, with all that is going on, but I can feel that the break is off-center. I need to move it back into place. I'll give you a shot that will deaden the pain."

He moved to a cupboard at the back and returned with a syringe. There was a welcome numbness, but even with the narcotic Florence gasped as the bone was aligned.

"I will put your arm in a sling and wrap it to your torso to keep the bone in place. This should hold everything for the month that it will take to set. You need rest for the next few days, Madame, and keep your arm as still as possible."

He bandaged her wrist, cleaned her face and hands with disinfectant, then dabbed the scrapes with iodine. He adjusted her blouse around her strapped arm and buttoned it. Florence wrapped her scarf around her neck with her left hand.

"Your wrist is sprained but try not to use it. I need to see you on Wednesday, to ensure that there is no other problem."

She picked up the satchel at the front door. "May I leave my suitcase? I'll send a friend for it."

The doctor agreed and moved to open the door for her. Florence walked slowly into town, trudging her way toward the apartment, keeping her head bent so her loosely hanging hair would hide her face.

General Jean Joseph Marie Gabriel de Lattre de Tassigny, leader of the Free French First Army, was astonished at the rapidity of the advance in Provence. He stood over a table with detailed maps, markers and tokens that showed the curves and zigzags of his French and Algerian forces' progress. He also knew that, due to the unexpected momentum of General Patch's American Seventh Army, the Allies were further inland than anticipated. Supply trucks were barely able to keep up.

Originally de Lattre de Tassigny and the two commanders had planned to attack the critical port cities of Toulon and Marseille successively. Two days before, he had decided that a simultaneous assault could be executed. Split into two units, the French First Army had encircled and attacked both towns. German troops defending the cities were in disarray, as they tried to organize a defense.

Stepping to the radio, he reported to Charles de Gaulle on developments as the troops fought to capture the ports.

De Gaulle was pleased--things were going well, overall. He had just spent a week badgering and negotiating so that General Philippe Leclerc's French Armored division would be the first to enter Paris, and he had finally triumphed.

When Madame Saint-Cloud walked up to the Domaine's front door and announced that Florence had broken her shoulder, Juliette brought her into the kitchen, gave her a glass of wine and peppered her with questions. As soon as she left, Juliette walked to the upper vineyard and told Jean-Pierre the news. They decided not to tell Gigi until they knew more.

Maurice was in the equipment barn stringing used corks on wire to be tied around the tire rim of his mother's bicycle, in place of a rubber tube. At the news, he quickly twisted the last of the wires, testing to be sure that they were tight.

When Juliette arrived in town, breathless from the ride, she left the bicycle in the entry and ran up the stairs. At the door, she winced at Florence's appearance.

"Juliette, do I look that bad?"

"Your face is very ornamental, my dear, almost cubist. How are you feeling?"

"I'm comfortable as long as I lie down."

Florence turned and walked back to her bed. Juliette fussed with the sheet and helped get her settled, then went to the kitchen to see what could be fixed for supper. A jar of canned tomatoes from the Domaine's garden and some dried lentils would make a decent soup. She took an apron from a hook and placed a pan on the burner of the stove.

GRAPES AND WRATH - 1984

Happily, the Laurent family swept me into its vortex from the day that I arrived as Maurice's wife. Their original curiosity at *l'Americaine* evolved into acceptance, and soon I became part of a routine and steadfast French life. His children wanted to 'lairn Eenglish' so I became the family's tutor.

However, for a year after I arrived at the Domaine, Gabrielle refused to come to Sunday dinners. When she and her children grudgingly realized that I was not going to go away, that Maurice and I were legally married not only in California but also in a civil ceremony by the mayor of Carpentras, they resumed coming a couple of times a year. As grandchildren arrived and careers accelerated, each family had different schedules so this wasn't as blatant an affront.

Neither Maurice nor I could understand the reason for his sister's animosity. I chewed over any number of possibilities, none of which made much sense. Sadly, she was not close to either of her brothers and acted aloof much of the time. Juliette seemed protective and anxious to mollify her daughter's behavior, making excuses for her.

Every month Juliette spent a week at the Thibault's impressive villa, perched on a hill near Aix-en-Provence. I became chauffeur and drove the three-hour round trip, at first without being invited inside even for a glass of water. After the second year, Gabrielle invited me in and regaled me with her children's accomplishments.

I learned from Amélie that Juliette's reference to the 'difficulties' Gabrielle suffered during the war were due to her having been a German officer's mistress. This explained much, from the rift between her and Francois to Gabrielle having had many lovers. Amélie said that she bragged about sleeping with thirty-four different men before getting married. Her husband had been her employer, an older widower with two teen-agers. His and Gabriel's children were Audrey and Gerard.

Over the years, as Juliette and I shelled peas, made jam or canned vegetables, I heard about the father-in-law I never knew, a solidly built man with a quick temper and a passion for his vines. During our kitchen chats she talked about people that they hid in the cellar during the war, about Francois' and Amélie's romance. I learned about Brigitte, her solitary, self-contained character, her interest in music.

After a couple of years and feeling well accepted by the family, I cautiously touched on the Gilles-Martin family. The Laurents, including my sweet husband, barely mentioned Brigitte's parents other than saying that they liked Cousin Florence and thought that Brigitte was much like her. Henri was described as 'opinionated, conservative, an opportunist'--but never as a 'collaborator.' Amélie, whom I knew had told Florence of Henri's *liaison* with a German officer, never once mentioned this to me. As time went on I became sure that only she and I knew about this, and only I knew that Henri had been murdered.

The French guarded many secrets from wartime. Post-war attempts to heal wounds and hide crimes imbued them with a fear of disclosing too much. It didn't take long before I became as adept as the Laurents in keeping confidences. Incidents and impressions, gathered up one stem at a time, gradually formed a bouquet of personalities heavily influenced by their choices during the German Occupation. I, too, was keeping a journal.

Then, in August 1984, Maurice received a letter from Gabrielle.

"What is this? Did you take her pearls on your last visit to the villa?" Maurice frowned. "She's says that you hid them in the 'deux chevaux.' We haven't had that car for three years."

We looked at each other in astonishment. I read over the scribbled note, shrugging my shoulders. "I imagine that she's misplaced them and they'll turn up."

"You're right. Let's just forget it."

The following month Gabrielle came for Sunday dinner with Audrey, Pierre and their two children. A few days later I realized that a set of antique silver spoons was missing. I asked Juliette if she had moved them. She hadn't and we searched all the drawers. Without telling me, Juliette called Gabrielle. She admitted taking them and sent them back by mail.

After the opening of the annual Truffle Market in November, Maurice received another letter stating that she wanted me to immediately return the fur coat that I'd stolen on my last visit. She was sure that I'd also taken a box of valuable old books. She ranted for a full page that he was to make me stop going through her armoires and chests.

"I've not done any of this. What do you think is going on?"

The year before Gabrielle had tripped in her garden, sprained her ankle then started taking prescription pain pills. I'd seen boxes of pharmaceuticals in her purse when she'd left it on a hall chair. We noticed that she drank a Vodka cocktail before mid-day dinners, followed by several glasses of wine, and she was gaining weight. We were suspicious that she was beginning to show signs of dementia.

Maurice grumbled, "I think that I'll call Gerard and ask if the family is aware that his mother is acting confused at times."

Gerard was huffy and said that the incidents regarding the pearls and the fur coat were between his mother and me. She seemed perfectly fine, in his opinion, although he admitted that she sometimes rambled when she was overly tired. (I thought to myself, 'drunk,' you mean.)

Maurice called Audrey and skirted around the possibility that her mother might be on the verge of a nervous breakdown. I could tell from his expression that this did not go well either. Audrey had hung up.

In mid-December, at two o'clock on a Sunday morning, our phone rang. We both jolted upright.

Maurice grabbed it, "*Oui?*"

I could hear his mother's voice, normally so calm, crying.

"What are you doing there? Where is Gabrielle?"

I heard a mumbled explanation then Maurice stated, "Arrange for a room and get warm. I'll pay when I get there."

"What happened?"

"Gabrielle. She tried to force mother to sign a document and threatened to kill her if she didn't do it. *Maman* snuck out of the house in the middle of the night, walked to an inn on the road to Éguilles and woke up the owners. She sounds exhausted."

"Maurice, she's eighty-six years old! It's freezing cold!"

"Get dressed. We've got to go get her."

A distraught and exhausted Juliette slept all the way home, curled up under comforters on the back seat of the car. We put her to bed with a heating pad and Maurice gave her a drink of mulled wine.

Gabrielle called at six o'clock in the morning in a panic, reporting that her mother had been kidnapped and that she had called the police. I overheard Maurice explain what happened. He murmured a series of 'umm-humms,' 'I see,' and then simply said, 'goodbye, Gabrielle.'

I tiptoed back into the kitchen and heard him walking around the stairs toward his den. After Juliette awoke and ate, she and Maurice talked privately. He told me that his mother did not want anyone else in the family to know what had happened and he couldn't tell me. I agreed, but was as curious as could be. What did his sister want Juliette to sign?

Christmas holiday routines occupied thought and time, although Juliette was not her usual self. Maurice and I noticed that she repeated stories, sometimes had difficulty answering questions and was often quiet. Because Christmas at the Domaine was always cheerfully active, nobody else paid much attention.

On Christmas Eve Juliette gave me an antique pin of her mother's, an especially sentimental gift that I treasured. She had previously given Maurice his grandfather's gold pocket watch and said that these gifts were intended to be passed on to future generations. Maurice planned to give his watch to three-year-old Lucien when he was grown up. I stated that I would give the pin to little Chloe, his sister, when she married.

Juliette patted my hand as she nodded, "*Parfait!*"

As the year went on I noticed that Juliette was relieved when I took over most of her tasks around the house. She seemed more tired than usual; however, Maurice and I didn't worry when she failed to come into the house after breakfast the last week of April. When I opened the door to announce that lunch was ready there was no response. The curtains and shutters were still shut and the apartment was cold. Juliette Laurent lay with her head on her pillow, her eyes shut, and a peaceful expression on her face. We learned later that she'd had a heart attack.

The French name for mother-in-law is *belle-mere*, 'beautiful mother,' and Juliette epitomized this to me. I was as bereft to lose her calm presence as anyone, especially having lost my own mother far too early.

The memorial mass for her was to be held at Saint-Siffrein Cathedral. Maurice thought that wearing the pin she had given me was a lovely tribute to Juliette, so I fastened it to my black winter coat's lapel. Family members were meeting by the stairs of the church's entrance shortly before the service. Marie-Laure came from Paris and had arrived at the *mas* the day before. Julien and Martine, Joseph and Cécile, Francois, Amélie, their children and spouses, began to merge with us as we walked along the rue de la Republic.

As I greeted Gabrielle's daughter Audrey by the church steps, she suddenly reached over and grabbed my shoulder.

"Give me that pin this instant! How dare you take my grandmother's jewelry and brazenly wear it, today of all days!"

She reached for the pin with both hands as I backed up.

"But Juliette gave this to me!"

Maurice and Francois stepped between us. Francois spoke in a soft voice as he grabbed her elbow and pulled her back.

"Audrey, this is no time to act like this. Be respectful!"

Maurice reached for his wallet and removed five hundred francs. His anger was palpable and unusual. He held the money in her face.

"Here, Audrey, this should cover the cost of buying one for yourself."

Now Francois had the job of keeping his brother apart from the flushed and tearful woman. People walking by began to stare. I stood behind

Maurice's shoulder. A grim-faced Pierre, Audrey's husband, marched up and took her arm then led her back to Gabrielle's family group. She mopped at her cheeks with a scrunched handkerchief as her mother, her face puffy and reddened, looked angrily over at us as she leaned on a cane. I watched shakily as Gabrielle spoke to those around her, her mouth tight, bitter. Of the beauty she had once had, little remained.

Maurice stuffed the money in his pocket, took my elbow and marched us up the steps and down the aisle to the front pews. We sat far to the left side. Francois and Amélie followed and sat in the seats to our right. Gabrielle and her brood filled a row of pews in the center. I bowed my head and sat back against the hard wood, using Maurice's shoulder as a barrier, hoping to be out of the Thibault family's sight.

Even with this horrific beginning, the mass for Juliette was comforting. The priest had known her for years. All three of her children gave short eulogies. Gabrielle, standing by aid of her cane, managed to make hers sound more about herself than her mother. Church bells tolled their usual mournful refrain when we exited the front doors. Many good friends came: the Bertolinis, the Duprés, the Rousseaus and the Napiers, as well as owners of farms and vineyards around Beaumes-de-Venise and Aubignan. Maurice and I greeted them, talking quietly. Elderly men from Francois' *Maquis Ventoux* network surrounded him and Amélie.

Gabrielle did not seem to know many people and stood off to the side with her children. Yvette, now married to a car salesman, stood with them and blew a kiss to Maurice. Then Audrey's husband marched up to Francois and stated that the family had decided not to come to the reception at the Domaine. While I ached for my husband, he and his children seemed glad to not have to put up a civil front under the circumstances.

Over the next few months our lives moved on. Then in mid-summer we received a terse letter from Audrey saying that Gabrielle had lung cancer. The cards that we sent, extending sympathy at the news, were returned, unopened. After she died, neither we nor Amélie and Francois received the usual black-edged announcement card, but the Napiers showed us theirs.

Sometimes when I reflected back on Gabrielle's life, I wondered how her experience during the war years affected her? Certainly the drinking and pills had an impact. Is it simply that some people endure torment and hardships and rise above them, while others seem to never shake off demons from the past?

THE VAUCLUSE – 1944

AUGUST 22, TUESDAY:

'Plan Violet,' the destruction of train tracks that were critical for the German Army's success, was going well. Almost as soon as a section of rail was repaired, it was rebroken, as with the telephone lines.

Roland Najarian, now twenty-three, had been in the Resistance since he was twenty. His knowledge of the terrain between Mont Ventoux and villages dotting the plains of the Rhone Valley distinguished him as an expert. He had climbed the rocky and *garrigue* covered canyons of the Vaucluse from the Dentelles de Montmirail in the north to Gordes and the *route national* in the south; from Sault in the east to Avignon in the west.

Over 650,000 Frenchmen had been shipped to labor camps in Germany. According to Roland's calculations in the past months, half of the men volunteering in the Resistance were due to the STO. This night, the *reseau* had another mission, to damage a track near Le Thor. At three o'clock in the morning, Roland and three others stealthily wound their way through the high brush, following a trail made by sheep that had roamed the area before the need for meat meant their end. They wore mended boots and shoes, patched trousers, berets and armbands emblazoned with the 'cross of Lorraine.' Rifles were slung across their backs.

A German detachment that patrolled the road between Carpentras and Cavaillon had been tracked for several days. Pre-dawn, it was heading south toward L'Isle-sur-la-Sorgues. The men moved cautiously, pausing often to listen. The week before a German patrol had attacked a part of the *Groupe-franc Kleber* and two men had been killed. There was suspicion, as always, that they had been betrayed, or it could have been simple negligence.

Often when on a sabotage mission *Petrarch* thought of their comrades who were dead: *Denis, Jacques, Diego* the Spaniard; but there were plenty of new *refractaires* filling in. Two of the latest were on this trip. *Ferdinand* was a taciturn kid of seventeen whose Jewish parents were in hiding. *Spartacus*, maybe fifteen years at the most, had been in the network a year. His nickname seemed fitting in that he was spunky and rebellious, a street urchin who had run afoul of the law at some point.

Leading the mission was *Centurion*, their seasoned leader and a former student of mathematics who had escaped arrest during participation in an anti-Nazi protest in 1941. He held up his left hand and motioned downward. Petrarch did not hear anything at first, then the faint clop of horse hooves invaded the silence. Several Germans were riding at a fast clip on a farm road further down the hill. They were heading north toward their garrison near Carpentras after a night roaming roads, looking for saboteurs.

Centurion indicated that they should stay put. Mouths parched from the hike and anxiety sipped from canteens. After fifteen minutes and no further noise, their leader gestured for them to rise. They walked bent over, gliding between scrub brush and low trees. Eight miles of the ten to their destination were behind them but the next two were the most risky, crisscrossing fields and farm roads, fording creeks, avoiding buildings.

On a hand-drawn map *Centurion* showed the creek that went under the main road. He whispered instructions that *Petrarch* would lead the way followed by the others in five-minute intervals. They would meet at a forest thicket on the opposite side of the train tracks. *Spartacus* carried a canvas rucksack with their explosives, a reel of wire, and detonators, called *crapauds* or 'toads,' hidden under innocent looking schoolbooks.

Crouching as he left the protection of the shrubs and trees, *Petrarch* made his way across the corner of a dirt clod and hay stubble field. He edged down an incline to shallow water and stepped from rock to gravel back to rock, trying to keep his boots dry. Ahead was the faint outline of an ancient stone bridge. *Petrarch* crept under it and paused. Leaning against the arch, he felt a faint vibration. It was not his imagination; something was coming. Soon he heard the rumble of heavy machinery. He looked back up the stream, hoping that *Ferdinand* would not come closer.

Within minutes the noise became thunderous. Tank treads rolling above him shook dirt loose onto Roland's head and shoulders. A second tank crossed, then a third, followed by motorized vehicles. The rolling noise diminished, became a mild vibration and then a hum.

A splash then a whispered *'merde'* announced *Ferdinand*'s arrival.

"Did you see what went by?"

"There were three armored tanks and four artillery vehicles. Maybe something is going on near Pernes-les-fontaines."

"Or the Germans are leaving!" *Petrarch* peered further down the creek. "I'll go on ahead. If *Spartacus* arrives before five minutes are up, make sure that he waits and gives you a head start."

Roland crept downstream. Soon the waterway widened and babbled noisily. He searched for a break in the trees along the bank and found one leading to the orchard marked on the map. He crept from tree to tree, stopping as he reached the safety of each trunk. At the orchard's edge was an embankment that led up to the railroad bed. This was the place.

In the distance a dog bayed. Suddenly a group of birds flew into the air down the tracks. Roland dropped to the ground and inched into nearby bushes and reeds. A thorn raked his forehead as he heard soft footfalls coming from down the tracks. A moment later he saw, through intertwined leaves, the outline of a soldier holding a rifle and bayonet. The man turned and motioned to another. They stopped every few feet, peering into the grasses and shrubs, moving to look into the forested area on the other side of the tracks or staring into the orchard. Roland held his breath, closed his eyes.

He heard a whispered conversation in German then suddenly the sound of the men running.

"Halt! Halt!"

Shots rang out and Roland watched the figures run in the other direction, firing into the orchard. They dropped below the embankment, firing wildly and continuing to shout. In the distance more dogs barked, a horse whinnied. Roland knew that Ferdinand had probably been sighted. He clambered up and ran across the railroad tracks toward the trees.

The pain was sharp and Roland's knees hit the ground suddenly. His right arm with the gun kept him propped upright. His left arm sagged and he watched dark stains ooze down his sleeve and the left side of his shirt. He crawled a few yards dog-style to a large rock. He backed up to it and pulled his rifle into shooting position, pointing toward the orchard. The pain in his chest caused him to suck for air.

A spectral, lone figure with a rifle and a German helmet emerged from the misty trees. Roland put his weapon on his knee, aimed and pulled the trigger. The other man stood motionless for several seconds then slowly dissolved into the ground.

Juliette found a packet of powdered medicine that relieved Florence of the pain but they both spent a restless night. In the morning Juliette bought a piece of bread in the one remaining bakery. She managed to find a bit of ersatz coffee in a tin.

At the table Florence announced, "I want you to go on home and let Gigi know that I'm fine. The doctor wants to check my condition in the morning then I can leave. Can you come back tomorrow with the wagon?"

"What about food, Florence? There's some soup left but nothing else."

"See if you can get something at the little store out by Notre Dame d'Observance. I'm not especially hungry." She smiled, "You can fatten me up when I get to the farm!"

Juliette met Uncle Xavier as she walked down the *rue de la Republique*. He was upset when he heard about Florence's accident. He said that there were still major battles going on in Marseille but Pertuis, near Aix-en-Provence, had been liberated. He frowned and shook his head. "It's only a matter of days, my dear, a matter of days."

"Uncle Xavier, why not come stay with us until after the fighting is over? I'll be coming back with the wagon tomorrow."

"Oh? Yes, ummm, maybe I should do that. Perhaps I can help you and Jean-Pierre." He nodded as he put on his beret. "I'll go pack up some things and be ready."

Juliette was mentally counting, "Let's see, that makes…eight of us. We can manage that."

ADIEU, MON CAPITAINE

FEBRUARY 1988:

Sitting at the kitchen table after breakfast on February 20, I read in the morning paper that René Char had passed away the day before. He'd been hospitalized in Marseille for a heart attack then flown to a Paris hospital. His public funeral and internment were to be held on February 24 at his home near L'Isle-sur-la-Sorgues. An incredible emptiness came over me, as if I had lost a good friend even though I had only met him that once.

Hundreds of people gathered at *Les Busclats* to bid the poet farewell. Standing at the back, Maurice and I were able to occasionally get a glimpse of the light colored casket as people milled about.

Char had married Marie-Claude de Saint-Seine the previous fall, a woman thirty-six years younger whom he'd met a decade before when she worked as his editor at Gallimard. His friend Claude Lapeyre had arranged a secret marriage ceremony to avoid intrusion and publicity. We saw Claude and his wife Renée standing by the coffin near Madame Char.

Many important people were there, certainly people important to Monsieur Char during his complicated and adventurous life. Only a few were recognizable to me. I identified Jean Garcin, bald, distinguished looking; the former *Colonel Bayard* was now *Consul General* of the Vaucluse. Maxime Fischer, around seventy-five years old, was slightly bent, his left arm hanging limply while his right one clutched a handkerchief. Lapeyre later told me that one of Char's last visitors, at his request, was this old friend, *Anatole* of the Maquis Ventoux.

A few years before, René had sold his astounding collection of paintings and drawings to a collector for an undisclosed but apparently substantial amount. So typical of his generous nature he had used the money for close friends and people in need. He bought a house in Malaucene for Tina Jolas, a French-American translator with whom he had a long relationship, producing hundreds of letters between them over a thirty-year period. Anne of the unknown name, who had lived with him for two decades and separated from him right before he married Marie-Claude, also was given a house. The poet insisted on buying the Lapeyres a couple of new windows for the farmhouse that they had inherited from Renée's family. The new Madame Char was given *Les Busclats* as well as the responsibility of overseeing and protecting all of Char's prolific works.

The press published a series of articles lauding René Char's poetry. Prime Minister Jacques Chirac was quoted as saying that he was 'the greatest French poet of the 20th century.' Most mentioned that he had been awarded a Medal of the Resistance and the Croix de Guerre and was named to the Legion of Honor. Our *Capitaine Alexandre* had been 'larger than life' with a generosity of spirit and a vision of the world that would continue to be enjoyed by future readers and writers.

Back at the house, Maurice pulled out the copy of *Feuillets d'Hypnos* and we spent the evening sitting by the fire and sipping muscat, reading his prose to each other and talking about that long ago history. We talked more about Francois' time in the Maquis and reflected on what of Char's stories he might recognize. Sometime, perhaps he would tell us more.

THE OUTSIDER
TRISTAN TZARA

Tristan had been running and hiding for almost three years but thought that his current refuge was a safe one. He was shocked to find an article published in the May 21, 1943 edition of '*I Am Everywhere*,' a collaborationist journal, stating: '*For several weeks a new guest has installed himself in Souillac, in the Lot Department, Tristan Tzara in person. A boarder in the main hotel in town, he carouses about surrounded by a half-dozen of his co-believers, groaning about Fascist persecution and prophesying an American rescue... They are like a tribe of 'intellectual' Jews at ease in the Free Zone.*'

Souillac had seemed like a perfect place in which to disappear, a *village perché* halfway between Avignon and Bordeaux in the Dordogne region. Medieval and eighteenth century buildings roosted on rock outcroppings of a steep hillside high above the tranquil Lot River and below a wilderness. It had an active anti-German population, although the Gestapo was headquartered barely fifty miles away in Cahors.

Tzara rented a room in a pension and ate his meals in a nearby hotel. Life seemed much less threatening than when he had bounced around Provence. Although he used his real name, he kept a low profile. Well, his real second name, he reminded himself. Born Samuel Rosenstock, he had never fit in his native Romania with a Jewish population of less than twelve percent. He excelled in his French private school and was considered a 'nerd.' Added to this, he was short and not athletic, so it was not surprising that he became introspective, rebellious and creative.

Tristan sighed as he closed the clasps on the suitcase and hefted it down from the bed. He placed an envelope on the lamp table with enough francs to cover the rent. Shrugging on a coat and then a fedora, leaving his trademark monocle in his jacket pocket, he quietly opened the door and listened. He stepped close to the wall and edged along its side to keep boards from squeaking. Stepping carefully down the stairs to the kitchen, he felt along a chair rail to the rear door. Tristan squeezed through, being careful not to bump anything with his suitcase.

The tiny garden backed up to a hillside covered in spindly trees. Three feet below the rear wall was a rough and rarely used path. Standing on a stone bench by the wall, Tristan eased his suitcase over. As he struggled to pull himself to the top of the wall and sling his legs over, he admitted that it was not merely his stature and his sedentary life that was limiting him; he was also nearing fifty years old.

Pausing to get his breath, the co-founder of the famous Dada literary movement of 1916 pushed graying but still thick hair out of his eyes, picked up the suitcase and started walking along the overgrown path. It was after curfew and he did not expect to run into anyone until he made contact with 'Bizet,' who was to take him to an isolated Resistance camp.

He thought back to his extraordinary life. Little Samy Rosenstock had devoured works by Charles Baudelaire, Stéphane Mallarmé, Arthur Rimbaud, Paul Verlaine and translations of Edgar Allen Poe. By the age of sixteen he had published his own poetry in French. At the age of nineteen, he changed his name to Tristan Tzara and left Romania for Zurich, Switzerland, on a journey toward what would become his future as a leader of the modern written word.

The 'Samy' underneath the Tristan façade accepted that he would be looked upon as an 'odd duck,' so he played the part. Blessed with fine features, a well-formed nose, full lips, he wore raised shoes, dressed in black and sported a monocle.

In Zurich, young Tzara joined a crowd dedicated to radical talk and pursuit of new thought that met at the *Café Voltaire*. They thought of themselves as messengers intent on waking their fellow man to new ways of looking at life. It was necessary to annihilate and destroy the values of the current culture in order to produce a more just future, so they became communists. It was here that the 'Dada movement' began, with Tzara credited as the founder.

Dadaists promoted art and writing with no apparent meaning. The term may have come the first word spoken by a baby, or from the Russian for 'yes-yes,' or from the French word for 'hobby horse.' A literal interpretation did not conform to the 'nothingness' preferred by the founders. Tristan composed a *'Manifeste Dada'* in 1918 in which he stated:

> *'Those who belong with us must guard their freedom, we do not recognize any other theory. We have had enough of the academic cubists and futurists' laboratories of formal ideas. Let each man cry out, there is great destructive, negative work to accomplish. Sweep out, clean out.'* (45)

During the spring of 1924 he met twenty-one-year-old Greta Knutson at a party in Paris. She was tall, elegant, articulate and bohemian. Her healthy Swedish looks, light brown hair and blue eyes, her creativity, her wittiness, drew Tristan to her like the proverbial moth to a flame. An artist who spoke several languages, she shared Tristan's passion for invention and transformation. By the end of that evening they were a couple. They married in 1925; their son was born in 1927. Her inheritance made it possible for them to build an elegant home up on the Montmartre hillside.

The marriage worked for a while but within ten years the two fought constantly. Greta flew into rages, Tristan argued back or distanced himself. When they went to Nice in 1935 with Paul and Nusch Eluard and René and Georgette Char, Greta and René had an affair. Greta fled to the Dali's home near Barcelona, Spain. In 1937 the Tzaras officially separated.

Tristan spent almost two years in Spain during the civil war. He came face-to-face with the gritty reality of bloody fighting, fleeing refugees, hardships, starvation and poverty. Just as Picasso painted 'Guernica' and Hemingway wrote 'For Whom the Bell Tolls,' Tzara's prose took on an even more anti-fascist slant.

As soon as Germany occupied France Tzara knew that he would become a target of the Nazis so he headed south to the 'free zone.' In Sanary-sur-Mer, a town on the Mediterranean coast, a local gendarme told him that he would be imprisoned if he didn't leave immediately. He went to St. Tropez and tried to get help from American friends in Paris, to no avail. In 1941 he and his son, fourteen-year-old Christophe, sought refuge with his estranged wife Greta in Aix-en-Provence where her lover René Char had ensconced her. There he was arrested. Aided by local friends who convinced a clerk that Tzara was an important writer, he was released. He immediately headed west to Souillac.

When he lived in Provence the poet lay low, not wanting to draw attention. But when he arrived in Souillac and felt more secure, he fought back with words. Along with fellow communists Paul Eluard and Louis Aragon, he contributed to literary reviews such as *Confluences, Les Lettres Françaises, Les Etoiles*. His poetry became a weapon and he commented that it was 'plunged into history up to its neck.'

This night, shortly after midnight, *Bizet* met him as planned. They trudged for many miles to a dilapidated stone building tucked against a rugged cliff, edged by thickets of oak and chestnut trees. A motley group of communists, anarchists and supporters of General de Gaulle surrounded Tzara, all united by the same purpose—liberation from the Germans. He was not expected to participate in raids led by the *Armé Secret* (AS) or the various independent *Maquis* groups in the area. He was to continue his work, writing to friends and to his publishers.

When young Maquisards sat down with him, curious about what he was doing, he shared his poems and his philosophy on writing. It seemed that the heart of a poet resided in many of the boys brandishing weapons.

"Monsieur, how did you happen to come to France?" Inquired a boy called '*Janvier*.'

"I was invited by the Surrealists André Breton, Paul Eluard and Pierre Soupault. They were impressed by our Dadaist ideas so I left Zurich and came to Paris in 1920. We used to meet at lively cafes in Montparnasse, at the Café

Cyrano or the Bar du Chateau, or at Breton's apartment. It was quite a life! There were delightful young women, soirées with fabulous food, wine and laughter, animated discussions. We teamed up with many of the great artists who illustrated our work."

A former teacher of French literature stated wistfully, "How I wish that I could have been there. Those must have been amazing times.

"It wasn't always amiable," Tristan admitted. "In 1922 André Breton tried imposing his rules on the modern arts' movements. We Dadists abhorred the idea of conformity, regulations and structure, and refused to participate. The following year, in revenge, Breton, Aragon and Benjamin Péret disrupted my play 'The Gas Heart.' They jumped on stage and attacked the actors who were encased in cardboard boxes."

"What happened then?"

"This ended any chance of a continuing relationship between the Surrealists and the Dadaist movement," Tzara sighed. "We've gone our separate ways."

Tristan knew that a man in his resistance camp had shot an Alsacien *collabo* who tried infiltrating his team. There were rumors of others killed when it was proved that they were Nazi informants. Occasionally one of their men would not return from a mission. To avoid detection, they frequently moved and established a new camp.

In late October there was chatter back and forth between England and constantly roaming radio operators. Then in mid-November, news came that a major parachute drop of thirteen containers filled with weapons had occurred near a town fifty miles directly east. Tzara also learned that his son Christophe, now barely seventeen, had joined the *Franc-tireurs et partisans (FTP)*. Half Jewish, standing out due to his father's unusual family name, he had few options.

Members of the American OSS (Office of Strategic Services) were flown into the heavily forested *Causses de Quercy* to increase sabotage. The first two arrived in January 1944, followed by four more in March. The Normandy Invasion on June 6th was cause for an enthusiastic celebratory toast, as the Allies' progress was followed intensely. Tristan sensed that Resistance activity in the area was increasing dramatically.

On July 14, Bastille Day, the *Maquis* learned of another arms drop less than twenty-five miles east of their current camp. Near the chateau-topped village of *Loubressac*, Flying Fortresses sent down so many containers of armaments that it took an entire day for volunteers to gather them up and distribute the contents. Within a week, planes tossed out leaflets warning of a secondary invasion coming from the south, advising residents to flee strategic towns.

The two hundred foot span of the graceful *Viaduc de La Motte* that crossed the valley leading into Souillac was in constant use by armored trains with German canons. On August 2, fifty Maquis and two Americans, in what was called 'Operation Emily,' laid explosive charges on the tall pylons holding up the bridge. The span collapsed perpendicularly into the valley, still attached to its frame.

The invasion of Southern France on August 15th resulted in the swift advance of American troops. When Toulouse and Cahors were liberated on the 20th, Tristan Tzara came down from the mountains to Cahors with its damaged buildings and rubble-strewn streets. He arrived to a jubilant celebration and was welcomed as one of the men who had encouraged the rebirth of his adopted country and given hope to many.

Tristan's old friend, the former director of the Museum of Modern Art, had been gravely wounded in the battle for Toulouse. He was among those responsible for conveying over three thousand paintings and art objects from the Louvre Museum to warehouses in Southern France. After the Occupation of 1942, priceless works of art were distributed among villages throughout the Lot Department. Trustworthy residents hid some of the world's finest art: the 'Mona Lisa;' 'The Holy Family' by Rembrandt; Cezannes, Watteaus, Millets, Rubens. In addition, personnel from the National Museums were welcomed into discrete and tight-lipped families who sheltered them until the war ended.

Tzara leaned against the side of a building, watching the activity, the coming and going of people finally released from Nazi control. American and French flags flapped, sharing their red, white and blue with the wind. He planned to meet with colleagues at the *Centre des Intellectuelles* that had been publishing his work while he evaded capture. He had handfuls of poems to be printed and old friends to contact. His work was not yet done.

⚉

<u>Anecdote</u>

giants of rain coolness of summer
oh vain sparkling depths
still I go tempting the most certain falls
do I not see from far away my own living and dying
    so I go leafing through landscapes to come
    tearing torn faithful
    made of dead wood flesh earth
    badly off persevering
    from one halt to the next
I am a horse I am a river
I go on clumsily nevertheless I live   (46)

Tristan Tzara   1896 – 1963

THE VAUCLUSE - 1944.

AUGUST 23, WEDNESDAY:

Alone in the apartment, Florence curled up and groaned in pain. Occasional twinges that had started the evening before were now severe cramps. She dressed then eased down the stairs, stepping unsteadily along the street toward boulevard Jean Jaurés, determined to be at the doctor's when he opened his office.

Desjardins poked and prodded gently. When he asked 'are you possibly pregnant?', Florence took a deep breath and was silent for several seconds.

"I'm not sure. I could be."

"I think that you should be seen at the Moricelly Clinic in case you are. If it is an internal problem they are better equipped to help you. The Germans are still occupying the main hospital."

He turned away to wash his hands. "Would you like me to call someone to help you down the street and up the clinic's stairs?"

"I'd like to contact a young nun called Sister Monique, but I'm not sure how to reach her."

He looked at her oddly for a minute. "I believe that I can get in touch with her. Please wait in the other room while I make a phone call."

LIZ KONOLD

From a letter found on a courier captured near Gigondas on August 23, written by a Caporal Pichlmeier, date August 22, 1944:

'Actually, every half hour, 8 to 12 fighter planes attack us. We are not able to work and everyday we retreat, fighting around 60,000 (sic) terrorists who are joined by hundreds of English paratroopers. Not a single German plane! And still bombardments! It is unimaginable. We are obliged to advance step by step: everything is mined! We just put our gun batteries in position. I am curious to know if they will succeed in stopping the enemy. We have two dead and many wounded. Our vehicles are still being bombed. A complete burned out mess. I hope to continue to be lucky. The 19th we climbed to a new location. At 7 o'clock already the first enemy aircraft were there, and not a bit of shelter. It was almost incredible how quickly I dug a ditch. When one is afraid, one does things much faster. Our courier cannot leave and we are almost completely encircled. It is for this that we must fold back, retreat. I do not know the name of the hollow in which we find ourselves. I will give this letter to a buddy who is leaving for Germany.'

(Exerpt translated from <u>Maquis Ventoux</u>, Claude Arnoux, 1994)

Sister Marie-Gabriel, director of the maternity hospital located behind the *Hotel Dieu*, folded her arms under the dark tunic of her habit as she stood at the window of her office looking at the morning sun filtering through the leaves of the plane trees.

It seemed impossible that the *Clinique Moricelly* was already ten years old, and that she was now sixty years old herself. Under different circumstances, the entire community would have celebrated this special anniversary. Instead, Sister-Marie Gabriel and her staff had quietly sipped champagne in her office, raising a toast to their patients, to many successful births, to obstacles overcome.

Rose Courveille had arrived in Carpentras at the age of twenty as a member of the Augustine Convent where she had lived a gentle life and worked as a caregiver at the Hotel Dieu. Then, in the 1920's when the charity hospital needed more skilled staff, she had been sent to Avignon, at forty years of age, where she trained as a nurse, a midwife and a pharmacist.

Funds donated for the Hotel Dieu decades before by the wealthy industrialist Isadore Moricelly and his wife had been used to build the maternity clinic in order to ease over-crowding in the main hospital. Sister Marie-Gabriel had been selected as the director. However, she had never been trained for what had become her most demanding mission.

The modern building was designed with a long tower-like center structure and two-story wings on either side. At the top of the tower above the registration and office areas was an attic, ostensibly for storage. This was where she and three trusted aides (two midwives and her young niece in training to be a mid-wife) cared for abandoned Jewish babies and infants.

A doctor in Avignon who treated Jews being held for transport to German death camps had set up a surprisingly efficient system. Desperate mothers, knowing the fate awaiting them, begged for their children to be saved. Nurses smuggled out toddlers and babies in large baskets, under flowing capes, in oversized medical bags. They were brought to the doctor's house then immediately taken to Chateau Husson, a Chateauneuf-du-Pape winery located close to the town of Courthezon, 15 miles northeast of Carpentras. The Chateau, a collection of rambling buildings dating back to 1890, also housed a number of young Luftwaft pilots who were given significantly large amounts of wine on a daily basis.

The winery's delivery van took the infants to Carpentras and Sister Marie-Gabriel. There they were nursed and cared for until an enclosed, gaz-o-gene car could transport them to another contact's remote chateau in the Lozére, a mountainous region west of Avignon. So far, no one else in the clinic had been aware of anything out of the ordinary.

Children were not the only people smuggled out of the area via the clinic. Eduard Deladier, prime minister at the time of the 'phony war' with Germany, arrived in Carpentras to see his son who was living with Deladier's sister. The clinic's women helped him escape to a nearby farm after the visit, although he was later captured and imprisoned in Tunisia.

Pregnant gypsy women knew that they could give birth at the sanitary Moricelly Clinic, if needed, during their annual pilgrimage to Saints-Maries-de-la-Mer. Any number of gypsy babies had been born on the third floor, hidden from prying eyes that would have been askance at seeing mothers-to-be in ruffled, flowery skirts and fox fur draped jackets. Sister Marie-Gabriel had been midwife for many of these births.

She shifted toward a shaft of sunlight at the window and contemplated the day ahead. Her niece Odette Courveille, dressed in a white uniform and headscarf, waved on her way to the German military office in the *Hotel Dieu* where she worked as the director's secretary and funneled information to her aunt.

Sister Marie-Gabriel mused, "She must be having a busy week!"

Not far behind was another of her contacts, a young woman going by the name 'Sister Monique,' who was heading intently toward the center of town. The clinic's director turned back toward the door to the dim reception hall and juggled keys in a pocket of her robe on her way to unlock the front doors.

The Moricelly Maternity Clinic, Carpentras

One of the first to arrive the morning of August 23 was a petite, dark-haired woman wearing a man's shirt that covered her bandaged right arm and shoulder. Helping her up the steps and into the registration office was Sister Monique, a courier for the *Maquis*. The two nuns greeted each other with nods then the younger woman kissed the injured lady and exited without saying anything more.

Sister Marie-Gabriel stepped into the hallway as the new patient registered. The woman suddenly bent over and moaned, leaning against the desk with her left arm.

"My dear, you need to lie down. Hold on to me and I'll take you to a room."

Florence looked into the welcoming face of an elderly nun who radiated kindness and reached for her elbow as the worst of the cramp dissipated.

"Now, tell me what seems to be wrong?"

Florence explained that she had broken her clavicle in a bike accident and possibly might have internal injuries.

"Mmmm," the nun mused as she patted Florence's hand. "I see. One of our nurses will bring you a gown and help you change then we can check you over."

As Florence lay down, curtained off from other beds in the room, a midwife in a white uniform checked her vital signs, probed her stomach and asked questions. Florence admitted that she could be pregnant. The nurse stated that Florence needed an X-ray to determine treatment. Half an hour later another nun bustled up and pulled the curtain aside. "Madame Gilles-Martin? I'm to take you to the radiation room."

After the x-ray, Florence was taken back to the room where, behind a far curtain, a new arrival cursed in between sobs and moans. A midwife was checking on her, murmuring encouragement and asking her to try and not swear. Florence climbed into her bed, curled into a ball and waited. An hour later she sat up as a sharp stab in her abdomen caused her to gasp.

She pulled back the curtain and called, "Could someone help me? Something's wrong."

Within minutes the midwife probed Florence's body once more. She murmured as she looked up from the chart. "No internal injuries appear on the x-ray but it looks like you're having a miscarriage. We have a doctor available in the surgery and can get this taken care of swiftly."

Florence was wheeled into a large, bright room with a man in a mask and cap standing by a well-lit, sheet-covered surgical table, a nurse in a stiff white cap and white uniform at his side. The mid-wife handed over the chart and

Florence was lifted up to the table, her broken shoulder handled gently, as a mask was placed over her nose and mouth.

When she roused, Florence was back in the maternity hospital's bed and a volunteer aide sat on a stool beside her. The woman, with light tan skin, dark eyes, curly short hair under a stiff white cap, looked up from a book and smiled.

"Ah, Madame, welcome back to the world. The doctor said that the curettage went well, he got all the tissue out and you will be fine in a day or two. Would you like a pill to help with the pain? Some sips of water?"

Florence swallowed the pill and sat back. As the aide closed the curtain and moved away, tears rolled down her cheeks, dampening the pillowslip, the ache in her abdomen pulsating through a fog of sadness.

TIME MARCHES ON -- 1992

Though barely in our sixties and still active, after Juliette's death in 1984 Maurice and I turned over the main house to Julien and his family. My sweetheart and I moved into Juliette's old apartment, a combined mid-18th century animal shelter and a 19th century add-on. The remodeled 'American' kitchen, tucked into a corner, has a two burner stove and a microwave. The main room has a large fireplace and windows overlooking vines to the southwest. The bedroom and remodeled bathroom are in the 1920's extension. An outside door and a few stairs lead to a rock wall enclosed terrace. Maurice and I built our offices under skylights installed in the attic roof. It is private, cozy and perfect for us two.

The house's communal space is available as much as he and I wish—another tradition in multi-generational families. Most days we eat meals together in the kitchen, the dining room or outside on a terrace. The arrival of Pierre Maurice Louis Laurent the summer after René Char passed away, in 1988, filled another upstairs bedroom and added to our joy.

Martine had quit teaching and found a new enterprise. Her apricot jams and chutneys are sold at the Beaumes-de-Venise Tuesday market and she has built up a loyal clientele. I work as 'sous chef' and assistant cashier some of the time. We've developed a close friendship; I admire her even-keel personality and intellect, traits I would have loved in a daughter of my own.

Lucien, now eleven years old, Chloe, now eight, and Pierre, four, call me *Mami* or *grandmére,* having never known any other. I am the one who provides the afternoon snack of *pain au chocolate* when they return from school, the one who washes and bandages scraped knees, the one who reads them stories before bedtime and the one who is teaching them to speak English.

Maurice's daughter Marie-Laure, married to a successful businessman in Paris, gives piano lessons and cares for their two children. Jean-Paul is the same age as his cousin Pierre; his baby sister Giselle has barely been introduced to her family circle but will soon spend summer months weaving in memories of a childhood at the Domaine. Joseph is a professor of anatomy and physiology at the School of Medicine in Montpelier; his wife Cécile is a professor of mathematics. They apparently don't plan on having children, happy to be a doting aunt and uncle during holidays and family events.

Shortly after little Pierre arrived in 1989, JT and Martha's first child, Mathew James, was born. As close as I had become to Maurice's grandchildren, there is nothing quite the same as welcoming your own child's child into the world. As I stood at the hospital nursery's window I could see that he was perfect, handsome, and showing signs of intelligence on his first day on earth--even if he did sleep most of the time.

Then Vivienne Louise made her appearance this past June, a few weeks after Giselle was born. Again, I flew to Boston and held the tiny, precious bundle a few hours after her birth. I had a hard time leaving. Happily JT and his family visit us for several weeks every summer and the American grandchildren, who are learning French, think of the Laurent children as their 'cousins.' My father, Roselyn and my brothers come to France for periodic visits and I make an annual trek to San Francisco to see them.

Elodie, the cook, housekeeper and mainstay for many years, retired within a year of Juliette's death. She comes as our guest for many events. Martine and I, with Elodie's help, found a replacement. Maria, in her forties and with grown children, helps on occasion and has learned to cook our favorite recipes with a slightly Spanish touch.

Sophie and Georges continue to be our best friends and we regularly see each for a game of *belote,* take vacations together or meet for long, conversational dinners. Maurice and I often see Katie and Andrew Franchini, exchanging visits to our respective vineyards every few years.

I thought back to shortly after Maurice and I were married. We were wandering in among the vines, clipping and tying up branches. It was a cold day in spring and we worked in tempo, entertained by pesky magpies that darted in and out of the rows further down the hill.

Maurice stopped suddenly and tipped his head to the side. "Are you sorry that you married me? That you gave up the interesting life that you had?"

I was startled, wondering what had caused him to say this. "Maurice, I have never regretted being your wife for one second. Being with you has enriched my life in unimaginable ways."

I remember pulling off a glove, saying, "I can hardly remember what it was like, that other lifetime. Our lives are so full here--the seasonal rhythms, the sense of community, wonderful times with our families, the beauty surrounding us, the warmth and kindness of our friends."

I remembered putting my glove back on and reaching across the wire, touching his cheek and saying, "Most of all, I love the wonder of us."

My 'other' life had been blessed, in many ways, and I did not regret the paths that I chose, but what I told my Maurice was the truth: that being with him, facing ups and downs, ins and outs, being part of our combined families and 'living off the land' was immensely fulfilling. In the midst of the journal that I kept sporadically, I had written a short poem reminding me of my blessings:

Today and today and today and today,
An endless string of beads
Forever behind, forever in front, forever 'today.'
Fondle them gently, hold them close,
Warm them with the blood of your heart
Before they slip their clasp. (47)

THE VOYAGER
PHILIPPE SOUPAULT

T he adjunct professor sat at his desk in a classroom overlooking the autumn colors and green lawns of Swarthmore College, a liberal arts school a few miles from Philadelphia. He twirled the globe of the world on the left corner, sliding his finger along the continents, the places that he had been.

He loved to travel. He had realized, decades before, that his was a restless soul determined to explore the world. In his new book he had written: '*Obliged to suffer because I was locked away, I understood at that point that I was a vagabond. Meant to wander. Not accepting, not able to accept staying immobile. To change scenery and thoughts, to not cease to move: to live!*'

He stopped the globe and traced from Texas through Mexico, down to Brazil then up at an angle through the Caribbean to Florida and New York. The latest trip had been spectacular.

Dressed in a dark suit and subdued tie, Philippe Soupault pulled a packet from his desk drawer, withdrew a cigarette then lit it with a gold Cartier lighter. He was part of a privileged turn-of-the-century family used to luxuries, classical educations at the Sorbonne and the means to use what they learned. Studying in London then in Germany, he was fluent in their languages. In summers, the family had vacationed at expensive hotels on the Normandy coast.

Sometimes he wondered how differently his life would have turned out had he followed his family's anticipated career as a lawyer or businessman, instead of traveling and reporting on what he found. He certainly would have made more money! He might have continued in a comfortable bourgeois lifestyle, the son of a respected doctor, brother of an attorney and a business owner, a nephew of Louis Renault of automobile fame who was making a fortune manufacturing tanks for the Germans.

As a young man he'd had almost anything that he wanted and was able to be generous to others as well. When he and André Breton wrote and published in the 1920's, it was his money—his family's money—that provided funds to print their first manifesto, *The Magnetic Fields.* He had never been penurious about helping friends in those early years.

He, too, had been conscripted in World War I but not until late in 1917 when he was sent to a regiment that still wore metal armor around their torsos. He swept the courtyard, peeled potatoes and polished armor. When he volunteered to be inoculated with a new typhoid vaccine, the ensuing fevers and damage to his lungs caused numerous hospitalizations. While in those wards, he was brought face-to-face with bloody young men splayed out on stretchers, boys damaged by mustard gas who would never breath normally, some with missing legs and arms and eyes. Families were decimated as their men were used as cannon fodder in an old man's war.

Having nothing to do but read, Philippe immersed himself in literature and composed his first prose. He returned to Paris, at barely twenty years old, with an expanded perspective. Although he worked in his family's printing company and, for a short time, was director of a petroleum shipping service, it was not long before he gave up his expected career. Instead, he became a co-founder of the Surrealist poetry movement along with André Breton and Paul Eluard. He pursued a career as a novelist, journalist, publisher and radio commentator. And now, he thought somewhat ruefully, he was a professor at an American college.

Soupault stood and walked to the window, breathing out a waft of smoke, contemplating his latest book. Called 'The Age of Assassins,' it was to be published in the United States. He was very hesitant about having the book published in France considering the horrors that his countrymen endured under the Nazis, what all of Western Europe had been subjected to, what was being discovered in various prisons and camps. In contrast, his stay in the Tunisian prison seemed insubstantial even though being arrested and condemned to death had not appeared so at the time. The book's theme was the prisoners that he knew and the prison mentality that developed among those with shared beliefs.

With the Allies in control of France and on their way to Germany, Soupault hoped that his stay in the United States would not last long. He walked to his desk, putting the cigarette out in an already overloaded ashtray, and thumbed through the first pages of *The Age of Assassins*. It brought back many good memories.

Even before their marriage, while waiting for his second divorce, he and Ré had traveled extensively. They hiked and skied in Norway and Sweden; took jaunts through Austria and Germany, England and the United States. In 1935, Philippe wrote on events in Norway, Germany, Czechoslovakia, Great Britain and Spain, with Ré providing photo coverage. Then in 1936, shortly after they were married, Philippe was asked to set up Radio Tunisia. France wanted to establish a station broadcasting information to counter Mussolini's pro-Nazi propaganda from Tripoli.

Under Philippe's guidance, the programs were in Arabic as well as French. North African music and Fauré were given equal time. News broadcasts attempted to be factual, not just propagandistic.

An independent woman who had had her own dress shop and clothing line in Paris, Philippe's wife had enthusiastically climbed onto the rear of his motorcycle, camera equipment in hand. She had photographed men, women and children in the bazaars, pilgrims on route to Mecca, women in the 'reserved quarters,' those without protection who turned to prostitution and were treated cruelly.

Photos in their apartment and his office showed a handsome, relaxed couple in exotic settings. Philippe sighed as he picked up one, realizing that this marriage, too, was likely to end. Ré had not been able to continue her career in the United States and it was clear that she felt isolated and depressed. At least in New York there had been things to do, there was a social life.

The writer flipped through more of his manuscript, reliving the shock of those years as a journalist and his realization that Hitler was determined to control Western Europe. Then, when Petain capitulated in 1940, the *Marechal* agreed that the French Empire in North Africa should be sheltered under the Nazi umbrella. After Vichy-selected officials were installed, bit-by-bit Philippe's control over radio broadcasts diminished. By early 1941 Soupault realized that he was under suspicion. He contacted the American consulate but the earliest passage out via Lisbon was not until January 1942. He wrote a Surrealist novel about the future and sent off reports and poems to friends in France. Ré took more pictures. They read voraciously. And they waited.

The evening of March 12, the couple took a walk in the colorful streets surrounding their home. Three policemen wielding pistols met them when they returned. The goons ransacked every room, overturning mattresses, pulling out books, going through letters. Although they found nothing incriminating, Philippe was hauled off to a local jail. Ré was told to remain in the house.

Soupault was interrogated for hours about a man named Roquemare to whom he was supposed to have provided incriminating documents. The next morning he learned that the son of a former secretary had denounced him, a boy who was also under arrest and willing to point the finger at anyone suspicious.

After a lecture on treason by a stern judge, he was taken to the military prison where he spent forty-five days without any visitors except for an attorney. For prisoner number 1234, the sun became his clock; the meals and exercise time his only diversions. He got to know the dissidents incarcerated with him: French, Tunisian, Legionnaires, nomads, Bedouins, royalists, de Gaullists, members of resistance groups. All detested Petain and the Germans; all wanted to be outside fighting for independence.

Taken before another magistrate, Philippe finally learned the details of his 'treason.' The man who had been introduced as a fellow journalist, whom he had casually welcomed months before in his role as director of Radio Tunis, had been gathering information for de Gaulle and the Allies. Testimony from Soupault's colleagues that they were not acquainted was not enough to dissuade the judge from continuing his imprisonment for subversion. His attorney could not get a straight answer regarding the charges against his client or when, if ever, there was to be a trial.

Six more months passed. Philippe mulled over what might happen: would he be shot standing up against a wall? When and where would it be? Would Ré even know if he had been killed?

Finally Philippe received a package from Ré with clean clothes, toiletries, food--and cigarettes. When he finally got some books, he read two or three a day. After six weeks he was taken from his cell and permitted to see Ré, who told him that she had not known where he was until the day before she sent the package.

After Ré's visit one evening, a guard took him out to the courtyard. The judge's lackey that Soupault disliked intensely, a malicious, unctuous man, stood by a pillar. He smirked and said, "I have news for you."

Philippe waited to hear the worst.

"The judge has signed your release." He waited for a reaction. Seeing none, his mouth turned down, his eyes flickered sideways. "You are free; you can leave this evening."

When the German Luftwaffe bombed Tunis, he and Ré learned that the Allies' 'Operation Torch' against the Germans in North Africa had begun. In November 1942, the Soupaults boarded a crowded bus heading toward Algeria, taking only what they could carry. They got out of town barely ahead of Rommel's troops. At the border they caught a train to Alger. They crowded in with friends and Philippe continued writing articles, another novel and a poem dedicated to the bombing of London.

A representative of de Gaulle's arrived in Alger to organize an information network in North Africa. The man suggested that Soupault organize a similar system for the French information agency in North and South America. This way, his and Ré's visas to the USA could be expedited. Philippe agreed.

After the Allies captured Tunis, Soupault went back to the city with an American in charge of 'psychological warfare.' The Soupault's former home had been pillaged. Everything was gone, including his novel on Surrealism and Ré's equipment and photos.

In July 1943 he and Ré boarded a boat, part of a flotilla of thirty that carried wounded men, refugees, prisoners of war and civilians unwilling to stay. It was like being in prison again, confined to a cabin except at mealtimes, required to wear a life vest and to observe night long 'black outs.'

In New York the Soupaults mingled with old friends before starting their trip south. André Breton was working as an announcer for the 'Voice of America.' He had married a Chilean pianist, Elisa Claro, after Jacqueline dumped him for an American sculptor. Max Ernst also was remarried, to the wealthy art collector Peggy Guggenheim whom he'd met on the boat when leaving France.

Philippe contacted intellectuals, writers, journalists and artists in Latin America and constructed a web of sources for what would become known as *l'Agence France Press*. The Soupaults traveled through Mexico, Guatemala, Panama; they visited Bogota, the Andes, Lima, Santiago, Buenos Aires, Montevideo, Rio de Janeiro, Bahia, then up to the mouth of the Amazon River. From Trinidad they flew to Miami then back to New York.

Instead of accepting a job offer that involved more travel, here he was at a desk, his book reminding him of the unease and terror that he felt as a caged bird that craved flight. Although he liked teaching American students--there were any number of attractive and smart young women--he felt out of place in the cloistered academic environment. It was another form of captivity.

As soon as the War was over he would return to France. He was not yet fifty years old. He had more to accomplish, more places to go. Whether Ré was with him or not, he would move on.

LIZ KONOLD

Poems from Saint Pelagia Prison
translation by Paulette Schmidt (48)

I.
Wednesday on a barge
and you Saturday like a flag
the days have crowns
like kings and dead men
lissome as a kiss my hand
rests on chained foreheads.
    A child cries for her doll
    and we'll have to start over again
    Monday and Tuesday cold-blooded
    four Thursdays off from work

II.
A thread unravels
A shadow falls
A butterfly explodes
Chrysalis or glow worm

    III.
    Who mounts the storm
    a balloon
    honey or silver moon
    four by four.
    Let's look for the children
    the parents of the children
    the children of the children
    the bells of springtime
    the beginnings of summer
    the regrets of autumn
    the silence of winter

an elephant in his bathtub
and the three sleeping children
singular singular tale.

Philippe Soupault 1897–1990

THE VAUCLUSE - 1944

AUGUST 23, WEDNESDAY:

A woman groaning in a room down the hallway was the first sound Florence noticed in the morning. Pale light from windows across the room filtered through white curtains at the end of the bed and Florence followed the shadow patterns shifting on the blanket covering her. Her room was silent. The woman in labor in the other bed had either been moved or the baby had been born. Florence didn't want to know. She reached for the glass on the table. It was empty. She called out, as loudly as she could.

"Nurse? Nurse? Can you help me, please?"

Sister Marie-Gabriel, who was making rounds that morning, pulled back the curtain and reached for the pitcher. Then she stopped and took out a thermometer from her pocket. "Let's take your temperature, dear, before you drink."

She left to check on other patients then returned, looked at the thermometer and frowned. Putting it in its container then in her pocket, she poured some water and handed the glass to Florence.

A midwife in her white outfit, stethoscope in hand, woke Florence a while later, saying, "Madame, I need to check your heart rate and your blood pressure. It seems that you have a fever."

She placed the stethoscope's cup on Florence's back. She asked if her throat was sore and Florence murmured that it wasn't, although she did have a headache. The midwife took her blood pressure and wrote notes on the chart. She poked her abdomen, pulled down the covers and examined her. The midwife looked up reassuringly.

"Everything seems normal, Madame. I imagine the fever is temporary. I'll give you some pills."

———

Juliette and Maurice Laurent arrived back in Carpentras to pick up Florence and Uncle Xavier as planned. Maurice staked Clotilde to graze and waited under a tree along the Auzon River, holding a hefty tree branch to fend off thieves.

Surprised that no one was at the apartment, she assumed that Florence was still at the doctor's office and walked to his *cabinet*. Desjardin told her that Florence was being checked for internal injuries at the Moricelly Clinic. There she was told that Florence had undergone minor surgery, was sedated and needed rest. Juliette went to her room and stood by the bed, shocked at how small and fragile her cousin looked. She stroked her hand. Florence rolled her head and moaned but did not open her eyes.

As Juliette walked back through town along side streets, out of the path of the retreating German troops, she cringed at the sound of planes flying low overhead, the occasional far-away thrump of an explosion and sounds of gunfire. Thankfully they had insisted that Gigi stay at the Domaine. She went to Xavier's apartment and he followed her down to the river, with suitcase in hand. She told Maurice and Xavier to go to the Domaine. She would stay and watch after Florence.

If his father felt it was safe, Maurice could come back on his bicycle with food and clothes. Then, when Florence was ready to leave, he could go back to the farm for the wagon.

"Maurice, don't draw attention to yourself and try to get off the main road as soon as possible. We can't afford to have Clotilde and the wagon confiscated. Please be careful."

Her teen-aged son nodded, speaking in his most mature voice, "The road toward Caromb shouldn't be busy. I'll head there and cut through the groves and orchards. It will take longer but we'll be fine, Maman. Uncle Xavier can help me."

He handed the heavy branch to a delighted Xavier.

"Your sister Madame Laurent is here to see you again."

Florence blinked and mumbled, "Cousin. She's my cousin."

Juliette tried not to look shocked. "Florence, I am so sorry that you had to have surgery. How serious was it?"

"Something about my spleen but I'm all right now," Florence fibbed. She reached for her hand and used Juliette's grip to pull herself up against the back of the bed.

"I must look simply awful. Help me fix myself up."

Juliette darted outside the curtain and came back with another pillow. Taking a comb and lipstick from her purse, she sat on the edge of the bed and worked on Florence's hair. She adjusted the gown and wrapped the scarf around her cousin's bandaged neck. Pleased at the improvement, she stepped back.

"That looks much better. In a few more days Provence will be completely liberated and our lives can return to normal. Just think, Florence, only a few more days!"

Florence's smile widened and Juliette felt reassured as she sat on the edge of the bed. She held Florence's hand as she told her how well Gigi was doing, that Uncle Xavier was now staying with them, and Amélie was nursing Francois who was still recovering. Everyone at the Domaine seemed safe and they were anxious for her to join them.

AUGUST 24, THURSDAY:

The inhabitants of Cavaillon had felt under siege for weeks. The Allies seemed intent on destroying their graceful modern suspension bridge over the Durance River. Planes would periodically swoop low over the town followed by a series of detonations at the river. So far the *pont* had remained intact. Fires raged at two train depots and explosions reverberated from Nazi munitions depots as former workers torched them. Machine gun fire constantly rat-tatted in the distance.

Around two o'clock in the morning Gabrielle was awakened by a series of loud explosions coming from down river, one after the other. Within half an hour she heard the pounding of boots, the smacking of sabots, the clop of horses, the grumbling rasp of vehicles in high gear, gruff and panicked shouts. The smell of cordite and smoke drifted into her room. She pulled the sheet over her head and plugged her ears.

When she woke up later, the town was eerily quiet. She crept to her window and opened the shutter a crack. In the pre-dawn, there was no one on the street. Not a soul. Gabrielle pulled the shutter closed and dressed in the dim light, in the brown skirt that she had worn the day before.

Carrying her brown pumps in her hand, she crept down the stairs. Putting on her shoes, she walked toward a main square, turning to see if anyone else was emerging from one of the houses. At the square, a few people that she did not recognize stood by a man on a motorcycle with an FFI emblem on his arm. As she edged closer she heard one ask a question.

"Yes, yes, I told you," the member of the Resistance was beaming. "They're already in Cheval Blanc. They'll be here in a few hours. You are free!"

He gunned his motorcycle, turned in a half circle and headed toward a group of young men with rifles. As those around her scattered, Gabrielle felt a shiver of fear combined with relief. She wasn't sure how the Americans would act and worried that they might be aggressive, that they might take hostages. But at least this meant that she could go home soon.

She stopped at a bench under a leafy tree, wondering what she should do. The sudden opening slam of shutters across the square startled her as a couple shook out a French flag and fastened it to the edge of their window. Within a few minutes, a shop owner stepped out and started planting small French flags on posts along his store. Bells throughout town began to ring.

Gabrielle Laurent looked around and realized that there were no more swastikas. Anywhere.

⌇

Maurice jostled his bicycle into the storage room of the Gilles-Martin's building. Upstairs, his mother was relieved to see him and reached for the parcels that he had brought. He told her that Gigi was not happy at having to stay at the farm. Juliette was not surprised; it had to be hard on her.

"I will probably be at the Clinique Moricelly for most of the afternoon, helping Florence."

"How is she doing?"

"She was injured more than we thought but it looks like she will be fine once her bone mends. The nurse thinks that she can leave tomorrow morning. Although it is miserably hot, I hope that you'll stay here in the apartment or at least stay out of the Germans' way."

"Is it all right if I go to the Rousseau's to listen to the radio? I know they are still in town."

Juliette looked at him, raising her eyebrow as she kissed his cheek and agreed. "Just stay out of any trouble!"

After another warning from Josian's mother to be careful, the boys got permission to watch the Germans march through the town as long as they stood at a distance. They walked to the *rue du Musée* and past the commandant's headquarters where two large trucks with ribbed canvas tops were parked. Boxes, paintings and furniture from the *hotel particulier* were being piled inside.

German soldiers, often in dirty, torn uniforms, had rumbled, tramped and stumbled through the streets of Carpentras for days. They headed northeast for the D7 past Beaumes-de-Venise; others loped northwest toward Orange. They grabbed anything with wheels to hasten their retreat. They helped themselves to products left in the cheese shop, boulangeries and charcuteries with little opposition from shopkeepers who simply wanted them to leave. One soldier was seen trundling along the road pulling two cases of wine on a delivery trolley.

Sentries were still posted by a machine gun at the southern entrance at the *rue de la Republique* and at a second one by the bridge at *Notre Dame de Santé*. Those patrolling the streets seemed nervous, touching pistols in a reflex motion, serious and unsure. Although the summer was one of the hottest on record, chimneys spewed ash and smoke over tile roofs and into narrow streets as functionaries rushed to destroy damaging information.

A handful of regulars, some of them old veterans with eye patches or a missing appendage, sat under awnings in front of cafés. Sweating in the heat, drinking and smoking, they looked pleased to see the Nazis in disarray. Young women stood in shadowed doorways talking and crying, some hugging German soldiers. A couple of the girls were obviously pregnant. Villagers en-meshed with the Germans--owners of businesses that had profited, the mayor of the town, the police who collaborated with the Vichy government--were in conversation with irritated Nazi officers. Others were at home, scrabbling through closets for old outfits, destroying clothing, insignia, documents and any indication of collaboration.

Maurice and Josian decided to watch the departure from the relative safety of shops west of the *Café du 19ème Siècle*. Auguste, an older boy smok-ing a cigarette in a doorway, joined them. The three boys minced their way south and peered through low foliage and trees at the northwest corner of the square. Across the road an officious German shouted commands and a handful of men thumped their way toward the northern exit. A single tank puttered to the east along the large boulevard. Two Milice wandered back and forth on the sidelines.

Josian pointed to a lanky man leaning against a tree on the *place de Champville*, west of the *rue de la Republique*. Maurice recognized René Pasculin, the son of a carnival owner who had set up his attractions in a nearby field. Auguste whis-pered that they were 'buddies,' *copains*, and had once knifed the tires on a German truck. He giggled, looking smug, as Maurice and Josian stared, not sure if he was telling the truth.

"Honest!" Auguste bragged, "He really hates the Germans!"

René casually strolled past the fountain and across the street. As a group of defeated looking soldiers marched onto the square, René withdrew some-thing from his pockets. He fumbled with a match and lit some objects, pos-sibly firecrackers or detonators, then tossed them. They hissed and began to explode. Maurice dropped to the ground, his friends piling on top of him.

René jumped up on a stone bench, raised his fist and shouted. "Vive la liberté!"

All hell broke loose. Soldiers hopped and leaped, several dropped to the cement, one shot into a tree trunk as he tripped over a foot. Others stepped back from the spit-spat crackle of the *petards*. The Milice pulled out pistols and waved them around. Oberschutze Schmit ran toward René as he raced up the main street with Milice following.

"Halt or you will be shot!"

"Come on, I was only kidding around." René tried smiling, "Nobody got hurt, eh guys?"

Gunther Schmit's face was a mottled red as he shouted, "You and your Resistance thugs have done the last damage you will ever do to our forces. Take him to the Commandant's house. We'll let him decide this terrorist's fate."

They marched toward a staff car with René loudly protesting. One man reached up and gun butted him in the face. A trickle of blood ran from his nose and down his chin. He was shoved into the back of the car and driven north.

Auguste, Josian and Maurice did not move for many minutes. As the Germans milled around the square, the boys slid back, crouching and crab crawling along the building to a small square at the rear. Jumping up, they ran toward the *Chapelle des Penitents Noirs*. Ducking into a carved stone doorway, the trio paused to catch their breath.

Josian grabbed Auguste's shoulder, "They won't shoot René because he set off firecrackers, will they?"

No one said anything. Then Auguste wrapped his arms around his chest and stuttered, "My dad would kill me if he knew that I was down there when that happened. I'm going home."

Maurice turned to Josian. "Come on! Let's go see what they do to René."

Josian hesitated a second then followed his friend across town to the Commandant's house. They lurked behind a building on a quiet side street, trying to appear inconspicuous. At three o'clock they saw Pasculin shoved down the steps to a waiting truck and heard one soldier yell up to the driver to go to the *Etablissements Unatiers,* used for interrogations.

In whispered conversation the boys decided to walk up to the building to see if René was released. Time passed slowly. The boys periodically meandered down the street across from the building then disappeared into adjoining streets to wait. Maurice bought *ersatz* cigarettes and they stood on a corner and smoked. Tension evolved into silliness, a pushing match, sexually tinged jokes.

At four-thirty in the afternoon a battered René, his shirt bloodied, his hands tied behind his back, was shoved once more into the back of a truck. It lumbered south, turning out of sight at a corner. Josian and Maurice raced along the street until they were breathless. Not knowing where the vehicle had gone, they turned and walked back into town.

Josian bent his head. "Poor guy! What can we do?"

Maurice responded, "Nothing, Josian. Not if we don't want to get in trouble ourselves. We'd better go home. I've been gone too long and I know that *Maman* will be upset."

They separated and Maurice returned to the Gilles-Martin's apartment. His mother sat at the dining table and smiled a wan smile. He walked over and bent down for a kiss. Clasping his hand, Juliette admonished him.

"Maurice, *mon cher fils,* I was worried. What in the world were you doing?" Without waiting for an answer she continued, "Aunt Florence seems much better and probably will leave the hospital tomorrow. You look flushed—have you been running in this heat? Sit down and have a drink."

Maurice poured a glass and gulped the water, his hand shaking slightly. He did not mention the event by the Café of the 19th Century.

At five o'clock that evening those living along the southern edge of *avenue Jean Jaurés* heard a volley of shots echo from below the ancient city wall that supported the *allée des platanes*. Shutters along the street snapped shut as quickly and recurrently as a row of dominoes fall.

Here

August 24, 1944

Shot by Nazi barbarians

The young patriot

René Pasculin

Age 19 years

Let us remember

REALIGNMENT

JUNE 1998:

The phone started ringing. I wiped my hands on the towel hanging from my apron sash as I turned from the stone kitchen sink of the *mas* where I was cleaning carrots pulled from the *potager*. I walked quickly to the front hall table.

"*J'arrive!*"

My brother's voice echoed on the line. "Claire? It's Bill."

"Bill! Good to hear from you."

"I have bad news, I'm afraid, Claire. Our father is gone. He passed away this morning."

I pulled the long phone cord into the parlor where I sat down stiffly next to the marble-topped chest. Bill's steady voice explained that our father had died of a heart attack as he was pruning and tying up climbing roses along a fence. He and our brother Alain would make the funeral and memorial arrangements. Could I fly home?

"Of course. I'll be there as soon as I can. When is the funeral?"

"We'll delay it a few days so that you can be here. Friday is about the latest date. Will that work?" I agreed. "And what about John Theodore?"

"I'm sure that both he and Martha will want to come for the funeral." I put my forehead on my hand. "Oh, Bill! It doesn't seem possible. He seemed in such good health on their last visit."

We spoke for a few minutes longer, the bonds of family made more taut from the shock and loss.

"I'll make a reservation on the *Minitel* then call you back to say when I'm arriving."

Replacing the receiver, I sat with my hands on my lap. The still calm of the empty farmhouse echoed with a sudden void. Only the family cat stirred, sitting with paws turned inwards on the back of the couch, looking over at me with unemotional amber eyes.

I called JT at his office in Boston. He and Martha would meet me in San Francisco. Within minutes, the *Minitel* on the desk in the back room pulled up Air France flights. I found one leaving in two days and booked the fast train, the TGV from Avignon directly to the Charles de Gaulle Airport. This new spur had opened just four years before, along with one going from Paris to London in the 'chunnel.'

On his last visit to France, my Dad had been spry enough to ramble up and down the rows of vines with Julien and Maurice. He and Roselyn had wandered Carpentras' Friday market, amassing souvenirs and trinkets. Dad was energized by his ability to talk with vendors in his halting French, Roselyn impressed and adoring. My sweetest memories were evenings sitting under the old *platane*, sipping wine and reminiscing about our time in Paris and life in San Francisco. He repeated his favorite stories, for perhaps the umpteenth time, and reveled in the audience that appeared to enjoy them as much as he enjoyed re-telling them.

The sound of our new truck pulling up the gravel driveway startled me and I opened the apartment door leading to the main terrace. I walked quickly toward Maurice as he stepped down.

He looked puzzled and hugged me, "Ma cherie, what is wrong?"

"My father died."

Maurice held me close, rocking me from side to side.

———

The funeral was over. JT and Martha had flown east. Our nephews and nieces had left for their homes. Roselyn, having difficulty coping and consumed with grief, had moved immediately to her daughter's guesthouse in Santa Barbara. Bill, Alain and I were left with the task of sorting through our father's things and selling the house.

Looking through our childhood home, full of antiques and oriental rugs, treasures from travels, paintings, hundreds of books and at least four sets of 'good' china, we three siblings shook our heads and concurred that there were very few items that we wanted. Bill was trustee of the estate; Alain was managing the sale of the house and household items. I volunteered to inventory everything.

Starting with stuff stored in the attic, I bent down and brushed cobwebs and dust from the top of a cardboard banker's box. With a start, I realized that it was the one that I had left when I moved to France in 1979. The tape around the top was yellow and brittle. Inside, I found a handful of out-of-date reference books and biographies, a batch of file folders, each labeled with the name of the poet or writer painstakingly researched during the sabbatical in 1978. I pulled out 'Louis Aragon' and glanced inside at the published article, faded and dated looking, remembering his long marriage to Else and his involvement with young men after she died.

Since René Char's death there had been a resurgence of interest in his works and someone would surely write a book about him at some point. I spent almost an hour skimming over what I'd written about these amazing, adventurous characters.

A large envelope with brittle, glueless tape held the journal of Florence Gilles-Martin. I thought of talks with my mother-in-law, gradually piecing together the story of Brigitte. Maurice's children sometimes talked about their mother and, after the first few years, I ceased to think of her as a youthful murderer. She was simply Maurice's first wife, of whom the family spoke with affection. In all these years I never mentioned what I knew to either Maurice or to Sophie. It had been relegated to the attic in the house and the attic of my mind.

As I flipped through the journal's pages, written in Florence's tiny, spidery handwriting, her comments seemed poignant. One paragraph was vaguely humorous when describing the deprivations, what was available to eat. I knew that her family had never known of her work as a courier for the

Resistance or her affair with the Jewish document maker 'A,' nor how Henri had tried to kill her. This testament in simple daily entries evoked her fear combined with courage. And then there were her poems:

> From a Train Window
> Undulating cypress trees, darkened, point the way,
> A silver-winged bird soars toward heaven
> Blocked by gathering clouds
> Then falls
> There is an end to wounds that fill the earth.
> Reflections of shadows in rainwater pools
> Dark leaves that memory has left behind
> The gathering clouds turn the mirror white
> And we will soon forget.   (49)

At the end of the box was *Chants de la Balandrane*, the book that Claude Lapeyre had given me when we first met. I looked at the front page, the dedication to Claude and his note to me. Now and then he and I would cross paths at one of the conferences that he periodically scheduled to promote Char's prose and poetry. I decided that I would call him when I returned. We would have a good time reflecting on what René would think now that President Jacques Chirac had decided that the ageing nuclear missile silos should be dismantled from Char's beloved Plateau d'Albion. The poet, once again, had been prescient.

Putting the lid on, I carried the box and inched down narrow steps to the second-floor. In the den I sealed the journal inside a new envelope then taped the lid to the cardboard box, tightly, solidly. With a felt marker, I wrote my name and 'ship to France.' I had no plans to do anything with this ancient collection of 'stuff,' and certainly no plans to share what I knew with the Laurents. However, collecting the materials, researching the information, had helped define my own life and I didn't want to part with it yet.

THE VAUCLUSE - 1944

AUGUST 25, FRIDAY:

Michel Perrin, *Baptiste*, had not been back in his hometown since he and Francois Laurent had joined the Maquis sixteen months before. He, Étienne Bertolini and others from his *reseau* had joined a couple of other groups from the Venasque, Pernes and Carpentras triangle knowing that the towns had been evacuated by the Germans hours before. They marched ahead of everyone else, wanting to be among the first to announce the liberation and set the bells of St-Siffrein to ringing out the good news.

Not a single straggler let alone a sniper had been seen as they'd walked from below the cliffs of Venasque through flat Saint Didier's tree-lined main street and up the road toward Carpentras. Étienne had said that the Germans were heading for Montelimar further up the Rhone and planned to mount a defense from there. Michel was amazed at the accuracy of the information *Brioche* seemed to know but was glad that most of the fighting seemed over. They'd lost several men over the past six months, and a number, such as Francois, had been wounded.

Looking around as he marched between familiar buildings, Michel nudged Étienne. "Glad to be back?"

The baker's son nodded, not able to speak.

To the west was the backside of the Hotel Dieu. Up ahead, to their right, was the city's south wall topped with big-leafed trees, the *Allée des platane*. In the faint pre-dawn light the southern-most row of buildings along *boulevard Jean Jaurès* was cloaked in gray. The silence made it seem as if the town had been cast under a spell.

Walking at the edge of a field along the roadway, Étienne glanced over and saw what looked like a man crouched behind a bush at the base of the wall. He signaled to Michel and two other guys to hunker down as they crept over, rifles poised. Whoever he was, a young guy in baggy pants with suspenders, he had been dead for hours. There was blood spattered on the wall above him, blood dried around several holes in his shirt. As Michel turned him over, he noticed a bullet hole under one eye.

"Hey! I know this guy!"

Étienne looked more closely. "Yeah, isn't he René Pasculin who runs the traveling carnival with his dad?"

Michel blurted out as other young men gathered around, "What the hell do you suppose happened?"

Vinnie chimed in, "Three guesses and they all start with a 'G.' He obviously made somebody mad."

"Too bad he couldn't have waited a day," said another man.

Michel breathed out a huge sigh, "Let's leave him for the time being. After we've gotten someone to open the church and start ringing the bells, we can send a truck to pick him up."

Six men on motorcycles waved as they sputtered past, on their way into the town center. Michel watched as someone tentatively opened a shutter on the top floor of one of the buildings behind the trees.

"Let's go guys! We've got a celebration to start!"

Maquisards in front of the *Grand Café du 19*^{eme} *Siècle,*
Carpentras, France, August 1944.

As the day dawned, Private John Evans couldn't believe that it had been only ten days since he'd first slogged onto the sandy beach in Southern France. The platoon's sergeant kept telling the guys that it had been 'a piece of cake.' Maybe from the generals' points of view at a safe distance, thought Johnny, but they should have been in his shoes. He didn't even want to know how many miles he had logged in dirt encrusted boots that weighed down his legs. Every now and then he and a couple of the guys would hitch a ride on a jeep or a troop truck for a few miles but relief only came when the company halted for a meal or slept, often out in the open, curled up on grass or hay.

Lugging around a pack, a heavy weapon and a metal helmet that could cook an egg in the heat was not what Johnny would call 'a piece of cake.' Yet it was true, over all, that most of the enemy had skedaddled except for a handful here and there. The German troops they'd rounded up as prisoners of war included Poles, Czechs, Ruskies, some of them either pretty darned young or almost decrepit. Separated from the German troops many of these men stated that they hated the Nazis, that they had been forced to fight. One man showed Johnny cigarette burn marks on his arms and neck;

another had lost part of his ear. He saw a sad older man kneel on the dirt and grasp a chaplain's hand, muttering '*danke, danke.*'

Resistance groups rang church bells if Germans had evacuated a town so his patrol had simply walked through a number of villages and hamlets. Residents ran out with bouquets and backslaps, handshakes and kisses, waving French and American flags. Johnny didn't mind when the girl was good looking but a couple of old women with bad breath had kissed him and babbled in his ear. Still, he liked the good feeling that you brought them something special, that they truly were thrilled to see you. The girls seemed to favor tall, carrot-topped Sam who got kissed a lot. Johnny kidded him about it. Sam grinned and made a snappy comment that French women knew a good thing when they saw it.

There had been some heavy action in a couple of the bigger towns. A bunch of men in his unit had gotten it, including Stevie who had prayed every time that he could. It didn't do any good, Johnny realized, especially since Vinnie seemed to be a lucky son-of-a-gun and he had the ethics of a rattle-snake. Johnny knew at least a dozen men wounded badly enough to be sent to the hospital tent, some of them to be shipped home. They nicknamed them 'million dollar wounds.' If you got a minor wound, a medic would come by and stitch it up, maybe give you a shot for pain or infection, slap on a bandage, and you were expected to keep going.

The platoon had plodded through a series of pretty towns, or towns that had once been pretty, you could tell. Bombs did a lot of damage. And the Germans seemed to always leave something destroyed whether it was a smol-dering barn or a broken down truck set on fire.

Ahead was an enormous rock plateau sticking above the edge of the riv-er in the early morning light. A sign with an arrow pointed to 'Cavaillon.' Johnny Evans saw the outline of a former railroad depot and a round house, a shell of what-had-been with twisted, jutting rails that looked like care-lessly tossed sticks. The Americans walked past piles of stone and chunks of cement next to buildings with no roofs, sides missing, gaping holes for windows and doors, a shutter hanging by a single hinge. Then the build-ings began to look nicer, more normal, and people appeared, streamed out, throwing flowers, waving flags, yelling '*merci.*'

Johnny looked back at Vinnie and Sam as he was embraced by a couple of young women. He stopped for a hug, more kisses and a wilted bouquet. One man had set up planks between two tables and was offering drinks of beer as they walked by. Some of the cafés with tables under big Sycamore trees looked mighty appealing, but the platoon had miles to go before they could rest that night.

Men wearing berets and armbands emblazoned with the cross of Lorraine circled on motorcycles or marched in formation with rifles on their shoulders. Occasionally the sound of the *Marseillaise* could be heard: a flute, a group of singers, a motley and enthusiastic crowd.

When they reached a central square Johnny was shocked once again at how some of the women were treated. This wasn't the first place where he'd seen them up on a raised deck of some sort. There were seven in this square in the midst of having their heads shaved. Two of the girls crossed their arms over bare breasts; black swastikas decorated their foreheads and backs.

An extremely pretty girl about his age stood with shoulders bent forward trying to hold a torn blouse across her chest as her red-auburn hair was roughly scissored by an angry older woman. Johnny gaped as one of the men reached his arm around her neck to hold her still while he shaved the stubble down to bare skin. Her pale body and brown skirt dripped with black dots. Black swastikas covered her arms and cheeks. One of her brown shoes was missing and she balanced on her left toes.

Johnny stopped and watched, bothered at seeing such a pretty young woman treated so cruelly, although he understood that she was a collaborator, a Nazi's whore. As the man finished shaving her head, he pushed the once beautiful girl over to line up with the other women to be paraded through the town.

She saw Johnny watching her and glared for an instant, her green eyes spilling tears. Then she turned her head away. Johnny stood watching for a minute, shifted his pack, adjusted his rifle and joined his platoon in their march on to the next skirmish.

Among those gathered in Carpentras' square that morning was Benjamin Landau with his daughter, Sylvie. At the sound of bells ringing they had emerged from cellars on the southeast edge of town, much more pale and thin then when they had arrived in May. The former 'Antoine Dupont' was anxious to contact Florence Gilles-Martin to let her know that he was safe. He left Sylvie with a cluster of townspeople watching the Maquis and FFI strut in formation around the square, motorcyclists circling, tri-color flags unfurling from balconies and rooftops.

He knew the Bertolinis were good friends but their bakery was closed. He came back to the 19th Century Café and saw Marcel Alibert, asking if he had seen Madame Gilles-Martin. He was shaken when he heard that Florence had been in an accident and was at the Moricelly Clinic.

At the reception desk he gave his name as Antoine Dupont and said that he was a close friend. Sister Marie-Gabriel told him that an aide would check on her condition. Within minutes the aide, a chirpy young woman, came back.

"Madame Gilles-Martin seems well this morning. I think that the news of our liberation did it. We are all feeling better!"

She chattered on about how wonderful it would be to be free again, how glorious the day had become. Through the open windows happy sounds drifted in: the pealing of bells, singing, the cacophony of excited and celebratory voices, an occasional purring or grinding of a vehicle as it went by. Antoine followed her into a large room with curtains flittering and a number of empty beds stripped down to stained mattresses. At the fourth cubicle, the aide pulled back a curtain and announced to Florence that a Monsieur Dupont was there to see her. Benjamin stepped up and she clasped his hand, her eyes wide.

"You're safe!"

"Yes, yes, Sylvie and I are both safe. But what happened?" He leaned over, gently took her chin, kissed her on both cheeks then briefly on her lips. "You're all banged up."

"I had a bicycle accident and have a broken collarbone. I should be fine in a day or two."

Florence stroked his hand, smiling as Benjamin explained where he had been for the past months and that he'd been unable to send a message to her. When Florence added her news, that her husband was dead, his brows raised in surprise.

"He was drunk and died from a fall down the stairs."

"I guess that I should say that I'm sorry. Yet, in a way, it is good news. While Sylvie and I were in hiding we talked about what we might do when the war ends. Several people discussed moving to Palestine. I know that it is risky, unsettled at times, but a lot of Jews are moving there. If you and Gigi came with us we could start a new life." He kissed Florence's hand, "What do you think?"

She closed her eyes then opened them, murmuring, "It sounds like a good solution, Benjamin. I'm not sure that I want to stay here any longer, with all that has happened."

"Sylvie and I will be going back to Avignon to see how our house fared and start planning for the future. Our future!" Benjamin reached over and brushed a lock of hair from Florence's forehead.

"We need something happy to look forward to, don't we? Benjamin, the poetry books that you loaned me are in my bag. I've even written some poems, myself. Maybe I can read them to you later?"

"Of course, *ma chérie*." Benjamin leaned to kiss her on the forehead. "As soon as you feel better."

Florence fumbled toward the bag under her bed then Benjamin reached down and put it on the coverlet. She brought out two slim books.

"I've marked a couple that reminded me of you."

He opened a page with a paper bookmark and read out loud part of Paul Eluard's:

I have the power to exist without destiny
Between forest and dew between oblivion and presence
Coolness and warmth I care nothing for them
I shall send far across your desires
The image of myself you offer me
My face has but one star.... (50)

His eyes blurred and he paused. "Thank you, dear Florence. My wonderful student, you continually amaze me. We'll have so much to talk about when you are well."

As he slipped his hand out of hers, Florence looked up. "Benjamin. Thank you. Thank you for everything."

"I am the one to thank you. Being your tutor brought me great joy. I hope that we will share many more poems together over the years." He slid through the curtains, waved and blew one more kiss to her.

As Florence rolled over on her side, her knitting bag slipped to the floor spilling some of the contents. An hour later, a volunteer aide checked on the sleeping patient and gathered up the ball of yarn and knitting needles, her purse, a sack of jewelry, and carefully placed them inside the bag. She did not notice the composition book that had fallen far under the bed.

⁂

Late Friday afternoon, Johnny Evans and a handful of his platoon drove up an *avenue Victor Hugo* in the latest town. It had a name like 'Carpenters.' Johnny wondered if it had been built by a bunch of woodworkers. At least it was somewhat pronounceable. A crowd was waving American and French flags in a large square straight ahead. Members of the FFI and Maquis Ventoux stood in loosely assembled groups, rifles on their shoulders. A few men circled on motorcycles, stopping for kisses from girls.

As Johnny's truck got closer someone shouted, *"Les Americains sont ici! Les Americains sont ici!"*

Johnny and his buddies' hands were grasped and shaken, their cheeks kissed and the word *'merci'* repeated over and over again. As tanks and jeeps arrived and more American soldiers meandered in, townspeople surrounded them, cheered, leaned from balconies and waved tricolor flags. Some stood on vehicles parked on the sides. The Allied officers greeted the FFI commanders, shook hands and milled about in the middle of an open space.

It appeared that an improvised ceremony was to take place. The *Marseillaise* once again wafted from a choral group hastily assembled, bouquets were handed to Allied officers standing with French dignitaries. American soldiers and French partisans were photographed as they shook hands, smiling to the point of discomfort.

Suddenly a man, perspiring in a dark suit, stepped up on a jeep and yelled loudly. The crowd quieted. The man announced that General de Gaulle with General Philippe LeClerc and their Free French troops had entered Paris. The Nazi Colonel in charge of the city had surrendered. Paris and Carpentras had been liberated on the same day.

Carpentras, France celebrating liberation by the American 3rd Army

AUGUST 26:

When General Charles de Gaulle entered Paris, his head was high above those surrounding him, amid a cheering, flag waving, flower strewing, and ebullient crowd. As he walked the eleven miles from the Place de l'Étoile to Notre

Dame Cathedral on the Ile de la Cité, a sniper at a window fired a shot that narrowly missed him. De Gaulle did not waver and continued in his dignified manner along the route.

It had been a long, difficult four years but at last *la belle France* was free again and her people, all those who cherished the principles of *liberté, fraternité, egalité*, would be united under one purpose. The upstart general knew that he would still need to deal with the Americans but, regardless of how the Vichy government had portrayed him, he had returned victorious in his view and a hero in the eyes of the majority of his countrymen. He was firm that this new government must be inclusive and that, regardless of one's position during the war, all voices would be heard.

PASSING THE TORCH

AUGUST 2014

Vivienne parked her rented Twingo car on the now paved driveway with its wide parking area, west of the old arch. I watched as she opened the trunk, hauled out a suitcase, bumped it to the ground and wrestled its wheels toward the terrace where I stood. It seemed almost impossible that my 'little' granddaughter was so tall, so independent, so self-assured.

She waved and called out, "Bonjour, Mimi."

My American grandchildren's name for me was close to the Laurent's '*mémé*.' And I was now subject to another name since Chloe's baby had arrived a few months before. Befitting a great-grandmother of eighty-one years, my short hair was silvery-gray, my face lined, my mind astonished.

Sweet Vivienne—here she was: blue-eyed, wide of mouth, a streak of some reddish color on one side of her flowing brown hair, a row of graduated studs marching up her ear, a tattoo on her shoulder, as she presented her cheek to be kissed.

"Oh, Mimi, it's so wonderful to be back at the *Domaine*!" She looked around the terrace, motioned toward the vineyard below, "It seems like it has hardly changed since I was small."

I chuckled at that. "It has been improved a lot since. You remember the stucco pool in the field and the exposed rocks on the *mas'* façade?"

"I remember that it was like visiting a fairyland when we first came to see you and *Papi Maurice*. I'm so sorry about him, you know that?"

"Of course, darling." I couldn't say anything more. Widowhood was too new and I was not adjusting to it very well.

We stood for a moment, looking over the heat-sprinkled landscape, the vines lushly green, stretching out for miles. Linking my arm in hers, I gazed into her smooth, fresh face as we turned toward the front door.

"I'm so glad that you have a few days to spend here before you start graduate school.

Martine fixed up a room for you in the main house. Go get settled and change into a bathing suit and we'll walk down to the pool."

At the cabana next to the filtered swimming pool, I stirred a pitcher of lemonade that had been sitting in the patio refrigerator. Vivienne emerged from the water, wiping her face on a towel, her bikini barely covering the essentials.

"I made us something cool to drink, *ma chérie*. Let's sit here at the table with the umbrella. Now, tell me about your plans. At your college graduation we didn't have time to talk."

Vivienne stretched out her legs toward the sun. "I'm thinking of a thesis on something that combines American and French history or literature, since I'm fluent in both languages. Didn't you do research on French Surrealist writers when you were a professor?"

"A long time ago, yes. You remember the stories that I told you and Mathew when you were growing up, about how I met Maurice and ended up living in France?"

"Of course! But most of the time it seemed that raising grapes and making wine was the center of your world. I remember a lot of talk about getting recognition for your blends, not to mention the 'tastes' and 'bouquet.' I remember how pleased *Papi Maurice* was that your region was granted an *AOC Cotes-du-Ventoux*."

"That was a wonderful accomplishment, something that he, Julien and the other vintners worked hard to get. Look at the new label." I held up the bottle. "The name has been shortened to *AOC Ventoux*. And the muscat continues to get more recognition as a *cru* of the *Cotes-du-Rhone*."

"They both still taste great regardless of what the label says!"

We talked intermittently, listening to the *cigales* give their afternoon concert, refilling our glasses. I savored the warmth of the sun and the joy of our camaraderie, a tiny slice of heaven. My granddaughter suddenly leaned toward me and smiled her wide smile.

"Tell me again, what had you had planned to do with that research when you first came here?"

Memories. Faded, sharp, surreal, deep. I reached into the past and began to retell the story of my sabbatical project when I came to Carpentras in 1978, so long ago.

"Wow," she said, when I finished. "I might use some of that for a thesis. René Char sounds like a particularly good subject if I can find enough information."

"He was very private for a long time; however, about ten years ago a man wrote his biography. I'll give you a copy."

"Do you still have those papers, the notes and all?"

"Yes, they are in a box up in the apartment's attic. You're welcome to look over what is there. I also have a journal written during the war by the mother of Maurice's first wife. It described what it was like during the Occupation here in Provence and refers to a number of poets that the author studied. She also wrote several poems."

Was Florence Gilles-Martin's journal even readable? Had mice or insects ravaged the probably dry and yellowed papers? I felt a wave of melancholy, the knee-jerk reaction to overlook the worst that happened, to keep the secrets of wartime.

"I've not talked about this journal for years. The author was in the Resistance, covered up a murder and had an affair. You could use some of the information but perhaps not the personal part...."

Vivienne sat up in her chair. "Mimi, you've known about this all these years and never said anything?"

"Disclosing what happened would have hurt and upset a number of people. Even now, although the others of my generation are gone, I'm not sure the rest of the family should know." I paused then added, "Over the years I've jotted down stories about the Laurent family's experiences during the war, whenever they confided in me. Perhaps you could use some of this as background information if you decide to focus on writers during wartime. But not everything."

Hesitant, I waited before continuing, "I also recently learned something new about René Char. It's supposed to be a secret although the gossip is pretty rampant."

"Well...?," Vivienne looked over with raised eyebrows.

"He evidently had a daughter. Her mother apparently never made any demands on Char and he never acknowledged the child. However, now that this woman is a grandmother, the rumor is she wants his grandchildren and great-grandchildren to know about their heritage. I've heard this from a couple of people although it's not known publicly."

"That's interesting. I'd like to look at your papers," she remarked as she sat back in the chair, sipping her drink. "I suppose a lot depends on what I learn in class, what else I find that I might want to pursue. There have been a lot of studies and new information since the 1970's. May I take some of the research back with me, in case it seems relevant?"

"Of course. If it would be the least bit relevant that would be wonderful." I opened my hand toward Vivienne. "Perhaps your generation can learn from our past, perhaps take on the task of never letting such horrors be forgotten or repeated. The world constantly needs to be reminded how easily humanity can slide into the most base and evil actions against one another."

Seventy years had passed since the Occupation had ended, since Florence had filled a journal with her thoughts and her poems, since the Laurents had reunited as a family and moved on. Cities throughout Provence were currently in the midst of celebrating the Liberation's 70th anniversary with speeches, parades of military vehicles, flags and banners, the visits of elderly American soldiers and recognition of the remaining Maquisards. Still, it seemed to me that the writers of the Resistance were revered more for their later literary contributions than for their fight against Fascism.

Even though the residents of the Domaine had not been greatly affected by political upheavals over the past decades, we were very aware of the desecration and damage of Carpentras' Jewish cemetery in 1990 by a handful of neo-Nazis, the riots in 2005 throughout France by children of immigrants from North and Sub-Saharan Africa, the emerging influence of the *Front National's* zenophobia in recent elections.

What, I wondered, would these poets of the Resistance think and write about today? As I reflected on some of their poems and prose, their words were still fitting, their sentiments a caution that was still relevant.

⚬

"To see, to hear, means nothing. To recognize (or not to recognize) means everything. Between what I do recognize and what I do not recognize there stands myself. And what I do not recognize I shall continue not to recognize.'
André Breton, Surrealism and Painting (1928).

'Those who cannot remember the past are condemned to repeat it.'
George Santayana, The Life of Reason (1905-06)

THE VAUCLUSE – 1944

SEPTEMBER 1:

The acrid smell from the fire at the *Chateau de Barroux* wafted over the fields and into the Domaine de Lauritaine's rooms. It had been eight days since the Germans had torched their headquarters in the magnificent 12th century monument and it was still smoldering. Juliette Laurent sniffed at the scent mingling with the atmosphere of wounded souls in their home.

She stood before a bedroom mirror and pulled a long pin from her black straw hat. After she took it off, she reattached the pin, smoothed the veil and placed the hat on a table. Mumbling noise came from the crowd downstairs, assembled for the luncheon that she and Jean-Pierre were hosting for their family and a few friends after the funeral mass that morning in Saint Siffrein.

She still could not quite accept that Florence, whom she had known since she was a baby, was no longer with them.

Right after the Liberation, Florence seemed better and was scheduled to leave the hospital. Suddenly her fever shot up, she went into a coma and passed away within two days. Sister Marie-Gabriel explained that the staff had not realized how serious an infection had become, what she called 'septicemia.' The reasons could have been numerous: bacteria that thrived in hospitals, the warm weather, an internal injury, Florence's frail health. The departing Germans had stripped the pharmacy of the sulfa that might have saved her. There was nothing that they could have done, Sister Marie-Gabriel told Juliette.

The compassionate aide who stood by Florence's bedside at the end said that Madame Gilles-Martin did not want her family to know about the miscarriage. Sister Marie-Gabriel concurred. They did mention a grief-stricken friend who had come by then walked out with his hands held over his face. Juliette did not recognize the description and there was no name, so she passed it off as a concerned neighbor or parishioner.

Gigi was now an orphan, without siblings, and fully dependent upon the Laurents. Juliette did not know how to sooth her. At first Gigi cried broken-heartedly then she retreated into an almost frightening silence. Attempts to talk with her resulted in a chin tucked to her chest, a muttered 'don't bother me,' 'I don't want to talk about it,' 'leave me alone.' She insisted in staying up in her attic hideaway, not wanting to be around anyone. She picked at the plates of food placed by her door. Sometimes squeaky music could be heard as she played her father's violin. Juliette felt that she could stand some practice but was grateful that the music consoled her.

Juliette's other great sorrow and worry was her own daughter. When Gabrielle arrived home she literally sobbed on her mother's shoulder, holding on like a forlorn child, saying 'I'm so sorry' over and over. Her father, shocked at the significance of his daughter's appearance, had wept and then avoided her, spending much of his time wandering around checking vines. Francois, appalled by Gabrielle's affair, had at first yelled at then refused to speak to her. He reclined on his bed in the downstairs room for hours on end, a book in hand, crutches at his side. Maurice, at an age when tears and conflict were difficult to interpret, went off on long walks into the hills.

To Juliette's relief, her parents, Annette and Nicolas Boisseau, had arrived four days earlier from a remote hamlet northeast of Sisteron where they had lived in her brother's vacation cottage, supplied with a well, a tiny garden, three chickens and a neighbor who was a poacher. Upon returning, they came to help Juliette and Jean-Pierre.

Over the past week Juliette and her mother had cared for everyone, serving meals in bedrooms, not asking questions. At the kitchen table, conversation seemed limited to requesting that a dish be passed. Jean-Pierre's lone subject was the muscat, the possibility of the AOC having been granted and the harvest ahead. Juliette's father, a reticent man to begin with, retired to a corner of the salon reading books from their library.

Juliette straightened the front of her black dress, smoothed the skirt and walked down the stairs to greet guests. Elodie, the new girl that she'd hired to help, needed guidance on what to do with the bouquets and gifts. Family and guests needed to be reassured and thanked.

A tear-stained, nervous Anne-Marie Bertolini greeted Juliette with a box of pastries as she and Émile arrived in the entry hall. She had been devastated to learn of Florence's death, and whispered to her husband over and over how fortunate that they and their children had survived. Their unspoken anxiety was of being accused of collaboration. Dozens they knew had been attacked or were in jail. News of executions by former Resistance groups ran rampant.

Uncle Xavier sat in a stiff-backed Jacobean-style chair looking dazed. Juliette was suspicious that he had suffered a minor stroke since arriving at the Domaine. His left hand trembled and his speech seemed slurred. He looked up as she walked over and patted him on his shoulder.

"Ah. My dear Juliette. The war is over, isn't it?"

She nodded, not wanting to explain more, and moved on to greet Étienne and his fiancée, Laurianne, who clung to his right elbow like a mussel to a rock. They murmured their sympathy and mentioned how much Florence would be missed. Across the room Jean-Pierre and Maurice stood by Francois, who sat with his wrapped leg straight in front of him, Amélie at his side. Three men from his Resistance *reseau* stood in a half circle, among them his former classmate Michel Perrin. Juliette guessed that they were talking about their friend Roland, who hadn't survived.

Juliette greeted their neighbors the Napiers, standing with glasses of rosé and puzzled expressions, still unsure about surviving unscathed.

"We're so sorry about Florence," Madame Napier murmured. "But you must be relieved to have your children back at home. We think that Mathieu is still in the German town where he's been working and hope that the *Croix Rouge* will be able to find out for us. With all the fighting it's been difficult."

"I know that you will be so glad to see him come home! Let's hope it happens quickly, that the war will end soon."

Juliette touched her hand and moved on to greet Doctor Blum and his wife, who stood next to her parents.

"Doctor, thank you again for fixing Francois' leg."

"Madame Laurent, we will be forever grateful for the time that you hid us until we found a place to stay. We made it through those difficult days thanks to your parents. Their friends were wonderful to us and our son."

He dipped his head almost in a bow. Juliette's mother mumbled a few words in response then edged her daughter to the side. "Darling, your father and Uncle Xavier are both tired so I think that we'll leave soon."

"Thank you so much for being here and helping care for everyone. I am so glad that you are back and we can be together again, *Maman*."

They kissed cheeks as her mother said, "How terribly sad that Cousin Florence is not here to celebrate France being free."

"It's not over yet. I imagine that shortages and difficulties still lie ahead. It looks like it will be months before the Nazis give up."

Her father spoke up, "The Americans have almost succeeded in pushing them back into Germany. What brave and generous young men! We owe them a huge debt."

Juliette agreed, moving toward the hallway to ask Elodie to pass another plate of *hors d'oeuvres*, and saw Gigi standing at the entrance to the main room.

She wore a simple black sheath with cap sleeves and a pair of her mother's black high-heeled sandals from the mid-thirties, her big toes sticking out a fraction. Her hair was pulled back in a chignon and the gray pearl earrings that she had borrowed from Juliette added an air of sophistication to her solemn, teen-aged face.

As Monsieur Bertolini greeted her as '*ma petite Gigi*,' Juliette was surprised to hear her loud response.

"That was my nickname as a little girl. My real name is Brigitte. Please, I want to be called Brigitte."

Juliette stepped toward the girl who stared at her, her chin firm, her reddened eyes resolute. Juliette smiled and put her arm around her rigid shoulders and gave her a kiss on the cheek. They walked into the living room, arm in arm, and began to greet their friends and thank them for expressing their sympathy.

THE END

ACKNOWLEDGEMENTS

T hanks go to many people in France who helped with information or shared their stories that inspired this book: Malika del Amo, Amaury de Cizancourt, Rose Eravanian, Raymonde Franchini, Claude and Renée Lapeyre, and Steve Patris. Albert Cordola kindly gave me a copy of his auto-biography, *Quelques passages de ma simple vie,* in which he recounted his life in prison, ending up at Dachau.

I can never thank friends from the France-USA Committee enough, as knowing them has added richness to my life: Michel Alcide, Pierre and Anita Caillet, Brigitte and Roger Charlet, Andrée Chenal, Michel Cokelaere, Nina Eldridge, Elisabeth Fabre, Laurianne Gardet, Delphine Kurtzman, Francoise Marchal, Michel and Marie-Christine Pacros, Steve (whose father was an American paratrooper) and Joelle Patris, Philippe and Michelle Saleille, and Patricia Seaux. A huge *merci* to the Favier-Ligier family that warmly welcomed me to their beautiful *hotel particulier,* where I have spent many happy months.

In the USA my deepest thanks and appreciation go to the 'Town and Gown Book Club' members, from whom I received an education on good books and good writers. I owe a 'bouquet' to another group of avid readers, 'The Aspiring Minds,' for the years we shared a love of women authors.

Two wonderful groups of 'Francophiles' inspired me with their spirits of adventure, their life stories, their encouragement and help, as I strove to improve speaking the French language: Peggy Rocha's private French class (Pat, Maria-Elena, Frankie, Laurie, Vava, Chris) and the 'French Club' (Mel, Paul, Anne, Devin, June, Sherman, Francoise, Roger, Jo, Steve). You've enriched my life! How fun it has been, hosting several of you in Carpentras.

I especially want to thank readers who spent valuable time and effort making helpful suggestions and corrections: Susan Benedetti, Pat Cox, Durlynn Anema Garten, PhD., Beth Gregory, PhD., Valerie Hogan, Pat Kim, Joyce McAllister, Chris Olin, Teri Oppenheimer, PharmD., Frankie Parker, Douglas Pressman, PhD., Barbara Schwartz, and Peggy Traverso.

A heartfelt 'hug' to John Shirley, DVM, whose experiences as a young soldier in Provence, August 1944, served as inspiration for Johnny Evans in this book. He survived a prolonged battle in Montilimar, marched up to Northeastern France where his platoon was captured. Wounded in the jaw and bleeding, John clobbered his guard and ran into the maze of destroyed buildings. He made his way into nearby woods, found a group of American soldiers and was flown to London. After surgery and time to heal he returned and continued fighting until the end of the war. Back home he married his sweetheart, became a veterinarian, had three children and was elected mayor of his town. He has returned to France every five years to visit French friends and commemorate a period in his life that marked him forever. The most touching tribute was a square named in his honor in the village that he helped liberate in the Alsace-Lorraine region, where he was wounded. His courage and patriotism are exemplary! Thank you, John.

Arnaud Lemaigre of the *Centre d'Interpretation du Patrimoine* in Carpentras was very helpful in locating publications, documents and photographs. The archivists at the *Musée Departmental d'Histoire Jean Garcin 39-45* provided numerous articles and books. I found several references at the d'Inguimbert Library. Librarians at the University of the Pacific, Stockton, California were incredibly patient and forgiving as I checked out bibliographies from their stacks. UOP's Writers' Conferences were helpful—featured speaker John Lescroat was an inspiration, as I had followed his career from (almost) its inception. Paul Lundborg provided helpful guidance on how to publish the book, after the success of his own. Dare I thank Wikipedia for the ability to quickly fact check?

Last, and certainly not least, thanks go to those who lived during World War II in Provence and to those who fought against oppression in whatever way they chose. Vive la France!

Liz Konold
2016

APPENDIX

NON-FICTION CHARACTERS

Alibert, Marcel – Co-owner of the Grand Café of the 19th Century (*Grand Café du 19eme Siècle)* in Carpentras, rendezvous spot of Resistance groups in the Vaucluse. Rene Dulfour was his father-in-law.

Arnoud, M. – Mayor of Carpentras under the Vichy administration.

Bernard, Jacqueline (dates unknown) – executive secretary of the underground newspaper *Combat*, Paris; born in Lyon of Jewish parents. Arrested and sent to Ravensbruck concentration camp, she was released in 1945.

Bernard, Roger (b. 1921, d. 1944) – poet, member of the Resistance, shot by the Germans on June 22, 1944.

Beyne, Philippe (b. 1896, d. 1967) – Retired Lieutenant-Colonel in the French Army Reserves who served with distinction in World War I. Former tax collector of the town of Sault. Co-founder of Maquis Ventous with Maxime Fischer. Code name: *d'Artagnan.*

Blanchard, Georges – known as *Mekan*, Blanchard was in the Resistance Movement in Carpentras. Little information was found.

Bonin-Pissarro, Claude (b. 1921) – grandson of the painter Camille Pissarro, he served in the *Maquis Ventoux* under Fischer and Beyne. Works from the Louvre Museum and the Calvet Museum, Avignon, were hidden at the Chateau de Javon where he lived during WWII.

Caillet, Robert (b. 1882, d. 1957) – curator and director of the Bibliotheque d'Inguimertine, Carpentras; father of Maurice Caillet (b. 1910, d. 2008), Inspector General of French Libraries

Castaud, Louis (b. 1891, d. 1959) - instrumental in obtaining an AOC 'cru' label for Beaumes-de-Venise Muscat wine; owner of the *Domaine de Bernardin*.

Cat, Gaston (b. 1905, d. ?) - Owner of a transportation company in Carpentras and a member of the *Maquis Ventoux;* code name: *Antoine.*

Corbin de la Mangoux, Commander Gonzague (b. 1903, d. 1966) – coordinator of the Maquis Ventoux with Major John Goldsmith, prior to the invasion of Provence 1944. Code named *Amict.*

Courveille, Rose (b. 1884, d. 1946) – Sister Marie-Gabriel of the Augustine Convent, Carpentras; director of the Clinique Moricelly maternity hospital 1934-1946 who helped save Jewish infants.

Deladier, Eduard (b. 1884, d. 1970) – born in Carpentras, Prime Minister of France in 1933, 1934, 1938-40.

de Boiseaumarie, Baron Pierre Le Roy (b. 1890, d. 1967) - the co-founder of the *Institut National des Appellations d'Origine* (INAO) who guided the creation of the *Appellation d'origine contrôlée* (AOC) system which controls French wine laws.

Dulfour, René – Co-owner of the *Grand Café du 19ᵉᵐᵉ Siècle* in Carpentras. Code name: *Maxmillian.*

Durand, Albin – A farmer from Sarrian who helped the Resistance. He was brutally tortured and murdered by the Milice in 1944, using his own mechanical saw to cut off his extremities. A street in Carpentras bears his name.

Fenouil, Paul and Émile – owners of the Fenouil Nursury in Carpentras in late 1800's, early 1900's; known for importing California grape vines resistant to phylloxera; builder of the mansion 'La Roserie,' currently owned by the City of Carpentras.

Fischer, Maxime (b. 1913, d. 2005) - Attorney from Paris, co-founder of Maquis Ventous with Colonel Philippe Beyne; code name: *Anatole.*

Garcin, Jean (b. 1917, d. 2006) – Leader of the *Group Franc,* code name: *Colonel Bayard.* His family owned paper mills and factories. His father was mayor of Fontaine-de-Vaucluse, was arrested by the Nazis and died in Buchenwald concentration camp. He served as a member of the General Council of the Vaucluse, 1945-1998.

Goldsmith, Major John (b. 1909, d. 1972) - a British agent for the Special Operations Executive (SOE) helping to coordinate Resistance groups.

Grangeon, Lucien (b. 1911, d. 1975) – Capitaine of 1st Battalion, *Maquis Vasio;* code name: *Antoine.*

Komornica, Yvonne (b. 1898, d. 1994) – chief of the *Combat Group,* code name: *Kleber.* She and two daughters (Wanda and Christiane) helped wounded prisoners, contacted families of Resistance members and distributed propaganda. Arrested in October 1943, she survived internment and medical experiments in Ravensbruck and was liberated in July 1945.

Lapeyre, Claude – close friend to René Char, former professor of mathematics, former mayor of Pernes-les-fontaines.

Lapeyre, Renée – wife of Claude; also the daughter of a former mayor of Pernes-les-fontaines.

Leyris, Monsieur – President of Carpentras' civil courts, arrested for aiding the sabotage of train engines in Avignon, 1944. Dates and survival: unknown.

Moulin, Jean (b. 1899, d. 1943) – a former town administrator from the Pyrenees area, he established MUR, the *Movement Unis de la Resistance,* from Marseille to Lyon, code name: *Max.* In June 1943 he was arrested, tortured and murdered by Klaus Barbie, the 'butcher of Lyon.'

Pasculin, René (b. 1925, d. 1944) -- The son of a carnival owner, he was assassinated the evening before the Liberation of Carpentras. There is a square in his name and a plaque on the lower city wall of Carpentras where he was shot.

Pons-Sedoine, Marcelle (b. 1916, d. 2011) -- René Char's partner while working in the Resistance, in the hamlet of Cereste. A seamstress, wife of a prisoner-of-war and mother of Mireille Sidoine Audouy, she and Char were together for about ten years.

Roux, Gaston – farmer; one of his fields was used for the 'spitfire' parachute drop site.

Seghers, Pierre (b. 1906, d. 1987) – Publisher of wartime poetry in *Les Editions du Tour*, Villeneuve-lès-Avignon. Founder of *Editions Seghers,* Paris.

FICTIONAL CHARACTERS

Marie-Laure (children: Jean-Paul, Giselle)
Adele Laurent Chevalier (sister of Jean-Pierre; died in 1918)
Xavier Chevalier (married to Adele Laurent)

The Boissieu Family:
Annette and Nicholas Boissieu, parents of Juliette Boissieu Laurent

The Gilles-Martin Family:
Henri Gilles-Martin (from Alsace-Lorraine)
Florence Gilles-Martin (wife of Henri)
'Gigi' (Brigitte) Gilles-Martin (daughter)

The Dupont/Landau Family:
Antoine Dupont (aka Benjamin Landau)
Silvie Dupont/Landau (daughter of Benjamin Landau)

The Bertolini Family:
Emile Bertolini (owner of the *Boulangerie Bertolini*)
Anne-Marie Bertolini
Etienne Bertolini (son, POW, marries Laurianne)
Amélie Bertolini (daughter, marries Francois Laurent)

The Najarian Family:
Anton Najarian (Communist, imprisoned in Lyon/Dachau)
Roland Najarian (Communist, member of the Resistance)

Miscellaneous: The Rousseaus, the Napiers, the Merciers, the Grimauds, Yvette La Pierre, Michel Perrin and his uncles, the members of Francois Laurent's resistance group, Colonel Dietrich von Hellman, Commandant Schneider, Oberstleutnant Erik Ziegler, Gunther Schmit, Madame Poitier, Klaus (German guard), Sister Monique, Harlan the professor, Elodie, Maria.

POETRY AND QUOTE REFERENCES

(1) Breton, André and Soupault, Philippe. Quote from *Magnetic Fields*. www. mariabuszek.com

(2) Breton, André. 'Fata Morgana,' excerpt from *Poems of André Breton, a bilingual anthology*. Translated by Jean-Pierre Cauvin and Mary Ann Caws. Austin, TX: University of Texas Press, 1982.

(3) Baudelaire, Chárles. 'The Enemy,' *Dictionnaire de la poesie française*, Paris, Maxi-livres, 2002. Translation: Liz Konold, all rights reserved.

(4) Eluard, Paul, 'Obsession,' permission to reprint by translator A. S. Kline. www.poetsofmodernity.xyz.

(5) Rimbaud, Arthur. 'A Dream for Winter.' www.allpoetry.com

(6) Eluard, Paul. Excerpts from 'Liberty.' www.poemhunter.com

(7) Soupault, Philippe – 'Tomorrow is Sunday.'

(8) Aragon, Louis - - 'Else at the Mirror,' A. S. Kline, www.poetryintranslation. com

(9) Caws, Mary Ann and Jolas, Tina, Editors. 'Refusal Song,' *Poems of Rene Char.* New York. New Directions Publishing, 1992

(10) Giono, Jean. *Jean Giono: Recits et Essaies.* Paris: Gallimard, 1986: Excerpt translated by Liz Konold, all rights reserved

(11) Aragon, Louis. 'I Salute You My France,' translation by Liz Konold. www.reseau-canope.fr/

(12) Aragon, Louis. 'Lilacs and the Roses,' A. S. Kline. www.poetryintranslation.com.

(13) Char, René. 'Feuillets d'Hypnos, #15,' *Fureur et Mystere.* Paris: Gallimard, 1962. Translation by Liz Konold.

(14) Manouchian, Missak. Excerpt from 'Privation,' translation by Liz Konold

(15) Camus, Albert. *Resistance, Rebellion and Death.* Translation by Justin O'Brien. New York: Vintage Books, 1974.

(16) _____. *Resistance, Rebellion and Death.* Translation by Justin O'Brien. New York: Vintage Books, 1974.

(17) von Goethe, Johann Wolfgang. A. S. Kline, translator. www.poetryin-translation.com

(18) Greilsamer, Laurent. *L'éclair au front: René Char.* Paris: Chez Fayard, 2004. Translation by Liz Konold.

(19) Char, René. 'Venasque,' *Le Nu Perdu.* Paris: Gallimard,1978. Translation by Liz Konold.

(20) Manouchian, Missak. 'une poem – 1934,' vlabbe.blogspot.com 2010. Translation by Liz Konold

(21) Desnos, Robert. 'Mobius Strip,' excerpt from EAT IT ALIVE, published by University of Colorado, Boulder Creative Writing Program, Volume 3, Issue 5, December 1981. Amy Levin/Johannes Beilharz 1981/2010. www.albneckarschwarzwald.de/surrealism

(22) Desnos, Robert. Excerpt from 'Last Poem.' A. S. Kline, translator. www.poetryintranslation.com

(23) Desnos, Robert. 'Epitaph,' A. S. Kline, translator www.poetryintranslation.com

(24) Eluard, Paul. 'The World is Blue as an Orange,' translation not attributed. www.poemhunter.com

(25) _____. 'Nusch,' translation not attributed. www.poemhunter.com

(26) Manouchian, Micha. 'Letter to Melinee.' Translation by Mitch Abidor. www.jewishcurrents.org.

(27) Aragon, Louis. 'The Red Poster Affair,'A. S. Kline, translator. www.poetryintranslation.com

(28) Apollinaire, Guillaume. 'Clotilde,' translation by Liz Konold

(29) Greilsamer, Laurent. *L'éclair au front: René Char.* Paris: Chez Fayard, 2004. Translation by Liz Konold.

(30) Char, René. 'Feuillets d'Hypnos, #222,' *Fureur et Mystere*. Paris: Gallimard, 1962. Translation by Liz Konold.

(31) Giono, Jena. *Song of the World*. Paris: Gallimard, 1934. Translation by Liz Konold

(32) Char, René. 'Feuillets d'Hypnos, #146,' *Fureur et Mystere*. Paris: Gallimard, 1962: Translation by Liz Konold.

(33) _____. 'Feuillets d'Hypnos, #138,' *Fureur et Mystere*. Paris: Gallimard, 1962: Translation by Liz Konold.

(34) Konold, Liz. 'Apparition.' All rights reserved.

(35) Konold, Liz. 'Temporal.' All rights reserved.

(36) Beckett, Samuel. *Watt*. New York: Grove Press, 1959.

(37) Greilsamer, Laurent. *L'éclair au front: René Char*. Paris: Chez Fayard, 2004: Translation by Liz Konold.

(38) Appolinaire, Guillaume. 'One Evening,' Translations by A. S. Kline. www.poetryintranslation.com

(39) Breton, André. Quote from *Nadja*. Translated by Liz Konold. www.goodreads.com/author/54133.AndrBreton

(40) Reverdy, Pierre. "The Dry Tongue," translated by Kenneth Rexroth, from SELECTED POEMS, copyright ©1969 by Kenneth Rexroth. Reprinted by permission of New Directions Publishing Corp.

(41) Vaughn, Hal. *Sleeping With the Enemy : Coco Chanel's Secret War*. New York: Vintage Books, 2011.

(42) O'Hara, Frank. *Lunch Poems*. San Francisco: City Lights Pocket Series, 1956

(43) Reverdy, Pierre. 'In a Lower Voice,' from *The Song of the Dead, 1946*, translation by Mary Ann Caws. *Pierre Reverdy*. New York: New York Review Book, 2013

(44) Malraux, André. *La Condition Humaine*. Paris: Gallimard, 1933: Translation by Liz Konold.

(45) Buot, Francois. *Tristan Tzara: L'homme qui inventa la revolution Dada*. Paris: Bernard Grasset, 2002.

(46) Caws, Mary Ann. *Tristan Tzara: approximate man and other writings*, Detroit, MI: Wayne State University Press, 1973.

(47) Konold, Liz. 'Today,' all rights reserved.

(48) Soupault, Philippe. Translation by Pauline Schmidt. www.cse.iitk.ac.in/users/amit/books/forche-1993-_against-forgetting-twentiethcentury.html.

(49) Konold, Liz. 'From a Train Window,' all rights reserved.

(50) Alexander, Lloyd. 'Untitled, page 51.' *Paul Eluard—Selected Writings*. Nortfolk, CN: published by James Laughlin.

REFERENCE MATERIALS

Alexander, Lloyd, translator. *Eluard—Selected Writings*. Nortfolk, CN: New Direction published by James Laughlin.

Bair, Deirdre. *Samuel Beckett*. San Diego, CA: Harcourt Brace Jovanovich, 1978

Balakian, Anna Elizabeth. *André Breton, Magus of Surrealism*. New York : Oxford University Press, 1971

Beaudelaire, Charles. *Les Fleurs du Mal*. Paris: Librio, 2012,

Beckett, Samuel. *Collected Poems in English*. New York: Grove Press, 1977
_____. *Watt*. New York: Grove Press, 1959

Berthon, Simon. *Allies at War: the bitter rivalry among Churchill, Roosevelt and de Gaulle*. New York: Carroll & Graf Publishers, 2001

Breton, André. *Poems of André Breton, a bilingual anthology*. Translated and edited by Jean-Pierre Cauvin and Mary Ann Caws. Austin, TX: University of Texas Press, 1982

Bronner, Stephen Eric. *Camus, Portrait of a Moralist*. Illinois: University of Chicago Press, 1999

Brun, George. *Carpentras 1914-1948*. Carpentras: Le Nombre d'Or, 1986

Buot, Francois. *Tristan Tzara: L'homme qui inventa la revolution Dada*. Paris: Bernard Grasset, 2002

Canfield-Reisman, Rosemary M. *Critical Survey of Poetry: Surrealist Poets*. Massachusetts: Salem Press, 2012

Camus, Albert. *The Stranger*. Paris: Gallimard, 1942

Carroll, Sean B. *Brave Genius: A Scientist, a Philospher, and Their Daring Adventures from the French Resistance to the Nobel Prize*. Ne York: Broadway Books, 2013.

Caws, Mary Ann and Jolas, Tina, Editors. *Poems of Rene Char*. New York. New Directions Publishing, 1992

Caws Mary Ann. *The Inner Theatre of Recent French Poetry*. New Jersey: Princeton University Press, 1972

_____. *Tristan Tzara: Approximate Man and other writings*, Detroit, MI: Wayne State University Press, 1973

_____. *Pierre Reverdy*. New York: New York Review Book, 2013

Char, René, *Fureur et Mystere*. Paris: Gallimard, 1962

_____. *Le Nu Perdu*, Paris: Gallimard, 1978

Chevassus-au-Louis, Nicholas. *Le Midi en Resistance*. Villeveyrac, France: La Papillon Rouge Editor, 2011

Cordola, Albert, *Quelques passages de ma simple vie*. Pernes-les-Fontaines, France: Association des déportés, internes, résistants et patriots de Vaucluse.

Desnos, Robert. *Contre suivi de Calixto*. Paris: Gallimard, Edition by Marie-Claire Dumas, 2013

DiPierro, John C. *Structures in Beckett's Watt*. South Carolina: French Literature Publications Company, 1981

Eluard, Paul. *Selected Writings*. Translations by Lloyd Alexander. Paris: Henri Marchand & Co., 1956

Fageot, Christelle. *La Milice en Vaucluse*. France: Etudes Comptadines, 2008

Gildea, Robert. *Marianne in Chains: Everyday Life in the French Heartland under the German Occupation*. New York: Henry Holt & Co., 2004

Giono, Jean. *Jean Giono: Recits et Essaies*. Paris: Gallimard, 1986

Golsan, Richard J. *French writers and the Politics of Complicity*. Maryland: Johns Hopkins University Press, 2006,

Greilsamer, Laurent. *L'éclair au front: René Char*. Paris: Chez Fayard, 2004

Gueno, Jean-Pierre. *Paroles de l'Ombre, lettres, carnets et recits des Français sous l'occupation 1939-1945*. Paris: Librio, 2009

Jenkins, Cecil. *André Malraux*. New York: Twayne Publishers, 1972

Kedward, Rod. *France and the French: A Modern History.* USA: The Overlook Press, Peter Meyer, Publishers, Inc., 2005

Kline, A.G. www.poetryintranslation.com, Translations.

Lacouture, Jean. *André Malraux.* Translated by Alan Sheridan. New York: Pantheon Books, Random House, 1975

Lin, Dominique. *1939-45 en Vaucluse: nous étions des sans-culottes.* Orange, France: Elan Sud, 2014

Madsen, Axel *Malraux, A Biography.* New York: William Morrow and Co., Inc., 1976

Malraux, André. *La Condition Humaine.* Paris: Gallimard, 1933

Mathews, J.H. *Surrealist Poetry in France.* New York: Syracuse University Press, 1969

Mathieu, Marie-Yvonne. *Carpentras: Reflets du XXe Siècle. Association* des Cartophiles et Collectionneurs de Carpentras, 2000

Mousli, Béatrice. *Philippe Soupault.* Paris: Gallimard, Groupe Flammarion, 2010

Nugent, Robert. *Paul Eluard.* New York: Twayne Publishers, Inc., 1974

Ray, Lionel. *Louis Aragon.* Paris: Editions Pierre Seghers, 2002

Rexroth, Kenneth. *Selected Poems: Pierre Reverdy.* New York: New Directions Publishing, 1969

Rhein, Phillip H. *Albert Camus.* New York: Twayne Publishers, Inc., 1969

Résistants et Collabos: 1943 La France déchirée. Paris: Le Nouvel Observateur, 2013

Sadoul, Georges. *Aragon*. Paris: Editions Pierre Seghers, 1967

Stoltzfus, Ben. *Hemingway and French Writers*. Ohio: Kent State University Press, 2010

Todd, Oliver. *Albert Camus: A Life*. New York: Alfred A Knopf, 1997

Vaughn, Hal. *Sleeping With the Enemy : Coco Chanel's Secret War*. New York: Vintage Books, 2011

www.goodreads.com

www.wikipedia.com

www.carpentras-ventoux.fr/carte -- for a more precise map of the town of Carpentras

Made in the USA
San Bernardino, CA
23 July 2016